PRAISE FOR

GLORIOUS

"*Glorious* has all the elements of a fabulous western: compelling characters, br̶ ̶ ̶ ̶ ̶ ̶ ̶ ̶ ̶ ̶ ̶ ̶ ̶ ̶ ̶ ̶ ̶ ̶ blinking take on t̶ ̶ ̶ ̶ ̶ ̶ ̶ ̶ ̶ ̶ ̶ ̶ ̶ ̶ ̶ ̶ ̶ ̶ thor of the ̶ ̶ ̶ ̶ ̶ ̶ ̶ ̶ ̶ ̶ ̶ ̶ ̶ ̶ ̶ ̶ ̶ *ngmire*

"*Gloriou̶ ̶ ̶ ̶ ̶ ̶ ̶ ̶ ̶ ̶ ̶ ̶ ̶ ̶ ̶ ̶ * ̶earted, optimist̶ ̶ ̶ ̶ ̶ ̶ ̶ ̶ ̶ ̶ ̶ ̶ ̶ ̶ ̶ ̶ ld. It's wonderf̶ ̶ ̶ ̶ ̶ ̶ ̶ ̶ ̶ ̶ ̶ ̶ ̶ ̶ ̶ ̶ acters, and read̶ ̶ ̶ ̶ ̶ ̶ ̶ ̶ ̶ ̶ ̶ ̶ ̶ ̶ ̶ ̶ ̶ thor of ̶ ̶ ̶ ̶ ̶ ̶ ̶ ̶ ̶ ̶ ̶ ̶ ̶ ̶ ̶ ̶ ̶ e Cold

"I've lon̶ ̶ ̶ ̶ ̶ ̶ ̶ ̶ ̶ ̶ ̶ ̶ ̶ ̶ ̶ ̶ s of the America̶ ̶ ̶ ̶ ̶ ̶ ̶ ̶ ̶ ̶ ̶ ̶ ̶ ̶ ̶ ̶ I was thrilled ̶ ̶ ̶ ̶ ̶ ̶ ̶ ̶ ̶ ̶ ̶ ̶ ̶ ̶ ̶ redible research̶ ̶ ̶ ̶ ̶ ̶ ̶ ̶ ̶ ̶ ̶ ̶ ̶ ̶ ̶ of the America̶ ̶ ̶ ̶ ̶ ̶ ̶ ̶ ̶ ̶ ̶ ̶ ̶ ̶ ̶ ̶ thor of ̶ ̶ ̶ ̶ ̶ ̶ ̶ ̶ ̶ ̶ ̶ ̶ ̶ ̶ ̶ ̶ rsaken

"[Guî̶ ̶ ̶ ̶ ̶ ̶ ̶ ̶ ̶ ̶ ̶ ̶ ̶ ̶ ̶ ̶ ative, and er̶ ̶ ̶ ̶ ̶ ̶ ̶ ̶ ̶ ̶ ̶ ̶ ̶ ̶ ̶ ̶ rican West.'̶ ̶ ̶ ̶ ̶ ̶ ̶ ̶ ̶ ̶ ̶ ̶ ̶ ̶ *News*

"An a̶ ̶ ̶ ̶ ̶ ̶ ̶ ̶ ̶ ̶ ̶ ̶ ̶ ̶ ̶ ̶ d by the en̶ ̶ ̶ ̶ ̶ ̶ ̶ ̶ ̶ ̶ ̶ ̶ ̶ ̶ ̶ ̶ fond of Glo̶ ̶ ̶ ̶ ̶ ̶ ̶ ̶ ̶ ̶ ̶ ̶ ̶ ̶ ̶ *Post*

"A wo̶ ̶ ̶ ̶ ̶ ̶ ̶ ̶ ̶ ̶ ̶ ̶ ̶ ̶ ̶ ̶ some *Dove* ̶ ̶ ̶ ̶ ̶ ̶ ̶ ̶ ̶ ̶ ̶ ̶ ̶ ̶ *Times*

"Delightful . . . wonderfully appealing. *Glorious* is an old-fashioned western with likable characters who, because Guinn projects a trilogy, will return shortly."
—*Booklist*

"The Wild West comes alive in this novel of prospectors, desolate cavalry posts, rotgut saloons, and Apache raiders . . . The plot is classic . . . Good fun."
—*Kirkus Reviews*

"This first installment in a trilogy will delight historical fiction fans longing for the return of classic westerns. This entertaining outing is sure to keep the saloon doors swinging for more entries in the genre."
—*Library Journal*

PRAISE FOR

THE LAST GUNFIGHT

"A gripping revisionist account of the famed 1881 showdown . . . Exhaustively researched, stylishly written . . . As grimly compelling as a Greek tragedy."
—*Publishers Weekly*

"Jeff Guinn has come up with a new angle and approach to the events of that bloody day in Tombstone. Without that gunfight, Wyatt Earp would have never become a household name a hundred years later. Guinn delves into the myth and separates it from the facts. A terrific read about the West's most famous lawman."
—Clive Cussler, #1 *New York Times* bestselling author of *Ghost Ship*

"Jeff Guinn took readers down the back roads of Louisiana in his book *Go Down Together: The True, Untold Story of Bonnie and Clyde*. He's back in *The Last Gunfight*, displaying the impeccable research that is his trademark . . . Guinn's story is what really happened . . . A terrific read."
—*USA Today*

GLORIOUS

JEFF GUINN

BERKLEY BOOKS
New York

THE BERKLEY PUBLISHING GROUP
Published by the Penguin Group
Penguin Group (USA) LLC
375 Hudson Street, New York, New York 10014

USA • Canada • UK • Ireland • Australia • New Zealand • India • South Africa • China

penguin.com

A Penguin Random House Company

Berkley trade paperback ISBN: 978-0-425-27542-9

The Library of Congress has catalogued the G. P. Putnam's Sons hardcover edition
of this book as follows:

Guinn, Jeff.
Glorious / Jeff Guinn.
p.   cm.
ISBN 978-0-399-16541-2
1. Fortune hunters—Fiction.   2. Gold mines and mining—Fiction.   I. Title.
PS3557.U375G57   2014   2013037961
813'.54—dc23

PUBLISHING HISTORY
G. P. Putnam's Sons hardcover edition / May 2014
Berkley trade paperback edition / May 2015

PRINTED IN THE UNITED STATES OF AMERICA

10 9 8 7 6 5 4 3 2 1

Cover design by Richard Hasselberger.
Text design by Meighan Cavanaugh.

For Ivan Held

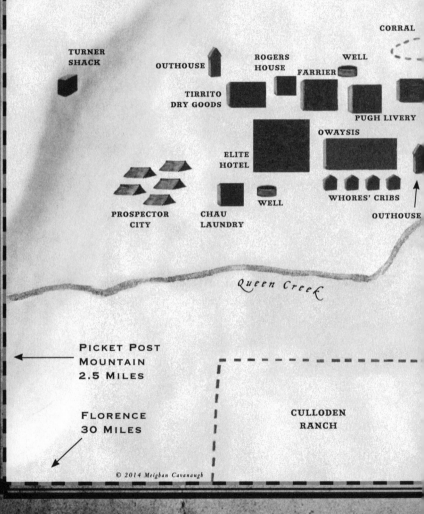

CAMP MCDOWELL
70 MILES

GLORIOUS

CORRAL

TURNER
SHACK

OUTHOUSE

ROGERS
HOUSE

WELL

FARRIER

TIRRITO
DRY GOODS

PUGH LIVERY

OWAYSIS

ELITE
HOTEL

WELL

WHORES' CRIBS

PROSPECTOR
CITY

CHAU
LAUNDRY

OUTHOUSE

Queen Creek

PICKET POST
MOUNTAIN
2.5 MILES

FLORENCE
30 MILES

CULLODEN
RANCH

© 2014 Meighan Cavanaugh

PINAL MOUNTAINS

Queen Creek

APACHE
LEAP

Canyon

STALLS

JAIL

CHINESE
CAMP

N

W   E

S

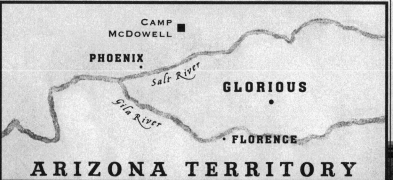

CAMP
McDOWELL

PHOENIX

Salt River

GLORIOUS

Gila River

FLORENCE

ARIZONA TERRITORY

GLORIOUS

———◆———

1872

They took Tom Gaumer late in the morning.

He shouldn't have been out alone. Like all the other prospectors in Glorious, Gaumer knew the area was crawling with Apaches. You didn't have to see them to know that they were there. In the three weeks since he'd arrived in the tiny town, Gaumer went out on his daily hunt for silver with four other prospectors, all of them frontier veterans who observed the proper precautions: stay together, make as little noise as possible, take turns acting as lookout. The Indians generally didn't bother well-armed men working in groups. They wanted easier white prey.

But the day before, Gaumer had noticed a particularly promising bit of oxidized, black-lined rock, typical of potentially significant silver content. He and his informal partners—they'd all met on arrival in Glorious—were working about three miles northeast of town along the banks of Queen Creek, in an area where the creek cut around the base of the Pinal Mountains. Bossman Wright was on lookout, and Oafie and Archie and Old Ben and Gaumer were chipping away on a ledge, each no more than ten yards from the others because the Apache could snatch anyone straying too far in an eye blink. When Gaumer's pick dislodged the first black-lined rock chunks he drew breath to holler out the news to the others, and then thought better of it. None of the others were turning up anything interesting; that was the way of even the widest silver seams, to have surface concentration in one small spot, and it was his luck alone to find it. These men he'd been working with were fine fellows, but Gaumer had a wife and two daughters back in Minnesota who lived in near poverty while he was away trying to strike it rich for them. So Gaumer took a good look to mark the exact place in his mind, then casually said, "Nothing's here. Let's try farther downriver." Much to his relief, the others muttered agreement and moved on.

The next morning in the prospectors' tent city just beyond the few permanent buildings in Glorious, Gaumer told the other four to go on without him, he had stomach trouble and would rest all day. He lay in his blankets until everyone in the prospectors' camp was gone, all of them disappearing into the vastness surrounding Glorious. Then Gaumer jumped up and started back toward his secret treasure spot, keeping a sharp eye out for anyone who might be exploring the same general area. But his luck held. By the time he was back on the ledge he felt certain that he was miles away from anyone else. It was risky to be out alone, but Gaumer didn't care. In all his years of prospecting, he'd never seen such strong silver sign. He soon lost himself chipping away at the black-lined rock, the lines getting tantalizingly thicker and more numerous: my God, there was going to be a fortune in silver here! He'd done it! This was it! As he was exulting, they came quietly up behind him. A rope snared Gaumer's arms to his sides and just like that he was helpless.

They took their time with the torture and mutilation. First they built a fire and used the brands to burn the soles of Gaumer's feet. He screamed, but his screams were lost in the cliffs and canyons. They amused themselves for a while removing Gaumer's fingers one joint at a time, and then there was some skinning, parts of his chest and back. By then he was periodically passing out from the pain, coming to when they briefly stopped, shrieking when they resumed until the agony was too overwhelming and blessed blackness descended on him again.

His captors knew their business. It was almost nightfall when Gaumer finally succumbed. His last sensation was of fresh pain. One of them was dragging a sharp knife along the hairline of his forehead. Gaumer only spoke English, not their language, but he'd been in Arizona Territory long enough to comprehend meaning if not individual words. Gaumer thought one of them was saying, "Stop—Apaches don't scalp."

Then the final darkness swallowed him.

PART ONE

ONE

Shortly before the morning stage left Florence for the thirty-mile trip to Glorious, Mr. Billings, the depot manager, took Cash McLendon aside.

"I hope you've taken advantage of our privy, sir," Mr. Billings said. "Passage to Glorious is wearying at best. You'll want to avoid additional discomfort."

The suggestion surprised McLendon, who replied, "I'm not concerned. Today's is only a short trip, every depot along the way will have facilities, and in between scheduled stops I can always tap on the stage roof and signal the driver to pull over."

Mr. Billings, a square-shaped man with muttonchop whiskers, shook his head. "I see from your ticket that you've come to us all the way from Texas. Up to now, you've followed mostly well-established routes on decent roads. But the way to Glorious is rough travel, very hard going, and there are no depots along the way. You'll not find another privy between here and there."

McLendon was bone-weary from riding inside cramped stagecoaches during the three weeks it had taken him to get from Galveston to Florence in Arizona Territory, and he was further discomfited by the memory of why he'd fled St. Louis nearly two months before that. Throughout much of this wretched time, he sustained himself with the belief that if he could only get to Glorious, everything might yet be all right. All he knew about the place was its name, but that was enough. He wanted to board one last stagecoach and find out what was going to happen, one way or the other.

"Even with no depots, the matter of a comfort stop seems simple enough," McLendon said, hoping to convey through a friendly but firm tone that the subject was closed. "I'll bang on the roof and the driver will accommodate me." But Mr. Billings shook his head again.

"We leave the matter of such pauses to the driver's discretion, and of course you can signal him all you like," the depot manager said. "But on this route it's unlikely he'll rein in on passenger request, and even if he would, as a sensible man you'd not want to step down from the stage and remove yourself even a short distance to take your stance or squat. That's due to the Apaches, of course. They're always alert to pick off any white man who foolishly separates himself from his companions."

"I suspect that you exaggerate," McLendon said. "I saw no sign of Apache on the journey here from Tucson, and it's my understanding that most of them ride with Cochise well away to the south and east."

"Please observe the sign," Mr. Billings said, and pointed to a large poster by the depot door. In all capital letters it warned:

YOU WILL BE TRAVELING THROUGH
INDIAN COUNTRY AND THE SAFETY
OF YOUR PERSON CANNOT BE
VOUCHSAFED BY ANYONE BUT GOD!

"Those are the truest of words," Mr. Billings said. "You have no idea of how dangerous this country is. I assure you that these savages lurk behind every rock and bit of brush between here and Glorious, and the thing about Apaches is that you don't see them until they're upon you. The savages got a prospector just outside of Glorious not two weeks ago, and they butchered him up like a hog. Trust me on this, sir. If you require additional testimony, inquire of your driver or anyone else with some experience in this region. Make use of the privy here, and then remain alert all the way to Glorious, where I doubt you'll want to linger very long."

McLendon reminded himself that the man was trying to be helpful. "And why is that, sir?"

"Why, there's nothing to the place," Mr. Billings said. "Don't let the braggardly name deceive you. A few buildings and some prospectors' tents is all of it. We run this stage once a week because you never know what may happen with these meager little towns. Most vanish right off the map in a matter of months when no significant lodes of ore are discovered. But on those rare occasions when a major strike is made, why, it seems that everyone on earth immediately wants to hurry to the spot, so we have a Glorious route in place just in case. Meaning no disrespect, you seem to me more likely a businessman than a prospector, and someone accustomed to a degree of comfort. There's none of that in Glorious, I assure you." Mr. Billings paused, waiting for McLendon to mention his reason for such an unlikely destination. When he didn't, the depot manager continued: "Well, then, I'll inform you that the stage and driver will remain in Glorious overnight and return here tomorrow. After that, it's another week before our next stage arrives. Should you decide to come back in the morning and spare yourself such a long delay, the fare is three dollars, the same as you're paying to make the Glorious trip today. Just give the money to the driver, as we have no formal depot there. And now I thank you for your business, and wish you the best day possible under the circumstances in which you'll presently find yourself."

McLendon waited until Mr. Billings disappeared inside the chinked wood depot before hustling to the rank privy behind the building. Even though the ride to Glorious surely wouldn't take too long—it was only some thirty miles, and McLendon knew that stages routinely covered ninety or a hundred miles in a day—it was disturbing to learn that there would probably be no relief stops along the way. His digestive system was in a disrupted condition brought on by the meals he'd consumed since Galveston. Depot food was expensive, sometimes as much as a dollar a plate—twice the price of a meal at a decent hotel—and the fare was almost always limited to bacon, beans, biscuits, and foul-tasting coffee or tea, with the occasional substitution of tough, stringy beef or salty sowbelly as the main course. Because depot stops were usually limited to twenty minutes while fresh teams of horses were hitched to the stage, there was never time to wander off in search of more palatable meals. McLendon couldn't remember the last time he'd eaten a vegetable other than the ubiquitous mushy depot beans. In recent days, the constipation he had endured since the beginning of the trip from Texas was replaced by periodic piercing urges to evacuate that struck without warning. As he closed himself inside the fly-infested outhouse, he reflected that for the moment, at least, he feared the Apache far less than he did ruining his remaining pair of relatively clean trousers.

AFTER MCLENDON finished his business in the privy, he went back inside the depot and collected his valise. When he'd fled St. Louis, the bag was shiny and redolent of expensive leather. Now it was gashed in several places, and the handle was held in place with twine. Stage travel was hard on luggage. Each passenger was allowed twenty-five pounds of baggage, but McLendon's battered valise was considerably lighter. It contained only a book, the sheet music for "Shoo Fly, Don't Bother Me," four shirts, some drawers, the denim jeans he'd purchased in New Orleans while working on the docks there, a few pairs of socks, some toiletries, and the suit he was saving to wear when he surprised Gabrielle in Glorious. It was an expensive suit, hand-tailored to fit his slender frame, and McLendon hoped the prosperous appearance wearing the suit gave him wouldn't be offset by any stench acquired from the long-unwashed clothes packed around it. The valise also contained the .36 caliber Navy Colt he bought in Houston after observing that all of the passengers on the westbound stage were armed, including the women, and a box of cartridges he'd purchased at the same time. One handgun was the same as the next to McLendon, who'd never owned or even fired one before. The shop owner assured him that the Navy Colt was popular among frontier travelers, and particularly excellent protection for a beginner marksman—"Just cock, point, and pull the trigger." For the first few days McLendon concealed the weapon in his coat pocket, but the sagging weight of it was distracting and he decided to carry it in his bag instead. Since he rode with the valise crammed behind his legs underneath the stagecoach bench, he could get to the gun quickly if the need ever arose, which fortunately it so far hadn't. McLendon's remaining money, a roll of about eight hundred dollars in greenbacks and a few gold double eagles, was kept in his trousers pocket. He'd left St. Louis in February with nearly two thousand dollars, and now it was May; life on the run was proving expensive.

McLendon carried his valise over to the Glorious stage, which was being loaded by a depot crew. The appearance of the vehicle gave him pause. Until now, the stages he had ridden to Arizona Territory from Texas had been stout, impressive conveyances, with wide wheels and sturdy carriages and varnished sides that glistened in the sun. Their appearances had given a sense of reliability. But this one looked rickety in the extreme. The driver's bench sagged on one side, and the sides of the carriage were so stained with streaked dirt and dried clots of mud that it was impossible to tell what shade of paint or varnish might lie beneath. McLendon feared that the thing might collapse entirely the moment he stepped aboard, but apparently the fragile-looking vehicle was able to support modest loads. During previous stops on his long journey, he'd seen stages laden with mailbags, but this time there was only a small mail pouch. The citizens of Glorious didn't receive many letters. The stage roof and boot were being packed with wooden crates. According to labels, these contained mostly canned food—peaches, pears, and tomatoes. He saw several marked SUGAR and COFFEE, while a large crate was mysteriously labeled MISCELLANEOUS. Next to the stage, two wagons were hitched together, and these, too, were being loaded with crates of canned goods. The depot workers also hoisted bulky wooden casks onto one of the wagons. From the sounds of sloshing liquid, McLendon guessed they held whiskey or beer, probably both. Perhaps Glorious had a saloon. He already knew there was a store in town, because Gabrielle and her father, Salvatore, ran it.

The clopping of heavy hooves caught McLendon's attention. Four Army cavalrymen pulled up alongside the stage and wagons. McLendon knew as little about horses as he did about handguns, but even he could tell that the soldiers' mounts were the next thing to broken-down. Their coats were dull with age as well as dust, and when their riders dismounted, the horses hung their heads listlessly. The cavalrymen were equally unimpressive. Their uniforms were patched and filthy; one appeared to be drunk. Another of the raggedy soldiers exchanged friendly greetings with the grizzled fellow who was apparently going to drive McLendon's stage. "An Army wagon is taking supplies and messages from Camp McDowell to Camp Grant, which is southeast of Glorious," a worker loading cases told McLendon. "As a courtesy to civilian stage operations, the Camp McDowell commander is sending his wagon and some cavalrymen partway with your stage as an escort."

"Can those sad creatures they're riding keep up with the stage?" McLendon asked. "I doubt that they can even trot a little, let alone gallop."

"Sorry as they are, they'll keep the pace with this team," the worker said, and gestured to the depot corral, where four rawboned braying mules were being forced into harness. "There's little opportunity for galloping or trotting on the way to Glorious. The trail's too rough. Your typical team of horses would all go lame. Mules, though, can pick their way forward. It's travel slow but sure."

"How slow?" McLendon asked. "It's still early morning, and with a trip of just thirty miles I thought that we'd easily reach Glorious by noon."

"A bit before dark is more likely, and that's if the stage or one of the wagons don't throw a wheel," the man said. "You best get some food for along the way." McLendon had hoped for a more appealing meal when he reached Glorious, but the worker seemed positive that the trip would take all day. So McLendon bought food from Mr. Billings, tossed his valise up through the open stage door, and clambered inside the carriage. There were only two benches there instead of three; the stages from Galveston to Tucson all seated nine, three to a bench, with facing passengers interlocking knees because of limited space. In several instances there were too many passengers to squeeze onto the benches, so the overflow perched atop baggage tied to the roof or else wedged themselves on the outside bench between the driver and shotgun guard. But besides McLendon, the morning stage to Glorious had only one additional passenger, a tall red-faced fellow in a checked suit who nodded companionably as he sat down on the opposite bench and stowed his own case underneath. The stage rocked as the driver and shotgun guard climbed up to their outside seats. McLendon pushed the cloth window curtain aside and stuck his head out to watch as drivers took the reins of the two wagons, which were also pulled by teams of mules. The four cavalrymen nudged their horses up, two ahead and two behind the three-vehicle convoy. The stage lurched slowly forward with the wagons directly behind. McLendon expected the stage driver to quicken the mules' pace as soon as they were clear of the Florence depot, but he didn't. The convoy headed slowly east and a little north; McLendon was certain that if he jumped out and walked, he'd be faster than the mules.

For all Mr. Billings's dire warnings about rough terrain, the going seemed easy enough. There was very little to look at as the stage crept along except sandy flats speckled with scrubby cactus and brush. It was going to be a long, tedious trip, and McLendon sighed as he pulled his head back inside and tried to settle himself with some minimal degree of comfort on the thinly padded seat. Enjoying elbow room for a change, he pulled a battered book from his bag: James Fenimore Cooper's *Last of the Mohicans*. McLendon loved the story's vivid descriptions of valorous acts and appreciated its unhappy ending, which struck him as truer to real life than a triumphant climax.

He'd read the book so often that he had memorized many passages. In recent months, with everything else in his life so desperate and changed, he'd drawn comfort from the familiarity. Now, nerves on edge since his arrival in Glorious was finally imminent, McLendon tried to distract himself again with the exploits of Hawkeye, Uncas, and Chingachgook, but it proved impossible. Even on fairly level ground the stage bumped along, and without being braced on his bench by other passengers, McLendon found his head and shoulders bouncing painfully off the cab doors and roof. He sighed and tucked the book back in his valise.

As soon as he did, his lone fellow passenger struck up a conversation. William Clark LeMond identified himself as a salesman of "luxury sundries, scented soaps and lotions, and the like." He explained that he currently lived in Tucson but made regular trips around the rest of the territory, attempting to place his wares in dry goods stores "mostly in the larger towns like Florence and Prescott and Arizona City out on the California border, but also in the smaller places that could one day prove significant. That's not to say I linger in any that clearly have little promise. Phoenix, in the Salt River Valley, for example, is nothing but farmers, none of them men of ambition, and so it's destined for well-deserved oblivion. On the other hand Glorious, where we're currently bound, has considerable potential."

"Mr. Billings back at the Florence depot would disagree," McLendon said.

LeMond straightened his bowler hat, which had just been knocked askew by a particularly violent bump. "Yes, well, that's Dick Billings. He's a failed prospector, you know, wandered the territories for years and never found any color to speak of. Men like Dick just plain give up after a while, settle in wherever they happen to be and spend the rest of their days pissing on the ambitions of others. Dick's not a bad fellow, just a disappointed one. Glorious is all right. There's silver in the mountains around it, that's common knowledge since two years ago, when one of General Stoneman's men found considerable rich rock specimens practically lying on the ground. Up to now fear of the Apaches has kept most people away, and they do pick off a poor soul every now and then, but that won't last much longer. Someone's going to make a grand find, word will spread, and so many prospectors will come flooding in that the damned Indians will get brushed aside like flies. The businesspeople and lawyers and whores and the like will be right on their heels, ready to suck up every cent of the money that the prospectors all of a sudden have to spend. Practically overnight, humble little Glorious will have gourmet restaurants and gambling casinos and theaters with shows put on by the finest traveling troupes—high-class civilization. And when it arrives—when folks want to end the workday by cleaning up and going out to enjoy an elegant time—they'll wash off the dust with my fancy soaps, which will by then be stocked everywhere in town, thanks to the diligence that I currently exercise."

"You're a hopeful man," McLendon said.

"That's what you've got to be, out here in the territories. Hope is what makes the present discomfort tolerable."

Having told something of himself, LeMond tried to draw out McLendon, who said that he was going to Glorious to see an old friend and didn't expect an extended stay.

"I hardly blame you for that," LeMond said. "As much as I'm optimistic for the future of Glorious, at present there's little in the way of leisure comfort to be found there, only a cramped saloon and a hotel of sorts. Tomorrow morning I'll call at the town dry goods store, leave some further items for sale if they'll have them, and then it's right back to Florence on the stage."

"Tell me about this store," McLendon said, trying not to sound too eager. "Does it carry a good variety of wares? Are you familiar with the owners?"

"Like the rest of the town except for the hotel, it's an adobe structure," LeMond said. "A man named Tirrito and his daughter, Gabrielle, are proprietors. He's Eye-talian with limited English, but pleasant nonetheless. She's quite delightful, and I might add very sensible for a woman. When I explained how stocking fine soaps would ensure the business of future customers more civilized than your typical hardscrabble prospector, she was forward-thinking enough to take some bars on consignment. I'm hoping they've since sold a few and want more. Even if they don't, I'll share some conversation and continue building a relationship for future business, so the time spent on this trip won't be wasted. Now, what friend do you seek in Glorious?"

"I intend to call on a lady," McLendon said.

"Miss Gabrielle, then," LeMond observed.

"What makes you so certain?" McLendon asked. "I specified no name."

LeMond grinned. "If the location is Glorious, the term 'lady' can't as yet be widely applied." McLendon wasn't sure how to respond, so he pulled the window curtain aside and stared out at the nondescript countryside. LeMond didn't seem offended, and they rode in companionable silence.

About three hours into the trip, McLendon felt the stage tip slightly upward. Since he was seated on the inside bench facing forward, by peering out the window he could see that they'd reached a long, gradual incline.

"We're now almost halfway to Glorious," LeMond said. "But from here the going gets more difficult, with steeper slopes and finally the mountains. Keep the window curtains drawn from now on if you would, since the higher we go, the stronger the winds, and so more dust will be blown. I prefer to make my sales calls in a clean suit rather than a filthy one." McLendon initially obliged him, but with the curtains closed the carriage quickly became stifling and he began oozing sweat. Along with perspiration came waves of nausea. LeMond didn't seem as affected; clearly he was more used to the furnace-like heat. McLendon stood the discomfort as long as he could, then yanked the window curtain open. When he did, the resulting gush of molten air carried with it a thick cloud of dust. McLendon coughed; LeMond covered his nose with a handkerchief, then reached over and tugged the curtain shut.

"The mule team and the cavalry riders in front kick up most of the dust," LeMond explained. "Our choices are to bake or to choke, and baking is the lesser of these evils. Buck up if you can, for I'm sure they'll soon call a stop. Then we can eat our lunches and have a pee."

"Mr. Billings told me there would likely be no rest stop," McLendon said. "He spoke of near-certain Apache assault."

"Counting the soldiers and the stage crew and the wagon drivers and ourselves, in all we number ten," LeMond said. "That should be sufficient to discourage any lurking Indians. They generally attack lone travelers, or those who wander off from a main body. Just make sure that when you relieve yourself, you do your business close and in plain sight. Don't act modest."

McLendon's bowels were rumbling. "I won't," he said, and made sure when he bolted from the stage a few minutes later to stop only a few feet away, his urgency such that he truly didn't care who could see. When he was finished, everyone else took a turn, one at a time, while the others stood guard. Afterward the drivers watered the mules from casks brought for that purpose, and all the men ate lunches. Grateful to be out of the boxy stage carriage and refreshed by the warm breeze in his face, McLendon found that his nausea eased and he had an unexpected appetite for his cold bacon and thick-crusted bread. LeMond produced several tins of sardines and shared the tiny olive-oil-drenched fish among the group. That encouraged one of the wagon drivers to pass around a canteen he promised was full of "*special* water," and when McLendon took his swallow he discovered it was wine instead. Despite the heat and dust they passed a friendly half hour before the stage driver announced it was time to be moving on. He added to McLendon, "Prepare for some bumps," and pointed east. McLendon saw what appeared to be a gigantic lump of something purplish-brown. "Picket Post Mountain," the driver said. "Monstrous big thing. Then rough ground for some time and the Pintos and the Pinals beyond that."

As the way grew steeper and more rugged, the stage rocked harder. Inside the passenger carriage, McLendon and LeMond held on as best they could. With the window curtains still pulled tight, McLendon could only imagine the terrain outside. His nausea resumed, more intense this time; the rancid tang of greasy bacon and sardines was thick in his throat, and he particularly regretted the lunchtime gulp of wine. "Are we going up a mountain?" he finally gasped, and LeMond laughed and replied that they were still in the foothills. He suggested that McLendon take slow, deep breaths: "That'll help settle your belly." Then the stage came to a lurching halt and they hopped outside. A rear wheel was caught between two rocks; while the stage and wagon drivers struggled to pry it free with metal crowbars, McLendon looked ahead and was astonished to see Picket Post Mountain looming less than a mile away, craggy and intimidating. The huge hunk of rock seemed to have exploded out of the desert floor. Even more amazing was a sprawling mountain range farther east that LeMond identified as the Pinals; compared to them, massive Picket Post was an isolated pebble. It was another two miles from Picket Post to Glorious just before the Pinals, the salesman said.

"The Army had a small camp near the Picket Post lower base before they closed it last year," LeMond told McLendon. "Sometimes they climbed up near the summit and signaled with mirrors to other camps and patrols many miles away; the heights commanded a wide view."

"I suppose the residents of Glorious depended on the Army at Picket Post to protect them from the Apaches," McLendon said. "They must have resented the closing of the camp, even if its soldiers were all as disreputable as those cavalrymen who've ridden with us today."

LeMond snorted. "In the event of an Indian attack, in the hour it would take for cavalry from Camp Picket Post to get word, saddle up, and ride to Glorious, everyone living there would already have been turned into food for buzzards. Apaches swarm in fast and lethal. I noticed you attempting to read that Fenimore Cooper book. I'm a reading man myself, and familiar with the Mohican yarn. Apaches are nothing like Cooper's made-up Indians, who make long speeches before they strike. The savages out here prefer attacking over talk. There's also the matter of the Army mounts. You see the cavalrymen with us on the dray draggers the government has issued them to ride. Those Morgans are probably left over from service in the war. It's cheaper for the Army to send the surviving steeds here to be ridden during the final days before they drop instead of paying for new, fresh stock. In this region, the cavalry presence is mostly for show only, to discourage bandits riding up from Mexico and to at least give the appearance that they're on the lookout for Apaches."

"Then what prevents the Indians from falling on a town like Glorious?"

"There's a large ranch, the Culloden, across the valley, just on the other side of Queen Creek," LeMond said. "Its owner employs a number of seasoned vaqueros. I guess their presence discourages any full-scale Apache assault, though of course the savages still skulk in the area and present constant danger. To live out here is to accept their proximity. Some of them are certainly watching us now."

"Mr. Billings at the Florence depot mentioned that a prospector was recently killed by the Indians just outside of Glorious."

"That's true. They carved him up and played with the pieces. But he was careless and went out alone. Even the Culloden vaqueros can't be everywhere at once. Common sense is still the best defense against the Apaches."

When the wagon wheel was finally freed the trip continued, with the mules maintaining a methodical pace as they skirted rocky inclines and eased through gaps between piles of boulders. McLendon no longer scorned their limited speed; the beasts were amazingly sure-footed. Just southwest of Picket Post, the cavalry and Army wagon veered off toward the southeast, leaving the stage and the remaining wagon to go on alone. There was less dust without the cavalry mounts plodding in front of the stage, so LeMond suggested that McLendon pull back the curtains and take in the view. He did, hopeful of taking his mind off his still-unsettled stomach, but what McLendon saw failed to cheer him. Unlike the rounded summits McLendon previously associated with mountains, the Pinals rose in a series of jagged, jutting peaks that seemed to him like serrated teeth.

Menacing saguaro cactus dotted their slopes. The predominant color
of the rock was rusty red, similar to dried blood. The Pinals seemed
to go on forever; they were too much, too intimidating, and they were
still some distance away.

"They do loom, don't they?" LeMond commented, and waited for
McLendon to offer some praise of the scenery. When none was forthcoming, the soap salesman took a watch from his vest pocket, checked
the time, and added, "As soon as we top the next rise we come to a
long valley, and Glorious will come into sight at the far end of it. If
there are no further emergency stops, we'll arrive right around dinnertime."

McLendon nodded and began pondering the specifics of his
imminent reunion with Gabrielle. He alternated between thinking
she'd be thrilled that he'd come and being certain she'd send him
packing—which, when he was being honest with himself, he knew
that he deserved. When and how should he surprise her for maximum odds of success? As soon as he arrived in Glorious, possibly
interrupting the Tirritos' evening meal? That would be dramatic.
But his clothes were saturated with sweat, he suspected both his
breath and his body smelled awful, and every inch of his exposed
skin was caked with dust. Far better to take a room at the hotel
LeMond had mentioned, have a hot bath and a good dinner and a
solid night's sleep between clean sheets, then in the morning don
his fine suit and call on Gabrielle feeling and looking his best.
McLendon would acknowledge the terrible mistake that he'd made,
then point out that he'd come all the long, weary way to Glorious to
get her back. He hoped that when he finally spoke to Gabrielle, he'd
find the right words; the power of persuasion had always been his
greatest gift.

After some time LeMond asked McLendon, "Where will you stay tonight in Glorious?"

"I thought I might take a room in the hotel you mentioned. Is that where you'll be too?"

"I didn't mention earlier that the hotel is unfinished," LeMond said. "On my last trip to town I arranged other accommodations. The livery owner lets me to take my rest wrapped in blankets on soft straw in his stalls. It's quite comfortable if you don't mind the rustling and snorting of his mules, which, as a heavy sleeper, I don't. The stage and wagon driver will sleep there too. I imagine that Bob Pugh, the owner, would let you join us. He's a friendly fellow."

"Does the hotel have real beds?" McLendon asked. "If it does, that's my preference. I've spent far too many recent nights trying to sleep on moving stages, or else curled on a rough pallet in the corner of some depot. I want sheets and a pillow if I can get them."

"Oh, you can get those at the hotel, but there are other considerations," LeMond said. "I'll let you discover them, and if you pick the livery stable instead, it won't be hard to find."

"I appreciate the suggestion, but I'm sure I'll choose a pillow and sheets over straw," McLendon said. "However, I'll ask a favor of you. Should you encounter Miss Gabrielle before I do, could you please not mention me? I hope to surprise her tomorrow."

"Glad to oblige," LeMond said. "I expect to call on her and her father at their store quite early in the morning. They have to be open by dawn; that's when the prospectors begin their treks out of town in search of color, and most stop by the store to buy their necessaries for the day. I'll be done there by nine, and ready to board the stage for Florence. It usually departs about ten. Perhaps if your visit with Miss Gabrielle is concluded promptly, you'll be joining me on the return journey?"

"I think not," McLendon said. "I expect I'll have some things to arrange."

"Well, fine," LeMond mumbled, and looked down at his hands. "Arrangements can be confounding. I wish you well."

McLendon, adept at interpreting gestures and tone, wondered why the man seemed doubtful.

THE BATTERED LITTLE STAGE rocked along; after another half hour the ride again leveled out. McLendon tugged the curtain aside to peer out the window and was startled to see, about a half mile in the distance, two armed riders seemingly trailing the stage.

"There may be bandits," he said to LeMond, who leaned over him to look.

"No, those are Culloden vaqueros," the drummer said. "They're out on patrol. Nothing coming into or out of the valley escapes their scrutiny. Say, put your face right out and look straight ahead, just below the Pinals. You may have to squint a bit."

McLendon craned his head out the window and blinked against the blowing dust. He raised his hand to shield his eyes and stared until his eyes burned and watered.

"Nothing," he called in to LeMond.

"Study the base of the mountains, not the mountains themselves," the salesman said, and McLendon tried. After several moments he noticed what appeared to be smudges at the far end of the valley. These gradually came into sharper focus: a few very low buildings, lighter in color than the bloody Pinals, and also flapping shapes that he recognized as tents. McLendon kept staring, waiting for the actual town to come into view, something considerably more substantial than what he'd seen so far. When nothing did, he sat back in the carriage and wiped his eyes, which ached from the strain.

"There are some outskirts, but I failed to sight the town," he said. "There must be another rise or two remaining for us to climb."

LeMond chuckled. "No, what you saw is what there is. That's all of it. That's Glorious."

TWO

The Florence stage didn't clatter into the main street of Glorious because there was no formal street there. Instead, the town began with a few dozen tents and lean-tos gathered in a haphazard clump, and then came a dozen adobe buildings and one large wooden structure whose second story was topped by loosely cinched canvas rather than an actual roof. A few of the adobe buildings were whitewashed. The others were dull brown. There was also a shack atop a hill fifty yards from the rest of town. It seemed to be constructed from slabs of wooden packing cases. The driver eased the stage past the tents and most of the buildings before reining in the mule team in front of a structure identified as Pugh Livery by a sign swaying in the stiff breeze.

"Here we are," LeMond announced to McLendon. "Climb out and look around. As you can see, it won't take long."

McLendon disembarked, rolling his shoulders and neck. His entire body felt battered from the daylong ride. A small smiling man with a mustache curled at the tips emerged from the livery building and waved to the stage and wagon drivers. "Welcome, boys!" he called. "Good trip, was it?" He clapped LeMond on the back, said it was fine to see him again, and then extended his hand to McLendon. "Bob Pugh," he said. "Always glad to meet a newcomer to our town. Hope you like it enough to stay or at least return often to do business. Call on me if I can be of help."

"Kind of you," replied McLendon. He shook Pugh's hand and looked past him at the windswept, dismal little settlement. Except for a few ragged men slouching around the tent area, no one else besides Pugh and the arrivals from Florence seemed to be stirring. To the west there was nothing but the hulking silhouette of Picket Post Mountain. To the north was a steep hill that fed into the jagged mountain range, and after a few level miles there were also mountains to the south. Directly east of town was the steepest sheer cliff that McLendon had ever seen, like some stark monstrosity in a particularly disturbing nightmare. The cliff would have dwarfed a sizable city beneath it, and Glorious was only a speck of a town.

Pugh helped the stage crew and wagon driver unhitch their teams. LeMond said to McLendon, "Well, I'll drop off my bag and sample case at the livery office, then repair to the saloon for refreshment. Care to join me?"

"There's really a saloon?" McLendon asked. "Here?" Despite the sloshing barrels he had seen loaded back in Florence, he found it hard to believe that such a ratty place as Glorious had amenities.

"Of course," LeMond assured him. "Where there's prospectors, there's whiskey. It's right over there." He pointed to a sprawling, squat adobe building next to the canvas-covered wooden structure. There was a hand-lettered sign out front: OWAYSIS. "Crazy George, the owner, can't spell worth a damn, but he serves an honest drink at a reasonable price. George even has girls there if you're of a mind for that sort of sport. On the other side of the Owaysis is the Elite Hotel, which as you can see still has the top floor unfinished. Major Mulkins will rent you a room if you're set on staying there, but haggle with him on the price. He's money-mad, though inoffensively, if such a thing is possible. The Chinese laundry is between the hotel and the tents, fast and efficient service offered by the yellow folk who run it. Across from us is the jail. Just a little place with two cells, I believe. Next to the livery right here is the farrier's, and then the place where he lives with his wife, and adjacent to them is the Tirritos' dry goods store. The shack you see up the hill, the one made of scrap wood, belongs to one of the prospectors, who's a mean-spirited loner. His name is Turner, and it's a challenge to make him converse, even a single word. And that covers everything. See you soon in the saloon, perhaps? The first drink's on me."

"I think I'd rather a bath and a meal," McLendon said, "assuming that these can be had in Glorious."

"Major Mulkins will offer both," LeMond said. "Remember to negotiate. And also remember that the return stage to Florence departs at ten tomorrow morning. If you like, I can ask the driver to linger just a little longer in case you complete your business with Miss Gabrielle quicker than expected. Since you don't wish to encounter her now, I'd suggest that you step lively to the hotel. After their teams are installed in Bob Pugh's corral, the stage and wagon drivers will start unloading supplies for the Tirritos' store, and the lady and her father will come out to assist them."

"I'll be on my way to the hotel, then," McLendon said. "Thanks for all your courtesy, and don't concern yourself with having the driver wait tomorrow." He shook LeMond's hand, picked up his valise, and walked twenty dusty yards to the self-styled Elite, which, to his surprise, did not seem entirely undeserving of the name. In contrast to the mud-colored adobe buildings that made up much of Glorious, the Elite was constructed of fine wood planks, all smoothly cut and varnished. There were stairs up to a wide front door, and McLendon stepped inside to a lobby where a man stood up from behind a desk and introduced himself as "Major Mulkins, proprietor." Mulkins wore a suit and cravat. His red beard was neatly trimmed, and he was the first person McLendon had seen since Tucson who wasn't covered with a layer of dust.

"Would you want a room for the night, sir?" Mulkins inquired. "We have a fine selection still available. Since I anticipate a late rush of new guests, I advise you to make your selection promptly."

McLendon couldn't help grinning. "Are other stages expected to arrive in town this evening? I hadn't realized that Glorious was situated at a busy travel crossroads."

Mulkins grinned too. "The number of daily visitors varies. Meanwhile, here you are, in need of first-class accommodation. Our rooms suit every budget. Though I perceive that you're too much the gentleman for the least of the selections, I'll mention that a place upstairs with canvas rather than a wood-and-shingle roof overhead goes for a mere six bits. There are actually those who tell me that they prefer our upstairs rooms, what with fresh air being that much more present under the canvas. Downstairs rooms are a dollar fifty, much snugger and with dust swept out daily. I'd suggest that you spring for one of the three first-class rooms with real glass windows; they'll allow you to enjoy a view of our ruggedly beautiful surroundings. Two dollars, and a bargain at the price."

"It'll soon be dark, so there will be nothing to see," McLendon said. "Four bits extra for a window of such little use seems steep."

"The windows furnish ambience," Mulkins said. "A bit of sophistication out here in the wilds. There are no glass windows to be found anywhere else in town. It cost a fortune to have the panes shipped here from Tucson. Take a windowed room, sir—you'll revel in the luxury of it. Given my personal pleasure at having you as a guest, I'll ask just twenty-five cents additional, a piddling amount to invest for a night of royal comfort."

McLendon laughed and agreed. Mulkins produced a guest register and peered at McLendon's signature.

"Welcome to Glorious, Mr. McLendon," he said. "Will your stay be extended? Shall I reserve this fine room for a week, or perhaps even longer?"

"It's hard to say," McLendon replied. "Let me take it for tonight, and tomorrow we may discuss an additional reservation. Though should that be the case, I'd hope that the rate might be adjusted accordingly."

Mulkins led McLendon down a hall to a room that contained a bed on a wood frame, a dresser with four drawers, and the promised window that, in the late afternoon, offered a view of the Owaysis saloon. There were candles, a pitcher, a basin, and a small hand towel on top of the dresser, and lace curtains on the window.

"Is a bath possible?" McLendon asked. "I've got nearly a month's worth of travel dirt stuck to my skin."

"I'll have a tin tub in your room promptly," Mulkins said. "A dime for its use, of course. And I'll get water boiling on the stove out back, another nickel for the water. Soap's a dime, too, but it's delightful soap, scented with rosewater. A drummer brought a supply of bars to the dry goods store here about a month back, and they've proven very popular with my guests. And of course you'll be wanting a bath towel—a mere penny for its use, seeing as you're in my finest room."

McLendon calculated. "So you're charging me twenty-six additional cents to bathe?"

"I forgot the dime for the firewood," Mulkins said. "It's a total of thirty-six cents in all. I have to go out and cut the wood in the mornings; the dime is to compensate me for that time and effort. You're getting quite the bargain. Visiting a hoity-toity bathhouse in Tucson would set you back fifty cents."

"Will you also charge for the air that I breathe as I bathe?"

"Oh, no. Air is free at the Elite Hotel."

Despite the additional expense, McLendon enjoyed his bath. The water Mulkins brought to the room was steaming hot, and the soap did smell delightful. William Clark LeMond hawked a splendid product. McLendon lingered in the tub, washing his hair and using scissors and a small handheld mirror from his valise to trim his dark hair and beard. Feeling refreshed, he dried himself with the bath towel provided by the Major, then put on his good suit. As he had feared, it was somewhat wrinkled, but any smells acquired from dirty clothes packed around it were offset by the strong scent of roses that still clung to McLendon's skin thanks to the perfumed soap. By the time he'd smacked as much of the dust as he could from his hat and made his way back to the hotel lobby, it was fully dark. Mulkins sat behind the desk, scribbling in a ledger by the light of a kerosene lamp.

"Your bath has worked wonders, Mr. McLendon," he said. "In your new attire you're every inch the gentleman. It's such a privilege to have a guest of your quality in my hotel."

"Are there currently any other guests, Major?" McLendon asked. "If so, I fail to discern them."

"This may be a night of late arrivals," Mulkins said. "If you've already retired, I'll caution them to step quietly so as not to disturb you. Meanwhile, what services may I offer you further?"

"Having suffered through so many indigestible stage depot meals,

I long for a decent supper," McLendon said. "Perhaps you might suggest a place where I could eat?"

"There's only one actual dining establishment in Glorious, and it's here, of course," Mulkins said. "The dining room is down the corridor to your right. At some point I intend to employ a fine chef, but for now I handle the cooking. Let me get you seated, and I'll see to your meal."

Mulkins led McLendon to a room lit with several kerosene lanterns, which emitted yellow, smoky light. "The wicks need trimming," Mulkins said. "If it's all the same, I'll deal with that tomorrow."

"You're the complete hotel staff, then?" McLendon asked.

"Not entirely. There's a Mexican woman from the ranch across the creek who comes in to sweep every morning, and she also changes the sheets on such beds as have been used on the night previous. As the town grows and visitors become more numerous, I intend to employ courteous professional staff who will pamper my guests at every turn. For now, I'm honored to be at your beck and call." Mulkins ushered McLendon to one of five tables. No one else was there. "Are you ready to eat? The stew is warming in the kitchen."

"Is that the extent of the menu? I had in mind something grander."

"It's very good stew," Mulkins said defensively. "It contains sizable hunks of beefsteak and substantial portions of carrot and potato. The vegetables were picked fresh today in the Chink camp by the creek. Potatoes are scarce in this area; most of the ground is too warm for proper planting. The yellows somehow manage it, so this delicacy is available from our kitchen. Though if you prefer, I could instead give you bacon and biscuits. The stew is two bits, bacon and biscuits a dime. I heartily recommend the stew."

"If it contains vegetables, I'll gladly have it," McLendon said.

"With what will you wash it down? I have coffee, tea, or water. If you prefer beer or stronger spirits with your meal, I can send over to the Owaysis."

"Coffee, I believe," said McLendon. "How much additional will that set me back?"

"Not a cent more," Mulkins said indignantly. "This is a class establishment. So long as I don't have to buy it on the spot from Crazy George, the beverage is included with the meal. And now I'll fetch your supper."

Besides the three guest rooms, the Elite also had glass windows—large, impressive ones—in its lobby and dining room. As he waited for his supper to be served, McLendon stared out the dining room window. It was very dark and there were no streetlamps, so he couldn't see much, mostly the campfires in the tent area and flickering candlelight behind oilcloth curtains in some of the adobe buildings. These curtains were pulled tight over openings cut into the walls. Besides Major Mulkins, nobody else in Glorious seemed able to afford window glass. McLendon wondered what Gabrielle was doing—probably fixing supper for herself and her father. Perhaps tomorrow night he'd share their evening meal.

Mulkins, now wearing an apron over his suit, placed a bowl of stew and a cup of coffee on McLendon's table, cheerfully wished him a mispronounced but sincere "Bone appetite," and left him to eat. As the Major promised, it was very good stew. McLendon especially savored the vegetables. The coffee tasted fine, too, and was a definite improvement over the sour sludge he'd been choking down at the stage depots.

A few other diners drifted in, prospectors by the look of their patched, dusty clothes. Mulkins greeted them warmly and made jokes about the heat. The newcomers looked exhausted. McLendon noticed that they all chose bacon and biscuits over the pricier stew.

He guessed that they probably could ill afford a hotel meal, but were so worn out from their day's sweaty labor that they had no energy left to cook for themselves over a campfire.

McLendon was only halfway through his own meal when Mulkins ushered in three additional diners, escorting them to an adjacent table. Their clothes were much cleaner than the miners'. As Mulkins took their orders—all three ordered the stew—McLendon studied them out of the corner of his eye, aware as he did that they were surreptitiously inspecting him too. The trio consisted of two men and a woman. One of the men was pouch-eyed and dressed in overalls; the other was slightly built to the point of appearing skeletal. He wore dungarees and had something pinned to his checkered shirt. McLendon couldn't tell what it was because the light in the room was so smoky from the kerosene lamps. The woman was stout and wore a tentlike dress. It was hard to tell where her several chins ended and her neck began.

McLendon ate slowly; there was no reason to hurry through his meal. The men and woman at the next table talked quietly and tucked into their stew when Mulkins brought it to their table. Moments after McLendon finished his last tasty bite, the man in overalls stood up and came over. He extended his hand and said, "Charlie Rogers, mayor of this town. We're always glad to greet new arrivals. Has Major Mulkins made you feel welcome? Was your dinner satisfactory?"

"Yes, and yes, though haggling over price seemed obligatory," McLendon said, and told Mayor Rogers his name.

Rogers chuckled. "Well, that's the Major for you. Will you take a cup of coffee with us? Pleasant conversation is the best aid to digestion." Waving McLendon to an empty chair between the thin man and the obese woman, he said, "Cash McLendon, meet my wife,

Rose, and also Joe Saint, our town sheriff." McLendon saw that the object on Saint's shirt was a metal star, though the badge was badly battered. One of its five points was bent at an odd angle, and another was broken off completely.

"Saint is a curious name for a sheriff," McLendon said. "I expect you take some ribbing about it."

Sheriff Saint had lank blond hair and wore wire-rimmed spectacles; his beard was sparse and there were several bare patches on his cheeks where whiskers refused to grow. McLendon estimated Saint's age to be in the early thirties. "It's no more an unusual name than Cash," the sheriff replied. "Because of it, do people take you for a gambler? Have you come to teach our citizens the treacherous arts of cards and dice?"

"Not at all," McLendon replied. To divert the inevitable queries about why he'd come to Glorious—if he admitted he was there to see Gabrielle, these people might alert her and spoil his opportunity to surprise her in the morning—he added, "Tell me about your town." It was McLendon's experience that people proud of their titles usually couldn't resist invitations to talk.

Mayor Rogers launched into a rambling account of how, just about eighteen months earlier, he and Major Mulkins and Bob Pugh met in Tucson, where all the talk was about some silver-laden rock found up in the Pinals by a soldier. Even before that, Rogers said, everybody in Arizona Territory knew that there were vast seams of silver—and probably copper, too—all through the Pinals, but dread of the Apaches kept everyone away. He and the Major and Bob decided that, to hell with it, they'd accept the risk in anticipation of great reward; a town had to be established in this rich region so that when the inevitable first strike was made, there'd be local services available. Rogers was a farrier by trade, and Bob Pugh had a great deal of experience working with mules. The Major—that was Mulkins—had a little money and was willing to invest it in a hotel; well, he at least had enough capital on hand to start building one.

"That's why the Major fights now for every extra cent," Rogers explained. "He needs to buy additional materials and hire work crews from Florence to come out and finish the Elite."

The new friends rode up into the Pinals and discovered a promising spot, a valley in the shadow of the mountains so prospectors would have proximity to the areas where silver was likely to be found. A site adjacent to Queen Creek meant that water wouldn't be a problem. When they returned to Tucson they were lucky enough to make the acquaintance of Sal Tirrito and his daughter, folks experienced in the dry goods trade who'd come west from St. Louis, and with them on board they had the makings of a small but select business community. They loaded up, came back to this far end of the valley, and picked a town name, and so Glorious was founded.

"The prospectors come and go for now," Rogers said. "That's the way they naturally are. They poke about in one place and if they don't find color after a few weeks they wander on somewhere else. But someday soon one of them will hit it big here, and when that happens, word will spread and you'll see hundreds more pouring into town every day. And some of them will make additional strikes, and then will come the crews to build the mines and the miners to dig the ore and the workers to process it, and Glorious will grow and in time rival places like Virginia City. And here we founders will be, doing great business and making our own fortunes. You may call it a dream, but it's going to come true."

"Perhaps you're right," McLendon said. "I sincerely hope so. But the Apache threat must remain a deterrent. As I understand it, around here a man risks his life straying even a few yards on his own. Perhaps you feel safe here in town, but what about the prospectors as they make their way across the valley or up in the mountains?"

Sheriff Saint, who had been polishing his glasses with one of the hotel's cloth napkins, said, "We're fortunate in that Mr. MacPherson, owner of nearby Culloden Ranch, employs some of his men to patrol the area. They have some experience fighting Indians, and their presence seems to generally discourage the Apaches, though of course we have occasional incidents."

"I saw two of those riders on my way into town," McLendon said. "That's quite generous of this Mr. MacPherson."

"He's a true benefactor," said Mayor Rogers. "Ah! Here's Major Mulkins to offer dessert."

The three men declined Mulkins's suggestion of canned peaches or pears but accepted more coffee. Rose Rogers, who'd been silent while the men at the table conversed, asked Mulkins in a surprisingly high, girlish voice to bring her "the usual." Mulkins nodded and returned in a few moments with a jar of jelly and a spoon. McLendon thought she would spread the treat on biscuits, and tried hard not to look astonished when Mrs. Rogers ate the jelly straight from the jar. She emptied it in moments, sighing with satisfaction as she gobbled each spoonful. When the last delectable blob was consumed, she delicately dabbed her lips with a napkin. Her husband said it was time for them to go.

"We have a small place just behind my shop," he told McLendon. "Should your stay here extend, feel free to call. It's always pleasant to see a fresh face."

McLendon pushed back his chair, too, but Sheriff Saint signaled Mulkins for another coffee refill and nodded for the Major to also pour more for McLendon. Well-versed himself in the arts of indirect manipulation, McLendon guessed what was going on. Major Mulkins undoubtedly told Mayor Rogers that a stranger had arrived in town, obviously not a prospector, but someone well heeled enough to afford a hotel room with a window, and a bath besides. At this early, critical juncture in Glorious's existence, the mayor would want to meet such an intriguing visitor. Having done so, Rogers now left it to the town sheriff to take McLendon's measure. Saint's first words after Rogers and his wife left the dining room confirmed that conjecture.

"You've failed to mention your reason for coming to Glorious," the sheriff said, studying McLendon through the thick lenses of his eyeglasses. The magnification made his blue eyes look enormous.

"That's correct," McLendon said. "Don't worry, it's an errand of no concern to the law. Just personal business."

"The territories draw all kinds, and confidence men are always attracted to mining towns. I'm glad to hear you say that your purpose is law-abiding."

"But you'll be watching me," McLendon said, enjoying the verbal sparring.

Saint nodded and said, "I will, but now that we've talked, I'm sure that I won't see anything troubling."

"It must be stressful to keep constant lookout for miscreants," McLendon said. Joe Saint was impressive. For all his physical frailness, the sheriff packed sufficient intellectual muscle for sharp conversational counterpunches.

For the first time Saint smiled. "For now, my job is more ceremonial than anything else. Most newcomers are prospectors, and they rise before dawn and are out until dark. When they return at night they're too worn-out to do much beyond cook some beans on their campfires and fall asleep in their tents. Sometimes one of them takes a glass too many at the Owaysis and I lock him up until he's sober. As the town grows, so will my responsibilities."

"What qualities recommended you as sheriff?"

"Someone had to take the job. We're looking to the territorial legislature for official town status, and that requires local law enforcement. I was passing through, liked what I saw, and wanted to stay. So I'm the sheriff. Perhaps you'll want to stay too."

"Perhaps," McLendon said noncommittally. "Well, Major Mulkins is charging me dearly for my room, so I think I'll turn in and get my money's worth. It was a pleasure to meet you, Sheriff Saint."

"Likewise." The men stood and shook hands. McLendon walked back through the hotel lobby and was stopped there by Major Mulkins.

"Off to bed?" Mulkins asked. "Could I interest you in a cat for your room?"

"Why would I want a cat?"

"It's an unfortunate fact that we, like most isolated frontier towns, have a problem with pests and vermin," Mulkins said. "There are scorpions. Be certain to shake out the bedclothes before you pull them over you, because scorpion stings are nasty. Rats are a particular nuisance. I set traps, of course, but there are too many to get them all. Many of my discerning guests like a cat in their rooms at night, to keep the rats under control. Just a dime will get you a fine feline, and thus assure a more peaceful night's slumber."

"I believe that I'll pass on the cat," McLendon said. "I've seen no rats in your hotel."

"That's due to my efforts to keep them away, but I admit that during the dark of night too many elude me," Mulkins said. "Even the finest hotels in Tucson offer cats. You'd be well advised to take one. Rats are well known to bite."

McLendon sighed and said that he'd take the cat. Mulkins fetched a near-feral calico from a cage he kept behind the hotel. The animal's occasional yowls and the constant sound of its sharp claws scrabbling on the floor kept McLendon awake for much of the night. He spent the sleepless hours remembering all that had happened back in St. Louis, and in particular the tragedy that had him on the run ever since.

THREE

Cash McLendon wasn't certain how old he was. His mother died when he was an infant, and his father, Caleb, cared more about drinking than celebrating birthdays. In May 1872, when McLendon arrived in Glorious, his best guess was that he was about twenty-eight.

His early childhood consisted of getting his perpetually drunk or near terminally hungover father to work at a series of St. Louis factories. Sometimes Cash failed, and on those occasions it was the boy's responsibility to convince the factory foreman that Caleb was sick again, another bout of the grippe or recurring neuralgia. All the foremen eventually got fed up with the excuses and fired Caleb, and then there were near-starving nights spent sleeping in alleys until the son heard of another factory that was hiring and talked a new foreman into giving his father a job there. When sober, Caleb McLendon was a good worker, particularly skilled at fitting small machinery parts. But he wasn't sober very often. It was lucky that there were so many factories in town; St. Louis was the manufacturing capital of the

American West. There was always another prospective employer
Cash could cajole on his father's behalf. The lies he learned to tell
were effective ones, incorporating sufficient fact to allow him, in the
moment of the telling, to believe them himself. This made him look
and sound sincere, so he and Caleb usually had just enough money to
afford a place to sleep and something to eat. Like many of the city's
poor children, he never attended school. It was a hard, insecure life,
but it was all that the boy knew.

One night in 1855, Caleb McLendon disappeared. His son
searched in taverns and brothels and hospitals, but found no trace of
him. The police guessed that Caleb got drunk, fell in the Mississippi
River, and drowned. Cash had no money for shelter or food. He ate
what he could steal from markets and outdoor stands, and slept in
the saddle tack factory where his father had last worked, sneaking in
through a back window after the late shift left for the night, keeping
warm under the large squares of leather set out to be cut and shaped
the next day. A night watchman prowled the factory, and soon the
boy was caught. In the morning the watchman hauled Cash into the
foreman's office and suggested that the police be summoned; ragged
beggar boys like this one belonged in the poorhouse. But Mr. Hancock, the foreman, took pity on Cash. He knew him from the times
when Cash came to explain that his poor father was once again sick
in bed, very ill but surely able to work tomorrow. He asked if Cash
wanted a job sweeping out the factory and picking up the leather
scraps that piled up around the cutting tables. In return, he could
sleep there at night under a real blanket and earn a few pennies a day
for food. Cash gratefully accepted. He worked hard and soon became
a favorite of the adult workers. Even though they made barely enough
to feed and clothe their own families, they packed extra food for him
in their lunch buckets, brought him their children's hand-me-downs,

and chatted with him during breaks. The boy was a sympathetic listener who seemed fascinated by everything he heard. Within a month they were sharing with him their complaints about how little they were paid while working under very hazardous responsibilities: a shift seldom went by without one or two of them cutting themselves badly, and occasionally someone lost a finger or even a whole hand to the blades.

There was talk of organizing a strike. The trick was to get all the employees to agree before the foreman found out. Then they could stage a mass walkout; the owner would have to pay them better or else close the factory down, losing production time and profits. Cash was terrified. If the plant shut down, he'd be back on the street. The other workers were his friends and he cared about them; their complaints about working conditions were valid. But his obsession with self-preservation won out. After considerable soul-searching, he warned Mr. Hancock. Four of the would-be union organizers were summarily fired. Afterward, Mr. Hancock showed his appreciation by giving Cash a dollar. The other employees didn't know that Cash had been an informer. There was talk about a spy in their midst, but no one suspected the friendly young boy. They continued to give him food and secondhand clothes and talk unguardedly to him. So did the plant shift leaders and even Mr. Hancock. Cash never spent even an hour in a formal classroom, but he remembered and learned from everything he heard. He developed an extensive vocabulary, though he could neither read nor spell the words he understood and used in conversation. He learned arithmetic by looking over the shoulders of plant accountants as they kept daily ledgers. Over the next few years he occasionally had the opportunity to alert Mr. Hancock to other potential problems. Each time, he was praised and given a little money. Cash's conscience sometimes bothered him, and when it did he told himself that he was actually helping rather than betraying people who trusted him. It was in everyone's best interests that the plant operated at maximum profitability. That was the way to ensure that all the workers' jobs were safe, and they could keep on supporting their families. He'd learned this from listening to Mr. Hancock himself.

IN 1859, ST. LOUIS was swept with talk of imminent civil war. Missouri was bitterly divided between supporters of the government in Washington, D.C., and militants favoring the slaveholding South. There was one issue on which everyone agreed: St. Louis would be a vital supplier of military supplies to one side or the other. Abraham Lincoln's election to the presidency in 1860 precipitated a rush of seceding Southern states. Missouri wavered. Cash McLendon, now a teenager, had no interest in the plight of slaves or the question of states' rights. His concern was that he would be drafted into the Army and forced to fight. Having struggled so hard to survive in peacetime, he had no desire to die in a war. Mr. Hancock offered Cash a way out. The federal government was determined to keep Missouri in the Union fold, he told the youngster. Its factories and textile mills were vital to the Northern cause. There would soon be rich Army contracts coming up for bid. As it happened, the saddle tack facility was just one of several factories and mills owned by Mr. Rupert Douglass. A great patriot, Mr. Douglass wanted to win those contract bids and supply the finest-quality saddles and blankets and uniforms for the Union Army. The problem was in knowing how much to bid. Mr. Hancock had long observed how good Cash was at gleaning information, how people naturally told him things.

"What would you think, youngster, of going around to rival factories and taking jobs there, staying long enough to hear talk about contract bids, and then quietly sharing what you learn with me?" Mr. Hancock asked Cash. "I can then inform Mr. Douglass, and he can adjust his bids accordingly. It would be a fine thing to do for your country. The products produced by Douglass companies are far superior to those of the competition. If Mr. Douglass wins most of these bids, the Union Army will be better served."

"I could try, sir," Cash said. He felt doubtful and it showed in his voice. It was one thing to be helpful to Mr. Hancock by listening and reporting in a factory where he already knew everyone. The boy's hard life on the street had made him wary of strangers.

"Don't forget that everyone employed by Mr. Douglass will also benefit," Hancock said. "Perhaps you will most of all, since Mr. Douglass has ways of rewarding helpful young men. And, should you agree, I'll personally write a letter to the Army saying you shouldn't be forced to enlist, since you're providing vital services to the war effort. And that will be the truth."

Cash said he'd try. He infiltrated competitors' factories, and when he learned something useful, he passed it on to Mr. Hancock. He found that he enjoyed the challenge of discovering key information, and that now he didn't need to feel troubled about informing on friends. Soon, in most contract competitions, the Douglass bids were a few pennies per unit lower than anyone else's. The war made Mr. Douglass fabulously wealthy. And, as Mr. Hancock had promised, he showed his appreciation.

One summer night in 1864, Cash McLendon met Mr. Hancock in a dark saloon well away from the St. Louis factory district. He told Mr. Hancock about plans at a competing button factory to add fifty workers, increasing output and enabling them to promise delivery to the Army faster than rival bidders. Armed with this knowledge,

Mr. Douglass could add more workers at his own button plant and beat the competition at their own game.

"This is very useful," Mr. Hancock said. "Now I have something for you. Tomorrow night, clean up and put a shine on your shoes. Mr. Rupert Douglass himself requests your presence at nine in the evening in his home."

"Why would Mr. Douglass want to see me?" Cash asked.

"I couldn't say, but be at your best tomorrow. This may be your opportunity. Go to the back door, of course. The front is for the society callers."

The next night McLendon cautiously rapped on the back door of a mansion that far surpassed any private home he'd ever seen. He was admitted by a forbidding-looking butler who didn't bother giving a name or asking McLendon for his. The butler escorted McLendon up a winding staircase and into a study lined with bookcases and paintings. McLendon was instructed to sit in a chair and wait: "Mr. Douglass will be with you shortly." Five nervous minutes stretched into ten. McLendon felt completely out of his element. Though there were stairs in the factories where he worked, he'd never been in a house with a staircase before. Even the chairs in the room were intimidating, with their great wide armrests and plush cushioned seats. The bookcases were dark oak. The titles on the spines of the books seemed like mysterious code. Having never set foot in a classroom, McLendon couldn't read. But the sheer number of books on the shelves astounded him. They were one more indication of unimaginable wealth. It amazed him that anyone could be rich enough to live in a house like this.

The door finally opened and Rupert Douglass stepped in. A tall, regal-looking man, he was dressed in a velvet smoking jacket. McLendon had never seen such a garment before, and found it hard not to stare.

"I'm having a brandy," Mr. Douglass said. "Join me?"

"I don't drink much, sir," McLendon said politely. "But thank you for the offer."

Mr. Douglass regarded him curiously. "Hancock says your father was a drunk. Is that why you abstain?"

"No, sir, and I don't entirely abstain. If the situation or the company requires, I'll sip a beer or wet my lips with hard liquor. But most often it's my job to listen, and for that I need a clear head."

"Then listen well," Mr. Douglass said. "You're a young man of some potential. I believe you can be of further assistance to me."

The war would be over soon, Mr. Douglass said. The South was licked; it was only a matter of time until they accepted it. Then the wartime bidding would be done with, so it was time to look ahead. It was Mr. Douglass's intention to control St. Louis manufacturing. Competition was for lesser men. He sought total domination. And that would be best for everyone all the way down, from factory foremen to the lowliest line workers, because he was an honorable man who paid fair wages and provided sanitary workplace conditions. That was all any honest workingmen should expect. In return, he wanted no obstruction from unions, no grumblers hindering production. Did his young friend McLendon understand? If so, he could play a key role in all this.

"Go on being a sociable fellow in the factories I already own and the ones I contemplate acquiring," Mr. Douglass said, draining his brandy and lighting a dark, fragrant cigar. "Find out things that I need to know. Beyond whatever salary you earn at your day jobs, some additional pay from me will be involved. Nothing excessive to begin, but there will be more to come if you prove yourself worthy in this special duty. So long as you're efficient and loyal, you can always rely on Rupert Douglass—although in that regard, any form of betrayal would result in unpleasant rather than happy consequences. I'm a generous man, but not a foolish one. Never fail me. Have I your word?"

"You do, sir," McLendon said. His heart was pounding. It seemed too good to be true.

Mr. Douglass shook his hand and rose, indicating that McLendon should do the same. "Don't disappoint me. Do well and you'll be rewarded." Though McLendon hadn't seen or heard Mr. Douglass make any sort of signal, the door opened and the dour butler appeared to escort McLendon out. He followed him downstairs in a daze. Somewhere in the house a young girl was laughing, sustained euphoric peals. McLendon was too stunned to laugh himself, but he felt the same sense of euphoria. He'd been presented with a tremendous opportunity. He intended to make the most of it, and did.

McLENDON INFILTRATED over a dozen St. Louis factories. Sometimes he identified irreplaceable supervisors and workers so that they could be hired away by Douglass, simultaneously improving his boss's business operations and hindering his competitors'. If some new procedure improved product quality or production time, McLendon studied it carefully and then taught it to Douglass's workers. Because he was so ordinary-looking, average in height and build, he blended in at will. In conversations he always encouraged the other person to keep talking, to tell more. Cash was careful not to allow himself to form genuine friendships. Sometimes it was hard, but his loyalty to his real employer won out. He never indulged in casual chat; he spoke to others not for any social purpose but to glean information, anything to gain an advantage for Rupert Douglass.

One evening in the midsummer of 1866, Mr. Douglass summoned Cash to his home. "I'm about to acquire two new factories, and I need your help in a different way," he said. "This assignment will test your powers of persuasion rather than observation."

The two plants stood on adjacent lots near the river, Mr. Douglass explained. Together, they employed nearly three hundred workers, who would all benefit from the new ownership. But he had a concern: a half-dozen privately owned shops operated directly across the street from the main factory entrances—a boot maker, a milliner, a pharmacy, two groceries, and a dry goods store. After receiving their weekly pay packets on Fridays, the employees promptly spent most of their wages at these very convenient stores. McLendon's new assignment was to befriend the shop owners and convince them to sell their businesses to Mr. Douglass.

"I pay the workers' salaries, so they should spend the money in stores that I own," he said between puffs on one of his fine cigars. "You see the rightness of that, I'm certain. Win the trust of these shop owners, then identify yourself as my agent and help them understand it's in their own best interests that they do as I wish. Make it politely but definitely clear that if they don't, I'll build rival shops on the factory grounds and undersell them right out of business. That's extra trouble and expense I prefer to avoid, of course. And I'm really doing these people a favor. I'll pay them a fair price, so if they wish to try again, they'll have a stake to do so somewhere else."

Over the next four months, McLendon made friends with all of the shop owners. It wasn't hard. He began by dropping in on a regular basis, buying small items, and chatting companionably. Then he began to talk of the business opportunities in other parts of St. Louis, away from the airborne grit and choking smoke of the factory district. When, eventually, McLendon revealed that he worked for Mr. Rupert Douglass, and that Mr. Douglass was prepared to make very generous offers for their shops, five of the six shop owners soon agreed. New signs proclaimed DOUGLASS BOOTS, DOUGLASS MILLINERY, DOUGLASS PHARMACY, and DOUGLASS MARKET; the two small groceries were merged into one.

But Salvatore Tirrito, owner of the dry goods store, refused to sell. He and his nineteen-year-old daughter, Gabrielle, told McLendon that there was no reason to discuss it further.

"Perhaps you misunderstand," McLendon said. "Mr. Douglass is prepared to be quite generous. This is an excellent opportunity for you."

"We're not interested in your so-called opportunity," Gabrielle said. She spoke on her father's behalf because, thirty years after immigrating to America, he still had a limited grasp of English. "We're happy with what we already have, and with where we are."

"Be reasonable," McLendon said. "You're in business to make money. This sale will bring you a considerable amount, so much that you can go somewhere else and open a bigger, better shop that will bring you better profits than you can make at this location."

"For some people, though I suppose not for you and Mr. Douglass, there are other things more important than money," Gabrielle said. "My father and mother and uncle and aunt come from Naples. Papa worked on the docks here by day and patched sails for extra money at night. He and my mother saved every cent for almost twenty-five years to start their own business. When they did, it was the proudest moment of their lives. They spent more than they could afford for that carved 'Tirrito Dry Goods' sign hanging over the door. Mamma died of a fever right afterward. We honor her memory with every day that this store is in business. It doesn't matter how much Mr. Douglass offers. We're not going to sell."

"Mr. Douglass is a proud man, and won't react well to a negative response," McLendon cautioned. "Once he's chosen a course of action, he never gives up. He'll very likely open a better dry goods store than yours right across the street on the grounds of the factories, and sell products cheaper than you ever could. Then you'll have no business at all, nor the wherewithal to start another."

"We'll take our chances, Mr. McLendon. I'm sorry if we offend Mr. Douglass's precious pride, but my father and I are proud too."

Mr. Douglass took the news better than McLendon anticipated. He said that five out of six wasn't a bad beginning. McLendon should keep talking to the Italian and his daughter when he had a spare moment. They'd eventually come around. Meanwhile, St. Louis was booming and Mr. Douglass felt that the time was right to get into the construction business. McLendon was instructed to identify the best companies currently in local operation so that Mr. Douglass could acquire them. That took up much of McLendon's attention, but he didn't forget Salvatore and Gabrielle Tirrito. Three weeks after their refusal to sell, he dropped back by their shop. Gabrielle stood behind the counter, chatting animatedly in Italian with an older woman, who hugged her and left the store.

"Do you embrace all of your customers?" McLendon asked.

"Only if they shop here regularly," Gabrielle said.

McLendon thought she was a pretty girl. Gabrielle's complexion was olive, and her eyes and hair were dark and lustrous. "Then you're assured of my constant business."

"Well, you're not assured of ever being hugged. Anyway, that was my aunt Lidia, who lives next door with Uncle Mario, my father's brother. Not that it's any of your business. Can I help you with something?"

"You and your father could sell this store to Mr. Douglass. That would help me."

Gabrielle laughed, and McLendon found the sound delightful. "Sorry, no."

To prolong the conversation, he asked her to show him their selection of scissors: "I want to trim my beard."

Gabrielle showed him several pairs and suggested one in particular "because the blades are strong and suited for cutting thick tangles. Beards look best when they're close-trimmed and not bushy."

"Do you think mine is bushy?"

"I don't think about your beard at all. Do you want the scissors? They're fifty cents."

McLendon put the coins in her hand. "Perhaps, when I've trimmed my beard, I'll return to see if it meets with your approval."

Gabrielle raised her eyebrows in mock astonishment. "Come back anytime you like, so long as you don't pester us about selling our shop."

He began dropping by the store once a week, then every few days. He was careful not to mention Mr. Douglass or his offer. Instead, he and Gabrielle chatted and often sparred verbally on topics ranging from politics to the best brand of tooth powder. She was a young woman of firm opinions. McLendon wasn't a man of any particular convictions, but he liked pretending to be against whatever Gabrielle was for, just to engage in witty give-and-take. He'd never realized that talking for pleasure could be so enjoyable. McLendon began occasionally visiting in the evening, on his way back to his boarding-house. One night Gabrielle invited him to have dinner with her and her father. Salvatore went to bed early, but McLendon stayed late and the talk between him and Gabrielle bubbled on until nearly midnight.

The next week Gabrielle suggested that McLendon accompany her to a free concert in a city park. The band played a selection of popular tunes. McLendon enjoyed the music, and when he took Gabrielle home he was astounded when she sat down at a small piano and played some of the same songs. "Sing with me," she urged as she began to play "When Johnny Comes Marching Home." When he did, his horribly off-key warbling reduced them both to teary-eyed laughter. The piano was the centerpiece of the Tirritos' social life. Every Sunday they hosted relatives and friends for a boisterous dinner prepared by Gabrielle and her aunt Lidia, and afterward everyone gathered around the piano and sang while Gabrielle played. McLendon came and enjoyed the sense of warm camaraderie that was so different from the false relationships that were part of his working life.

On Tuesday and Thursday evenings, Gabrielle was never home. For a while she wouldn't tell him why. He suspected she was seeing another man, and felt jealous. One Tuesday night he waited across the street from the dry goods store and, when she left, followed her at a distance. Gabrielle walked a dozen blocks to the Catholic church that she and her father attended on Sundays. She entered the church through a side door. McLendon stood outside for a while. Then, overcome by curiosity, he went inside and found Gabrielle sitting on the floor surrounded by children. She looked up at McLendon and said, "I'm helping my small friends here learn to read. Come be my assistant." He excused himself because he didn't want to admit that he was illiterate. The next day she told him that she'd been giving lessons for years: "Reading opens up whole new worlds for poor children, who otherwise have difficult lives and little or no schooling. Most of their parents work in factories and have very little money to buy their children food, let alone books." Gabrielle used a small blackboard to display letters of the alphabet. Her late mother, Tina, had used the chalkboard as an aid in teaching her to read, Gabrielle said. "I'm doing this in part to honor her memory." But reading materials were necessary, too, so Gabrielle bought used copies of McGuffey's *First Eclectic Reader for Young Children* for a few pennies apiece. Because her funds were limited, she could afford only a few at a time, and her students had to share.

"How much do their parents pay you to teach them?" McLendon asked. "Couldn't you use some of that money for the books?"

"I don't charge for these lessons," Gabrielle said. "Haven't you heard the saying that good deeds are their own reward?" He had, but considered it a foolish notion. She suggested again that McLendon help with the classes, and when he declined, she insisted. So he came, ostensibly to remind the children to listen to their instructor, and found himself listening too. As a naturally quick learner, McLendon soon recognized letters of the alphabet and then printed words. When Gabrielle began lending him books and encouraging him to read them, he thought she must have guessed that he was unlettered but was considerate enough not to say so. Instead, she'd made him her helper, and in doing so taught him to read too. That Christmas she gave him *The Last of the Mohicans*, by James Fenimore Cooper, the first book that he'd ever owned. He read it over and over; she was so pleased that she continued to give him books—other novels by Cooper, *The Scarlet Letter* by Nathaniel Hawthorne, and collections of verse by the oddly named poets Longfellow and Tennyson. He gave her sheet music, more songs that she could play on her beloved piano, the single luxury in the Tirrito household. She told him that she loved him giving her sheet music because it showed that he understood her heart.

Free reading classes for poor children struck McLendon as such a good idea that he mentioned them to Rupert Douglass. He suggested that they be arranged for the offspring of Douglass factory workers; he knew someone very capable who would be glad to help get them organized. The cost would be negligible compared to the goodwill gained with employees. But Douglass refused.

"If too many of the lower classes learn to read, it will give them ideas above their station," he said. "My businesses need workers who are grateful for steady employment and have no ambition to be more than they already are."

For the first time McLendon dared to disagree with his patron. "Even working people need hope of opportunity, sir, or at least the belief that their children's lives may prove better than their own."

Douglass snorted. "The reality of the world is that most are born into the working lives that they deserve, which is servitude to their betters. There are infrequent exceptions, you're one of them. But don't go softheaded on me. I raised you out of the gutter and could return you there anytime. I'll hear no more about these reading classes."

McLendon never mentioned them to Mr. Douglass again. But he quietly arranged for some of the children of Douglass factory workers to attend Gabrielle's Tuesday and Thursday night classes, and he used his own money to purchase additional McGuffey readers. He knew that Mr. Douglass would be angry if he found out, but the pleasure he took in watching the little ones learn made it seem worth the risk. Besides, he was already tempting fate by his ongoing, evolving relationship with Gabrielle.

They understood themselves now to be a couple, and sometimes discussed a future together. On Sundays, Aunt Lidia took every opportunity to hint to McLendon that her niece would make a wonderful wife. Salvatore Tirrito warmed sufficiently to McLendon to offer him occasional glasses of homemade wine, which he'd previously shared only with blood relations. Gabrielle knew, of course, that McLendon worked for Rupert Douglass in a capacity he never clearly described for fear of disgusting her so much that she would have nothing more to do with him. Based on her own first encounter with McLendon, she was still able to guess the nature if not the extent of his questionable activities. Gabrielle began mentioning the satisfaction he might find in helping to operate a dry goods store. McLendon felt sure, though he didn't say so to her, that if he ever left Rupert Douglass for Tirrito Dry Goods, his former boss would stop at nothing to put his smaller competitor out of business, just to teach his former employee a lesson. Besides, for all his certainty that he loved Gabrielle, McLendon still couldn't help relishing the sense of power, of importance, that he felt working for Mr. Douglass. So he tried as best he could to live in both worlds.

ONE FALL NIGHT, Mr. Douglass summoned McLendon. They met in the book-lined study, and this time Mr. Douglass insisted that McLendon take some brandy.

"You've worked for me almost six years," Mr. Douglass said. "I've gotten a good sense of your talent, and I mean to make fuller use of it."

McLendon had been his eyes and ears in the factory district of St. Louis. Now, Mr. Douglass said, it was time for him to become something more. There were other aspects to conducting successful business. It was critical to pick out the important elected officials and the key power brokers and gain their support, through campaign contributions and gifts to their favored charities and occasionally with what the unenlightened termed "bribes." Mr. Douglass preferred the term "considerations," which sounded more civilized.

"Self-interest drives our great land," he said. "Why would anyone ever willingly do something for someone else if he himself doesn't benefit?"

As Mr. Douglass's holdings continued to grow, he needed the constant assistance of someone able to comfortably mix on all levels of business and politics—"Not only my eyes and ears, but sometimes my voice. My right-hand man will be you, McLendon. You'll extend my reach and have your fair share of all that you bring me. You'll have to work harder than ever before. I'll expect only the best results. Fail me and I'll discard you. Betray me and I'll destroy you. But serve me well and I'll raise you high."

Besides even longer work hours and frequent trips—sometimes all the way to Washington or Philadelphia or New York—the biggest change in McLendon's life resulted from Mr. Douglass's insistence that he move into the mansion: "I want you at hand for discussion or action at any hour, but it's not just that. If you're going to represent me at the higher levels, then you must learn proper manners: which fork to use, how to act like a proper gentleman around the better people." McLendon was given a room on the second story just over the kitchen, and woke in the morning to the delicious smells of brewing coffee and fresh-baked bread. Servants changed his bed linen daily, and he wore fine clothes handmade for him by Mr. Douglass's personal tailor. On most evenings he took dinner in the main dining room with Mr. Douglass and his wife and daughter. Mrs. Matilda Douglass was an elegant, mostly silent woman who wore jeweled necklaces and dangling earrings. Seventeen-year-old Ellen was given to sudden fits of uncontrollable giggling; it had certainly been her laughter that he heard on his first visit to the Douglass mansion six years earlier. She was blond and strikingly lovely, with prominent cheekbones and long, elegant fingers. Beyond her looks and laughter, McLendon learned very little about her. They were never alone together. Her mother or a stout black woman named Mrs. Reynolds was always with her. Mrs. Reynolds didn't live with the Douglasses but came whenever they couldn't be with Ellen. McLendon, who'd never encountered a very rich girl before, supposed that they were always closely chaperoned. Whenever Ellen talked to him, it was in a teasing tone, and he could never feel certain what she really meant.

"Do you like living here in our house?" she asked him one night at dinner. "How long do you think that you'll stay?"

"I like it very much," McLendon said, trying not to drip a spoonful of soup on the fine white linen tablecloth. "I'm grateful for your parents' hospitality."

"It's my hospitality too," Ellen said. "Are you grateful to me?"

"Of course, Miss Douglass."

Ellen giggled. "Then perhaps I'll allow you to remain."

Matilda Douglass spoke for the first time since the meal began. "Ellen, don't torment Mr. McLendon. Eat your dinner."

Ellen didn't say anything further to McLendon, but a few times during the rest of the four-course meal he caught her staring at him curiously, as though he were an exhibit in a zoo.

McLENDON'S NEW DUTIES limited his time with Gabrielle. He was expected to meet with Mr. Douglass every evening for an hour or so to discuss the business of the day; sometimes the meetings lasted much longer, causing him to miss Sunday dinners with the Tirritos and helping with Gabrielle's reading classes. She never complained, which made him feel guilty. He knew she was waiting for him to formally propose marriage, but that wasn't something he currently had time to think about. There was too much to do for Mr. Douglass. In particular, there was a problem with the owner of a metal foundry. Mr. Douglass had learned from a contact in the War Department that the government would soon call for bids on new munitions contracts. The Indians on the frontier were proving stubborn. President Grant was being urged by his confidants to blast them into extinction. The St. Louis foundry could be quickly converted to manufacture ammunition for cannons. Mr. Douglass wanted to acquire it, but owner Arthur Cory refused to sell. McLendon spent hours with Cory, pointing out the splendid profit he would make, but the man was adamant: He had worked hard to build his company, and he meant to keep it. After a week of nonstop effort, McLendon reluctantly reported to Mr. Douglass that Cory would not budge.

"Don't blame yourself; some men simply will not reason," Mr. Douglass said. "I think we must take another approach."

Two days later, Mr. Douglass welcomed a mysterious visitor to his home. The towering, thick-shouldered fellow was ushered into the book-lined study at the same time that McLendon routinely met there with his employer. Now he was kept waiting while Mr. Douglass and the newcomer met privately. McLendon paced restlessly in the vast backyard, poking at shrubs and croquet goals. Once, when he looked up, he spied Ellen gazing at him from an upstairs window. When she saw him looking back, she moved out of sight. Finally, a servant came to say that Mr. Douglass now required him.

"Meet Patrick Brautigan," Mr. Douglass said. "He's lately from Boston, and highly recommended."

Brautigan's hand was much wider than McLendon's; Cash flinched as they shook, as it was clear that Brautigan could have easily crushed his knuckles. But he exerted only enough pressure for a firm shake and then dropped back into his chair.

"A pleasure," he said to McLendon. There was a complete absence of emotion in his voice and in his deep-set, opaque eyes.

"Brautigan is a man of certain persuasive skills," Mr. Douglass said. "He joins us on a permanent basis. Initially, he will assist with this man Cory, who Brautigan will call on in the very near future."

"Arthur Cory is a decent man, but stubborn," McLendon said to Brautigan. "I'll come along with you, of course, though I doubt we can persuade him to be smart and sell."

"No need," Brautigan said. "I'll manage on my own." He stood and made a slight bow to Mr. Douglass.

"I want that foundry," Mr. Douglass said.

"I expect to soon report satisfactory results," Brautigan replied. He nodded to McLendon and turned to leave. Even though the floor was carpeted, Brautigan's heavy boots thudded as he walked. McLendon noticed that the toes of the boots were reinforced with polished steel plates.

Mr. Douglass handed a thick sealed envelope to McLendon. "Tomorrow, take this to police chief Kelly Welsh at City Hall. Be discreet when you do. We must always demonstrate respect for public officials."

Three days later, the St. Louis newspapers reported that Arthur Cory, the fifty-six-year-old owner of a local metal foundry, had been found dead behind a riverfront saloon. His head was so damaged by repeated strikes from some hard, blunt-tipped object that he had to be identified by the rings on his fingers rather than his pulped facial features. When he saw Brautigan that night, McLendon looked again at the plating on the toes of his boots. It seemed to him that the steel toe on the right boot was freshly scraped. Chief Welsh announced a full investigation, but nothing came of it. Not much later, Cory's widow sold the foundry to Rupert Douglass.

McLendon was so shaken that he confronted Mr. Douglass.

"Why has this happened, sir?" McLendon demanded. "Is the ownership of one factory among so many worth the cost of a human life?"

"It's not just the factory," Mr. Douglass said. "Word was around town that I wanted to buy it and Arthur Cory refused. If one man so publicly defied me, more might find the gumption to attempt the same. This act was necessary to send a message, and the blame for it is all on Mr. Cory. He would not let reason prevail."

"I thought that we respected the law," McLendon said.

"We do, lad, we do. It's a rule of mine that my people must never openly break or defy the law. It's just that as practical men we must sometimes circumvent it."

After that, McLendon rarely encountered Patrick Brautigan and was glad of it. He privately nicknamed the man "Killer Boots." For a while he was panic-stricken at the possibility that Salvatore Tirrito would be the hulking monster's next victim, and thought about warning him. But he eventually decided that Mr. Douglass wouldn't consider an obscure dry goods store worth killing for, if in fact he remembered Tirrito Dry Goods at all. Brautigan mostly kept busy discouraging union organizers at Mr. Douglass's factories. McLendon tried hard not to think about how Killer Boots served their mutual employer. He told himself that it had nothing to do with him.

THAT WINTER, McLendon accompanied Mr. Douglass on a train trip to Washington. They met with a highly placed official who coordinated government dealings with the railroads. A plan to place

additional tracks in St. Louis included the annexation of some factory property owned by Mr. Douglass, who didn't want to give it up.
During the meeting the official argued that Mr. Douglass couldn't
always get his way. Several of President Grant's closest friends were
involved in the railroad plan. Friends of the president got what
they wanted. Mr. Douglass would just have to be a good loser this
time.

McLendon made a suggestion. Mr. Douglass owned additional
property not a mile from the disputed site. There was room on it not
only for the new track but also for a fine new public park that could
be named in honor of the president. Wasn't President Grant planning
to seek reelection? In that eventuality, such positive publicity in a
major city like St. Louis would surely be helpful. Mr. Douglass would,
of course, need to be appropriately compensated by the railroad for
the land used for the track, but perhaps the park property could be
donated. The railroad would have its track, and the people of St.
Louis would enjoy a new park. Everyone would benefit, the president
most of all. The official took the offer to the White House. He
informed Mr. Douglass the next day that President Grant accepted
and was personally grateful.

"The president now considers you, Mr. Douglass, to be his friend," he
added. "If he can ever be of help to you, send word to him through me."

On the return trip to St. Louis, Mr. Douglass suggested to McLendon that they repair to the train's dining car. It was late at night, and
no one else was there.

"That was a most impressive performance," Mr. Douglass said.
"There is even more to you than I thought, and you've earned the
most significant of rewards. I propose that soon Mrs. Douglass and I
announce your engagement to our daughter."

Mr. Douglass said that he wasn't going to live forever. He'd worked every waking hour to establish and expand his business empire, and he was damned if he'd allow it to be frittered away after his death. On the contrary, he meant for it to flourish and grow further, securing comfortable futures for his daughter and the grandchildren that he hoped would come. What he needed—what he had to have—was the right husband for Ellen, and McLendon had just convinced Mr. Douglass that he was the one.

"In many ways, you and I are very much alike," Mr. Douglass said. "I myself started with nothing but my wits. There's one critical difference. You've got no stomach for the hard action that's sometimes required, and I doubt that you ever will. But when I'm gone you'll have Patrick Brautigan, who understands the need for a hammer when a smile's not enough."

For once, McLendon was at a loss for words. He finally managed, "But about Ellen, sir. Would she even have me?"

"She likes you well enough." Mr. Douglass lit a cigar and pointed the glowing tip at McLendon. "Take time to consider my offer, though not too much. I'm confident you'll have the sense to marry Ellen and give up your Italian girl."

In his confusion, McLendon hadn't thought about Gabrielle. He blurted, "You know about her?"

"You're not my only watcher. Put the Eye-tie aside."

McLendon's initial, private reaction was that he couldn't even consider marrying Ellen Douglass. He loved Gabrielle. He'd refuse Mr. Douglass's offer, leave his employment, marry Gabrielle, and help run the dry goods store. But then he considered Mr. Douglass's reaction if he refused. By whatever means necessary, Mr. Douglass would have revenge, at least by opening a rival shop and putting the Tirritos out of business—or even, if he were outraged enough, setting Killer Boots on Salvatore and Gabrielle and perhaps McLendon himself. By being noble and choosing Ellen, whom he didn't love, he might be saving the life of the woman he really loved, and her father's, to say nothing of his own.

He sent word to Gabrielle that he was ill and lay anguishing in his room at the imposing Douglass mansion. At first he thought mostly of how Gabrielle's entire face glowed when she smiled, but then he pictured Ellen, beautiful and mysterious. He contrasted the Tirritos' small house behind their shop with the imposing Douglass habitation, and the small family shop to the Douglass business empire. McLendon remembered being a panicked little boy whose mother was dead and whose father had disappeared, and the terrible feeling of being poor and helpless. Gabrielle was wonderful, but Ellen was so beautiful, and so very, very rich. . . .

Cash McLendon, who was so good at convincing others, convinced himself that it wasn't the Douglass fortune that was the deciding factor in his decision. He was sacrificing his own happiness to save Gabrielle and her father from the wrath of Rupert Douglass.

"I'll be a good husband to your daughter," McLendon told his employer.

Mr. Douglass looked hard at McLendon. "From this moment forward, have no contact with the Italian girl. I want your word on this."

McLendon took a deep breath, then said quietly, "You have it."

THE ST. LOUIS NEWSPAPERS made much of the engagement, noting that Rupert Douglass, father of the prospective bride, was a leading businessman and philanthropist. McLendon wondered if Gabrielle would read the stories. Because of his promise to Mr. Douglass, he couldn't tell her in person.

Cash McLendon married Ellen Douglass on a glorious spring day in 1870. Shortly before the ceremony, Mr. Douglass said there was something McLendon needed to know about Ellen's health.

"She's a high-strung girl, and always has been." Mr. Douglass took McLendon to his study. "My wife and I have been obliged to be vigilant with her, and now you must too. She has wild moods, falls into them without warning. Then there are dreadful scenes, and on rare occasions she has even tried to do harm to herself if she feels thwarted in her wishes." He opened a small safe and removed a stoppered glass vial filled with a light brown liquid. "To help keep her steady, the doctor prescribes laudanum, liquid essence of poppies. At breakfast and in mid-afternoon, Ellen takes three drops in a glass of water. The laudanum is kept in this safe because she likes it too much, and taking it in excess is very dangerous. Two doses daily, and never more. I'll give you the combination of the safe. Usually her mother administers the medicine, but sometimes the responsibility may fall to you. Remember: Never leave the laudanum bottle where Ellen can get at it." He shook his head and looked grim. "I adore my daughter, and expect you to cherish her, and to protect her from the slightest harm."

McLendon hoped that his father-in-law might be exaggerating. There was no honeymoon because Ellen couldn't be trusted to behave on a trip. Instead, Mr. Douglass took his wife away to New York for a week and the newlyweds stayed behind in the St. Louis mansion. Before leaving, Mr. Douglass reminded McLendon that Ellen could never be left alone.

"During this honeymoon, if you're sent word of some emergency in one of the factories, contact Brautigan and send him to sort it out," he instructed. "Be patient with her. When Ellen's in a fit, she doesn't know what she's saying or doing."

For most of the week, Ellen seemed happy, and McLendon did his best to feel the same. He still thought of Gabrielle sometimes, but his wife was beautiful, the suite of rooms they shared in the Douglass mansion was luxurious, and as Rupert Douglass's son-in-law he was now a man of considerable standing. Ellen docilely took her laudanum doses, and they seemed to have the required effect. In the afternoons they played croquet on the wide green lawn. He let her win because it pleased her. At night she made love with a ferocious energy that surprised him. He wished their conversations were more rewarding. Unlike Gabrielle, who liked to talk about almost anything, Ellen seemed interested in very little beyond what her parents would bring her back from New York.

McLendon wanted to be a good husband, and to come to feel the same genuine affection for Ellen that he had had for Gabrielle. The night before the Douglasses were due back from New York, McLendon and Ellen enjoyed a delicious meal. They were served coffee with dessert, and McLendon wanted a second cup. He rang a small bell to summon a servant, but no one came.

"I'd better see what they're doing in the kitchen," he told Ellen, and left the dining room. It turned out that the cook had accidentally spilled a basin of gravy, and she and the other three live-in staff were mopping it up. McLendon retrieved the coffeepot and returned to the dining room. He hadn't been gone more than two minutes, but in the interim Ellen had transformed from a happy bride to a screaming harridan.

"You've been with somebody else!" she shouted. Her eyes were wide and wild.

McLendon was caught off guard. "What? I just went for more coffee," he said, and held up the pot. Ellen screeched and knocked the pot from his hand, drenching the tablecloth and some window drapes with coffee. Then she charged McLendon, trying to scratch his face with her long nails. He caught her wrists and tried to hold her back.

"Stop, Ellen," he said, trying to soothe her. "What's all this? What's made you so upset?"

Ellen clawed at him a moment more, then wrenched free. "You fucked her!" she screamed. "You fucked her!" McLendon was astonished that she knew the word. It had never occurred to him that a fine society girl would.

"Stop saying that," he pleaded, but Ellen persisted, spitting out the same three words over and over again. Then, just when he thought she'd never stop, she did. She stood silently and stared at him for a moment, then began battering her head against the wall. Her forehead was bruised and her nose began to bleed. McLendon grabbed her again and wrestled her to the floor. She howled and fought him until McLendon suggested that she take some laudanum. Ellen stopped struggling at once and said, "Yes, please."

She'd already had her two prescribed daily doses, but he felt that this was an emergency. Ellen watched greedily as he measured out the drops into a glass of water. She gulped down the drink and almost immediately became drowsy. McLendon washed her bloody face, put her to bed, then called the servants to clean up the dining room. When the Douglasses returned the next day, McLendon told them what had happened. They weren't surprised.

"Ellen does these things," her mother said wearily. "We'd hoped being married might calm her. If this happens again while we're absent and you can't restrain her, call for Mrs. Reynolds. She'll help you."

McLendon asked, "Aren't there places where Ellen might go to be helped? With special doctors trained in this kind of thing?"

"You mean lunatic asylums," Mr. Douglass snapped. "Not for my daughter—ever. Be a good husband to her. Maybe it will help. And next time, no extra laudanum. She could become addicted."

. . .

McLendon realized that he had made a bad bargain. He was important now, and could have virtually any material thing that he wanted. But it was impossible for him to relax at home, because he never knew when Ellen would suffer one of her fits. They usually involved loudly accusing him in the coarsest possible terms of being unfaithful. Sometimes her parents helped gently subdue her, but usually they left it to McLendon. After each episode, he found himself remembering the sense of peace he'd found with Gabrielle. At home at night, when he needed time away from Ellen's tantrums, he closed himself inside a small room he used as a study and reread the books that Gabrielle had given him. Now, when he owned so many fine things, he realized that *The Last of the Mohicans* was his most prized possession. He thought how comforting it would be to see Gabrielle again, even as an old friend rather than a lover. But he'd promised Mr. Douglass that he'd have no further contact with her. It wasn't worth the risk.

In late 1871, McLendon had to meet with a foreman at the factory directly across from Tirrito Dry Goods. He'd consciously avoided going anywhere near there, but now had no choice. Though he couldn't talk to Gabrielle, perhaps he might catch a discreet glimpse of her. Surely Mr. Douglass couldn't fault him for that. He felt impatient during the factory meeting, finally cutting it short, and left the building through a side entrance that offered a clear view of the dry goods shop. He was stunned to see that it was empty. The door sagged open toward the sidewalk. The hand-carved sign in front was gone.

Stunned, McLendon walked into the store. There was dust and cobwebs on the shelves. It had clearly been empty for some time. He went outside and circled to the small house in back. It was empty too. A woman was sweeping the porch of a nearby house, and McLendon recognized Gabrielle's aunt Lidia. When he greeted her, she glared and said contemptuously, "You."

"They're gone?" McLendon asked, knowing that he sounded foolish and not caring that he did.

"You broke her heart, so they left. A letter I got says they're in that Arizona Territory, someplace called Glorious. They got another store. After what you done to her, she couldn't stay here."

"I thought her father loved this store."

"He loved the girl more, just like you should have. She's a good one, the best. Now go away."

FOR SEVERAL MONTHS after her wedding, Ellen continued having violent fits. McLendon wearily accepted them as a new fact in his life—and then they stopped. A week went by, then another, and Ellen remained calm. She was attentive to her husband, and talked in the evening about normal things like the weather and decorating the mansion for Christmas. She seemed so calm that one Sunday afternoon McLendon told Mr. Douglass that he thought he might take Ellen out for a short carriage ride. There had been snow during the week, and the countryside had taken on a festive white sparkle.

"That's a bad idea," Mr. Douglass said. "We generally try to keep her inside. If she's away from home, she may get in a mood and try to run. It's happened before."

"She's been doing very well," McLendon said. "I think that perhaps doing an ordinary thing like having a ride in the snow would be good for her."

Mr. Douglass stuck a warning finger in front of McLendon's face.

"You watch her every minute, and if she acts up in any way, bring her home immediately. I'll not have Ellen making a spectacle of herself where the public can see."

IT TOOK ALMOST AN HOUR for Ellen to get ready. She seemed pleased to be bundled in a heavy coat and fur hat as her husband helped her up into the carriage. McLendon tapped the horse with a whip and they rolled merrily out past the mansion gate. It was a lovely day, cold but sunny. He found himself enjoying the ride very much, being in such a fine gleaming carriage with his pretty, laughing young wife at his side. It was the first moment of complete contentment that he'd had since his marriage.

A few green sprigs of holly poked through the snow, and Ellen begged McLendon to stop for a moment so she could break them off from the bush. He did, and while Ellen fussed with the holly, McLendon idly looked back down the road. Several hundred yards behind them, sitting astride another horse from the mansion's stable, he recognized the unmistakable hulking form of Patrick Brautigan, Killer Boots, who must have been summoned by Mr. Douglass to keep watch over Ellen on her special excursion. McLendon raised his hand and waved at Brautigan, who didn't wave back or otherwise respond.

ELLEN CONTINUED to behave well, so much so that McLendon thought the time might come soon when she could be left in the care of the mansion staff or even completely alone for short periods, though her father was adamantly against it.

In February 1872, when Mr. Douglass went to Philadelphia for a meeting with potential investors in his St. Louis munitions factory, his wife went with him. She liked the city's shops and museums. Patrick Brautigan went too. Mr. Douglass felt that a bodyguard would impress the men he was meeting. They expected to be away for five days. Mrs. Reynolds would stay with Ellen at the mansion while McLendon was at work.

On the third day after the Douglasses left, Mrs. Reynolds sent word that she was ill and would be unable to stay with Ellen, so McLendon worked from home. It was enjoyable. Ellen sat in the study with him while he read reports and wrote out orders to suppliers. In the early evening they played croquet. After dinner, McLendon and Ellen had settled down for a pleasant night in their sitting room when they were interrupted. A messenger sent by the foreman of the munitions plant reported that there had been a chemical spill, and noxious vapors were sickening the late-shift workers. The foreman thought it would be necessary to close the plant until the mess was cleaned up, but he couldn't do so without permission. Was it okay with Mr. McLendon?

McLendon thought it over. He had no desire to risk the workers' health, but he wasn't certain that the foreman's judgment was reliable. The work that would be interrupted was part of an important new contract, the plant's first one from the Department of War. If the ammunition contracted for was delivered on time, it would probably lead to more lucrative business. A delay might very well have the opposite effect. There was always hot competition for government contracts. He decided he would go see for himself. But when he told Ellen that he had to go out for just a short while, she flew into a hysterical rage.

"You're going off to meet a whore!" she shouted.

"Of course I'm not. I just have to see about an accident at one of your father's factories. I'll be home before you know it."

"Your whore will have the pox, and you'll give it to me. You're not going, no, no, *no!*"

McLendon momentarily considered bringing Ellen with him, but she was so out of control that he decided he couldn't. Sighing, he chose another option. She'd already had her two daily doses of laudanum. If he gave her a third, she would probably nap until he returned. Her father had ordered not to exceed her regular dosage again, but this was an emergency and Mr. Douglass wasn't there.

"Would you like your special drink?" he asked. The question had the effect that he'd hoped. Ellen stopped screaming immediately and followed him eagerly to the safe in Rupert Douglass's study, where he dialed the combination and took out the vial of laudanum. It was almost empty. After he measured out three drops into a glass of water, only bare dregs remained in the vial, not enough for even one more full dose. In the morning he'd have to send one of the servants to get the prescription refilled. Ellen drank her glassful down, then docilely allowed McLendon to walk her to their bed, where he covered her with a comforter. He was impatient to get to the factory, and she seemed about to fall asleep.

"I'll be home soon," he said.

Ellen muttered, "Promise?"

McLendon hurried to the plant and ended up staying for several hours. First he summoned a cleanup crew and supervised as they worked. Then he gathered the plant workers who'd been milling outside and told them they could return to work. Some were reluctant, and he had to persuade them that the chemicals were cleaned up and the air inside was again safe to breathe. It was past midnight when he finally started home, and on the way he suddenly wondered if he'd locked the laudanum back in the safe before he left. He was relieved when he remembered that even if he hadn't, there'd hardly been any left. If Ellen did get at the vial, there wasn't enough to hurt her.

When he came home and rushed up the stairs to his father-in-law's study, Ellen's body was sprawled on the carpet, blood pooled around her and bits of broken glass vial scattered by her side. McLendon understood in an instant that she'd wanted more laudanum, was enraged when there wasn't enough to satisfy her, and in her fury smashed the vial and used one of the shards to slash her own wrists.

McLendon's knees buckled and he dropped to the floor beside Ellen's body. The magnitude of the tragedy overwhelmed him. His wife was dead and he was responsible, though unintentionally. He leaned away from Ellen, vomited, and then began to sob. It hadn't been Ellen's fault that she was sick. Why had he left the bottle out where she could get at it? The vial was just as potentially deadly as the drug—he'd never considered that. He'd seen how, in some of her fits, Ellen tried to harm herself. This time she'd succeeded all too well. God, what a shock this news would be to her parents when he wired them in Philadelphia. Mrs. Douglass would be devastated. And Mr. Douglass—

The harsh circumstances of his childhood imbued self-preservation as Cash McLendon's primary motivation, and as much as he was devastated by Ellen's death, in this awful moment he reverted to form. He would have done anything, made any sacrifice, to undo his fatal mistake and bring Ellen back. But there was nothing he could do for his dead wife, so he had to think of himself. Rupert Douglass, McLendon realized, would have no mercy on someone whose carelessness had resulted in his daughter's demise. To him, it would be the same as deliberate murder. Mr. Douglass believed in immediate retribution; he'd call on Killer Boots. Quite soon, McLendon's battered corpse would be found in some St. Louis alley, his features mashed into jelly by repeated thundering kicks.

He tried to calm himself and think. He didn't have to wire the Douglasses. Ellen often slept late. The servants were told to stay away from her room unless summoned by McLendon or one of Ellen's parents. If Mrs. Reynolds was still too sick to come to the Douglass mansion in the morning, Ellen's body might not even be discovered until late afternoon or possibly the evening. After that, it would take time to contact her father in Philadelphia, and most of another day for Mr. Douglass to return to St. Louis, learn what had happened, and set Killer Boots on McLendon's trail. By then he had to be well clear of the city.

McLendon crammed some clothing into a valise, along with *The Last of the Mohicans*. Besides Ellen's laudanum, Mr. Douglass always kept a few thousand dollars in the safe. McLendon stuffed the bills into his pocket. Then, after a last, sorrowful glance at where his wife's body lay, he locked the door behind him and crept down the stairs, trying not to alert the servants.

McLendon hurried to the river and bribed his way aboard a flatboat leaving at dawn for New Orleans. He stayed there for a while, working day jobs on the docks. Ellen was much on his mind; if, during their brief time together, he'd found some way to reassure her of his love, perhaps she would have been less self-destructive. He considered more than once returning to St. Louis and accepting Mr. Douglass's inevitable vengeance. Perhaps he deserved a horrible death from the feet of Killer Boots. But in mid-March, when the landlady of the transient hotel where he'd taken a room mentioned

that a big man with steel-toed boots was asking for him around the
neighborhood, McLendon ran again, and not back to St. Louis. In
the time that he'd been in hiding, he had also found himself obsess-
ing about Gabrielle and how much better it would have been to
marry her rather than Ellen. He couldn't make up for what he'd done
to Ellen, but perhaps he could make things right with Gabrielle.
Both of their lives didn't have to be ruined. New Orleans was an
obvious place for Killer Boots to hunt McLendon, since it was linked
to St. Louis by the Mississippi. But surely Mr. Douglass had never
heard of Glorious in Arizona Territory. McLendon would go to there,
reclaim Gabrielle if he could, and with her travel to one of the big
western cities—San Francisco, Los Angeles, San Diego—where he'd
make them a new life by using all the business wiles he'd acquired in
St. Louis. Though he couldn't ever completely absolve himself for
Ellen's death, at least he could in some sense atone for it by giving
Gabrielle the happiness she deserved.

That afternoon, McLendon boarded a steamship that took him
from New Orleans to Galveston, Texas. To throw Killer Boots off the
scent, he traveled under the name H. F. Sills, a railroad employee
he'd known back in St. Louis. Once in Galveston, McLendon
inquired at the stage depot about passage to Arizona Territory, then
took the stage from Galveston to Houston and on across Texas and
New Mexico into Arizona Territory, finally fetching up almost two
weary weeks later in the Mexican-influenced town of Tucson. From
there it was a short trip north to Florence, and finally the last thirty
dusty, jarring miles to Glorious. Now it was only a matter of waiting
until morning to surprise Gabrielle, attempt to win her back, and
hopefully put his St. Louis past and the appallingly primitive Arizona Territory behind him forever. How he'd convince her to forgive
him, and what if anything he'd tell Gabrielle about Ellen's death, he

still wasn't certain. If she refused him, as she had every right to do, he'd have to go on to California by himself.

McLendon lay back on his bed in the Elite Hotel, willing himself to ignore the noises of the cat in his room and get at least a little sleep. He finally fell into a fitful doze, only to jerk awake periodically, wondering if he had dreamed or really heard the scrape of heavy boots outside his door.

FOUR

Sometime after dawn, McLendon dragged himself out of bed, feeling groggy after such a fitful night's rest. He splashed water from the pitcher into the basin, washed his face, used his finger to scrub his teeth with his final bit of tooth powder, and dressed in his good suit. He checked his pocket watch: it was nearly eight. Yawning, he made his way to the hotel lobby, where Major Mulkins was waiting.

"Will you take breakfast, Mr. McLendon?" he asked. "May I offer you oatmeal this morning, or perhaps you'd prefer bacon and biscuits with your coffee?"

"Oatmeal would be agreeable," McLendon said. Mulkins led him into the dining room, which was deserted.

"Most everybody in town is previously breakfasted and gone," Mulkins said. "The prospectors like an early start, before the sun gets too high and hot."

McLendon was perspiring under the fastened collar of his shirt.

"It's already uncomfortably warm. Surely the heat can't get much worse."

Mulkins chuckled. "You're in for an unpleasant surprise. I'll bring your oatmeal. May I sweeten it with a bit of juice from a can of peaches? It's a nickel unsweetened, seven cents with the juice."

"I'll live recklessly this morning. Pour on the juice."

As he ate, McLendon looked out the window. His view was frequently obscured by clouds of dust blown by a strong wind, but there was very little to see anyway. A few prospectors fussed with tents or loaded saddlebags on mules. The stage was standing outside Bob Pugh's livery, but there was no sign of the driver or guard. Perhaps they were still asleep in the stalls.

McLendon dawdled over his last spoonful of oatmeal. Shortly before nine he watched William Clark LeMond make his way from the livery to Tirrito Dry Goods. The soap salesman held the handle of his sample case in his left hand and clamped his bowler hat on his head with his right. The wind was blowing very hard. McLendon accepted Mulkins's offer of more coffee and began thinking through what he would say to Gabrielle. He hadn't seen her for two years. He hoped the gift of the "Shoo Fly, Don't Bother Me!" sheet music he had tucked inside a coat pocket would remind her that he understood her heart.

Lost in imagining a joyous reunion, McLendon was startled when Mulkins reappeared at the table and asked if there would be anything else. He dug in his pocket and handed seven cents to the hotel proprietor, who asked, "Will you be wanting to retain your room for tonight, sir?"

"I'll inform you shortly," McLendon said. He went back to the room, fetched his hat, and waited out of the wind in the hotel lobby for LeMond to finish his business and leave the dry goods store. It took longer than McLendon anticipated. It was nearly nine-thirty when the salesman emerged and walked back toward the livery. McLendon went outside. His hat immediately blew off, landing almost directly at LeMond's feet. The salesman snatched it up and held it out to McLendon.

"Miss Gabrielle is behind the store counter," he said. "Don't be concerned—I didn't mention your presence."

"Obliged," McLendon said. He took his hat and banged it against his leg, trying to knock off the dust from the street.

"Remember that the stage back to Florence leaves at ten," LeMond said. "You see it just in front of the livery. They're hitching up the mules now."

McLendon said politely, "Safe travels." Then he turned and walked toward the dry goods store. He passed the farrier's shop; town mayor Charlie Rogers stood over a forge, banging at a horseshoe. He nodded at McLendon, who nodded back. Except for the clank of Rogers's hammer and the keening of the wind, there was no other sound. In a few more steps McLendon was in front of the store. He noticed with some pleasure that the familiar hand-carved TIRRITO DRY GOODS sign was in place over a wooden door hung by crude latches. He went inside and there was Gabrielle, taking canned goods out of a packing case and placing them on a shelf. He thought that she was a bit thinner and her hair was longer. She turned, saw him, and calmly said, "Oh. Hello."

Among all her possible reactions to his arrival, McLendon failed to anticipate no real reaction at all. "You're not surprised to see me?" he asked. "Did the soap salesman who was on the stage with me alert you, after promising me that he wouldn't?"

"Mr. LeMond didn't say a word," Gabrielle said coolly. "Aunt Lidia wrote that you disappeared from St. Louis, and Mr. Pugh, the livery owner, mentioned last evening that a stranger had arrived from Florence. It crossed my mind that you might come this way. You're quite predictable to anyone who knows you."

McLendon had imagined controlling the conversation from the outset, but she had him off balance. He said, "I've come because we have something to discuss," but before he could continue, a raggedy prospector came in and inquired, "Miss Gabrielle, did the stage bring 'em yesterday?"

Gabrielle smiled the great warm smile that McLendon remembered so well and said, "Yes, Mr. Haines. Will you have a penny's worth?" When he nodded, she took a small box from the counter and shook some of the contents into a canvas sack.

"I haven't the penny this morning, Miss Gabrielle," the man said. "Will you extend me credit? I'm sure to find some color any day now, and then I'll pay the debt promptly."

"Of course you will, Mr. Haines," she said. "I hope you have good luck today." The prospector touched his finger to the brim of his hat in a courtly gesture, said, "Ma'am," and left the store. Gabrielle's smile instantly vanished, replaced by her previous neutral expression. She arranged a few more cans on the shelf as McLendon gathered himself. After several long moments of awkward silence he said, "What did that fellow want?"

Gabrielle continued shelving cans. She said over her shoulder, "Lemon drops, the hard candies. The prospectors suck them to alleviate thirst in the heat of the day. If they don't have the candy, they must use pebbles, which don't taste as pleasing."

"He can't afford a penny?"

"Many of the prospectors need occasional credit. We trust them to pay us when they can. They're for the most part decent men, seeking their fortunes through hard, honest work. I wouldn't have Mr. Haines sucking pebbles for the lack of a penny. I realize this isn't the way that you believe in doing business." She put the last can in place, wiped her hands on an apron worn over her long dress, and said, "You mentioned something to discuss. Perhaps the death of your wife? Aunt Lidia mentioned her demise in the same letter that informed me you'd vanished from St. Louis. Let me express my sympathy for your loss. Does that conclude our business? If so, I believe the stage back to Florence is ready for boarding."

"No, we need to talk," McLendon said. "Can we go somewhere, do this in private?"

"My father is busy in the back storeroom, unpacking some of the boxes that arrived yesterday. I must remain on duty at the counter. You can say what you need to here, but be quick. I've a great deal of work to do."

McLendon reached for Gabrielle's hand, but she moved it away. "Then I'll begin by saying I'm sorry. I acted abominably. I've come all this way to make things right."

Gabrielle began arranging open containers of small items—nails, buttons, needles, and spools of thread—on the other end of the counter, keeping distance between herself and McLendon. "Oh, there's no need. I've gotten on with my life just as you have with yours. No cause to feel guilty where I'm concerned."

"But because of me, you're here."

"I'm happy here."

McLendon sensed an opening. "Of course you're not. No one with any sense could be. I'll take you away. This place is dirty and dangerous and the man who owns the hotel charges extra for bathwater—"

Gabrielle laughed. "Major Mulkins, that sweet man."

"Yes, Mulkins. And not just him. The mayor's wife gobbles jelly straight from the jar and the sheriff is a scarecrow with a bent badge and patchwork beard."

"I like the sheriff's beard. It has unique character, where ordinary beards such as yours do not. I appreciate the trouble you've gone to in making this long trip, and the effort I know that it takes you to sound so sincere. But I have no need or desire to be rescued. You can be on your way with a clear conscience."

"But I have plans—"

"Of course you do," she interrupted, and even though there was sarcasm in her tone, he welcomed it, felt glad for any reaction at all. "You always have plans. But they change in an instant, don't they, depending on your own best interests. I decline further involvement in your plans now or ever."

"That's too harsh. I'm a changed man from the one that you remember."

"Really?" Gabrielle asked, arching her eyebrows in mock astonishment. "You seem exactly the same to me."

A wizened man emerged from the storeroom. McLendon extended his hand to Salvatore Tirrito, but the old fellow ignored it.

"I'm just visiting with Gabrielle, Mr. Tirrito," McLendon said. "It's a pleasure to see you again."

Tirrito's English vocabulary was sufficient to spit out, *"Bastard!"*

Gabrielle said something to her father in Italian—McLendon had no idea what, because he'd never bothered to learn any of the language during his time with her in St. Louis. She apparently assured the old man that things were fine and he could return to his work in the storeroom. Tirrito fixed McLendon with a baleful glare and stalked away.

"Let me be clear," Gabrielle said to McLendon. "This current plan you have for me—for us—is that you swoop into Glorious, rescue me from this hideous place, and carry me away to some great city where we're to live happily ever after. Is that correct?"

"Though you're mocking me, yes, that's the concept in general. California is my preferred destination. I'm sincere in this intention."

"And does any aspect of this plan include my father?" Gabrielle asked. "How would he fit in?"

"I suppose he would stay on here, operating his store," McLendon said.

"You think that I would abandon my father to go with you? That I would leave him all alone? You plainly have a low opinion of me."

"On the contrary, I have tremendous respect for you," McLendon said, marveling at how Gabrielle had seized and held the upper hand. "Come with me now and after we're settled somewhere we'll send for your father, or do whatever you want concerning him."

"What I want," Gabrielle said briskly, "is for you to get back on the stage to Florence, and from there go on to California or wherever you like. Your ultimate destination is of no consequence to me. Leave my father and me alone. We don't in any way require your attentions or concern. I find your attitude to be offensive."

"Don't be offended," McLendon pleaded. "What I want to do is correct my errors of the past. Far from intending any insult, my being here is a compliment to you. I believe you're so special that you're worth my coming all this way to be reunited. This is the sum of my thoughts and my entire intention."

Gabrielle came out from behind the counter. She was a tall woman and McLendon a man of average height, so their eyes were level. Hers stared hard and unblinking into his.

"I'll tell you what you thought and what you intended. You thought I was a lowly Italian who would never get over the pain of losing her man to a rich white girl. You intended to come here to Glorious and sweep me off to California because that was what you wanted, never considering whether it was best for me. Well, I'm happy here; I'm staying. If you need forgiveness, then fine, I forgive you. And now I have work to do." She opened another box and resumed putting cans on shelves, pointedly turning her back on McLendon.

He remembered the gift he'd brought. "I have something for you: sheet music." He took the pages out of his coat pocket and smoothed them out on the counter. "This song 'Shoo Fly, Don't Bother Me!' has become quite popular. It's a sprightly tune, and will sound well when played on your piano."

Gabrielle continued unpacking cans. "Thank you for the gift, but it's of no use to me. I no longer have my piano."

"Why not? I can't imagine you giving it up."

She glanced briefly at the sheet music, gently touching the pages with her finger. "Oh, it was too unwieldy to bring west. We sold it to help pay our way here. I really must get back to work." She took more cans from the box and put them on the shelf, turning each carefully so that its label faced out.

McLendon blurted, "Your aunt Lidia told me that I broke your heart."

Without turning around, Gabrielle said, "Hearts mend." A burst of wind gusted through the open doorway and blew the sheets of music off the counter.

McLendon stared at Gabrielle's back for a few moments, and then, not knowing what else to say or do, he left the shop. He thought he would return to the Elite Hotel, retrieve his valise, and get out of Glorious, but then he looked west, past the cluster of prospectors' tents, and saw the Florence stage disappearing over the horizon toward Picket Post Mountain.

FIVE

McLendon stumbled back to the Elite Hotel. He passed Major Mulkins in the lobby without speaking, closed the door to his room, and sat on the bed with his head in his hands. He had to get out of Glorious immediately. McLendon thought that his head would explode if he saw Gabrielle again. He should have known that she'd be too proud to take him back. What had he been thinking of? He took a breath and tried to compose himself. All right, it was Tuesday. The Florence stage wouldn't return until the following Monday, and then there would be another interminable night before he could finally leave the town behind—much too long. He'd find another way back to Florence. Thirty miles wasn't that far. Glorious had a livery. He'd rent a mount and make the ride. He grabbed his valise and hurried to the lobby, where Major Mulkins busily rubbed a rag over his prized windows.

"I'm checking out," he told Mulkins. "Let's settle my bill."

"Won't you be needing the room for some time further?" Mulkins asked. "I believe the Florence stage has departed."

"I don't need the stage to get out of this damnable place," McLendon said. "Let's conclude our business."

"Just as you please," Mulkins said agreeably. "It's a dollar fifty for the room, two bits for the window, and a dime for the cat. Total of one eighty-five." He took the coins McLendon handed him and added, "I'll hold the room for you anyway. You may be wanting it back."

"Hardly," McLendon said. He snatched up his valise and stalked back into the street. It was brutally hot. The wind intensified rather than tempered the searing heat. Without looking across at Tirrito Dry Goods, McLendon marched past the Owaysis saloon to the livery. Bob Pugh sat inside, picking at loose threads on a saddle blanket.

"I want to rent your fastest horse to ride to Florence," McLendon said. "I won't be coming back, but I'm sure the animal can be tethered to next week's stage and so will be returned to you."

Pugh glanced up from his work. "Let's consider that request for a moment. I believe you labor under certain misconceptions."

"There's nothing to consider. I want to be on my way. Rent me the horse."

Pugh grinned, a friendly smile. "Well, that's the first consideration. Come with me." He led McLendon to a corral in back. "Do you observe any horses in there?"

McLendon didn't. Instead, there were perhaps a dozen mules, each bonier-looking than the last.

"Not much call for horses around here," Pugh said, his smile still in place. "It's such rugged going in the high desert and the mountains. Only the real light, nimble mounts bred in Mexico are up to it over any significant distance, and they're too dear for me to afford. You may recall that your stage had a mule team. So the fact of it is, I have no horse to rent you."

"I suppose a mule, then," McLendon said, feeling dubious. He thought the mules had a contrary look. "Can you put a saddle on one of them?"

"I could, but let me ask this: Are you much of a rider? Have you some experience in the saddle?"

McLendon had never ridden a horse in his life, let alone a mule. "No, I haven't, but how hard can it be?"

Pugh chuckled. "Someone like you who's not especially saddle-broke, well, you might be able to climb aboard, and that's not guaranteed, since a mule may sense hesitation and buck. But after a short while, if you do get on, your behind and crotch will begin to ache from contact with the saddle, then they'll hurt powerful bad. And after you manage to either climb down or the mule pitches you off, you'll walk in considerable pain for some time to come. If I rent you a mule to ride, you won't make Picket Post Mountain, let alone Florence."

"Is there no alternative transportation available?"

"I've got a buckboard. Mules can be hitched to a buckboard."

"I'll rent the buckboard, then. I believe I can maintain my seat on that."

Pugh shook his head. "I said I had a buckboard, not that I'd rent it to you. Buckboards are hard to come by out here. Mules too. I'd have to rent you a pair of 'em to pull the buckboard, and I can't afford to lose them, either."

McLendon's impatience boiled to the point of near rage. He wanted desperately to get out of Glorious. The vast valley to the west and the towering cliff face to the east made him feel simultaneously marooned and claustrophobic. He said sharply, "I told you that I'd leave your property in Florence. Some arrangement could be made to return the buckboard and mule team to you. I have money. I'll pay any fair rental."

"You misunderstand me, sir," Pugh said. He grinned again and put a comforting hand on McLendon's arm. "I don't doubt you'd pay whatever I charged, or that, once you reached Florence, you'd make certain my mules and buckboard got back to me. But you wouldn't ever get to Florence. You wouldn't make it more than a mile or two out of town before the Apaches got you. They're always lying in wait for someone to venture out of town on his own."

"Don't the prospectors go out all the time?"

Pugh nodded. "True, they do, but mostly in small groups. They've spent years in these sorts of dangerous places, so they know how to be properly watchful. Even the most experienced are at awful risk if they're on their own. Perhaps you've heard that just a little while back one of the prospectors went out alone and was captured. Tommy Gaumer's body when we found it was a horrible sight. The prospectors who came upon it puked on the spot. Tommy was an experienced man. He knew all the tricks and the Indians got him anyway. I mean no insult, but someone like you, why, the Apaches'd pull you off that buckboard and hack you up in the most painful and brutal of ways, and afterward they'd have the mules for dinner. Apaches are powerfully fond of mule meat."

"I have a gun in my valise," McLendon said. "A Navy Colt—the storekeeper I bought it from in Houston assured me that it was a dependable weapon. I could defend myself."

"You wouldn't have a chance, because you wouldn't see the Apaches in time. So I won't rent you mules or a buckboard. You could try to walk it, but you'd soon wear out in the heat and the Indians would get you all the same. So I guess you've no option other than to stay in town for a week and wait for the next Florence stage."

"I don't want that," McLendon said. "There must be some other way."

"There isn't," Pugh said gently.

McLendon had never felt more helpless—or hopeless. He was completely out of his element. None of the manipulative talents that served him so well in St. Louis seemed of any use in Glorious. Smiling, weather-beaten Bob Pugh suddenly seemed to McLendon like the sole voice of reason in a vastly confusing new world.

"What should I do now?" he asked plaintively.

"First thing, you go back to Major Mulkins and tell him you need a room until next Tuesday," Pugh said. "He'll give you a better rate if you request one. And then you'll meet me at the Owaysis and I'll buy you a drink to settle your nerves a bit. You'll feel better after that. Glorious ain't bad, really. You just have to get used to us, and now you've got a whole week to do it in."

McLendon sighed. He picked up his valise and retraced his steps to the hotel. He passed Sheriff Saint, who walked by, nodded, and continued on to the Tirrito Dry Goods store, then went inside. McLendon wondered what the sheriff was there to buy, and if Gabrielle was still at the counter to sell it to him. Thinking of her was painful and he made himself stop.

In the hotel lobby, Major Mulkins said that he'd kept McLendon's room for him as promised. "It's hard for people to find their way here to Glorious, and it's also hard for them to leave. I'm sure you'll continue enjoying your fine window view of our town."

"I don't know that I can afford more nights in a room with a window," McLendon said, remembering that his funds were limited. "It might be that I'll take one of your upstairs rooms with the canvas overhead. Six bits, is that the charge?"

"Ah, as a weeklong guest I'll let you have your current downstairs room for the unwindowed rate," Mulkins said. "The room will be ready for you to reoccupy in an hour or so, after the Mexican woman changes the linen and sweeps. And now, why don't I hold on to your valise while you head over to the Owaysis?"

"How did you know I was going there?"

"You already visited the dry goods; I saw you go in and then leave. You've been to the livery and talked to Bob Pugh. Saw you do that too. You don't have a mount to shoe or prospecting tools to mend, so there's no need for the farrier, and you ain't been in town long enough to break the law, so the jail is out as a destination. You clearly don't feel inclined to stay here and visit with me. That pretty much leaves the saloon."

THE OWAYSIS WAS a single wide, low adobe room. Oilcloth curtains were pulled over the window holes, and three widely spaced kerosene lanterns provided minimal light. McLendon stood inside and blinked rapidly while his eyes adjusted to the gloom. There were a dozen battered tables surrounded by rickety chairs. The tables had oilcloth covers similar to the curtains. A stooped man dipped shot glasses and beer mugs in a bucket of soapy water placed on a long plank, and the plank was balanced on top of two high stools; this evidently was the bar. There were three women in the saloon, and one came over to McLendon. Even in the poor light, he could tell that she was older than she appeared at first glance. Her bright lipstick and powdered cheeks couldn't conceal the lines of middle age on her face.

"Welcome to the Owaysis," she said, her voice pleasant but grainy. "What's your pleasure? A drink?" She gestured at the other two women, who stood out of the lantern light. "Some time with one of our pretty girls?"

"I'm meeting someone," McLendon said. Bob Pugh came through the door and hugged the blowsy older woman.

"Mary, you just get more beautiful," Pugh said. "I want you to meet Mr. Cash McLendon, who arrived from Florence yesterday and will be spending the week in our town. Don't look so concerned, Mr. McLendon. I got your name from the hotel register."

"Pleased to meet you, Mr. McLendon," the woman said. "I'm Mary Somebody."

McLendon thought he'd heard wrong. "Mary who?"

"Mary Somebody. We're all somebody here in Glorious."

"Let's introduce our new friend around," Pugh said. "Mr. McLendon, this fellow behind the bar is George Mitchell, known to most as Crazy George. He and Mary own the place as well as each other's hearts." Mitchell gingerly extended a soapy hand. Bald, bespectacled, and with a long nose, he seemed to McLendon to exactly resemble a sunlight-shy mole interrupted in its subterranean digging.

"And here," Pugh continued, "are the loveliest two ladies imaginable." A strawberry-blond girl, perhaps eighteen, boldly held out her hand and said in a pronounced British accent, "I'm Ella, Mr.—?"

"McLendon."

"Well met, Mr. McLendon. I certainly hope to know you better. All arrangements through Miss Mary, of course." She saucily shrugged her shoulders forward; the low-cut, ruffled dress she wore showed off her bosom to great advantage.

McLendon was familiar with the ways of whores—St. Louis had innumerable bawdy houses—but he'd seldom encountered one so forward or pretty. He wondered what bad luck had brought Ella to a dive like the Owaysis.

"And hanging back a little because she's so shy, this here is Girl,"

Pugh continued. He and Mary Somebody made coaxing noises until Girl finally took a hesitant step toward McLendon. Her face was void of any expression other than a childlike blankness.

"Girl don't talk too much, but she's sweet as can be," Mary Somebody said. "If Ella's busy when you're in the mood and you decide to go for Girl instead, there's some special rules about things you can't do with her. But she's cheaper, just a dollar to three dollars for Ella."

"Why is she called Girl?" McLendon asked.

"Because she is. So, what's it to be? Refreshment, or frolic?"

"Just libation, I think, at least for now," Pugh said before McLendon could respond. "Our *amigo* here's had a hard morning and needs himself a bracer. Beer, Mr. McLendon, or something of a stronger nature? I'm buying the first one."

McLendon saw no reason for caution. Gabrielle didn't want him, he was stuck in Glorious, and alcohol suddenly had great appeal.

"I'll commence with beer," McLendon said. "Where my selection follows from there, I can't predict."

"Sure you can," said Mary Somebody. "We got beer and red-eye whiskey. None of that fancy shit like in Tucson bars, brandy smashes and the like. But at a nickel a beer and eight cents a shot, we've got the kind of prices that let you indulge without great expense."

Pugh led McLendon to one of the tables and they sat down. "It'll be quiet in here until four or five or so," he explained. "That's when the prospectors start drifting back into town. Then it'll get noisy and Ella will do some business. Maybe Girl, too, though most of the regulars think of her as more of a mascot."

Mitchell brought two mugs of beer to the table and ambled back behind the bar. He peered into the pail, apparently trying to tell if any glasses remained in the soapy water.

"That man is near blind, even with his specs," Pugh said. "I got no idea how he finds ol' Mary in their blankets at night, or even his own pecker when he needs to pee."

"He seems meek, not crazy," McLendon said. "Is his nickname deliberately inappropriate?"

Pugh took a long sip of his beer. "Since you'll be with us for a week, I expect that you'll discover the reason we've dubbed him Crazy George," he said. "In the territories, it's not considered polite to ask too many questions. Keep that in mind. But if you pay attention, you generally learn whatever you really need to know. You'll notice that I haven't asked after your purpose in coming out this way."

McLendon sipped his own beer. It was warm and bitter. "Is that because you don't consider it any of your business?"

"No, it's because I already know as much of the answer as I require. So does everybody else in town. You came from St. Louis to try and win Miss Gabrielle, who sent you packing. Now all you can do is lick your wounds until the Florence stage next week."

"That bastard LeMond," McLendon grumbled. "What, did he spend last night telling everyone in town? I swore him to secrecy."

"As he explained it, you requested that he keep mum to Miss Gabrielle but didn't specify anyone else," Pugh said. "So the case can be made that he didn't betray his promise. He did not mention you to her. But by the time you were walking into the Tirritos' store this morning, the rest of us in town were all peeking out windows and around corners to observe the result."

"You had nothing better to do?" McLendon said, drinking more beer.

"Here in Glorious, we welcome whatever show presents itself," Pugh said. "We're all so familiar with each other that any newcomer provides entertainment of some sort. It's harmless fun. For the rest of your stay, no one will jeer you for the failure of your suit."

"I'll still be embarrassed for the duration." McLendon drained his beer mug and gestured for Mitchell to bring him another. He took a sip of the fresh drink and thought that it was better than the first; perhaps it came from a different barrel. "Even if you don't mock me to my face, everyone will laugh behind my back."

"Not true," Pugh said. "In fact, you're only the second outsider who's failed in a recent attempt to rekindle romance. Three months ago, our mayor suffered quite the love embarrassment."

"Mayor Rogers? I thought he was married to what's her name, Rose."

"He is, or so he says," Pugh said, polishing off his own first beer. "One Monday evening, the stage pulls in from Florence and this short woman hops out. She starts screaming that she's come to find her husband. Says her name is Sweet, and she married Charlie Rogers back in San Angelo, Texas. Claimed he deserted her to come west and she tracked him to Glorious."

"What did Mayor Rogers say to that?"

Pugh accepted a second beer from Mitchell. "Not a word. He bolts from his farrier's shop and closets himself in the little house beside it that he and Rose live in. Sweet sees him run, follows him, and stands outside hammering on the door. I don't know where Rose was—I guess inside with Charlie. Anyhoo, Sweet pulls an over-and-under derringer from the front of her dress—the dress damn nears falls off, now *that* would have been a sight—and swears she'll shoot Charlie whenever he comes out. That's when somebody sends for Sheriff Saint. We don't hold for shooting here in Glorious. The sheriff tries to calm her, she keeps yelling and waving the gun, and finally a bunch of us, me and Major Mulkins and Crazy George and the sheriff, grab her and take the gun and lock her in jail. We have a jail with two cells across from the livery. A very good jail for a place this size. Anyway, the next morning some prospectors with a wagon are moving on from town, and they say they'll take Sweet and drop her off somewhere on the other side of the mountains. We had to toss her in that wagon all tied up and yelling, but we haven't seen her since. If it weren't for the trouble it would cause Charlie, some of us wouldn't mind if Sweet turned up again. It was exciting."

"Afterward, did the mayor ever confirm or deny her claim?"

"We never inquired further. It don't matter whether Charlie's married legal or joined otherwise to Sweet or to Rose or to neither one or to both. He's a good man and Rose herself is all right. They say they're man and wife and that's enough for us. See, there's the lesson. Nobody leaves the states for the territories because they were happy with where or what they were. We've all got mistakes in our past or at least things we'd rather forget. So we keep our secrets and respect those of others." Pugh cleared his throat and slapped his hand on the table. "I don't know about you, but I'm hungry. How about some lunch?"

"At the dining room in the hotel?"

"No, the Major doesn't offer a noon spread. But we can get something here." He looked over at Mary Somebody, who was leaning on the bar, whispering to Mitchell. "What's on hand for a midday meal?"

"I hard-boiled some eggs bought fresh yesterday from the Chinks," she said. "There's pickles in the crock. I can put some of each on plates if you want."

Pugh said that would do. The food cost two cents a plate. McLendon learned that hard-boiled eggs and pickles made a fine lunch if they were washed down with enough beer, which tasted better the more that he drank.

SOMETIME LATER Pugh said that he had to be getting back to the livery. He'd rented a few pack mules out to prospectors and they'd be returning them soon. McLendon gulped some last swallows of beer and stood up. His legs felt rubbery. He wasn't exactly drunk, but he was definitely off-kilter.

"A nap might be in order for you back at the Elite," Pugh suggested. "Have some dinner after, and then get yourself back here. There'll be more folks then, and we'll have some social time."

"Would Gabrielle be among them?" McLendon asked. "Due to our conversation this morning, I don't relish another encounter."

"Someone of Miss Gabrielle's character don't frequent saloons," Pugh said, sounding offended at the thought. "Where there's drinking and use being made of the whores, it's not appropriate for a fine lady to be present."

"Yes, she's a fine lady," McLendon mumbled. He tried and failed to choke back a beery belch. "What the hell. See you later." He made his way to his room, which was airless and stifling. McLendon was too tired to care. He lay down on the bed and almost instantly fell asleep. When he woke, it was nearly sunset. He looked out the window and saw people moving about, mostly prospectors but also a few diminutive individuals with long braids of dark hair dangling down their backs. In St. Louis McLendon had heard of the Chinese, but he had never seen any. He supposed they must have come into Glorious from their camp by the creek. He couldn't see the dry goods store from his room, which was a comfort, but then Gabrielle appeared, carrying a tray covered with a cloth. She looked very pretty.

Gabrielle walked past the Owaysis and toward the livery, smiling and exchanging words with everyone she encountered, seeming, to McLendon, somewhat like a queen graciously greeting her subjects. The dusty, ragged men all touched the brims of their hats with their fingers as they replied. Gabrielle stopped at an adobe structure across from the livery and went inside. McLendon wondered for a moment, then recalled Bob Pugh mentioning the town jail. What was she doing there? It was almost fifteen minutes before she emerged without the tray and walked back in the direction of the dry goods store. McLendon watched until Gabrielle, still smiling and briefly chatting with others, finally passed from his line of sight.

Though his stomach was unsettled by the lunchtime combination of hard-boiled eggs, pickles, and beer, McLendon thought he'd get something to eat in the hotel dining room before returning to the Owaysis. His options were spending the evening in the saloon or in his hotel room, and if he was alone in the room he knew that he would think too much and become more depressed than he already was. There were a few people in the dining room, all prospectors digging into bacon and biscuits. Major Mulkins told McLendon there was still some stew available, along with lettuce and cucumber salad he'd fixed with vegetables from the Chinese camp garden. McLendon said that he'd just have the salad, hold the stew. He ate his light supper—the cucumber was surprisingly crunchy—and left the hotel for the saloon.

Because there was little besides Picket Post Mountain to break the long western horizon. The upper rim of the sun was still barely visible. There was a violet twilight glow on the little town; McLendon found the effect disconcerting. Though the wind had lessened, it remained very hot. He was still wearing his good suit. The other clothes in his valise were too soiled to put on. A suit wasn't the right thing to wear in such broiling weather. McLendon had left his tie in his room and had his collar unbuttoned, but he still sweated profusely. There were some people out and about and everyone nodded or murmured a greeting as they passed. He thought everyone he saw must be prospectors, with two exceptions. A pair of Mexicans on horseback, obviously Culloden Ranch vaqueros, had reined their mounts in in front of the tent city on the west end of town. The horses looked wiry and much smaller than the plodding Morgans ridden by the cavalry escort for the Florence stage. Their riders calmly surveyed Glorious's limited evening bustle. They had rifles in saddle scabbards and pistols in holsters slung on their hips. Bandoliers stuffed with cartridges hung from their shoulders. It seemed to McLendon that there was an ominous air about the mounted men, a disturbing sense of barely suppressed brutality that reminded him, just a little, of Killer Boots, though these fellows obviously didn't compare in terms of potential menace. Besides, none of the townspeople seemed intimidated by their presence.

In contrast to his earlier visit, this time the Owaysis was crowded. Every table was filled and there were more drinkers milling around the bar. The buzz of combined conversation and raucous male laughter was so loud that it took McLendon several moments to realize that someone was calling his name. Bob Pugh sat at a table with Mayor Rogers, and waved him over to join them.

"Things get to hopping here after dark," Pugh said. "The prospectors have put in long, hot, dry days and feel thirsty and ready for fun. Crazy George about wears his arms out pouring drinks. Will you have one?"

McLendon still felt rocky from the lunchtime beer. "Is something nonalcoholic available?"

"Mary always has a pot of coffee going for the nondrinkers," Mayor Rogers said. "Let's call her over and get you some."

McLendon drank his coffee while the mayor and Pugh sipped whiskey. There were card games in progress at a few tables. In the far corner of the saloon, Ella took a man by the hand and led him off through a curtained exit.

"Crazy George and Mary got four little whores' cribs out behind this main building," Pugh said. "They don't need 'em all right now, but they put them up anyway in anticipation of increased future trade. Ella gives fifteen minutes for the three dollars and she gets as creative as you please. I consort with her myself on occasion and always consider my money well spent. You ought to take a turn."

"She's a pretty girl for a whore," McLendon said. "Why would she ply her trade all the way out here? I expect she'd make more money in a real city."

"Some bastard brought her all the way to the territory from England and promised he'd marry her when he made his fortune," Pugh said. "As I understand it, he threw her over for a Mexican girl in Tucson and there young Ella was, far from home and no one to turn to. Mary was in Tucson looking for a girl to work the Owaysis, so there was a natural fit. The city brothels often cheat their girls. Here, Ella's treated honest. She gets her room and board and a dollar for every man she does. Mary holds the money for her all proper. Ella thinks that in maybe another six months she'll have enough for passage back home."

McLendon thought about that until Ella came back into the saloon and took her next customer's hand. "It's a hard way she's taking," he said.

Mayor Rogers said, "Everything out here is hard," and signaled for another drink. He spoke a little about what Glorious was going to become: not only a mining town but a good place to live, one where men were comfortable bringing families. "When we've got enough kids to open a school, that'll be when I know we're on our way," he said. "At present we've not one child in our midst, but that's going to change. I wish you'd be here to see it."

"Well, I won't," McLendon said. "Soon as that Florence stage comes back, I'm off to California."

"You'd do well to reconsider," Rogers said. "Whatever you want out there, I believe that you'd stand a better chance of finding it with us. The territories are about the last places left where a man has a decent chance of *becoming*. Nothing's easy, but everything's possible."

After a while Pugh took McLendon around the room, introducing him to some of the other customers. Most were prospectors— Archie, Old Ben, Radko, Doughty, all grizzled men with dust in their beards. Bossman Wright, whose brows were so thick it seemed that a long, fat caterpillar had nestled above his eyes and across the bridge of his nose, leaned against one end of the plank bar and explained without McLendon even asking that he had earned his nickname by insisting on basic rules in every prospectors' tent camp that he lived in: "No shouting near anyone trying to sleep if it's well after dark. No flaunting mail from back home if you're lucky enough to have some. Above all, no drunken pissing in the immediate vicinity of another person's tent."

"These are sensible rules," McLendon agreed.

"Such courtesies are what separate us from the savages," Wright said.

A half-dozen latecomers surged through the saloon door. One, who Pugh introduced to McLendon as Oafie, joined Wright in leaning against the bar. McLendon was surprised by their body language. Though they did nothing overt, their shoulders bumped gently in what he recognized as a signal of physical intimacy. He looked closer at Oafie, the only beardless prospector he'd met so far, and wondered why Oafie had no whiskers, when he made out two barely discernible lumps under her filthy shirt.

"That's a woman," he whispered to Pugh.

"Damn sure is. When she first came to town with Bossman, we thought they were what you might call funny boys until we got a closer look at her. Women prospectors are rare. Oafie's our only one here. Works hard, drinks hard, so she fits right in."

"That's fine," McLendon said politely. "You know, I still don't see why you call that bartender Crazy George. He seems the furthest thing from it."

"I expect that you're about to find out," Pugh replied. "Keep a sharp eye on that fellow mishandling Girl."

Ella had just taken her latest customer to the whores' cribs behind the saloon, and one particularly hulking, hairy prospector seemed disinclined to wait for his turn with her. He grasped Girl's wrist and began talking to her, his bearded face pushed aggressively next to hers, and she tried to pull away. Mary Somebody hurried over. She said something to the prospector; McLendon couldn't make out the words over the ongoing drone of conversation throughout the room, but Mary seemed to be explaining that Ella would be back soon and that Girl wasn't suitable for him. The prospector pushed Mary away and grabbed at Girl again.

"Call the sheriff," McLendon said to Pugh and Mayor Rogers. "That man's going to hurt someone."

"Sit tight and watch," Pugh said, and gestured toward the bar. "It's about to get real good."

McLendon had taken Mitchell for a small, hesitant man, but now the barkeeper straightened and McLendon could have sworn that his back and neck swelled with new muscle. Mitchell tossed aside his glasses, reached down and pulled a length of lead pipe from his boot, and vaulted over the bar. Roaring with inchoate fury, he took hold of the prospector's collar and raised the pipe to strike. The prospector, suddenly appearing much smaller, let go of Girl and fled from the saloon while the other patrons hooted and cheered. Mitchell stood with the lead pipe raised until Mary Somebody patted his back and whispered something to him. Then he pushed the pipe back into his boot and walked behind the bar, seeming to deflate with each step. Someone handed him his glasses; he put them on and resumed nearsightedly pouring drinks as though nothing had happened.

Pugh laughed and said to McLendon, "Like I told you—Crazy George."

Six

As he served McLendon his breakfast of coffee and biscuits on Wednesday morning, Major Mulkins said, "I hope that you're finding your stay in our community to be acceptable."

"The Owaysis was diverting," McLendon said. "Crazy George Mitchell is worthy of the name. But I still look forward to boarding the stage back to Florence. My first act on arrival will be seeking out a laundry. Every item of my clothing is soiled from travel and constant heat."

"Florence is the bigger place, but we're not without our own conveniences," Mulkins said. "A laundry operates behind this hotel, on the fringes of the prospectors' tents. If you take your dirty clothes there after you finish your breakfast, they'll likely be returned clean and fresh-smelling to you around dinnertime. It's a Chink laundry, to be sure, but I think you'll discover that the pigtailed race has a knack for efficient service."

After eating, McLendon rolled most of his clothing into a loose bundle. He located the adobe laundry just where Mulkins said. He went inside and found it difficult to breathe in the ferocious heat. Water boiled in a huge kettle over a fire. Two large tin tubs stood against the back wall. An elderly Chinese woman bent over one of them, wringing out a pair of overalls. She carefully hung the overalls on a line stretched along a side wall; they dangled there alongside several other pairs as well as a number of dripping shirts and drawers and a few dresses. McLendon thought he recognized the daring frock worn the day before by Ella in the Owaysis.

The elderly woman noticed McLendon and held out her hands for his bundled clothing. She picked through, separating drawers and shirts and pants, and said, "Two dolla."

Two dollars seemed steep to McLendon, but he needed clean clothes. "All right," he said. "When will my laundry be ready?"

She frowned and repeated, "Two dolla."

"I understand the cost. I'm trying to determine when I'll get the cleaned clothes back. Major Mulkins mentioned one-day service."

"Two dolla."

A younger Chinese woman came in, hauling two sloshing buckets. She said to McLendon, "My mother wants you to give her two dollars now. She requires payment in advance because too many people have cheated her, taking their laundered clothes and then refusing to pay."

"I wouldn't do that," McLendon said.

"I'm sure, but Mother still wants the money now." She watched as McLendon handed over two dollars, then gestured to several piles of clothing stacked near the washtubs. "There are some things to be laundered ahead of yours, but if you come by around late afternoon your clothes should be ready. Washing dries quickly in this hot climate. Now, if you'll excuse us, we'll get back to work."

The morning stretched ahead for McLendon. He thought it was too early to go into the saloon. Instead he wandered to the farrier's shop, where he watched as Charlie Rogers mended a cracked pickax head for a waiting prospector. Rogers used tongs to place a strip of heat-softened metal over the crack, tapped it firmly into place with a hammer, and then plunged the ax head into a bucket of water to cool.

"There you are," he said to the prospector. "It'll be three bits. Shall I put it on your tab?" The prospector, dark eyes glittering on either side of a hooked nose, nodded, took the tool, and left the shop without saying a word.

"Is the fellow a mute, or merely rude?" McLendon asked.

The mayor blotted perspiration from his forehead. "Oh, that's just Turner. He never talks much. But among all the prospectors so far, he's the one who most believes that he'll make his fortune here." Rogers motioned for McLendon to follow him outside, and pointed to a small shack apparently constructed from rough wood planks and parts of packing cases. The shack was about fifty yards beyond the rest of the prospectors' tents. "He proved he's here to stay when he put up a permanent place on the hill. I suppose he built it some distance away because he don't often care for company. It's all right. We welcome all kinds. Meanwhile, I hope you're enjoying a pleasant morning?"

"I've just dropped off laundry with the old Chinese woman. She was adamant regarding payment in advance."

"Well, you can't hardly blame her. They set up that shop maybe two months ago, and some of the early customers neglected to pay. Many have no respect for the yellows—don't think of them as real people. Myself, I'm glad we've got some. Their vegetables and the laundry come in mighty handy. Rose has got a delicate constitution. I wouldn't want my jelly bunny wearing herself out over a washboard."

McLendon passed the rest of the morning in the hotel lobby, chatting with Mulkins and reading *The Last of the Mohicans*. Mulkins was impressed.

"It's a fine thing to be an educated man," he said. "I can read some myself, but I never took to books as such. What's that one about?" After McLendon summarized the story, Mulkins said, "That sounds like a stem-winder. We've got a few readers in town, the sheriff especially, and others who aspire to the skill."

"Are there many books here to be read? I assume that they're in short supply."

Mulkins mopped his brow with a bright blue cloth. It was very warm inside the hotel. "Well, the sheriff has some, and also Miss Gabrielle. They share with the few who can sufficiently decipher them. And, thanks some to him and mostly to her, more can all the time. What they do is—"

The Major was interrupted by the Mexican woman who cleaned the Elite. She asked in halting English if Mulkins wanted her to mop the floor of the lobby or the dining room next.

"I think the dining room, Mrs. Mendoza," Mulkins said. "Take your time and make a thorough job of it. Now, Mr. McLendon, I was telling you about Miss Gabrielle."

McLendon was trying hard not to even think about Gabrielle. To change the subject, he said, "You mentioned earlier that Mrs. Mendoza lives on Culloden Ranch across the creek. Does her husband live there too?"

"Quickie Mendoza is one of the vaqueros employed by Collin MacPherson to protect his ranch and, happily, this town," Mulkins said. "I believe that there are about twenty vaqueros in all, separate from the several dozen hands he employs to tend his cattle. Mr. MacPherson sells beef to the Army at its various camps and also to us here in Glorious. Without that, we'd be mostly reduced to eating jackrabbit stew, if we were able to catch the rabbits."

"I saw two riders in town last night that I took for MacPherson vaqueros," McLendon said. "They struck me as sinister."

"They look like hard men because they are, and that's what's required to keep the Apaches at bay. I understand Mr. MacPherson's foreman recruited them right out of Sonora in Mexico, where they fought Indians on a daily basis. He mounts them on the best horses and arms them with the finest weapons. Last night, did you notice the pistols those riders carried? They're double-action Remington-Riders, very costly and hard to come by out here. I believe they were ordered directly from the eastern manufacturer."

"I know very little about guns," McLendon admitted. "I have a Navy Colt that I purchased in Houston, and I know how to load and, I suppose, fire it. But I have no idea of what 'double-action' means."

Mulkins launched into an extensive explanation. Most frontier handguns, including McLendon's Navy Colt, were single-action. Their hammers had to be cocked by the shooter's thumb before he pulled the trigger with his index finger to fire—so that was one action at a time. Double-action models, just beginning to be widely manufactured, were better because pulling the trigger cocked and then fired the weapon—two actions in one. "That provides a faster rate of fire than single-action. I believe that within two or three years double-action models will be the rule rather than the exception."

"So Mr. MacPherson really does provide his men with the very best handguns."

"Yes, and the best repeating rifles as well. Most of us in Glorious have old-model Henry repeaters or shotguns. We're none of us gun hands, and unlikely to hit what we aim at. It's the town's good fortune that Mr. MacPherson looks after our welfare as well as his own."

They sat for a few moments in companionable silence. McLendon could hear the swishing sound of Mrs. Mendoza's mop on the dining room's wood floor. "I haven't seen any of the MacPherson vaqueros get down off their horses and spend leisure time in town," he said. "Are they forbidden to trade with you?"

"It's more that they have little need for such," Mulkins said. "The Culloden Ranch has its own blacksmith and cook, and there's a bunkhouse for the single men and adobe huts for the married men and their wives, so most of their needs are seen to there. And when they do choose to mingle in town, it sometimes gets uncomfortable. By nature they seem quick-tempered and prone to find insult where none is intended. We've had a few incidents, all thankfully resolved without too much damage. Sheriff Saint steps in, or if necessary we summon the ranch foreman. He's the hardest man of them all. Angel Misterio, 'the Mystery Angel' in English. If he's an angel, he's a dark one. But he keeps those vaqueros in line."

"You make it sound as though without MacPherson and his vaqueros, you might not have a town at all."

Mulkins finished his cigarette and began rolling another. "There's no way to know, but I'm glad we haven't had to find out."

McLendon took lunch at the Owaysis: more pickles and some spicy beef jerky. He drank beer, being careful to pace himself this time. Bob Pugh came in for pickles and jerky, and when he said he couldn't stay to talk because he had to muck out stables, McLendon offered to help. It was something to do. At Pugh's livery he took off his suit coat, rolled up his shirtsleeves, and set to work. The stables were behind the livery and next to the corral. Flies swarmed there, but the roof blocked the worst of the sun. After two hours Pugh suggested a water break and told McLendon that he was impressed.

"You may not be a rider, but you're a natural hand with a shovel and pitchfork," Pugh said. He and McLendon cleaned stalls, laid down fresh straw, and fetched water for the mules from a nearby town well. When McLendon finally glanced at his pocket watch, it was just after five.

"I need to go pick up my laundry," he said to Pugh. "Perhaps after dinner I'll see you back at the Owaysis."

When McLendon returned to the laundry and stepped inside, he was dismayed to see Gabrielle talking animatedly to the young Chinese woman. Gabrielle nodded at him politely, gathered up some laundered clothes, and left.

"Your clothes are ready," the Chinese woman said. She piled the folded shirts, drawers, and pants in his arms and said, "Thank you for your business. Come again."

Still unsettled by encountering Gabrielle, McLendon said, "You speak very good English."

She gave him a quizzical look. "Were you born in America?"

"Of course."

"So was I. We both speak good English."

McLendon, his arms full of laundry, retreated outside. He almost collided with Gabrielle, who was waiting for him.

"Let's not be foolish," she said. "We're not going to be able to completely avoid each other. This is a small place, and you're here until the stage leaves next week. We can say hello and be polite."

"After our previous conversation, I'll find that hard," McLendon said.

"It doesn't have to be. We'll keep it short and painless. I hope you pass a pleasant evening. Now I must go fix dinner for my father. Good night."

McLENDON WENT BACK to the hotel and changed into a freshly laundered shirt, drawers, and trousers. The clean clothes felt wonderful. He ate in the dining room and then decided to walk next door to the Owaysis. There didn't seem to be any other places in town to find evening diversion. But before he could go inside, he was hailed by a rangy fellow whose hatband sported a jaunty feather.

"Can we have a moment?" the man asked, extending his hand. "I'm Lemmy Duke, and I work for Mr. MacPherson of the Culloden Ranch. Perhaps we might have a word in a quiet place? The lobby of your hotel would do nicely."

They went back inside the Elite and sat in adjacent lobby chairs. Duke rolled a cigarette and offered the tobacco and papers to McLendon, who declined. After he had his cigarette properly lit and had asked McLendon's name, Duke said, "Those of us at the Culloden always take notice of unusual newcomers. You're not a prospector, it's clear, nor a drummer on a sales call. I hope it's not presumptuous to ask your purpose here in Glorious."

"I've already been asked this by the mayor and the sheriff. My response remains the same. I came to see an acquaintance."

Duke took a long drag on his cigarette and blew a perfect smoke ring. "So you don't intend, say, to open yourself a little business? Another hotel, perhaps, or a shop or dining establishment of some sort?"

"Hardly. I'm eager to leave, and intend to on next week's Florence stage. But I don't understand why my plans are of any interest to you or your boss."

"They aren't, so long as they don't pose a threat to the fine businesspeople here. Major Mulkins with this hotel, Mayor Rogers and his farrier shop, old Pugh with the livery, and the Tirritos with their store. These are fine people who've risked a lot to establish themselves, and who deserve the opportunity to prosper when this town does. They don't need competitors now when there's so little business to be had, and it's their right to reap the profits when that grand time comes. So we of the Culloden like to gently discourage additional businesses just now. Later on, I'm sure there will be no problem. But not at present."

"That's the opposite view of Mayor Rogers. He practically begged me to stay in any capacity that I chose."

"Mayor Rogers is a fine man who should be more cognizant of his own best interests." Duke carefully stubbed out his cigarette in an ashtray on the table beside his chair. "Well, Mr. McLendon, I'm glad we had this talk. Enjoy your brief stay in Glorious, and let us know at the Culloden if we can be of service." He tipped his hat, and moments later McLendon saw him on horseback, trotting out of town in the direction of Culloden Ranch.

THE OWAYSIS WAS even more crowded than the night before. Bob Pugh waved for McLendon to join him standing at the bar because all of the tables were taken.

"I just had a talk with a fellow named Lemmy Duke," McLendon said. "It was less a conversation than an interrogation."

"Lemmy's a curious man," Pugh said. "I've known him for some time, and he's always full of questions. Turn your attention to more important things. I believe you'll sample the stronger libations tonight. You earned the upgrade with so much hard work this afternoon on my behalf. George, my friend McLendon and I require servings of your finest." Crazy George poured whiskey into two shot glasses. Pugh handed one to McLendon, who recoiled at the sharp odor.

"It stinks like turpentine," he complained.

"You're not imbibing the smell," Pugh said. "Drink your whiskey."

McLendon gingerly touched the rim of the shot glass to his lips.

"No, don't delicate-sip it like a woman," Pugh said. "Toss it down." He raised his own glass and guzzled the contents. "*Aaah.* Do it like that. Get yourself the full effect."

"I'm not sure I want the full effect," McLendon said dubiously, but he noticed that Crazy George and Mary Somebody and many of the others clustered around the bar were watching, so he gulped down the shot of red-eye with the immediate resulting sensation of having swallowed liquid fire. He felt it sear his throat and then burn its way down into his entrails. He coughed convulsively while everyone laughed.

"It takes some getting used to," Pugh assured him, slapping McLendon on the back and signaling Crazy George for another round. "After the first five or six your gullet gets numbed up."

"I believe that five or six would kill me," McLendon gasped.

"Oh, hardly. Now settle down and let's drink."

McLendon found himself enjoying a convivial evening. Some of the prospectors talked of adventures in the Pinal Mountains and other parts of the territories, fine colorful tales of grizzly bears and flash floods and Indians and, always, the huge strikes of gold or silver that they just missed making—it was always the other fellow working nearby who had the luck. Each of them was positive that this time he'd be the fortunate one.

"I like these people," McLendon confided to Pugh.

"Most of them are good 'uns, though of course any crowd includes its share of miscreants," Pugh said.

Prospectors made up most of the bar crowd. Mayor Rogers sat at a table with Major Mulkins—"It's rare the Major emerges from his hotel," Pugh told McLendon. "He always fears he'll miss greeting a potential guest"—and three of the Culloden Ranch vaqueros drank at another table. They were the only patrons wearing holstered guns.

"Why are they armed and no one else apparently is?" McLendon asked Pugh.

"I expect that they finished their assigned patrols and wanted drinks before returning to the ranch," Pugh said. "The rest of us have no use for guns in town, though we certainly take them when we venture beyond it. Charlie Rogers and the sheriff are talking about a no-guns policy where all weapons have to be checked when anyone rides in. That would be sensible policy and I hope that it's imposed. Liquor and guns are a particularly bad combination."

Within minutes Pugh's words proved prophetic. A prospector who'd had too much stumbled into the vaqueros' table, spilling their drinks in their laps. One of the vaqueros jumped up and shoved the prospector, who lurched into another table. The men seated there stood and shouted at the vaquero, whose two companions rose and shouted back. Behind the bar, Crazy George peered nearsightedly in the direction of the disturbance and inched his hand down to the metal pipe in his boot. Bob Pugh leaned forward and murmured, "George, guns are to hand and that pipe won't suffice. Stay still and I'll run for the sheriff."

As Pugh hurried from the bar, a half-dozen prospectors and the three vaqueros continued to scream at each other. Someone shouted, "Take it outside!" and they did, spilling out into the inky night. Most of the Owaysis crowd followed. McLendon found himself swept up in the rush. Once outside, he sensed as much as saw that the prospectors and vaqueros were in the center of a spectator ring. As McLendon's eyes adjusted to the darkness, he saw that one of the prospectors waved a wide-bladed knife. A vaquero taunted him, making clucking noises and keeping his hand on the butt of his pistol. The other two Mexicans talked to their friend, apparently urging him to forget the gun. He pulled away, snarling at them in Spanish, and one of the vaqueros pushed through the crowd and ran to where three horses were tethered between the saloon and the Elite Hotel. He mounted and raced off.

"Yellowbelly Mexican's running from the fight," an onlooker told McLendon.

The prospector with the knife and the vaquero with his hand on his gun circled each other, barking threats. There was sudden rustling off to the right, and Sheriff Joe Saint slipped through the crowd. Saint stepped between the two men, holding up his hands and saying, "Stand down, stand down." He seemed to McLendon like a slightly built child attempting to break up a brawl between much older, tougher boys. "We'll go and talk," Saint said. "Whatever's happened, there's no need for this." There was a slight but discernible tremor in the sheriff's voice. He was, McLendon realized, afraid.

The angry vaquero knew it too. "Go back to your jail, Sheriff. This man called me a greaser. I will not be insulted."

"You *are* a fucking greaser," the prospector sneered, waving his knife. "Go ahead, pull that gun. I'll slice your nuts before you can shoot."

"We protect your white asses and you call us greasers. Show me how you can fight."

"Don't make me arrest you both," Saint said, pleading rather than warning. "Do the smart thing, walk away."

McLendon sensed that the prospector was ready to comply. He'd done plenty of posturing and the sheriff's presence gave him a plausible excuse not to fight. Without risking his life needlessly, he could return to the Owaysis and his friends would praise his courage. But the vaquero was different: he considered himself unforgivably insulted and intended to shoot. He smiled and said, "Remove yourself, Sheriff," and Saint took a reflexive step back. It was about to begin.

McLendon couldn't have explained why he did it. The vaquero

was going to kill the prospector, but it was none of his business. He hated being stuck in Glorious and was counting the hours until he escaped on the Florence stage. But Bob Pugh had been cordial to him, and so had Major Mulkins, and Crazy George and Mary Somebody and Mayor Rogers were all right too. If the vaquero shot the prospector, it would cause trouble for his new acquaintances. So McLendon shouldered his way inside the human circle and stepped beside the Mexican.

"You want some too?" the vaquero asked, and McLendon shook his head.

"I want to ask about that gun of yours," he said. "Double-action, is it?"

"What? Are you *loco*?"

"No," McLendon said, keeping his voice relaxed and friendly. "It's just that somebody was telling me about single-action versus double-action and I didn't really understand. Now, yours is double-action, right?" Bewildered, the vaquero nodded. McLendon kept looking at him, trying to hold the Mexican's full attention. From the corner of his eye he saw Sheriff Saint talking quietly to the prospector, moving him discreetly away. "I've got a Navy Colt, but before I shoot I have to cock it. But you don't have to do that with yours? Can I look at it?"

"Get away from me, *hombre*," the vaquero said, and pushed McLendon aside, but by then Saint had the prospector out of sight and the crowd began to drift back inside the Owaysis. McLendon stepped back in front of the Mexican and smiled.

"Let me buy you a drink," he suggested. "I want to learn about double-action."

"What the fuck?" the vaquero growled. "Get away, I'm going to kill that man."

"I don't think so," McLendon said. "The sheriff's taken him off and everyone's going back to the bar. It's all over. You might as well have a drink."

He led the thwarted shooter and the second vaquero back into the saloon, and soon they were seated at a table. Encouraged by McLendon, after only a few minutes of conversation both men displayed their pistols and earnestly explained to him why the guns' mechanisms didn't require cocking before firing. Bob Pugh and Mayor Rogers watched from beside the bar, shaking their heads in wonder. Juan Luis, the vaquero who almost fought the prospector, had just suggested he give McLendon some shooting lessons when another Mexican arrived. His lithe body had no angles at all, and he appeared to glide rather than walk. There was an air of authority about him. Everyone else in the Owaysis stopped talking and watched as he approached the table where the vaqueros and McLendon sat. The vaqueros jumped to their feet and stood at near-military attention as he sharply questioned them in Spanish. They stuttered replies in the same language. The man jerked his head toward the door and the vaqueros scrambled out. A moment later hoofbeats pounded toward the west. He'd clearly ordered them back to Culloden Ranch.

The man said to the mayor, "Señor Rogers, my *jefe* and I sincerely apologize for tonight's disturbance. Our men have instructions never to engage in unpleasantness in town, no matter what the provocation." Turning to McLendon, he said, "I am Angel Misterio, foreman for Señor MacPherson. What is your name?"

"Cash McLendon."

"Then allow me to express my thanks, Señor McLendon. I am informed that you prevented matters from reaching the point of actual violence, and you did this by asking Juan Luis about his *pistola*. Why did you attempt that subject?"

McLendon studied Misterio. The man was dressed in a dark shirt and trousers, with a gun belt on his hips and a long knife in a sheath. A thin scar ran from his right eyebrow across his cheekbone to his earlobe, and he exuded a sense of absolute self-assurance. Like Killer Boots in St. Louis, Misterio would murder without hesitation, but with quick strikes rather than bludgeoning.

"All men like to talk about what they love, and your vaqueros love their guns," McLendon said. "It seemed an obvious strategy."

"Obvious to you, *amigo*." Misterio looked around the saloon. "Gentlemen, my employer wishes to buy everyone here a drink. Again, we regret the unpleasantness and assure you that it will not be repeated." He dropped a fistful of coins on the bar and added to Crazy George, "Señor MacPherson especially wants to pay for all Señor McLendon's drinks for the rest of the evening." He bowed gracefully to McLendon, then to Mayor Rogers, and left the saloon.

Everyone surged toward the bar, hollering for Crazy George to fill their glasses. Bob Pugh stopped them with outstretched arms and said, "Boys, let the hero go first." Then he said to McLendon, "I advise drinking long and a lot. The whiskey always tastes better when a rich man's buying."

SEVEN

McLendon dragged himself out of bed late on Thursday morning. His last vague memory of the previous night was Bob Pugh helping him back to the Elite Hotel. Now he was paying for his night of overindulgence with a colossal hangover. He dressed, fumbling with various buttons, tried to shave, gave up, and stumbled into the hotel lobby, where Major Mulkins was, as usual, rubbing a fresh shine onto his prized windows.

"Do you want breakfast, Mr. McLendon?" Mulkins asked. "It being somewhat past eleven o'clock, there's no more oatmeal, but I could fry you up some bacon."

The thought of greasy bacon made McLendon's stomach lurch. "I believe I'll pass on breakfast."

Mulkins laughed. "That's not surprising, given your state last night. Bob and I had a time getting you to bed."

"I don't precisely recall," McLendon said. "I apologize for any inconvenience."

"Guests at this hotel never inconvenience me," Mulkins said.

"Besides, it was a special pleasure to be of some assistance to you after your actions in that scuffle. You demonstrated impressive coolness."

"You saw what happened?"

"I was inside at the time, but was soon told all about it. The word spread. You have the gratitude of everyone here in Glorious."

McLendon shook his aching head, hoping to clear it. He stepped outside and felt himself engulfed in heat. It was worse than any he'd experienced. For a moment he wondered why, and then realized that the high winds of previous days in Glorious had died down almost completely. Without the wind, searing as it was, the heat seemed to wrap around his body like a suffocating blanket. Oily, whiskey-scented sweat burst from all his pores. He thought he might faint. Then he heard someone call his name. Charlie Rogers, standing in front of the farrier's shop, beckoned McLendon over.

"I thank you again for last night," said the mayor. "We want a reputation as a safe town, a civilized place. The sort of incident you prevented is exactly what we want to avoid."

"Glad to help," McLendon muttered, blinking hard against the sun's glare, and from the sweat dripping down his forehead into his eyes.

Mayor Rogers grinned. "Perhaps you aren't real pert this morning? When I left the Owaysis near midnight you were still well into the merriment. Why don't you step inside my house over here? Rose will get us up some coffee. You may feel better with some inside you."

"I wouldn't want to impose," McLendon said. "Mrs. Rogers may be offended by my obvious condition."

"Not at all. My Rosie understands that we all sometimes take a glass too many."

The adobe dwelling was small and blessedly dark inside. Rose Rogers had the oilcloth curtains drawn against the glare. She put a coffeepot on to boil over a fire in a small woodstove and bustled about, fetching tin plates and pewter cups and placing them on a small handmade table. McLendon and Mayor Rogers sat on chairs. Rose, after she'd poured the coffee and put slices of bread and a jar of jelly within easy reach, perched on a wooden chest sturdy enough to support her.

"Will you take some sweetener in your coffee, Mr. McLendon?" she asked. "We have a pitcher of lovely sorghum."

McLendon looked doubtfully at the thick concoction on offer. "Thank you. I believe I'll take mine black."

"Just as you please," said Rose. She poured almost half of the small pitcher's gluey contents into her own cup. Her husband added a little to his coffee.

"I hope you didn't take last night as typical here in Glorious," Rogers said. "This is a very peaceable place. I especially hope that when you return to Florence next week you won't think the dispute worth mentioning."

Out of the sunlight, off his feet, and drinking coffee, McLendon did feel a little better. "I'll take your word that the incident is isolated, but I'm still troubled by one aspect. Surely the main responsibility of your town sheriff is to handle such events. Based on one brief conversation with Sheriff Saint, I found him to be intelligent, but clearly he's not skilled at the martial requirements of the job. Why make him the town sheriff? Surely there's someone . . . *harder*."

Rogers went to the woodstove and refilled his cup. "The role of a sheriff in a mining town, which we hope soon to be, is a prominent one. Such towns flourish or fail based more on reputation than anything else. The men who come, who work hard and risk so much with the Apaches, want to have fun at night. By fun I mostly mean drinking. And when they do, some quarreling is bound to result, and now and then it turns ugly. Usually if a prospector gets too much in his cups and acts mean, several of us get him subdued and drag him to the jail, where he sleeps it off in a cell. I admit that Sheriff Saint's not much of a hand in those situations, though, by God, the man tries. Joe's a good sort. He used to be a schoolteacher back east, he came out this way for whatever reason—of course, we don't ask—and happened to stop over soon after we set up the town. He liked us and we liked him, so we suggested he stay and be our sheriff."

"Why him?"

"Lots of towns hire badge-flashing mercenaries, testy sorts who come in and get paid to scare people. Hickok in Kansas, the ones like him. As a result, those places get notorious for daily shootouts in the streets. You can maybe get away with that if you're a buffalo or a cattle town, where little civilized is required, but here we're thinking higher-class, hoping to attract respectable businessmen who'll invest and stay. They won't want to settle in Glorious, let alone bring their families, if they think there're bullets flying all over. So we do our best to keep things calm and quiet, handling the flare-ups as best we can. Once the town's booming, then taxes are imposed to pay for the nice streets and real plank sidewalks and so forth. The sheriff levies and collects those. Joe's honest and smart. He'll keep good books and he's got the social graces to impress the businessmen. That's the kind of sheriff we want."

"You planned all this out?"

Rogers spread jelly on a slice of bread. "Some of it. Bob Pugh and the Major and I have bummed around considerably, we've seen lots of places and gotten the same impressions. But there's always luck involved too. This beautiful spot, well, we had no idea it was here until we stumbled on it. Even then it wouldn't have worked, what with the Apaches all around, if it weren't for Mr. MacPherson. He was here before we were—him and a few others who'd dared to set up ranches. With Queen Creek providing sufficient water, there's good grazing land on the flat. The beef shortage in this territory's terrible."

McLendon took a second cup of coffee. The throbbing in his head was slightly less intense. "I hear about MacPherson all the time. Where are the other ranchers?"

"Oh, he bought them out. Now he's got a considerable spread. We don't see much of him in town—he keeps to himself—but he's generous enough to hire vaqueros to keep the Apaches at bay. Without them, well, the Indians might be too much."

"The depot manager in Florence told me the Apaches got a prospector near here a couple of weeks ago."

"That was Tom Gaumer," Rogers said. "His demise is no reflection on Mr. MacPherson's men. Good as they are, they've got a lot of ground to patrol and can't be everywhere."

"If last night is any indication, they're a source of concern as well as protection."

"We have to accept that. Angel Misterio mostly keeps them under control. I admit that last night there was almost a serious fracas, and it would have been terrible. We've been here now well over a year, prospectors drifting in and out, many drinking hard at night, and there's not been a single shooting in town. We've lost two men to snakebite and Gaumer to the Apaches, but none to gunplay. It's a record we're anxious to preserve."

McLendon drained the last of his coffee. He set down the cup and said, "Well, I hope you do. Thank you for your hospitality, Mrs. Rogers."

"Come anytime," Rose replied, and reached for the jelly jar.

The heat outside was still oppressive, and glare from the sun almost directly overhead in a cloudless sky made it worse. McLendon tilted his hat for maximum eye shade. As he tugged at the brim, he heard footsteps, and then Gabrielle saying in a mock-playful voice he recalled too well, "So here is the hero. Why, you look unwell."

"Are you enjoying my suffering?"

"Not at all. After facing down a gun-wielding vaquero, who could blame you for indulging at the Owaysis afterward?"

McLendon tried to gauge whether she meant to be friendly or taunting. "I didn't face him down. I talked to him."

"Yes, you've always had talent for talk. Will you talk to me for a moment? I'm on my way to the Chinese camp by the river. Perhaps you could come along."

McLendon remembered the prospector ambushed by the Apaches. "Should I first fetch my gun? It's back in my room at the hotel."

"There's no need," Gabrielle said. "The camp is close, perhaps a quarter mile over that small rise. We'll be fine."

They walked past the Owaysis and toward the livery, moving as briskly as the heat allowed. McLendon wondered if Gabrielle might be warming toward him. He considered trying to take her arm, but noticed that an empty wicker basket hung from her elbow between them. Bob Pugh was in front of the livery, untangling several halters. He waved and called out, "Hot day for a stroll." Gabrielle waved back. The boxy jail was opposite the livery. Sheriff Saint was outside, too, leaning against a wall and, McLendon thought, glaring in his direction. "Hello, Sheriff," he said. In contrast to Pugh's effusive greeting, Saint responded with a curt nod.

"I suppose he's sensitive about last night," McLendon said to Gabrielle.

She shot a hard look of her own in Saint's direction. "Yes, I suppose." Then she smiled—to McLendon, it seemed a little forced—and called, "Sheriff, I'm sure I'll see you later." Saint nodded again and went inside.

At the top of the rise, McLendon looked ahead and saw Queen Creek winding in a sharp curve toward the mountains. The sheer cliff towered nearby.

"Some call that cliff Apache Leap," Gabrielle said. "As the story is told, Army cavalry trapped a band of Apaches up there on the precipice, and the Indians chose to jump to their deaths rather than be taken captive. It's a fable, of course. I doubt that the entire United States Army could corner a single Apache. They're too skilled at eluding pursuers. Apache Leap is a foolish myth, but one that people believe because it suggests that the Indians can be beaten. Why are you smiling?"

"We're having a conversation like we used to."

Gabrielle drew slightly away. "Don't misinterpret. I haven't in any way changed my mind about your selfish offer. But there is a matter to discuss, something of importance to me if not to you. Let me do a bit of business here and then we'll get to it. Isn't this camp an interesting place?"

McLendon agreed that it was. A half-dozen huts were grouped a short distance from the river. In contrast to the adobe buildings of Glorious, these were constructed of narrow logs chinked with clay. Their window openings were protected with swinging shutters rather than oilcloth, and several had small covered porches. Plants growing in small pots lined each porch, and beyond them, closer to the water, were gardens being tended by Chinese using hoes. In the slender shade of some small cottonwoods growing near the bank of Queen Creek, women sat cleaning carrots and cabbages, rinsing each vegetable in the creek water before piling them on a blanket. One of them looked up and called, "Gabrielle!" It was the same young woman McLendon had met in the laundry.

"Have you been formally introduced?" Gabrielle asked. "If not,

Sydney Chau, this is Cash McLendon, briefly visiting from St. Louis and soon to be on his way to California."

The young Chinese gave McLendon's hand a firm shake. "Were your clothes cleaned properly? Mother prides herself on good service."

"They were very clean, though I've already sweated through some again. I'll bring them back to your mother tomorrow." McLendon struggled to think of something else to say. His hangover hadn't completely dissipated. "May I ask about your name?"

"Sydney, with a *y*. Mother wanted me to have an American name and chose one without regard to spelling or appropriate gender."

"Sydney's parents came to this country from China and eventually worked on the railroad," Gabrielle explained. "She was born near Sacramento, and she's my closest friend here in Glorious."

"How did your family fetch up in Arizona Territory?" McLendon asked Sydney.

"When the rails from the West and East joined in Utah two years ago, the Chinese lost their jobs building them," Sydney said. "We went off in all directions. I think those of us here in camp are about the first in this territory, but as towns spring up, more will be coming. We do the work that white people won't, like laundry, and we grow the vegetables they want but are too busy to plant and tend themselves. For that, most people in Glorious tolerate Chinese, so long as we don't otherwise impose ourselves."

"Much the same as Italians in St. Louis," Gabrielle said, and McLendon flinched. "Anyway, Sydney is an especially valuable member of the community. She serves as our unofficial physician, tending to various injuries. Many of the prospectors call her Doc Chau."

Sydney laughed when McLendon asked where she'd studied medicine. "Not in any American school. My mother taught me about

herbs and poultices; railroad doctors refused to treat Chinese workers, so we had to learn how to heal ourselves. And a lot of it is just
common sense. Most prospectors can't remember to wash dirt from a
cut or open sore." She turned to Gabrielle and asked, "Are you here
for vegetables? We picked some fine cabbages today."

"Do you remember Mr. Haines, the prospector who requested
lemon drops on credit?" Gabrielle said to McLendon. "He's found
no silver since, but early this morning he shot a mule deer outside
town and he brought a haunch to my father and me as payment in
trade. I'm making a stew tonight, Sydney, so I suppose a cabbage, and
perhaps some carrots?"

Gabrielle stowed the vegetables in her basket and told Sydney
good-bye. Then she and McLendon made the short walk back into
Glorious. Bob Pugh was still untangling bridles in front of his livery.
Joe Saint was nowhere to be seen. McLendon joked, "I guess the
sheriff's taking a nap. He needs rest after his exertions last night."

"That's what I want to discuss," Gabrielle said sharply. "You have
the wrong impression of Joe Saint. Back east he was a schoolteacher,
and I'm sure a fine one."

"So I was told by the mayor. But the skills required to be a good
teacher and an efficient sheriff aren't the same."

"Joe is a very good man and doesn't deserve to be mocked, by you
or anyone."

"I'll grant you he's intelligent, but he plainly lacks nerve," McLendon said. It was still very hot, and his sweaty clothes were uncomfortable. "His voice shook last night when he tried to intervene between
the prospector and the vaquero. In times of crisis, it's important to at
least sound authoritative. As I told your mayor this morning, this
town would be better served by a sheriff with more backbone."

Gabrielle frowned. "And what was the mayor's response?"

"Something about towns getting reputations, and how business-men are put off by mercenary lawmen. Mayor Rogers thinks that Joe Saint is exactly the kind of sheriff that Glorious needs. I say that he lacks courage, but it's really no business of mine. As you mentioned to your friend Sydney Chau, I'm leaving soon."

"You have an incorrect interpretation of courage," Gabrielle said. "Courage doesn't mean never experiencing fear. Being courageous means trying to do the right thing even when you're afraid. Of course the sheriff was afraid last night. What sensible man wouldn't be? The vaquero had a gun and the prospector waved a knife. But Joe—Sheriff Saint—stepped between them anyway. And while it was you who received all the praise, did you fail to notice that while you diverted the Mexican, it was the sheriff who quietly removed the prospector from the scene? It was only because his rival was gone that the vaquero let go of his gun. So the sheriff was every bit as responsible as you for the satisfactory conclusion."

McLendon dragged a shirtsleeve across his sweaty forehead. "For someone who wasn't even there, you're very well informed."

For a fleeting moment he thought Gabrielle looked uncomfort-able. "I had the story from several people this morning, and from Sheriff Saint last night, though he was typically modest regarding his own crucial role. As a favor to me, please don't disparage him further to anyone. And now I must get back to the store."

McLendon had a sudden thought. "Wait a minute," he said, doing rapid mental calculations. Stage fare to California would be about sixty dollars, and then he'd need some money to live on while he looked for work. Still . . .

"I want to buy you a piano," he said to Gabrielle.

"Why would you do that?"

McLendon sighed. "I know how much you loved the one you had.

When you left St. Louis, you had to sell it. That was my fault. I've got some money, enough to order a piano from somewhere and get it shipped here. I know it won't make you forgive me, and it shouldn't, but let me do this, at least."

"You'd do that?" Gabrielle said in a wondering tone, and then, much more firmly, "No, I couldn't let you."

McLendon massaged his aching temples with his fingertips and squinted against the sun's glare. He badly wanted to find some shade.

"Why not? There's no strings attached, no obligation on your part."

"Thank you, but no. Think of the cost."

"That would be my concern, not yours." Ever since fleeing St. Louis, McLendon felt guilty about stealing from his father-in-law's safe. Ellen's death was burden enough on his conscience. This would, at least, be a positive way to use some, maybe most, of the remaining money. "Knowing your love of it, I don't see how you live now without playing music."

Gabrielle smiled. "Well, I still do, after a fashion, but that would be of no interest to you. Thank you for your offer, though I must refuse it. You'd better go rest. You look ready to topple over."

THAT EVENING, McLendon went back to the Owaysis. He was bored and couldn't think of anything else to do. With the remnants of hangover still lingering, he was determined to stick to coffee. But he found himself at a table with the mayor and Bob Pugh, and Major Mulkins came over to join them. Talk at the table soon bubbled over. McLendon realized that he liked these people and their innate hopefulness, though he believed that there was nothing about Glorious to encourage the slightest optimism. He kept that opinion to himself, and loudly agreed that the town's future was bright. The others wanted to toast to that, and McLendon felt that it was only polite to raise a glass of whiskey rather than a cup of coffee. He was careful to sip rather than gulp the red-eye.

It was a convivial evening. At one point McLendon endured joshing about his name. Bob Pugh suggested that since he was their friend, it made no sense for them to continue addressing him as Mr. McLendon, "and 'Cash' is a silly name." McLendon suggested that "Pugh" was, too: "And since you're with mules all day, perhaps you ought to spell it P-E-W." Everyone had a good laugh about that, and Major Mulkins suggested that they call McLendon by his initials: "Let's drink to our new friend, C.M." McLendon asked how much extra Mulkins wanted to charge him for the new name, and the Major said he thought a thousand dollars or a fresh round of drinks would do. Pugh bawled for Mary Somebody to bring them four more shots of red-eye, and the men giggled like schoolgirls when she asked who this goddamn C.M. was that Pugh said would pay for them.

"Charlie, why don't the town give C.M. a reward for his heroism last night?" Pugh asked. "It might encourage other civic-minded folk to step up as required."

"It's a fine thought, but the town coffers aren't currently flush," Rogers said. "He'll have to settle for our thanks instead of money."

"I hadn't a financial reward in mind," Pugh said. "Ella's looking especially pert tonight, and if each of us other three puts up a dollar apiece, we could treat ol' C.M. to a little of love's delight." Mulkins and the mayor immediately agreed.

McLendon peered at Ella across the smoky saloon. She did look enticing with her long, thick hair and sassy smile. It wasn't like he hadn't sometimes gone with whores back in St. Louis, before Gabrielle and Ellen. But he still hesitated. Everyone in Glorious knew everyone else's business. If he went with Ella, Gabrielle would surely hear about it. "No, I better not," he told the others at his table. "My head's still banging from all the drinking last night." Bob Pugh made a joke about another kind of banging being likely to get rid of McLendon's headache, but no one insisted that he change his mind.

"You're missing a good time, though," Major Mulkins said. "Ella's always a source of considerable pleasure."

"As you know from experience?" McLendon asked.

"Well," Mulkins said, "I believe just about every man in town would concur, with the exception of our noble mayor, who's faithful to his missus. Of course, the rest of us have no spouse as an option."

"My jelly bunny," Mayor Rogers mumbled, and signaled Mary Somebody to fetch another round of drinks.

McLendon was just thinking about saying good night when the sheriff came into the Owaysis. McLendon couldn't remember seeing Saint in the saloon before. Saint paused, looking around, and when he saw the table with McLendon, Rogers, Pugh, and Mulkins, he came over and joined them.

"Things are quiet, so I thought I'd have a short break," he said. The table wasn't large. The others had to scrunch to make room. The limited light from the kerosene lamps glittered on the thick lenses of the sheriff's eyeglasses. McLendon noticed again the pink fleshy gaps in Saint's beard.

"Is all well in our world, Joe?" Pugh asked heartily.

"It is. Just coffee, Mary," the sheriff said, and she brought him a steaming cup. No one at the table spoke for a few moments. The others sipped their whiskey while Saint drank coffee. Finally the sheriff said to McLendon in a grudging tone, "Last night I appreciated your assistance."

That's it, McLendon thought. *The mayor must have told him he had to publicly thank me.* "Glad to be of some small help, Sheriff. I thought you acted wisely in taking away the prospector. That defused the situation."

"Maybe so," Saint said. He drank more coffee.

"Well," said Major Mulkins, "are you fellows ready for the dance on Sunday night?"

"What dance?" McLendon asked.

"Ever' once in a while we have a little dance here in the Owaysis," Pugh explained. "We move back the tables and some of the prospectors who play instruments provide music. It's a nice departure from the usual routine. I'm glad you'll be here for it, C.M."

"'C.M.'?" the sheriff asked.

"Ol' Cash McLendon here. We could hardly keep calling him *Mister*."

"You're making friends, C.M.," Saint said to McLendon. "You make quite the good impression, I find."

"I try my best," McLendon said mildly. "Are these dances regular events?"

"No," Mayor Rogers said. "Usually someone proposes them, says it's been a while and the town could use some fun. In this instance Miss Gabrielle made the suggestion to me this afternoon. I asked George and Mary, and they said they'd make the saloon available. It's a financial sacrifice on their part, since for the duration of the festivities they won't serve liquor and Ella has to shut down whore operations. That's so the fine ladies of town can attend. Modesty wouldn't allow Rosie and Miss Gabrielle to set foot inside otherwise. Tomorrow we'll spread the word. On Sunday everyone in town will attend."

"Including that fellow Turner?" McLendon asked. "I had the impression that he never mingled."

"He won't talk to anyone, and he sure won't dance," Pugh said. "But he'll come listen to the music all the same. Even the pigtails from the creek camp will come, though of course they can't dance with white people. Will you dance, C.M.?"

McLendon imagined twirling Gabrielle across a dance floor, her eyes sparkling as they swayed in time to good music. "I will," he said.

"It might do to have a bit of adventure prior to Sunday," Sheriff Saint interjected. "Perhaps we should give C.M. a taste of prospecting, of the real life here in Glorious. Bob, Major, it's been weeks since we tried finding color. What about tomorrow? I'm sure C.M. would find it diverting, and he might bring us luck."

"Are all of you prospectors too?" McLendon asked. "I thought you provided services and stayed in town."

"It's impossible to be out here and not occasionally feel tempted to seek out silver ourselves," Mulkins said. "We figure on making our fortunes with a hotel and a livery and blacksmithing, but that would be nothing compared to the riches resulting from a big strike. So we go out once in a while. Charlie, will you watch the hotel? And Bob's livery? Same share promise as always. If we hit, Charlie will get a share for his trouble," he explained to McLendon.

Pugh said, "If we're going out tomorrow, we best call it a night. A long, hard day looms ahead."

"A lot of hot walking and work, not to mention the snakes," Saint said, grinning at McLendon. "Then there's the constant threat of the Apaches."

"Don't fail to mention the bears, Joe," Pugh interjected. "There's some of them out there too. C.M., should you happen to find yourself faced with the unwelcome choice of taking on either a bear or an Apache, my advice would be to fight the Indian. The Apache's still going to kill you, but he's not likely to eat you afterwards unless he's especially peckish."

"With four of us we ought to be all right, but you never know," said the sheriff. "Maybe C.M. would prefer not to come. He's a city gentleman, after all."

"I'll try to keep up," McLendon said. "What time and where will we meet?"

"Let's say my livery a bit after five," Pugh suggested. "We want to be starting at sunup and that's just before six. Major, you pack the food necessaries. C.M., bring along that Navy Colt you've mentioned. We'll all need arms. I've got the picks and shovels, and of course the mule."

"Any special dress?" McLendon asked. "My wardrobe is limited."

"Denim pants rather than those fancy trousers," Mulkins said. "There are considerable cactus stickers out there, and they tear right through flimsy material. Long-sleeved shirt to avoid the sunburn. I expect we'll work some by the creek and also up in the shadows of the mountains, but even so, it's going to be toasty."

Pugh raised his shot glass. McLendon, Mulkins, and Rogers followed suit. Saint hoisted his coffee cup.

"Here's to good fortune tomorrow," Pugh said. "Somebody's going to find silver around here. It might as well be us."

EIGHT

Major Mulkins pounded on McLendon's hotel room door at four-thirty, calling, "Up and at 'em, C.M. See you at the livery in half an hour." Thickheaded with sleep, McLendon pulled on clothes and rummaged in his valise for the Navy Colt. He couldn't decide how to carry it. The weapon was too big to put in the pocket of his denim jeans, but he surely couldn't hold it in his hand all day. He finally stuck it in his front waistband. He stuffed some cartridges in a pocket, sighed, and walked to the livery, the barrel of the Navy Colt jabbing the soft flesh of his lower abdomen with every step.

Mulkins and Sheriff Saint were already there, helping Bob Pugh load supplies on a mule. Besides canteens and cans of food, they tied three picks and two shovels to packs slung over the beast's back. Handles stuck out in all directions. It was hard to see the mule underneath.

"Where are the mules we're going to ride?" McLendon asked. "Maybe we could share some of that load among them."

The other men laughed. "Nobody's riding today," Pugh said. "On foot's the way to properly inspect the ground we plan to cover. And we're only walking about four miles out—why would we need riding mules for that short distance?" He gestured at the gun in McLendon's waistband. "Take that thing out of there right now. You trip, maybe even stumble wrong, and you'll blow off your pecker."

"I didn't know how else to carry it," McLendon said.

"In a holster, of course, like the sheriff's got."

"I don't have one of those," McLendon said. "I see you and the Major have shotguns, and the sheriff's got his pistol. I could just put my gun in with the supplies on the mule."

"We need all our arms handy," Mulkins said. "If the Apaches show up, you won't have time to fumble in a pack for your weapon. Let's stop by the dry goods store. The Tirritos will have some holsters for sale."

"Are they open?" McLendon asked. "It's not even six yet."

"They've been open an hour or more," Pugh said. "Some of the prospectors wanting the earliest of starts are on the move before five, and Salvatore and Miss Gabrielle need to be available to sell them necessaries. Let's get over there. We're about to be wasting daylight."

Salvatore Tirrito was behind the store counter. He greeted Mulkins, Pugh, and Saint, and ignored McLendon. "What you need?" he asked, and Pugh said that they wanted a holster. Tirrito rummaged in a box behind the counter and produced several. Pugh chose one that snugly fit the Navy Colt. "Two fifty," Tirrito said. The store owner still wouldn't look directly at McLendon when McLendon handed him the money.

Pugh showed McLendon how to attach the holster to his belt. The weight of the gun against his hip was annoying, but still a considerable relief from the discomfort of the barrel stuck in his waistband. He and his companions were just leaving the store when Gabrielle emerged from a back room. "Joe," she said to Saint, and she smiled at Pugh and Mulkins. Her smile froze when she saw McLendon, who was still fiddling with his new holster.

"Are you taking him out?" she demanded, glowering at the sheriff. "Is this your idea?"

Saint didn't respond, but Bob Pugh said gaily, "C.M.'s about to make his fortune, Miss Gabrielle. A sharp-eyed fellow like him, why, he'll spot silver sign where the rest of us would miss it, and soon enough he'll return to town all safe and sound and rich besides."

"Idiot," Gabrielle snapped. McLendon wasn't sure who she meant. She stalked into the back room.

"Well," Mulkins said, "I guess we better be on our way." McLendon was smiling as he left the store. Gabrielle clearly cared about his well-being. Maybe there was still a chance.

They went back to the livery to get the mule. Pugh led the animal by its halter as they walked northeast of town. The sky was lightening, and it was pleasantly cool. "We'll follow the river for a while toward where it cuts into the canyon," Pugh said. "Major, maybe you go first, then C.M. I'll have the mule, and Joe guards the rear. It's early for Apaches, but you never know. Ever'body stay alert."

"What am I being alert for?" McLendon asked.

"Anything out of the ordinary, something moving where it shouldn't be. Apaches. The occasional mountain lion. And mind your step, there's scorpions and rattlers all over the place."

"You mentioned bears last night," McLendon said.

"Oh, yes, and they're big ones. You'd think they'd claw or bite, but what they like to do is grab hold and shake you to death, like a dog with a rat."

"Oh, stop exaggerating, Bob," Mulkins said. "We're bent now to serious business. Where you have in mind for today?"

"Some ridges on the other side of the canyon seem promising," Pugh said. "There's climbing involved, but not much. We want to break C.M. in gradual. When we get a mile or two along we'll hopefully see some quality float and go from there."

McLendon wondered what float was, but didn't want to keep asking questions. He was busy enough alternately looking around for bears and down for rattlesnakes. As soon as they moved away from the river he had a new problem. The ground didn't lend itself to easy walking. It was solid in some places, but in others it turned unexpectedly into loosely packed sand and his boots sank in. After only a few hundred yards his hamstrings were twanging, and soon after that the sockets of his hips began to ache. He couldn't help lurching as he walked. The others didn't seem bothered. Bob Pugh, leading the mule and walking behind McLendon, said, "Don't try to go too fast. Just take real easy steps," but the advice didn't help. McLendon still lurched. "Don't fret," Pugh said. "You'll get used to it."

After an hour Pugh said, "Major, we ought to turn up here," and in the broadening daylight McLendon saw steep heights copiously studded with towering saguaro cactus.

"We're going to *climb* that?" he asked.

"It's just foothills," said Joe Saint, who hadn't spoken to McLendon since they left Glorious. "If it's too hard for you, I guess you can quit and go back to town on your own."

"Don't be teasing C.M., Joe," Pugh said, but McLendon thought that the sheriff wasn't teasing.

"I guess I can do it," he said. "Maybe I better go last, so if I come skidding down I won't plow into anybody else." Pugh and Mulkins chuckled, and Mulkins demonstrated how to clamber up sideways, making certain the back foot was solidly planted before pushing the front foot ahead. Cactus and ground plants thickened the higher they went, and McLendon's pants legs were frequently snagged by thorns. Sometimes the thorns ripped into his skin. The scratches were deep enough to hurt but not severe enough to be debilitating. Pugh assured him, "Just about ever plant out here bites."

By nine the sun was fully up, and it turned hot fast. Pugh called for a water break. They rested in the shadow of a particularly gargantuan saguaro. Pugh poured some water into his hat and held it for the mule to drink. "You always got to care for your animal first," he told McLendon. "This mule is working just as hard as we are, plus he's carrying the heaviest load."

"I still don't see why we aren't riding mules instead of walking," McLendon said. "Maybe you three are fine, but my legs already feel like they're broken."

"That's what you think now, but if we run into Apaches those legs of yours could still trot quite smartly," Pugh said. "If we have to run for it, mules might not cooperate. No matter what's coming behind them, they're only going to be rushed along so far and then they'll stop in their tracks, even if a thousand Indians are howling in pursuit. This here mule, he's fine so long as we keep a nice steady pace and water him now and then. Should Apaches appear, we'll leave him to them and try to save ourselves. Besides, once we get up to the ridges I have in mind, we need to pay attention to the rock, not a mule herd."

They climbed higher. McLendon, wondering how much farther it was to the top of the so-called foothill, looked up and saw mountain precipices high overhead. Mulkins saw him staring. "Don't be concerned," he said. "We're almost to where we're going, I believe," and in a few more minutes Pugh called, "Just over to the right, boys." A ledge curled around out of sight. It was wide enough for two men to walk abreast.

"I don't believe I'll tether the mule," Pugh said. "No sense leaving him as Apache bait. The ledge shouldn't narrow for a good bit. Let's take some refreshment and then get down to real work."

Mulkins used a knife to open a can of pears. The men fished bits of fruit out with their fingers, then took turns drinking the juice left in the can. McLendon was surprised to find himself enjoying the thick, cloying taste. His legs ached badly and he hoped that the break would last awhile longer.

"You're quiet this morning, Joe," Mulkins said to Sheriff Saint. "As a schoolteacher by former trade, why don't you teach C.M. what he needs to know about seeking color?"

Saint sat down next to McLendon. "There's a certain art to it," he said. "It starts with knowing what you're looking for."

"If it's silver, then I suppose I look for the gleam," McLendon said.

"You're thinking of horn silver," Saint said. "Very rarely there's a seam so pure that it's clean and shiny, and the silver's so soft that you can press your thumb down and leave an imprint. But it's hardly ever that way. What you want to look for is discoloration on rock, black patches and lines. That's a sign of possible minerals. The more discoloration, the more potentially rich the rock. If we find that, we use picks to break chunks off. We measure out and mark a claim, and then we take the samples to be assayed in Florence."

"Assayed?"

"An expert pulverizes the rock and puts it in a chemical wash to measure what minerals are in there, and to what extent. He might estimate that, based on a certain sample, there's sufficient silver in a sample to recommend full mining operations to dig down into the rock it came from and see how much of a deposit there is. You can't ever be sure—some of the richest samples are misleading and there's very little underneath. But if the assayer says a sample's poor, then you have to go back out and try again. That's by far the most common result."

Pugh said, "The sun's getting higher and the day's passing. We ought to be moving on."

McLendon had trouble getting to his feet. His back as well as his legs stiffened while he sat. Saint grabbed his arm and helped him up. "Try not to topple off the ledge," the sheriff said.

They worked their way along the ledge, Saint leading the mule now as Pugh and Mulkins peered at the rock wall. McLendon stared at it, too, still not certain what he was looking for. All of the rock looked the same to him, the color of dried blood. There were faint striations but no black blotches or lines as far as he could tell.

"There's Old Ben and some others in the valley," Mulkins said. "Bossman Wright and Oafie too. Don't recognize the rest." He pointed, and McLendon looked down. Far away a half-dozen blurry black dots were moving parallel to Queen Creek. He was amazed that Mulkins could identify anyone at such a distance.

"What if we bump into other prospectors on this ledge?" McLendon asked. "Will there be some question concerning who has right of way?"

"There's a lot of potential ground to be covered around here," Pugh said. He was squatting down, studying rock. "We all try to give each other room, and I suspect there's maybe five or six parties total out looking today, plus Turner, who always goes alone. There's little danger of encountering someone else, and if we did, we'd exchange greetings and go our separate ways."

"That's unless somebody thinks somebody else seems hot on a find," Saint said. "Then everybody tries to follow, and that's when hard feelings result. But first somebody has to discover significant color, and that hasn't happened around here yet."

They worked their way along the ledge. Twice Mulkins and once Saint thought a spot seemed promising enough to take a pick and break off some rock, but all three times they examined the resulting

pieces and decided that there wasn't sufficient discoloration to warrant staking a claim and taking samples to Florence.

"It was close, though," Pugh said after the third time. "A little bit
more and tomorrow we'd have been Florence-bound." McLendon
nodded but wasn't really sure. He hadn't seen any difference between
the broken bits and the rest of the rock wall. Pugh mistook his bewil-
derment for dejection. "Don't fall into a sulk, C.M.," he said. "We're
not skunked yet. I suggest we find our way down into the canyon
basin and explore for float there."

Before McLendon could ask, Saint explained that float was bits of
rock worn from higher elevations by erosion or water runoff. If they
found anything promising, they'd work their way back up in the
direction that the float might have come from.

McLendon found going down almost as difficult as clambering
up. Now he had to beware of losing his footing and sliding down the
steep slope into the prickly embrace of saguaro and other cactus. His
boots skidded and he almost toppled several times. By the time they
reached the base, he was panting and sweaty. None of his companions was even breathing hard.

"Now we need to arrange ourselves a bit different," Pugh told
him. "Down here the Apaches can conceal themselves pretty much at
will. So two of us will concentrate on float, one will hold the mule,
and one will be on lookout. We'll switch off as we go. Why don't you
start out on float patrol with me, the Major can take the mule, and
the sheriff will keep watch." He untied a shotgun from the mule's
load and handed it to Saint. With the river to their right, they moved
along what McLendon initially thought was blessedly flat valley. But
its appearance was deceptive. It was pocked with small hollows and
dips, each just deep enough to obscure someone down in it. McLen-

don suddenly understood how Apaches could seem to appear out of nowhere. The chilling realization distracted him enough so that he barely noticed a sudden brisk buzzing. Pugh yanked him aside and said, "C.M., watch your feet. You damn near stepped on that rattler. Keep your head out of your behind." Feeling doubly panicked, McLendon shuffled warily, hardly paying attention as Pugh picked up bits of rock, examined them, and tossed them aside.

"Major, C.M. and I aren't having a bit of luck," Pugh declared. "Why don't you and Joe take point, C.M. can haul on the mule, and I'll keep watch." It sounded good to McLendon until he had the mule's halter in his hand. The animal had followed Mulkins docilely enough, but now it yanked against the bridle and McLendon had to tug hard.

"He just wants to crop at some brush," Mulkins said. "Keep a steady pull, show him who's boss." McLendon thought it was the mule.

Just after one o'clock they took another break. The jagged summits on their left threw down wide blocks of shade, so they were able to enjoy welcome relief from the sun. They slumped on the ground, McLendon looking long and hard for snakes before he dropped down. The mule munched on some spiny-looking plants, and the four men shared another can of fruit, this time peaches. They had several canteens and drained two. Trying to be helpful, McLendon gathered all of the canteens, stood up, and began walking toward the Queen Creek about fifty yards away.

"Get back here!" Saint barked.

Seeing McLendon's startled, slightly hurt expression, Mulkins explained, "You never want to wander away from the group. Apaches could be anywhere, and if you stray they could pick you off before the rest of us could blink. You always have to presume that they're lurking nearby. When we're ready, all four of us will go to the creek and fill canteens. And we'll do it with our weapons handy."

"C.M., hand me the empty fruit can," Pugh said. "We can't leave anything that the Indians might make use of. They'd cut up that can and use pieces for arrowheads. Apaches can turn almost anything to a bloody purpose. They've been known to wield discarded hammers as war clubs." Pugh tucked the empty tin into the mule's pack. "All right, then. Let's fill canteens and go find ourselves some silver."

They continued prospecting along the canyon basin. Though he was determined not to say so, McLendon was ready to quit. His legs ached, and his eyes stung from the dust and glare. It was very hot now, and though the brim of his hat mostly shaded his face, the back of his neck was bare to the merciless sun. He tried to pull up the collar of his shirt, but it wouldn't stay in place. He could feel the exposed skin blistering.

They paused again when Bob Pugh thought he'd discovered interesting float. Pugh and Mulkins scrabbled among bits of rock, holding some up for closer inspection. McLendon held the mule's bridle and tried not to think about his considerable discomfort. He was surprised when Saint sidled up and said, "You need to tie a bandanna around your neck to block the worst of the sun. See, we all have one."

"I don't," McLendon said. "Like a holster, it's a key accoutrement that I foolishly neglected."

Saint dragged a bandanna out of his hip pocket. "I have an extra. Soak it with whatever water is left in your canteen and tie it on. That'll be of some help." McLendon did as Saint suggested and felt better. He hoped that the sheriff's attitude toward him might be improving, but afterward Saint continued to avoid speaking, unless it was to correct him.

Mulkins and Pugh decided that the float wasn't worth further inspection, and the group moved on. They crossed the creek and, to McLendon's immense, unspoken pleasure, began slowly wending their way back in the general direction of town. Then Major Mulkins, peering at a rock outcrop, summoned the others to come take a look.

"There's clear discoloration and some lines here," he said. Pugh and Saint agreed. Even McLendon could see the markings. Pugh tethered the mule to some scrub brush and took the picks and shovels from the pack on its back.

"We'll work this awhile, C.M.," he told McLendon. "Here, take this shotgun and keep watch. Look for any sudden movement. Call it out clear if you detect menace." Then he, Saint, and Mulkins began hacking at the outcrop. The sound of the picks striking rock rang out in the canyon. McLendon hefted the shotgun; it was very heavy. He scanned the canyon and the cliff face, half expecting to glimpse an Apache behind every cactus. The wind had picked up considerably, and clouds of dust rolled along the canyon floor.

The three men hammered at the outcrop for almost an hour before deciding there wasn't enough discoloration to warrant additional work. McLendon expected them to say they'd had enough for one day, but Pugh announced that they needed to "poke around" more. "Just because that one spot petered out, there may very well be another better one nearby. That outcrop is just too promising."

"Getting a little late, Bob," Mulkins said. "It's a couple of hours back to town. Maybe we should be going." Saint said the same, and McLendon was in wholehearted agreement, but Pugh said they ought to work just a bit longer.

"Think how we'd kick ourselves if somebody else sashayed in to this spot and found silver enough to rival the Comstock Lode," Pugh said. "What's another half hour or so of honest sweat? Do you want C.M. to think we give up so easily? Thirty minutes, no more, and then we'll start for home. C.M., can you stand watch just a little longer?"

McLendon did his best. The shotgun seemed heavier by the minute. He wanted to set it down but felt certain that the moment he did, Apaches would attack. He swept his eyes back and forth, trying to look in every direction. He was sweating hard now, and every muscle ached. Swinging picks pounded rock; the combination of noise and heat made his head hurt.

The others paused to examine the pieces of rock they'd broken loose, and in the sudden silence McLendon detected a scuffling sound. Heart pounding, he looked desperately for its source, and to his horror he saw slight but definite movement in a patch of brush less than ten yards away on the edge of a small arroyo. "There," he croaked, and raised the shotgun and pulled the trigger. The blast was deafening, and the butt of the gun recoiled painfully against his shoulder. The bush exploded; a cloud of dirt kicked up, and the wind whipped it back into the faces of McLendon and his startled companions. Saint's gun was drawn, and Mulkins had moved very quickly to grab the second shotgun. "There," McLendon said again, expecting a pack of Apaches to come boiling out of the arroyo. Instead there was only more brief, now frantic scuffling, and then a flashing glimpse of brown flattened ears and white fluffy tail streaking across the canyon.

After a long moment Bob Pugh observed, "Well, that is truly one scared jackrabbit. You put the fear of God into him, C.M."

McLendon sagged. "I thought it was an Apache."

"No, their ears are considerably shorter." Pugh took the shotgun from McLendon and said, "Let's pack up prompt, boys. Got to be moving. Ever' Apache within miles is on his way here to see what that shot was all about."

McLendon continued muttering apologies as they started back west down the canyon. They moved faster than they had going out. After a mile the river cut south and the canyon ended. Looking ahead, McLendon could see the adobe buildings and tents that composed most of Glorious.

"About another hour, C.M.," Mulkins said. He still held the shotgun, and McLendon noticed that the hotel owner looked around and behind as much as he did ahead. So did Pugh and Saint; Pugh had the other shotgun, and Saint held the mule's bridle with one hand and kept the other on the butt of his gun. The footing remained treacherous, but McLendon was getting used to it. Though his legs still hurt, he had no trouble keeping up.

The thump of hoofbeats came from behind them, and McLendon reached for his Navy Colt. His hand was shaking. Mulkins called to him, "Stand steady, Apaches generally aren't on horseback." Two horsemen trotted into view.

"Why, one of them's Lemmy Duke," Pugh said. "Holster your cannon, C.M., these men ride for MacPherson. I expect they were attracted by your blast." He waved at the two riders, who rode up and reined in their mounts.

Lemmy Duke leaned down from his saddle and asked, "Bob, did one of your party fire the shot? We've seen Apache sign in that area."

"We're responsible, Lemmy," Pugh said. "C.M. here tried potting a jackrabbit. We've explained how it's wiser to hold fire this far out from town. He's new to the region and didn't realize."

"You need to remember that, sir," Duke said to McLendon. "The Apaches are trouble enough without giving them encouragement.

There are plenty of jacks right around town if you're hungry for some. Now, I think you'll all be wanting to get back. Domingo and I took a turn through the canyon, and there's no Apaches behind you. You can enjoy the rest of your walk home. Bob, Major, Sheriff. Mr. McLendon." He and the Mexican vaquero wheeled their horses and rode away.

"He acted like he was our boss," McLendon said. "I didn't appreciate his tone."

"Oh, Lemmy's all right," Pugh said. "He rode down in Mexico for quite a while and is mostly comfortable with its people, but it still can't be easy living on the Culloden amongst all those beaners. Important thing is, he and the other one didn't see any Apaches coming our way. Joe, haul on that mule. There's beer at the Owaysis and I don't like to keep brew waiting."

It took another forty-five minutes to reach Glorious, time that Mulkins spent trying to lift McLendon's spirits. "So you fired a tick too quick, C.M.," he said. "No real harm was done. You conducted yourself well for your first prospecting attempt. It'll go easier next time."

"Maybe so," McLendon said, certain that there would be no next time. How, he wondered, did prospectors do it, go out and physically suffer and risk their lives day after day with so little possibility of success?

It was nearly five o'clock when they finally reached town. Saint went to the jail, where he evidently lived, and Pugh led the mule back to the livery. Mulkins and McLendon returned to the Elite.

"I've got dinnertime to prepare for, but first I'll boil you some water if you want a bath, C.M.," Mulkins said. "You'll feel better when you're clean."

"Don't you want a bath yourself?" McLendon asked. The usually dapper hotel owner was covered with dust.

"I'll make do with a quick washbasin scrub," Mulkins said. "Don't want to keep hungry people waiting. You go on. I'll have the tub and hot water to you directly."

McLendon went to his room and peeled off his sweat-soaked shirt and thorn-tattered denim jeans. The shirt could be washed, but the pants were beyond saving. He'd go to the dry goods store and buy a new pair. It would be a good excuse to see Gabrielle. He couldn't remember feeling more exhausted. After Mulkins dragged in the tin tub and filled it with several buckets of hot water, McLendon fell asleep in his bath and only woke up, prune-skinned, around nine. He climbed out gingerly; his legs still hurt.

When he felt able to leave his room, he wandered into the hotel lobby, where Major Mulkins sat reading his book. The proprietor now wore a suit, but McLendon noticed a rim of dirt still crusted behind Mulkins's ear. He'd missed a spot during his washbasin scrub.

"I hope you found your bath relaxing?" Mulkins asked.

"Too much so; I fell asleep. Let me pay you for it. I recall that your charge for a bath is thirty-six cents, including the firewood and soap?"

Mulkins waved his hand dismissively. "No charge."

"You'll never complete the second floor if you don't make money from your guests."

"That's so," Mulkins said. "But you acquired the dirt to be washed off not as a guest but as my prospecting partner."

A warm sensation spread in McLendon's chest. It was good to have friends. "Well, then, Major, let's go over to the Owaysis. Your prospecting partner wants to buy you a beer."

"There may not be any beer left on the premises," Mulkins said. "Bob Pugh might already have guzzled it all." But he hadn't. Mulkins and McLendon found the livery owner at a table, regaling Mary Somebody with tales about the day's adventures.

"Mary, these boys will confirm that we're hot on the track of a fortune in silver," Pugh said. "I can't say where, but we located some no doubt rich float. Next time we'll make a bodacious strike. C.M. took to prospecting like a Mexican to tortillas. We'll be hard-pressed to keep him from running back out tonight."

"Not true," McLendon said. "My legs still hurt so much that I may never run again. I suppose Bob's been telling you about my encounter with the jackrabbit?"

"This is the first I've heard of it," Mary said. "What about a rabbit?"

McLendon expected Pugh to launch into an outrageous description, but the livery owner said simply, "Oh, C.M. shot at a big jack. He wanted to bring home supper, but his aim was off. Nothing really to speak of. Now, how about some more beer? We've had ourselves a day of thirsty work."

After Mary brought the beer, McLendon said to Pugh, "You omitted certain comic aspects of my blunder. I thought that by now everyone in town would be enjoying a laugh at my expense. You've mentioned their desire for entertainment."

"You already provided your share of recent entertainment," Pugh said. "There was your failed suit with Miss Gabrielle and your actions with the vaquero the other night. So you get a pass on the rabbit. Drink your beer and let's talk of other things."

And they did, touching on several subjects. President Grant had recently dispatched one-armed General Oliver Otis Howard to the territory to attempt peace negotiations with the Apaches; Mulkins thought he had a chance to succeed, Pugh didn't. They wrangled a bit about whether Crazy George should stock and serve Mexican tequila as well as red-eye whiskey. Pugh swore that tequila would soon ruin any white man's stomach. Mulkins mused about several new glass windows he hoped soon to install at the Elite: "I'm using your room charges toward that, C.M." McLendon enjoyed the camaraderie. When he finally got to bed, just before falling asleep he thought that he'd miss Glorious after he left town on Tuesday.

NINE

Saturday was hard for McLendon. He woke from a series of troubling dreams, one particularly vivid: he was in a California city, being chased through its streets by Killer Boots. He ducked inside a doorway to escape, only to find Ellen Douglass, alive and dead at the same time, waiting for him there.

When he got out of bed, McLendon discovered that every part of his body ached: his back from swinging a pick, his shoulder from the recoil of the shotgun, his hips and knees from the long hike and climbing. The ubiquitous thorn scratches on his legs had bled onto the sheets. Major Mulkins would probably charge him extra for that. Hard-to-reach places itched; apparently he'd suffered insect bites that he hadn't noticed at the time because of all his other physical discomfort. How could prospectors endure such suffering on a daily basis?

Because it was almost noon when he got up, there was no breakfast to be had in the Elite dining room besides stale coffee and some tasteless tortillas. When McLendon went outside, he discovered that it was another blazing hot day. Perspiration trickled down his face and chest, soaking his shirt before he'd taken more than a few steps. What a god-awful hellhole this town had turned out to be.

He did his best to mop his face dry before entering the dry goods store, but the sleeve he used was saturated with sweat. McLendon wanted to buy a new pair of denim jeans and, hopefully, enjoy more conversation with Gabrielle. But her father, Salvatore, was behind the counter instead. When McLendon asked where his daughter was, the old man either didn't understand the question or chose not to answer it. "What you want?" he barked.

"Denim jeans, Mr. Tirrito."

"Don't got."

McLendon gestured toward a pile of them on a table in a corner of the shop. "Then what are those?" He wanted to try some on to ensure a reasonable fit, but Tirrito kept grumbling at him and it stung; McLendon didn't blame Gabrielle's father for loathing him. He ended up buying a pair that was too loose in the waist and short in the legs.

As he handed over the three dollars to purchase them, McLendon said hopefully, "Will you tell Gabrielle I send my warmest regards?"

"No. Get out."

McLendon went back to his room at the Elite and put on the jeans, which he cinched around his waist with the belt he normally wore with his suit. Then he wondered what to do next. For the moment, at least, the Owaysis held little appeal. He'd had more to drink since he'd arrived in town than he'd consumed in all the rest of his life. He could sit in the hotel lobby and leaf through *The Last of the Mohicans*, but it was broiling inside the Elite too. A walk down to the Chinese camp was a possibility; perhaps he could buy a tomato or some radishes for a healthy snack. But as he gazed out the window of his room he saw that the early afternoon wind was full of blowing dust, which he knew would sting his eyes and work its way into every crevice of his body, including the folds of his ears. Then he'd need another bath, and that meant having Major Mulkins haul out the tin tub and fetch buckets of hot water. The simplest conveniences in civilized places were complicated in Glorious. McLendon reflected that, here, even relieving himself was a struggle with the high-desert elements. By their very natures, outhouses anywhere were inhospitable, but the privies in Glorious were torture chambers. Besides the smells, heightened by the heat, and ubiquitous buzzing flies, users had to be wary of spiders, ants, and scorpions, all of which scuttled around the feet and, too often, up the legs of anyone seated for more than a few moments. It usually required all of McLendon's self-control not to bolt the privy with his pants bunched around his ankles.

And there were still three days to go before he could escape on the Florence stage. Reflecting on that, he wondered if there had ever been any chance that Gabrielle might leave with him. He'd once thought that he understood her completely, but now in Glorious he had no idea of what was going on in her mind. Surely she couldn't be happy in this crude, uncomfortable place, and yet she insisted that she was. What was this business about her suggesting a Sunday dance to Mayor Rogers? The Gabrielle who McLendon remembered from St. Louis had never mentioned dancing at all.

McLendon took off his boots, stretched out on the bed, and tried imagining what it would be like the next day in the Owaysis, with everyone packed inside and Gabrielle perhaps sitting off in a corner somewhere, since he recalled that she was a somewhat clumsy girl and probably not any good at dancing—if anyone asked her to dance. Perhaps that would be McLendon's opportunity. He imagined himself coming over to where she sat, asking her to dance, and then the two of them close in each other's arms and lost to the rest of the world. . . .

McLendon slept for a while, this time without dreaming, and when he woke it was dusk. He stood up tentatively and was relieved that he didn't hurt as much, although there were still dull aches in his joints and the bug bites itched. He pulled on his boots and went down to the dining room, where he ate biscuits and bacon, because that was all Major Mulkins had on the evening menu.

"I'm saving up most of my larder for tomorrow night," the Major explained. "After the dance, lots of folks will decide to conclude the big event by dining here. Dance days are especially good for business."

"Will you be serving anything especially good for breakfast?"

"No, the dining room is closed on Sunday mornings."

AFTER HIS UNSATISFACTORY MEAL, McLendon went outside. It seemed to him that the night temperature had dropped lower than usual, the most welcome relief of his day so far. He walked toward the Owaysis, hearing the laughter and raised voices inside, and then, on impulse, turned around and walked west instead, past the Elite and the Chinese laundry and Tirrito Dry Goods. It was quieter in that direction. He could hear his boots crunch in the dirt, and the calls of night birds. Just a sliver of moon was visible in the black sky, but there seemed to be an endless blanket of stars. Up the hill and to the right, light seeped through the slats of the shack where Turner, the unsociable prospector, lived, and straight ahead of McLendon was the cluster of tents where the other prospectors camped. He'd never been there and was curious to see how the men lived. A few of the tents were stout canvas, more were made of thinner material, and nearly all of them were patched. Some were supported by thick poles;

others sagged and seemed in danger of imminent collapse. A few prospectors were in the camp instead of the saloon, squatting beside small campfires and mending clothes, scribbling what McLendon guessed were letters home, or cleaning tools. He walked among the tents, greeting by name the men he recognized and nodding to those he didn't. One of these, seated in front of a particularly ragged tent, said cheerfully, "Sit and talk awhile. I've got coffee on the fire and beans if you're hungry."

McLendon peered at the man; all he could tell, by the light of the small blaze, was that he was older, with a seamed face and snow-white hair.

"The coffee is fresh," the man said pleasantly. "My name is Martin Sheridan, and I'd be glad if you joined me."

There was no reason not to. McLendon stuck out his hand, introduced himself, and sat down. Sheridan gave him coffee in a tin cup and said, "I believe you're the fellow who came here to call on the young lady at the dry goods store. You tried your hand at a bit of prospecting yesterday, didn't you? Then I expect you're feeling a little bit achy."

McLendon sipped some of the coffee, which was strong and very good. "That's a fact. I don't see how you fellows do it day after day."

Sheridan had very white teeth for a frontiersman. They reflected in the firelight when he smiled. "For many, it's an obsession. They're so determined to be one of the very few to strike it rich that they'll endure all sorts of pain in pursuit of the dream. Maybe one in a hundred does it, but that's enough to make all the others believe that they will too."

"Is that true of you?"

"Oh, I leave that up to God." Sheridan rummaged in a pack and produced a tin plate and spoon. "Let me serve you some of these beans."

McLendon held up his hand. "Thank you, no. I've eaten more than enough beans on my trip west."

Sheridan said, "What I suspect you're familiar with is stage depot beans, which are wretched fare. They just throw them in a pot of water and boil them into mush. Though pride is a sin, I have some confidence that you'll find my beans much tastier." He spooned some onto the plate.

McLendon couldn't think of a polite way to refuse. He took a tiny bite, chewed tentatively, and his eyes widened. He scooped several more spoonsful into his mouth before pausing to say, "You're right. These are delicious."

"Well, I cook them slowly so as to retain some firmness, and I season them with dried Mexican chiles. That gives them a little tang. There's no secret to it, nor skill. There are so many simple pleasures in this world to enjoy. We get caught up in bigger things and fail to notice them."

"Mmm-hmm," McLendon mumbled, eating fast and wondering if it would be bad manners to request a second helping if Sheridan failed to offer one.

A prospector came over to the fire and asked Sheridan, "Have you some thread to lend? I need to mend a shirt."

Sheridan produced a spool from his pack. "There you are, Archie. Will you join me and Mr. McLendon here for coffee and beans?"

"No, I've had my supper. I'll return your thread when my mending's complete. Thank you, Preacher."

As Archie returned to his own tent, McLendon put down his spoon and looked at Sheridan. "Preacher?"

"That's what most of them call me, because I share the Good Word. If I might ask, what's the state of your faith?"

One of those, McLendon thought. *And now here it comes.* "I really have none to speak of. I'm sorry if that offends you. I'll pay for the meal if you like."

"There's no need. And I'm not offended. I'll be glad to talk about what the Lord can do in your life, but if you'd rather not, you're not obligated. The God that I serve is a gentleman and doesn't want to be forced on anyone."

McLendon set down his plate by the fire. "That seems an odd attitude for someone called Preacher."

"It's my experience that the fire-and-brimstone types drive away many more than they reel in. I go out prospecting during the day, and at night I sit by my tent with my coffee and beans and the Bible close to hand. Everyone in camp knows that I'm here if they want to share a little Christian fellowship. And on Sundays we hold services in the dining room of the hotel. Major Mulkins makes it available for that."

"And do all the other prospectors come?"

Sheridan shook his head. "Not many. Mostly it's the women of the town, and a few others like the mayor. But it's important for everyone else to know that there's a Sunday place to worship if God puts it in their hearts. Perhaps you'll come tomorrow?"

"Perhaps," McLendon said noncommittally. "So you're a prospector by day and a minister by night? I mean no disrespect, and I understand it's the custom not to inquire too much into anyone's past, but was that always your intention?"

"I don't mind talking about it," Sheridan said. "Like others, I first came west after hearing of the big California strike in 1848. My family in New York was reasonably well-to-do and I was working in my

father's tailor shop. The idea of chunks of gold and silver laying out
on the ground, waiting to be picked up, seemed intriguing. I wanted
my life to be more exciting. So out I came, only to discover as everyone does that prospecting guarantees only backbreaking work, not
wealth. After six months I was ready to give up, but I couldn't give my
father the satisfaction—he'd predicted I'd come whining home, you
see. And so I stayed, working in shops as a clerk to save up some
money, then going out as a prospector when I had enough of a stake. I
did that in California and then in many of the territories. Nevada,
Montana, the Dakotas, now here."

"And have you ever hit anything significant?"

Sheridan chuckled. "In nearly twenty-five years, hardly a speck.
But that's true of most of us."

"Then if you know the odds are so much against you, why keep
trying?"

"Because God wants me out here. He has ways of letting us know
His will. I was in Nevada, down to my last cent, thinking it was finally
time to go home to New York. I had a letter from my brother saying
my father was sick, I should come back and help with the family business. I was ready. The thought of baths whenever I wanted them,
food cooked on a stove and not a campfire, clean clothes and no Indians and a comfortable bed to sleep in every night. No more trudging
across deserts and up and down mountains. But at night I'd been
reading the Bible by my tent, and it came to me just as clear as your
own voice this evening that it was the Lord's will for me to stay out in
the wilderness, making His Word handy to those finally ready to
hear it. I'm in a unique position to do this, you see. The usual preach-
ers, they visit the tent camps in their fine clothes and with their
holier-than-thou airs, telling men who've worked themselves into
exhaustion that day that they're nothing but disgusting sinners who

better change their ways entirely or get sent to hell. And then the fancy-pantsers leave with no converts but proud in the belief that they did God's good work and it was just that no one was smart enough to listen. Me, I'm out there with my friends, sweating in the hot sun and cracking rocks and walking back worn to nothing at day's end. I'm one of them. So when I ask if anyone wants to join me at my fire for food and maybe a word or two about the Lord, they're not insulted."

"And have you brought many of them to God?"

"I haven't, but that's all the more reason to keep trying."

"What brought you to Glorious?"

"I was in Tucson and heard tell that a new silver town was being formed. Such start-ups generally attract some of the prospecting crowd, so here I came. If nothing happens and the other prospectors drift off, I will too. I can't recruit for the Lord if there's no one around."

McLendon swallowed the last of his coffee. "But what about you? What if tomorrow you go out here in the Pinals or along the creek and you find yourself a colossal lot of silver? And you're all of a sudden a rich man, the one in a hundred—what would you do then?"

"Why, I'd let God decide. I expect He'd make it clear to me. Come to our service tomorrow morning, Mr. McLendon. It'll be a short one, what with everyone there needing to prepare for the afternoon dance. And it won't cost you a penny. We don't pass a collection plate."

"I'll think about it," McLendon said. "Thank you for the coffee and for the delicious beans."

Sheridan shook McLendon's hand. "You're always welcome here at my tent. By the by, if you come tomorrow, you'll hear some fine music. The mayor's wife will sing a solo, and of course Miss Gabrielle will play."

"Play what? She told me that she had sold her piano."

"Well, the Lord provides. You should come and see how He did for Miss Gabrielle. Ten o'clock sharp."

McLENDON DIDN'T PLAN to attend, but after his conversation with Preacher Sheridan he returned to the Elite and went to bed sober. As a result he was wide-awake at dawn on Sunday. It was too stuffy in his room to lie around in bed, so he got up, dressed, and went to the dining room before he remembered that no breakfast was being served. He sat in the lobby reading his book until ten, hearing people come and go through the hotel's rear entrance, presumably setting up the dining room for the service. McLendon thought he heard Gabrielle's voice and remembered Sheridan's comment that all the women in town would be at the dance. Since it was a chance to be with her, he decided to go after all.

Just before ten, people began coming into the lobby and walking down the hall to the dining room. Mayor Charlie Rogers and his wife, Rose, came first, then some prospectors, no more than ten, Bossman Wright and Oafie among them. Salvatore Tirrito, in a high-collared dress shirt, was next, accompanied by Sheriff Joe Saint, then Mary Somebody, Ella, and Girl. When McLendon made his own way back to the dining room, most of the seats were taken. The prospectors took up two tables, the Rogerses another, and the Owaysis bunch had the fourth. But Major Mulkins, resplendent in a chalk-stripe suit and seated with Mr. Tirrito and the sheriff, waved McLendon to an empty chair at their table. Saint nodded to McLendon; Tirrito ignored him.

"I hadn't realized that you were a fellow of such faith," McLendon said to Mulkins as he sat down. "By lending your dining room out on Sunday mornings, you're cutting into your precious profits."

"Well, hardly anyone turned up for Sunday breakfast anyway, what with Saturday night carousing," Mulkins said.

There was a table covered with a plain white cloth in front, with a Bible on it. Just to the left of the table, Gabrielle sat on a bench before a boxy-looking contraption. It had a keyboard, and underneath it a foot pedal connected to a bellows.

"What's that thing?" McLendon asked.

"It's called a melodeon," Saint explained. "It's sturdier than your usual piano and works the same way as an accordion. When Preacher started holding these services a few months back, we thought it would be fine to have music with our worship. Gabrielle said she used to have a piano back east, and somehow word got back to Mr. MacPherson out at the Culloden. He sent all the way to Buffalo, New York, for that fine instrument you see there. During the rest of the week it's at the ranch for safekeeping, and on Sunday morning a couple of his vaqueros tote it in on a wagon for the service. They take it back to the ranch right afterward. Here's Preacher, so we'd better hush."

Sheridan appeared out of the kitchen and stood behind the cloth-covered table. He smiled and said, "Let's stand and sing 'What a Friend We Have in Jesus.' Miss Gabrielle?"

Gabrielle's fingers struck the keyboard, her foot pumped the bellows pedal, and the melodeon emitted rich, organ-like notes. As she played, Preacher Sheridan called out each line of the hymn. After he recited it, the congregation sang the words and then paused while he told them the next line.

"What a friend we have in Jesus,
all our sins and griefs to bear!
What a privilege to carry
everything to God in prayer!

O what peace we often forfeit,
O what needless pain we bear,
All because we do not carry
everything to God in prayer."

McLendon did not even remotely believe in God. Back in St. Louis he had always refused Gabrielle's requests to accompany her and her father to church. But now, as he heard the people around him raise their voices in song, he was moved, thinking about how true it was that they all had sins and griefs to bear, himself especially. He'd come to the service to be with Gabrielle, but now he found himself thinking of Ellen, and the guilt about her death that he knew he'd carry with him for the rest of his life. Almost in spite of himself, he began to sing too. As always, he was terribly off-key, by far the worst in a room of mostly unskilled singers. Gabrielle twisted on her bench in front of the melodeon and, just for a moment, seemed stunned to see him there. Then she turned back to the keyboard, never missing a note.

When the song was over, Preacher read a little from the Bible, a psalm about the Valley of the Shadow of Death. The people gathered in the dining room that morning knew something about valleys of death, he said, since they lived in one themselves. They had so much to be afraid of: the Apaches above all, but also wild animals and falling off cliffs and many other threats to life. But the man in the psalm wasn't afraid because he had faith that God was with him, and everybody here in the room had that same protection if they shared the psalmist's faith.

"It's tough, I know," Preacher said. "We work hard without many rewards, if there are any at all to speak of, and we see friends die in tragic ways and wonder why God lets such things happen. That's when we feel the temptation not to believe anymore. I know you all want to get ready for the dance—have that chance to enjoy yourselves and put aside your troubles for a little while. When you're done dancing, those troubles will still be with you. But the good news is God will be too. After one final song I'm going to bless you and send you on your way, but take this thought with you. When those times come where you find it hard to believe that God exists, never doubt this. Even when you don't believe in him, God always believes in you. And now let's all take pleasure in a magnificent hymn sung by our very own Sister Rose."

The mayor's stout wife got up from her chair with some difficulty. Her husband had to stand and pull on her arm to finally get her on her feet. Then, with great dignity, Rose Rogers walked to where Gabrielle sat at the keyboard. Facing the small congregation, Rose said, "This is a favorite of mine, and, I'm sure, of yours." She nodded at Gabrielle, who coaxed great, soaring notes from the melodeon, and as the music swirled, Rose began to sing in scintillating soprano:

"Amazing Grace! How sweet the sound
That saved a wretch like me!
I once was lost, but now am found,
Was blind, but now I see. . . ."

Afterward, Major Mulkins served everyone coffee and biscuits. McLendon told Preacher Sheridan that he'd enjoyed the service, and Sheridan said he hoped to see McLendon again the following Sunday.

"I'll be long gone by then," McLendon said.

"Well, when you leave, I hope you'll take some of the Lord's spirit with you," Sheridan said.

"And if he does, maybe the Lord will finally grant him the ability to sing on key," Gabrielle added. McLendon hadn't realized that she was standing just behind him. "Right now, he remains the worst singer my ears have ever endured." To McLendon's immense pleasure, her tone was more affectionate than mocking. "It was a surprise to see you here," she continued. "You were never a churchgoer in St. Louis, no matter how much I asked you to accompany me."

"Given the opportunity, I'd continue demonstrating how much I've changed by surprising you in welcome ways."

Gabrielle studied his face. "So you say." After a long moment she said, "Well, I must get home to prepare for the dance. It will be great fun. Will I see you there too?"

"Of course," McLendon said. "You know, in recollecting old times in St. Louis, if I never went to church, I can't recall that you ever mentioned an affinity for dancing."

"Perhaps you're not the only one who's changed," Gabrielle said, arching her eyebrows. "Self-improvement should be everyone's goal." She seemed about to say more, but Salvatore Tirrito, exiting the dining room with Sheriff Saint, grasped her arm and tugged Gabrielle away.

TEN

The Sunday dance didn't begin until three that afternoon. Major Mulkins explained to McLendon that most of the prospectors who hadn't attended Preacher Sheridan's service wanted to get a half day's work in before returning to town. "Then they'll bathe in the creek, put on their nicest clothes, and head to the Owaysis. These dances are real dress-up occasions."

McLendon helped Crazy George and Mary Somebody move the tables back against the saloon walls. Mary asked McLendon to arrange a line of chairs along the farthest wall.

"That's where the Chinks will sit," she explained. "We let them come as a courtesy. Then put the rest of the chairs by the bar and over near the door. The prospectors will perch there while they wait their turns to dance."

"People have to take turns?" McLendon asked.

"You men do. We women can dance at every tune, there being so few compared to your numbers. Girl's too shy, but Ella will be in demand and even Oafie and Rose Rogers and me as well. There'll be a long line for Miss Gabrielle. She's the great prize, of course."

"Gabrielle? Explain that."

Mary set a chair near the door and crossed the saloon to fetch another. "Ella is a whore. I used to be, and I'm old. Ophelia, the one called Oafie, looks mostly like a man. Rose Rogers is fat and married to the mayor besides. Miss Gabrielle is the only decent, pretty, unmarried young white woman from here to Florence. Of course, every man who comes to town goes head over heels for her. I'll wager she turns down a marriage proposal a week, if not more. All the men dancing with her today will be hoping that something they say or do will win her love."

"Gabrielle," McLendon said again, trying to fit his mind around what he'd just heard. "I didn't realize."

"Then you ain't as smart as you clearly think yourself to be," Mary said disdainfully. "There's a great deal to notice about her. Pay attention at this dance. Maybe your eyes'll be opened."

By two p.m. there was considerable activity around the prospectors' tents. McLendon returned to the Elite to trim his hair and beard. When he came back outside he saw a half-dozen mounted MacPherson vaqueros led by Angel Misterio trotting into town. They struck McLendon as a solemn procession, observing the bustle without seeming in any way amused. Misterio nodded to McLendon as he rode past. He reined in his horse in front of the small jail and gestured for his men to wait while he went inside. In a few moments he and Joe Saint emerged. They talked briefly, and then Misterio began dispatching riders to various positions on the perimeter of town. They hobbled their horses, pulled rifles from saddle scabbards, and stood guard.

"That's another of Mr. MacPherson's courtesies," said Mayor Rogers, who walked up beside McLendon. "Everyone in town wants to
be at the dance, but the Apaches have no respect for our recreation.
So he sends some of his men to keep watch. That way, the rest of us
can relax for the duration of the festivities. They'll ride off when
we're done, which should be right around early evening. As a rule,
Apaches don't attack at night. Meanwhile, thanks to these vaqueros,
all's secure."

Just before three, McLendon returned to the Owaysis. Mary
Somebody was good-naturedly telling the prospectors outside that
they had to wait a few more minutes, but she let McLendon in. Ella
and Girl, both wearing pretty, conservative dresses, were sweeping
the floor. Crazy George arranged pitchers on the bar counter. Mary
said they were filled with punch, water sweetened with honey, and
the juice of oranges brought in by last week's Florence stage.

"There's not a lot, but everybody can have at least a sip," she said.
"When it's gone we'll wet our whistles with plain well water. But no
red-eye or beer until the dance is over. We want everyone to keep
their wits and mind their manners. Ah! Here's the band."

The band consisted of three prospectors, two with guitars and
one with a fiddle. Mary introduced them to McLendon: "Lynn Bai-
ley, Arnie Collier, and Bruce Dinges. Bruce here's the one who calls
the tunes."

McLendon took in the trio's battered instruments and asked dubiously, "Do you have much of a repertoire?" They looked puzzled.
"Do you know many songs?"

"Oh, we're adept at any number," Dinges, the fiddler, assured
him. "We'll commence with 'Oh! Susanna' to get all the feet to tap-
ping, and we'll just go on from there. Popular ones like 'The Lone
Fish-Ball' and 'Mollie Darling,' we play them all."

"Be sure and include some slow tunes," Mary said. "I want to dance close with my sweetie." Behind the bar, Crazy George beamed.

Charlie and Rose Rogers came in. The mayor wore a suit and string tie. Rose's billowing dress was bright blue, and starched petticoats peeked from underneath. "I think you better let 'em in, Mary," the mayor said. "If they get any more impatient, they may start jumping in through the windows."

"I suppose it is time," Mary said. "Ella, remember, you're not to do business. Don't let me catch you sneaking off with someone. This is strictly a social occasion. All right, open the door."

Laughing, whooping, the prospectors hurried in. None of them had suits and a few were still in dusty denims, but most wore clean shirts, some sported string ties, and many had slicked-down hair still wet from the creek. Oafie, hanging on the arm of Bossman Wright, wore men's denim pants and a broadcloth shirt, but she wore her hair down instead of under a hat. Preacher Sheridan told Oafie, Mary, Ella, and Girl how lovely they looked, then leaned comfortably on the wall nearest the door. After almost everyone else was inside, a dozen Chinese filed in and quietly sat on the row of chairs along the far wall. McLendon watched Sydney Chau lead her mother to a seat. A few of the prospectors called "Hey, Doc" to Sydney. She was the only Chinese anyone acknowledged. Turner, the hook-nosed, unsociable prospector, came in too. He stood by himself in a corner.

The musical trio pulled up chairs and settled themselves. McLendon expected them to begin playing, but they didn't. Major Mulkins in a fine gray suit and Bob Pugh in a baggy checked one hurried into the saloon. Pugh asked if they'd missed anything, and Mulkins asked Ella politely if he could have the first dance. The British girl winked at him.

Five more minutes ticked by without music. "What are they waiting for?" McLendon whispered to Mary Somebody.

"Hold your water," she said. "You're about to see."

Then Gabrielle swept in with her father and Joe Saint trailing behind. Many of the prospectors cheered, and Gabrielle smiled widely and waved. McLendon had never seen her look so radiant. She wore a crimson dress, and curled ribbons of the same color were threaded through her long, dark hair. There was stirring near the door where she entered; at least a dozen prospectors began forming a line. "Now," said Mary, and the musicians launched into "Oh! Susanna." The prospector at the front of the line bashfully approached Gabrielle and bowed. She curtsied and followed him onto the open area of the floor. Other couples joined them: Charlie and Rose Rogers, Oafie and Bossman, Ella with Major Mulkins, Mary Somebody with a prospector McLendon didn't know. Everyone else tried to clap in time to the music, but it wasn't easy. Each of the three performers played at a different tempo. The couples moving to the discordant sounds weren't dancing as McLendon understood the term. After becoming Rupert Douglass's right-hand man he'd attended several St. Louis balls, and dancers there followed carefully proscribed steps, moving smoothly and impressively in unison. The Glorious dancers bounded and twirled at random; their smiles indicated that they enjoyed every chaotic minute. Gabrielle in particular moved with more enthusiasm than grace, but the prospector dancing with her didn't mind. He grinned as though he couldn't believe his good luck in being her partner.

When the song concluded, everyone applauded. The prospector who'd danced with Gabrielle released her arm regretfully and hurried to the end of the ever-growing line. Her second partner approached her and bowed. Gabrielle curtsied again. Her face was glowing. Bob Pugh paired off with Ella, and Mary Somebody took a different partner too. Oafie joined Old Ben. Mayor Rogers smilingly handed Rose over to Crazy George, who nearsightedly poked his nose almost into hers.

"Folks, here's 'The Lone Fish-Ball,'" Dinges announced as he raised his fiddle to his chin. The guitarists blundered in, and to McLendon's ear there wasn't much difference between the new tune and the previous unwieldy rendition of "Oh! Susanna." But the crowd clapped along anyway, and the dancers didn't seem to notice.

When the second number concluded, Pugh handed Ella off to a prospector and came over to McLendon. "You better move lively if you want a dance," he urged. "The ladies will stay in considerable demand until the last number has been played."

"I'd planned to dance with Gabrielle," McLendon said. "I hadn't realized that I'd have to stand in line."

"Not to be disrespectful concerning either lady, but you'll have a shorter wait for Mary or Rose," Pugh said. "They both tend to become winded and need to sit awhile. Mary's getting up in years and Rose is, well, Rose. Catch one of them just as she recovers. That's the surest way to promptly get a partner."

"No, I've got my sights on Gabrielle." McLendon moved toward the saloon wall near the Chinese. Gabrielle's line stretched back that far. Sydney Chau and her mother were seated nearby, and he politely greeted them. "Are you enjoying yourselves?" he asked.

Sydney said, "The crowd keeps stepping on our toes."

"Then why stay?"

"My mother likes the music, awful as it is, and she won't come to these things if I don't."

"Maybe if you did some dancing you'd have a better time," McLendon suggested.

"Whites don't dance with Chinese," Sydney said. "And if Chinese danced with each other, the whites would think we were being impertinent."

McLendon didn't know how to respond to that, so he mumbled a good-bye and took his place in the line waiting to dance with Gabrielle. He counted; there were eight prospectors ahead of him. It would be a while. He passed the time by watching Gabrielle as she danced. For the duration of each song she focused completely on her partner, laughing if he told jokes, drawing him out if he seemed bashful. As his turn came closer—seven men ahead of him, now six, now five— McLendon began imagining what he would say to her. Acknowledge her popularity, of course, then praise for how pretty she looked. Then he'd suggest that after the dance they meet somewhere private to talk. . . .

McLendon was third in line when one of the guitarists snapped a string. There was a brief break while he replaced it. Gabrielle smiled and thanked the prospector she'd just danced with, then exchanged some words with Rose Rogers. She looked over Rose's shoulder and saw McLendon waiting in her dance line. He grinned at her. Gabrielle responded with a warning look and a subtle shake of her head: *Don't.* He thought about staying in the line anyway. She could hardly refuse to dance with him if he did. But she'd probably be angry—no, it wasn't worth the risk. He stepped out of the line. The prospectors behind him immediately surged forward and closed the gap. Gabrielle looked relieved.

Irked, McLendon stepped through the back entrance of the saloon to use the outhouse. There was a line there, too, but at least it moved faster than the one to dance with Gabrielle. Joe Saint stood just in front of McLendon, who told the sheriff, "I took the bandanna you lent me to be washed at the Chinese laundry. I don't have it with me now, but I'll return it to you tomorrow."

"No need," Saint said. "Keep it. I have several others." He was silent for a moment. "You know, I didn't think you'd last long out there on Friday, maybe give up before we'd even gone a mile. But you stuck it out."

"Well, Sheriff, I'm stubborn."

Saint nodded. "I've found that you are. But even stubborn men learn their limits. Are you enjoying the dance?"

"I'm finding it interesting. I haven't danced yet. Have you?"

"Not as of this moment," Saint said. "But I expect to very soon." McLendon, always alert to nuance in tone, thought the sheriff sounded self-satisfied, even cocky. It seemed out of character. But he was too preoccupied with thoughts of Gabrielle to dwell on it further.

McLendon and Saint reentered the Owaysis at the same time. As they did, band leader Dinges stood to make an announcement: "We're going to play a slow one, 'Jeanie with the Light Brown Hair,' and for this number it will be ladies' choice of partners. Will they please make their selections?"

Mary Somebody went behind the bar and collected Crazy George. Rose Rogers tapped her husband, Charlie, on the arm. Oafie took Bossman's hand. Gabrielle looked at the back of the saloon toward McLendon and he beamed. So that was it—she hadn't wanted him standing in her line because she was about to choose him for this dance. She'd forgiven him. While they danced she might even say that she'd decided to go to California with him after all. Now Gabrielle came toward him, the prospectors respectfully parting to make way for her, and just as McLendon stepped forward to meet her, she reached out and took Joe Saint's hand. McLendon, stunned, watched as she led the sheriff back to the dance area, then moved into his arms as the trio began to play.

There was a tap on McLendon's shoulder. Ella said, "Will you dance with me?" He stumbled after her onto the dance floor. A few feet away, Joe Saint whispered something in Gabrielle's ear; she smiled and whispered back.

"Is it too much to hope that you might look at me, Mr. McLendon?" Ella asked. "I realize you'd rather be dancing with the fine lady, but now you must settle for the likes of me."

"You're fine too," McLendon mumbled, suddenly remembering things: Gabrielle taking a dinner tray to the jail, the way Saint glared when McLendon and Gabrielle walked past him on their way to the Chinese camp. Obvious, so obvious. Saint didn't dislike him for defusing the showdown between the vaquero and the prospector outside the Owaysis. The sheriff detested having a rival for Gabrielle.

"Mr. McLendon," Ella said again. She was a slight girl, and moved gracefully in his arms. In other circumstances he would have enjoyed feeling her body brush against his. "Will you still be leaving Tuesday on the Florence stage?"

"I suppose."

"Do you find me so unattractive?" She giggled as Charlie and Rose Rogers bumped into them, and McLendon thought how young she was to be on her own in a foreign land, let alone primitive Arizona Territory. "I'd hoped you'd join me for some activity during your stay."

"My attention was diverted elsewhere," McLendon said. He tried not to stare at Gabrielle and Saint.

"That's been obvious. But now that you realize your attraction to her is unrequited, I hope you'll consider my company after all. Perhaps at the conclusion of this fete?"

"Didn't I hear Mary tell you not to do business during the dance?"

Ella giggled again. "But I'm suggesting a rendezvous afterward. In your hotel room, perhaps, not in one of those grimy cribs behind the saloon. If we're discreet, Miss Mary won't know a bit of it. Then I can keep all three dollars for myself and be that much closer to passage back home to England. I'll be well worth the price. I can please you in any way you like."

The song concluded. McLendon stepped away from Ella and said, "Thank you, but I couldn't."

She said pityingly, "There's no use in pining, Mr. McLendon. For now I shall dance with more appreciative gentlemen."

McLendon wasn't sure what to do next. He wanted to leave the dance, get out of the Owaysis, but his pride wouldn't allow him to. Gabrielle and Saint would surely see him fleeing and know why. He couldn't give them the satisfaction. But he didn't want to stand around looking like a fool, either. Gabrielle was dancing with adoring prospectors again, and Saint leaned against the bar talking to Crazy George. McLendon approached Saint and forced himself to smile.

"You and Gabrielle," he said. "Quite a surprise."

"Yes, I expect so," Saint replied. He grinned back at McLendon with the self-satisfied expression of a man who'd won. "You see, she didn't need rescuing after all."

"She told you about that?"

"She did," Saint said. "In the last few days she's told me quite a lot. At any rate, the Florence stage arrives soon, and you'll be off to California."

McLendon couldn't stand it. The patch-bearded, bent-badged sheriff was gloating. "I may go or I may stay awhile," he said, enjoying the flicker of surprise in Saint's eyes. "There's nothing urgent in California, and I've made some fine friends here."

"Stay if you like, but nothing will change," Saint said.

McLendon shrugged and walked away. He had no intention of remaining in Glorious a minute longer than he had to, but it felt good to unsettle the sheriff. He drifted around the periphery of the crowd and once again found himself near the seated Chinese. Sydney Chau looked just as ready to quit the place as he was. "Is it almost over?" he asked her.

She shook her head. "They'll go on until dark, probably another hour at least."

"That sounds like an eternity," McLendon said. He noticed that while Sydney had her hair pulled back, she hadn't woven it in a tight pigtail like the other Chinese. They were certainly the only two people in the Owaysis who didn't want to be there.

Back on the dance floor, Dinges bellowed, "Here's a real fast-stepper, 'Come In, Old Adam, Come In!' Let's see who can scoot the best."

Impulsively, McLendon held out his hand to Sydney. "Come on. Let's dance."

Her jaw dropped in shock. "No! Absolutely not!"

"Why not? It will give us something to do."

Sydney stood and hissed, "It can't be done, more for you than me. People will say I'm Chinese, maybe I don't know better. But you're a white man and they might never forgive you."

"I don't give a damn," McLendon said. "The hell with them. I'm leaving soon anyway."

"I've never danced," Sydney said. "I don't know how."

"Neither do any of them. They're skidding like cows on ice. You can't do any worse."

Sydney gestured toward her mother. "She'd be horrified. No."

"Yes," McLendon said. He grabbed Sydney's arm and pulled her through the crowd and into the dancing area. There were murmurs and a few catcalls as he put one hand on the Chinese girl's shoulder, the other on her waist, and began to dance. She stood stock-still; he urged, "Come on," and, after an apologetic glance toward her mother, Sydney did, moving woodenly but trying. "Just look at me, nothing else," McLendon said. They danced until the song ended, and when it did, McLendon realized that everyone had fallen silent and was staring at them on the dance floor. He bowed low to Sydney and said loudly, "Ma'am, thank you for the honor of the dance." Sydney turned and went back to sit with the other Chinese. McLendon went over to where Pugh and Mulkins stood. "Too bad there's currently no beer to be had," he said. "Dancing's thirsty work."

"Ain't it just," Pugh said. He leaned past McLendon and yelled to the musicians, "Don't just sit there, boys, play another. Something with spirit to it." The trio launched into something that vaguely sounded like "The Flying Trapeze." Pugh and Mulkins remained standing beside McLendon; he took it as a gesture of solidarity. McLendon was aware that other people were glaring at him, but he didn't mind, especially since he also noticed Gabrielle looking. For the first time since he'd come to Glorious, her expression seemed approving.

As SYDNEY PREDICTED, the dance broke up around dark. The three musicians announced a final tune, and several grizzled prospectors teared up as they sang along to "Old Folks at Home." Then

Mary Somebody hollered, "All of you clear out for an hour, and then we'll have this place back up and running." The saloon rapidly emptied. Gabrielle was escorted out by her father and Joe Saint. After everyone else was gone, the Chinese silently filed out. McLendon waved to Sydney, but she ignored him.

Crazy George, Mary Somebody, Ella, and Girl began pulling tables back into the center of the room. "Let me help," McLendon said. "Most of the town won't be eager for my company just now."

"Oh, I doubt that's true," Mary said. "Scandal's always diverting. Now they got something to talk about over supper. And if you had to pick a Chink to dance with, Doc Chau was the right one. They need her doctoring and her momma's laundry too much to hold a grudge for long. Now, help George drag this really heavy table, and you'll earn a drink for your trouble."

When all the saloon furniture was back in place, McLendon returned to the Elite. Most of the dining room tables were jammed with prospectors, still decked out in the good shirts they'd worn to the dance. When McLendon came in, they watched him carefully, as though they hoped he might do something else unexpected.

Mulkins, wearing an apron over his gray suit, told McLendon that only bacon and biscuits were left for supper. "Everything else has been called for and eaten up." McLendon said the simple fare would be fine. He took his time eating his meal. Most of the bacon was still on his plate when Charlie and Rose Rogers arrived. McLendon thought he'd invite them to join him, but when he greeted them Rose merely nodded and the mayor said, "Good evening, Mr. McLendon," with more than a hint of frosty formality. Then he joshed a little with the prospectors before sitting down with his wife at the table farthest removed from McLendon's. The Rogerses ate fast, Rose skipped dessert, and they departed before McLendon finished his second cup of coffee. He declined a third when Mulkins came by with the coffeepot.

"The mayor is displeased with me," McLendon observed. "My dance with Doc Chau has apparently dissolved our friendship."

The prospectors got up, nodded to Mulkins, took final lingering looks at McLendon, and left the dining room. Mulkins seemed thoughtful. He put the coffeepot down on McLendon's table and sat down.

"Don't be thinking too badly of Charlie Rogers," Mulkins said. "I don't think he really minds you dancing with Doc, but he's got the opinions of voters to consider. When the territorial legislature makes us an official town, he'll have to stand for election. So he's real sensitive to the local mood. Give him time and he'll come right back around, soon as he thinks people have forgotten."

"He'd better be quick about it, since I'm leaving day after tomorrow."

"Is that still the case? I understood that you might be staying."

"What, has Joe Saint spread the word already? I only told him that to upset him."

Mulkins chuckled. "Oh, I didn't get it from the sheriff. You two were at the bar when you made mention of maybe staying, and Crazy George overheard."

McLendon drank the last of his coffee. Mulkins gestured toward the coffeepot, but McLendon shook his head. "I'll be going on the Florence stage as planned. But even though things didn't work out here the way that I hoped—"

"With Miss Gabrielle."

"Yes, with her. But there are positive aspects to my short stay in Glorious, my new friendships with you and Bob Pugh among them. I hope we'll cross paths on other days in other places. Meanwhile, though I'm apparently an outcast to many here in town, would you be willing to come to the Owaysis with me now and let me stand you to a beer?"

"I've already spent more time away from this hotel today than I have in all the months since I opened it," Mulkins said. "I suppose another hour won't hurt. I'll buy the second round."

The last person McLendon wanted to see was Gabrielle, but when he and Mulkins left the hotel she was standing in the open doorway of the dry goods store, sweeping dust out from the front of the shop. A kerosene lantern inside the room offered just enough illumination for McLendon to see that she'd changed into a plainer dress. A kerchief covered her hair.

"Working late, Miss Gabrielle," Mulkins called.

She leaned on her broom. "Yes, with church and the dance, I had chores left."

"Work around here is never done," Mulkins agreed. "It's important for us all to have the occasional frolic, even C.M. here. He needed a change from sitting in my hotel lobby with that book he reads all the time, the one about the Mohicans."

Gabrielle stood up straight and leaned the broom against the wall. She asked McLendon, "You still have that book?"

"Yes. Always."

"You kept the book." For a long moment she seemed stunned, then recovered herself. "I'd best go back in. I wish you both good night."

As they continued on to the saloon, Mulkins said, "She sure reacted strange to hear about your book, C.M."

"Didn't she, though," McLendon said. His heart was racing, and he suddenly felt in a merry mood.

. . .

THEY MET BOB PUGH in the Owaysis and sat with him at a table. Mary Somebody brought them beers, and Girl surprised McLendon by coming up and patting his arm.

"You sure danced pretty," she said.

"Thank you so much," McLendon said. "I should have asked you to dance too." Girl blushed and scurried away.

"Why, that young lady fancies you, C.M.," Pugh said.

McLendon chuckled. "At least one woman in Glorious does."

"Don't beat yourself up over it," Pugh said. "You'd no way of knowing that Miss Gabrielle had settled on another. My opinion, the thing to do when a woman spurns you is to stay around awhile and discover new romance. Don't give her the satisfaction of seeing you depart all forlorn."

"Let's see," McLendon said. "Other than Gabrielle, there's Ella, who wants to go back home to England, and Girl, who's sweet but simpleminded. Rose Rogers belongs to the mayor and Crazy George would batter in my brains with his lead pipe if I tried sparking Mary. Doc Chau is forbidden. I believe that exhausts my possibilities."

"But those are just the possibles now, C.M.," Pugh said. "We're going to get big here if you'll just wait and see. Then there'll be women of all sorts, a corncuppa of females."

"Cornucopia," Mulkins corrected.

"Yes, that."

"As tempting as that sounds, there's still a practical concern that prevents me from staying," McLendon said. "My funds are limited. As much as I like my room with a window at the Elite, I can't afford to keep staying at the hotel. If I'm here much longer, I might not even have the price of stage fare to California. So I have to go."

"We could come to some arrangement, C.M.," Mulkins said. "Guests are currently scarce at the hotel. If you're truly approaching broke, you could even stay for free for a while. I enjoy your company."

"My pride wouldn't allow it, Major," McLendon said. "Charity from a friend is still charity. No, on Tuesday I'll start the journey to California."

Pugh took a swallow of beer and said, "You know, C.M., there's another way to skin this, respecting your pride and all. You pitched in just fine when you helped me clean stalls the other day. I got room at the livery. Right now I let the stage drivers and guards bunk overnight. How's this? You give me a hand with the mules and the upkeep, watch the place for me some if I go out with the boys to prospect, just generally do whatever needs to be done. I can't pay you, but you can sleep in the main room with me. I'll lend you blankets to roll up in. And you'll get meals too. Nothing fancy like the Major here serves in his dining room, but I've got a Dutch oven for biscuits and a little woodstove for other common fare. We can have this arrangement for as long or as little as you like. California ain't going away if you decide that's where you truly want to be. And," he added slyly, "if you give it a try, the sheriff can't think he run you off by besting you for Miss Gabrielle's affections."

"I thought Joe Saint was your friend," McLendon said.

"Oh, he is. But so are you. I'm not taking sides in the matter of Miss Gabrielle. I'm just getting myself some much-needed help."

"You already have so little to do that you spend most of your afternoons in this saloon," Mulkins pointed out.

"True," Pugh said. "But if C.M.'s working for me, I can leave him at the livery and come here to drink with a clear conscience."

McLendon laughed. "Since you put it that way, I'll think on it."

"Take all the time needed," Pugh said. "The offer will stand."

McLendon thanked him and meant it. After he was back in his bed at the Elite, he pondered the possibility of staying in Glorious— not permanently, just for a little while longer. Enough to take Gabrielle away from Joe Saint, or at least to know that he'd tried his best. Then, with or without her, he could go on to California and a fresh start on the rest of his life. Oh, he'd probably still leave Tuesday on the Florence stage. But maybe not.

ELEVEN

Early on Monday morning it rained in Glorious, first a steady patter of drops and then a punishing storm with booming, bone-rattling thunder. For a change, the window in McLendon's room came in handy. The ground that was mostly sand quickly turned to bog, and in the hard-packed areas the water didn't soak in and turned to writhing rivulets that washed about ankle-high. The lightning was spectacular. It leaped up wide and terrifying from the desert floor. Yet the prospectors still slogged their way out into the storm, determined to search out silver in spite of the weather. McLendon admired their pluck but felt no inclination to emulate it. He happily watched through his window for more than two hours until the storm passed and the dark clouds were almost immediately replaced by the bright, searing sun.

"If you went out into the mountains right now, you'd find much of the rock to be steaming," Major Mulkins told him in the dining room. "The heat's always extra fearful after rain."

"Will the stage still make the trip here today after the storm?"

McLendon asked. "I see all the mud and flooding. Perhaps they'll postpone the route this week?"

"Never a chance," Mulkins said. "The vagaries of weather are sometimes inconvenient, but we've learned to deal with them. The stage will be coming—perhaps a little later than usual but arriving all the same. This wasn't a severe storm, just a decent gully washer. A few months back we had a downpour that would have terrified Noah of the Bible. All the prospectors' tents were washed away, and most of their personal belongings. But the Tirritos lent the boys some blankets and I had some to spare as well. Many of the prospectors slept on the floor of my lobby and others in the Owaysis. A couple of weeks later we got some canvas delivered from Florence and new tents were fashioned. Everybody pitched in. Miss Gabrielle and Mary Somebody were particularly adept with their needles. Soon things were back to normal."

When he finished breakfast, McLendon strolled over to the livery, trying not to step in the worst of the puddles. The morning's heat was the most oppressive yet and he oozed sweat from every pore. He found Bob Pugh stuffing oats into feed bags.

"Mules don't require any fancy feed," he told McLendon. "They also need less grooming than horses. At present I may rent out only three or four mules a day to prospectors, but when the time comes that we're a growing community, I'll be making tidy profits. Have you decided to accept my offer of bed and board in exchange for daily assistance?"

"I'm still mulling it over," McLendon said.

"Take your time, you've got all day and most of tomorrow," Pugh said. "Come on inside. Familiarize yourself with your prospective accommodations."

The adobe hut in front of the corral and stalls served Pugh as both an office and a dwelling. There was a desk and chair—"My modest workplace"—and, in one corner, a low, narrow bed. A small wood-stove stood in the opposite corner. A chest apparently held Pugh's clothes and personal effects.

"I generally wash up outside in the trough," Pugh said. "On for-mal bath days I prefer a tin tub at the Elite to jumping in the creek. The Major will cut you a deal on bath charges if you're a regular. We would swap off nights on use of the bed; the other can wrap up with blankets on the floor. So you wouldn't be enjoying any luxury, but basic necessities would be satisfied. Perhaps you might take dinner here with me tonight to acquaint yourself with my cuisine. It'll be bacon and beans. That's generally the fare. I season the beans with chiles, a trick I learned from Preacher Sheridan, so they contain con-siderable kick. That makes it convenient following the evening meal to visit the Owaysis and soothe a scorched tongue with beer."

"You make it sound irresistible," McLendon said. "The beans, especially."

"They're quite tasty, what I call my Preacher beans. Dine with me tonight and see for yourself."

McLendon helped Pugh fill the feed bags and also to rake clean hay in some stalls. When the chores were done, he excused himself and went to the laundry, where Sydney and her mother were hard at work. The older woman glared at McLendon.

"Mother says that because you made me dance, now all the other white men think I'm a whore," Sydney said. "She says they'll be offer-ing me money to go off to their blankets with them."

McLendon was appalled. "I had no idea I was damaging your rep-utation in that way," he said. "What should I do to make things right?"

"Don't do anything," Sydney said. "Mother is just anticipating the worst; it's a natural expectation among Chinese in America. So far, no one's approached me in any indecent way, and if someone does, I'll discourage him. Meanwhile, are you leaving tomorrow or not? If you are and have clothes to be laundered beforehand, you should bring them to us now. The men who've gone out today will return fearfully dirty from the mud, and their laundry will have Mother and me fully occupied all day long tomorrow."

"I'm still thinking about it," McLendon said. "In any event, I apologize for whatever distress my impulsiveness yesterday may have caused."

"Oh, it was something to have danced," Sydney said. "Though I don't believe I'll ever do it again, I can see why people like it. I suppose I should be grateful that, in the most selfish, thoughtless way, you forced the experience on me."

McLendon went back to his room and gathered a bundle of laundry. He was probably going to leave, but even if he didn't he still wanted clean clothes. After he dropped the bundle off at the laundry, he went on to the Tirritos' dry goods store to buy a bandanna. He couldn't stand the idea of wearing Joe Saint's. Gabrielle was behind the counter. She handed McLendon a box of bandannas. He looked through them and selected one.

"Fifty cents," she said. He handed her the money. She put the coins in a cigar box under the counter and said, "Thank you for dancing with Sydney yesterday. It was a bold act and this town will be better for it."

"I fail to see how," McLendon replied. "Almost everyone there obviously disapproved, and the mayor is shunning me. Sydney's mother believes that I ruined her daughter's reputation."

"Nonsense. A white man danced with a Chinese woman and the world didn't come to an end. It will help everyone realize that the Chinese are human beings too. You did a good thing."

McLendon couldn't resist. "Would your sheriff have ever asked Sydney to dance?"

"We discussed it afterward. Next time he will. So, are you leaving tomorrow?"

McLendon shrugged. "I'm still deciding."

Gabrielle began rearranging small items on the counter. It seemed to McLendon that they were already properly in place, but she rearranged them anyway. "I hope that if you do choose to stay longer, it's not for the wrong reason," Gabrielle said. "You've startled me, because it seems as though you really may have changed, at least a little. But there's no chance that I'll change my mind. Do you understand that?"

"I can make you happier than Joe Saint."

"In your opinion, but not in mine. And my new attachment aside, you have more pressing concerns. Aunt Lidia's letter telling how you abruptly left St. Louis contained additional information. She wrote that, following your disappearance, a large, sinister man came to see her and Uncle Mario. He wanted to know if they had seen you or had some notion of where you might be. He mentioned a reward for useful information. You failed to tell me when you arrived last week that you're a fugitive from your father-in-law."

Even in the suffocating heat, McLendon thought of Killer Boots and shivered. "What did your aunt Lidia tell him?"

"She said that she had no idea where you were. But clearly Mr. Douglass has the notion that you're responsible for his daughter's death. Oh, don't worry. I know you're no murderer. Whatever happened, even if you were involved, must have been accidental. But don't you think I should have been told about this when you asked me to go off to California with you?"

"All that is in the past," McLendon said. "Powerful as he may be,

I doubt Mr. Douglass's reach extends to Arizona Territory and California."

"News out here may travel slowly, but it eventually gets around all the same," Gabrielle said. "You can't be certain that word of your whereabouts won't eventually reach Mr. Douglass in St. Louis. You're still in danger, and anyone with you will be too. So there's that, and also the other thing, what happened between us before. All right, you've changed, but how much? If I went off with you to some great city in California, what would prevent you from deserting me again the first chance you had to take up with another rich girl? No, we're done and I'm staying here with Joe."

"He'll never be anything but a small-town sheriff."

"Perhaps not, but when he says he'll love me forever, at least I know that he means it."

They were silent for a moment, and then McLendon said, "In your conversations with Joe Saint about me, did you mention that I'm on the run from Rupert Douglass? Because if the sheriff ever sent word—"

Gabrielle cut him off. "I've not told anyone—not Joe, certainly not my father, who despises you so much that he very well might contact Mr. Douglass if he knew. Though you treated me badly, my life has turned out better for it. I don't wish you any harm. Go to California."

MCLENDON GLUMLY REPAIRED to the Owaysis for lunch and a beer. He sat by himself at a table. The few other customers were prospectors who'd decided not to go out in the muck and heat, Old Ben and Archie among them. They leaned against the bar and talked about moving on to more promising places, maybe California City or the area near Camp Grant, where some sort of vigilante army had recently wiped out a large Apache band. It was likely, they agreed, that there were no vast silver deposits around Glorious after all.

"Bullshit to that," said Crazy George, who'd been listening as he washed shot glasses and refilled mugs of beer. "It'll happen here anytime now. You leave and you're going to miss out."

"Jesus, George, face facts," Old Ben retorted. "People have been out here looking for more than a year and nobody's found much more than the occasional trace. If you had any sense, you'd be ready to pull out too. You can't sell drinks in a ghost town."

George slammed down the mug he'd been washing. "Ben, you fucking give up if you want!" he bellowed. "Get your sorry ass out of my saloon and out of this town. Soon enough you'll regret it. You'll see. You'll see."

Mary Somebody hurried over and put her hand on George's arm. "Now, Sugar Pie, there's no need to be losing your temper. These boys are just hot and worn-out, that's all. How about a beer all around on the house and we're friends again?"

The prospectors were willing, and so was Crazy George, though he grumbled a bit and only poured the beer after Mary whispered to him a little more and kissed him on the cheek. When she was certain that things had settled back down at the bar, she came over to McLendon's table to take away his empty plate.

"Generous of you to be giving away beer," McLendon said.

"I'd rather have them drinking than bitching," Mary said. "What we don't need is people saying there's no silver. Talk like that can spread not just around here but out in the rest of the territory. George and me put every cent we had into building this saloon. This town has just got to work. But if somebody don't make a big strike soon, if the place dies and we have to move on, God knows how we'll manage. We won't have money to open a place somewhere else. George is near blind and I'm too old to earn a decent living whoring."

"Oh, now, you're not that old," McLendon said, not meaning it but wanting to soothe. He liked feisty Mary Somebody. She had considerable spunk for a woman her age, which he estimated was on the far side of fifty, maybe even a bit beyond sixty.

"I turn forty-three next month," Mary said. "Don't look so surprised. Life's hard on women out here in the territories. The sun and troubles wear us right down. If I have to turn myself out again, all I'll be able to get will be pennies from Mexicans."

"Maybe it won't come to that," McLendon said. "Some prospector might come back to town today with great news."

"I'm praying it's so. The thing is, in the last month, most of the prospectors here have stayed on, maybe twenty-five or thirty in all, but there ain't any more new ones coming in. They congregate around the assay offices and courthouses in Florence and Tucson waiting for word somebody's struck a seam someplace, and then they all rush off there to try and share in the find before it's overrun. While they wait, they gossip about all the places where they wasted their time. That's the goddamn beginning of the end—every prospector in creation will believe Glorious is a place to avoid. If we don't have some kind of find here, and soon, then we're done."

"Really?" McLendon asked, calculating. "How much longer, do you think, if there's nothing found around here and Glorious shuts down?"

Mary glanced at the prospectors grouped at the bar. They were laughing now, relishing their free beer, and Crazy George was laughing with them. "Two months more, three at most," she said. "Then one morning all the tents will be gone. George and me and the mayor and Rose, Bob Pugh and Major Mulkins and the Tirritos, will have to pack up what we can carry and take a stage out before the Florence office shuts down the route."

"I suppose Sheriff Saint would move on too."

"Like the rest of us, he wandered in and he'd have to wander out," Mary said. "But I won't waste further time on these depressing thoughts. You want another beer? Those goomers at the bar got one free, so I guess we can offer you one on the house."

"No, I want to support your business as a paying customer," McLendon said. "In fact, send the fellows at the bar another round of beer on me. Maybe that'll keep 'em better tempered so they don't go around talking Glorious down."

"Well, aren't you a sweetheart," Mary said.

IF ANYTHING, the damp heat intensified during the afternoon. McLendon spent much of it playing checkers with Mulkins in the Elite lobby. Mulkins won most of the time. McLendon was distracted and had trouble keeping his mind on the game.

"Major, Mary Somebody says that Glorious only has a few more months if nobody strikes silver soon," he said. "Are you in agreement with that?"

Mulkins's king took two checkers in a double jump, and the hotel owner celebrated by rolling and lighting a cigarette. "I try not to distract myself with negative thoughts," he said. "Imagining trouble often creates it. We're in a slow stretch, sure. You've been the only overnight guest I've had all week. But it's certain there's silver to be found here. There's too much sign, too much promising float, for it to be otherwise. And when it's found, word will spread, and then my second floor will be full each night and I'll probably have to add on a third."

"And if there's no strike?"

Mulkins sucked smoke deep into his lungs. "I've been out in the territories since right after the war. Glorious ain't my first time at the dance. Towns dry up overnight. When it happens, it's usually fast. It won't happen here. It can't."

"But what if there's no silver?"

"There's silver. Now pay attention to the checkerboard, because you're about to get whipped."

After a few more thrashings at checkers, McLendon excused himself and went to pick up his laundry. Then he had another beer at the Owaysis. The prospectors were gone and he was the only customer. Ella flirted with him outrageously and Girl beamed at him from afar. He drank his beer and thought about Gabrielle.

IT WAS ALMOST FULL DARK before the stage rattled in from Florence. There were no passengers, but the carriage was laden with boxes of supplies for the dry goods store, and several barrels of beer and whiskey were tied up top for the Owaysis. Bob Pugh greeted the driver and shotgun guard. McLendon, wearing his new denims, helped the livery owner and stage crew unload. Crazy George and Mary came out and rolled the barrels off to the saloon. Gabrielle and her father carried some of the boxes to their store. Joe Saint carried the others. The sheriff chatted a few moments with the stage crew and amiably bid Pugh good night. "You, too," he told McLendon.

"Joe, ain't we going to enjoy your company in the Owaysis tonight?" Pugh asked.

"No, I'm taking dinner with the Tirritos," Saint said. "Sal likes to be early abed, and after he retires, Gabrielle and I typically linger over coffee and conversation. It's the pleasantest of times."

"Don't be so quick to flaunt your dinner company," Pugh said. "My dining partner will be C.M. here, and as we've all learned, his conversation is among the most sparkling in the territory."

"A farewell meal?" Saint asked.

"Watch the Florence stage depart tomorrow morning, Sheriff," McLendon suggested. "That's when you'll find out."

As promised, Pugh served bacon and spicy beans. His beans, though decent, didn't rival Preacher Sheridan's, but McLendon didn't say so; he ate a big helping and praised Pugh's cooking.

After dinner, Pugh and McLendon moved the livery stock into stalls for the night, then strolled to the Owaysis. McLendon couldn't help staring at the flickering light behind the oilcloth curtains at the near side of the Tirritos' dry goods store. Pugh saw where he was looking and said, "It don't do no good to torment yourself. If you do stay, are you going to be mooning after Miss Gabrielle every waking minute?"

"As much as anything, the problem is the damned sheriff," McLendon said. "Every time I see him, he gloats."

"It seems to me that if he felt secure with Miss Gabrielle, he'd have no need for such posturing," Pugh said. "Now, let's drink beer and rise above distress over matters of the heart."

Inside the saloon, they saw Mayor Rogers at a table with Lemmy Duke from the Culloden Ranch.

"Charlie's got his head real close together with Lemmy's," Pugh said. "I wonder what that's all about. Let's join them."

"The mayor may object to my presence," McLendon said. "He was offended by my dance with Sydney Chau."

"Then go drink a beer at the bar," Pugh said. "I aim to learn what's afoot." McLendon got his beer from Crazy George and sipped it, watching as Pugh sat down at the table and joined the intense conversation. Duke talked low and vehemently, sometimes jabbing the tabletop with a thick forefinger. He spilled some small items out onto the table from a sack, pushing them in front of the mayor and the livery owner. Rogers looked appalled, and Pugh, who'd cheerfully backslapped both men when he first joined them, immediately turned serious. After another minute or two of conversation, with Duke doing most of the talking, the Culloden ranch hand walked out of the bar. Pugh saw McLendon watching and waved him over.

Rogers looked upset as McLendon sat down. "I didn't mean to offend you at the dance," McLendon said. "I was unaware of local dictates regarding the races. If you wish, I'll leave you entirely alone."

"Don't flatter yourself, C.M.," Pugh said. "Our mayor's got a concern that dwarfs your little floor turn with Doc Chau. Lemmy says he and the vaqueros found considerable Apache sign today not a mile west of town and brought some to show us. Lookie here—these are beads like the warriors wear on their deerskin shoes, and also some roll-your-own butts. They were found right where the creek cuts through the canyon. There were footprints all over. It seems that the miscreants might have some aggression in mind, and soon."

"The beads I understand," McLendon said. "But cigarettes?"

Pugh scowled. "The damn Apaches smoke more than white men. They suck on cigars and pipes when they can get 'em."

"This could be the ruin of us," Rogers moaned. "That's all we need, Apache attacks. That fellow Duke, he says Mr. MacPherson thinks Sheriff Saint and I should announce in a general meeting that anyone venturing out of town needs to be especially vigilant. That might be enough to run off all the prospectors remaining. No prospectors, no strikes, and no strikes, no Glorious. This Apache news comes at just the worst time."

"Like Lemmy told you, Charlie," Pugh said. "It might bruise our reputation some to warn of Apache activity, but it'd hurt it a hell of a lot more if we keep this news quiet and then have a bunch of prospectors massacred. Shit, all of 'em here already know the Apaches are lurking. There was no exodus when Tommy Gaumer went down. You and Joe Saint just remind everyone to be watchful, the Culloden vaqueros will be on extra-careful guard, and we'll get right through this. But you got to issue the warning. It's the responsible thing to do."

"Oh, I'm strongly considering it," Rogers said. "I sent Duke over to the Tirritos' for the sheriff, because Joe's at dinner there."

"That's a romantic supper all ruined," Pugh said, winking at McLendon. "So Lemmy's fetching the sheriff back here?"

"No, I don't want the sight of us together starting up speculation," Rogers said. "Duke and I are going to continue the conversation with the sheriff down at the jail. Then, if we decide to go ahead and make a general Apache warning, we'll call everyone together here at the Owaysis. I don't believe there's enough room for a full gathering in the Elite lobby. I'm off to the jail now, Bob. Promise you won't mention any of this until we come to our decision. It won't be long."

"I'll contain my socializing until your return," Pugh said. "Ol' McLendon and I won't leave this table. But just to make certain, on your way out you might slip Mary a dollar and tell her to keep the beer coming. I do tend to chatter when I'm thirsty."

Pugh kept his word. He wouldn't even discuss the new Apache threat with McLendon. "Enough of that for now," he said, and talked instead about the rising price of riding mules, up to almost $100 in both Florence and Tucson. A man couldn't find a decent bargain mule anywhere in the territory. When the big silver strike came, Pugh said, he'd need a lot more mules, and quick: the prospectors pouring in would need pack animals and he could charge a premium for their rental. McLendon only half listened, thinking instead about Gabrielle and Joe Saint. If he left on the Florence stage in the morning, any chance of getting her back was lost forever. If he stayed and the town should die, she might be more amenable to an offer of life with him in California. He didn't want bad things to happen to his friends in Glorious, but if it was inevitable that the prospectors were all going to leave, he might as well make the best of it for himself and the woman he loved. And now, with the increased threat of Apaches . . .

"Stop woolgathering, C.M.," Pugh said. "The mayor is back. What's the word, Charlie?"

"We're going to make the announcement," Rogers whispered. "Joe is rounding everyone up and sending them here. I think there's a way for us to come out of this stronger. Over at the jail, Duke revealed a wonderful suggestion from Mr. MacPherson. If he'd mentioned it sooner, I wouldn't have been so distressed. Duke's riding back to the Culloden now to report that I've accepted on behalf of the town."

"What suggestion was that?" Pugh asked.

"Let me tell everyone at once," the mayor said. "Look, people are coming."

Mulkins came into the bar, along with a few sleepy-eyed prospectors who'd turned in early. Rose Rogers arrived with Gabrielle and Salvatore Tirrito. Crazy George pulled the lead pipe from his boot and pounded it on the bar. Mayor Rogers and Sheriff Saint stood in front of the bar and faced the crowd.

"Is everyone here?" Rogers asked, and as he raised the question Turner stalked in. Then Gabrielle said, "Have we forgotten the Chinese?" and the mayor suggested that everyone settle down while the sheriff summoned them from their river camp. After twenty minutes the Chinese filed in, many of them with their hair loose instead of braided. They took their usual place along a back wall. Crazy George banged the pipe on the bar again. Mayor Rogers stepped up and cleared his throat.

"Folks, can you all hear me? Okay, earlier this evening I was informed that the Culloden vaqueros suspect the Apache are getting a bit more active. They found unmistakable sign. The first purpose of this gathering is to remind everybody to be alert when you're out, staying sensibly in groups as most of you already do. Those who usually don't, for the time being, attach yourself to others. That's the way it needs to be."

"Fuck that," Turner snarled.

Joe Saint said sharply, "Mr. Turner, there are ladies present. Moderate your language."

"Turner, nobody's ordering you to be smart, just strongly recommending it," the mayor said. "It's your call if you want to be stubborn at great personal risk." Turner snorted and walked out. "Well, then," Rogers continued. "It's not like we all haven't known anyway that the Apache are everywhere. This news from the vaqueros just confirms it. We should all go on about our business, keeping in mind that vigilance is part of our mutual quest for fortune. It's only a matter of time before something fortunate happens, and it's everyone's good luck to be in place to benefit from it. You prospectors, go out in safe groups tomorrow and find that silver. Back here in town, the rest of us will offer all the services you require to support you."

Sydney Chau stepped forward from among the other Chinese lining the back wall. "Mayor Rogers, in the event of Apache attack, may we take shelter in town?"

Rogers seemed uncertain, but Mulkins said, "Doc, at the first sign of trouble, you all just make your way into the lobby of my hotel. You'll be welcome there."

"Charlie, have any of those Culloden Meskins actually spotted Apaches, or have they just seen signs?" asked a prospector with long gray hair.

"Archie, it's my understanding that it's just signs. Lemmy Duke, the rider who brought me the news, said it was beads and footprints and so on. Just more of it than usual."

"So it might be nothing at all?" another prospector asked.

"Exactly right," Rogers said. "We all just need to exercise caution. And to that end, I have some very welcome news. As we're all well aware, Mr. MacPherson of Culloden Ranch has been a benefactor to our town. He now offers what can only be termed a blessing. Because this Apache sign is significantly closer to town than has previously been the case, Mr. MacPherson proposes that he build—at his own expense, mind you—small, stout structures immediately to the west and east of town and place in each of these two- or three-man vaquero teams, so that from dawn until dark we'll have skillful armed guards on hand to defend us in case of a town attack. This security—and I repeat that the cost of it will be entirely borne by Mr. MacPherson— ensures that we in turn can go about our business and make our town of Glorious as substantial as Tucson itself, if not more so. The Apaches, if they are contemplating mischief, will be discouraged, and we will be the safest people in Arizona Territory."

"When do these guard posts go up?" Bossman Wright wanted to know.

"I believe construction will begin in a few days," Rogers said. "Mr. MacPherson will send to Florence for planks and a work crew."

"Some of the Culloden Mexicans are bad apples," Mulkins said. "Sheriff, how do you feel about them being possible threats themselves? They're experienced gunmen—will they respect your authority?"

The light from the kerosene lamps reflected off Saint's spectacles.

"Well, Major, I believe Mr. MacPherson's discretion is such that he'll keep the ornery ones away on their usual area patrol. Angel Misterio can be counted on to help keep them in line. Duke assures me that vaqueros posted in town will observe our laws. And anyway, the worst of the vaqueros is still a pleasanter fellow than an Apache."

"I expect that's true enough," Mulkins said, and the meeting broke up. Just outside the saloon, the Florence stage driver stopped McLendon.

"We leave tomorrow morning at ten sharp if you're of a mind to come with us," he cautioned. "I ain't intending to wait around and play target for Apaches. My mules are going to *fly*."

"What's your decision, C.M.?" asked Pugh, who'd overheard the driver.

"I'm going to sleep on it," McLendon said, and went back to his room at the Elite. But he didn't sleep much. As he had on his first night in Glorious, he lay awake for hours pondering possibilities. He dozed a little, and in the morning packed his valise. Though he remained undecided, he knew it was his last night in Mulkins's room with a window.

HE ATE BREAKFAST in the dining room, a very good meal of biscuits and two hard-fried hen's eggs, which Mulkins had bought fresh before dawn from a Chinese who kept chickens in a pen by the creek.

"Even if I stay in town, I'm going to miss your fine coffee, Major," he said. "Bob Pugh's is poor by comparison."

"If you stay, you're welcome to drop in for a cup at your convenience," Mulkins said. "No charge." McLendon settled his hotel bill and went outside.

It was just before ten. The Florence stage was in front of the livery, its mule team already in harness. Bob Pugh talked with the driver; the guard, seated up on the cab, checked the load in his shotgun. Charlie Rogers hammered at a horseshoe in his forge. There was little other activity in town. McLendon glanced toward the dry goods store, hoping that Gabrielle would be outside, waiting to see what he did, but she wasn't. As he picked up his valise and walked toward the livery, though, Joe Saint emerged from the jail and watched him. McLendon called out, "Morning, Mayor," to Rogers, who waved red-hot tongs in reply, and then said, "Hello, Sheriff," to Saint. Even at this last minute he still hadn't made up his mind.

"Help you with your bag?" Saint said. The offer wasn't made in a particularly unfriendly or sarcastic tone, but it tipped the balance for McLendon.

"There's actually no need," he said, and walked past the stage to where Pugh stood outside the livery office. "Bob, can I pitch this in here? Then let's get the mules curried and fed. I've decided to stay on for a while."

PART TWO

———— ✦ ————

PART TWO

TWELVE

Bob Pugh snored, constantly and loudly. At least twice a night his thunderous blattings woke McLendon. Other than that, living and working with Pugh in Glorious was pleasant. The livery owner was generally in a good mood, the job itself wasn't onerous, and whenever he felt like it McLendon was welcome to take lengthy breaks sipping beer at the Owaysis or playing checkers with Mulkins at the Elite Hotel. At night he and Pugh ate simple suppers in the livery office, then usually repaired to the saloon for more extended social drinking. Pugh always went there, but sometimes McLendon varied his routine by dropping into the prospectors' camp to talk with Preacher Sheridan.

McLendon was pleased that his dance with Doc Chau was soon either forgotten or at least forgiven by the Glorious locals. Even Mayor Rogers returned to his old, friendly ways. Everyone seemed to think that his stay would now be permanent. Whenever he mentioned eventually leaving on the Florence stage, Pugh laughed and

said, "No, now you're one of us, C.M., a territory man to the bone."
He wasn't, but he was glad that they wanted him to be.

There were irritants. Gabrielle acted friendly but distant. When
they encountered each other at the dry goods store or laundry, she
greeted McLendon and asked how he was doing that day, but didn't
encourage more intimate conversation. It was obvious that Joe Saint
resented McLendon's presence and wanted him gone from Glorious.
At night in the Owaysis, joining Pugh, Rogers, Mulkins, and McLendon at a table, he would pointedly announce that he could stay for
just one beer, since Gabrielle was expecting him. The sheriff frequently asked McLendon when he was leaving town. Though he privately planned to stay no longer than a few months, McLendon never
let on to Saint.

"I'm having a good time here," he told the sheriff. "No reason yet
to be going." When he noticed that Saint liked to drop in at the dry
goods store every day around noon, McLendon began stopping by at
the same time, interrupting Saint's tête-à-têtes with Gabrielle with
requests for small purchases, like a needle and thread or buttons for
a shirt. Saint was always visibly annoyed, Gabrielle professionally
polite as she fetched his items. After the first few times McLendon
felt that she might be secretly amused. He couldn't be certain, but the
possibility was encouraging.

FOUR DAYS INTO McLendon's employment by Pugh, his raking of
stalls was interrupted by hammering on both ends of town. Work
crews from Florence were building wooden guardhouses. They were
small but solid-looking, boxy one-room structures, each with a water
trough and hitching post outside. When they were completed a day

later, they were manned by vaqueros from the Culloden Ranch, two or three at each post. The vaquero crews worked in shifts, beginning just before dawn and leaving at dusk. Mayor Rogers explained to McLendon that the guards weren't needed after dark because Apaches traditionally didn't attack at night: "I think that it's against their pagan religion." Almost everyone seemed to welcome their new in-town protectors.

Bob Pugh was an exception. "I don't like Charlie Rogers accepting Mr. MacPherson's offer on behalf of the town without consulting the rest of us," he complained to McLendon. "I know we told Charlie that he could be mayor, but it ain't like he had to stand for election. His ain't the only opinion that counts around here, and he shouldn't give permission all on his own."

"Something had to be done fast because of the Apaches," McLendon said. "A couple of guard posts are better than dead townspeople, don't you think?"

"So if Apaches presently abound, where *are* the rascals?" Pugh asked. "In the time since Lemmy Duke delivered that warning, have you seen any? Has anyone? It could be that all the sign, the beads and such, came from the whole caboodle of 'em heading southeast to join up with Cochise in the Dragoon Mountains a hundred miles from here. There might not be an Apache left in our vicinity. Meanwhile, we got strutting Mexicans with guns on either side of town. I don't see that as an improvement."

That night in the Owaysis, Pugh slammed down red-eye instead of beer and shared his thoughts on the MacPherson guard posts with everyone in the saloon who wanted to listen and all of the others who didn't. Mayor Rogers joked, "Bob, you're around shit so much in your mule stalls that I believe you've gotten full of it." Lemmy Duke joined in the derisive chorus, but McLendon noticed that soon afterward he slipped away. An hour later Angel Misterio came in, as usual seeming to glide rather than walk. He politely asked if he could join Pugh, Rogers, Mulkins, and McLendon at their table, and ordered a beer from Mary Somebody.

"Gentlemen, I hope that our new arrangement is proving satisfactory," he said. "Have my vaqueros conducted themselves appropriately? It is Señor MacPherson's wish that we look to your safety without in any way causing you inconvenience or concern."

"Everything is fine, Angel," Mayor Rogers said. "Couldn't be better, and we're grateful."

"Oh, I don't know, Charlie," Pugh said, exhaling boozy breath. "The boys renting mules from me this week, when they bring 'em back to the livery, they say they ain't seen a single damn Apache or even the slightest sign. I find myself beginning to wonder—maybe this Culloden bunch got it wrong."

Misterio smiled. "The sign my vaqueros found was quite clear, señor. There are Apaches all around. They are clever and know how to conceal themselves, that's all. Besides our people protecting your town, I have riders out searching. Whatever the *indios* intend, I believe we'll have more signs soon. In the meantime I request your patience." He took a swallow of beer, put down a mug that was still mostly full, bowed to the table, and left.

"That set your mind at ease, Bob?" Rogers asked. "I believe you ought to finish your drink and go off to bed. A good night's sleep is what you need."

"Less Mexican guards is what I need," Pugh grumbled. "If you'll notice, there's getting to be as many of them as there is of us, and yet not an Apache's to be found. I don't like it."

"Bob gets morose when he drinks too much," Mulkins said to

McLendon. "For a brief period his usual sweet nature turns sour. He'll be himself in the morning, won't you, Bob?"

Pugh responded with an inconclusive grunt.

"At least confine your doubting remarks to your friends, Bob," Rogers added. "We don't need Angel Misterio reporting to Mr. MacPherson that this town is unappreciative of his protection."

"Protection, my ass," Pugh said. He tossed off the last of his drink and got unsteadily to his feet. McLendon and Mulkins each took one of his elbows so he wouldn't fall. "If those Mexicans want me to believe, they damn well better show me some Apaches."

TWO DAYS LATER Joe Saint was at the livery, idly talking to Pugh and pointedly ignoring McLendon, when Ella came running in.

"Miss Mary needs you at the saloon, Sheriff," she said. "The cruel-looking Mexican gentleman and some of his people have arrived with something in a wagon, and you're wanted at once."

Saint, Pugh, and McLendon hurried to the Owaysis. Misterio, Duke, and two vaqueros McLendon didn't recognize stood outside with Mayor Rogers, Crazy George, Mary Somebody, Girl, and Ella. Everyone was staring at the wagon bed, which was covered with a dark green canvas tarpaulin. Misterio looked up and said solemnly, "*Hola*, Sheriff. This morning some of my men patrolled the mountains just north of the creek, and there they encountered an Apache war band. The Apaches meant to surprise some of your prospectors, but the vaqueros surprised them instead. After an exchange of shots the *indios* broke and ran. Two were unsuccessful in their flight, as you may now see." He grasped a corner of the canvas and pulled it back, revealing the bodies of two Apaches. Girl shrieked and clapped her hands over her eyes. Mary gestured for Ella to take her inside the saloon. The English girl did so reluctantly, staring back at the Apache corpses in the wagon as she pulled Girl through the door.

McLendon, looking at the bodies, felt mildly disappointed. In his mind, Apaches were fearsome copper-skinned giants. These dead Indians were surprisingly small. One had part of his skull blown away. Bits of brain matter oozed out the gaping hole. The other had several bullet wounds to his chest. Both wore calico shirts exactly like the ones the Tirritos sold in their dry goods store. The Apaches' lower bodies were clad in cloth breechclouts and deerskin leggings. They wore deerskin boots on their feet and their long black hair was tied back with leather thongs.

"They appear to be unarmed," Joe Saint said.

"Not so," replied Angel Misterio. "We took these from them after they were dead." He handed the sheriff two wide-bladed butcher knives and an ancient, battered shotgun. He gestured at the body on the left and said, "This one has five shells for the shotgun in that pouch you see at his waist."

Saint glanced briefly at the weapons and asked, "Was that all? Two knives and a shotgun? That's not much in the way of weapons for members of a war party."

"Apaches don't require many weapons when they kill," Misterio said. "They doubtless expected to arm themselves with the rifles of their victims. And these are only two of a larger group. I believe my men counted nine or ten in all. The others escaped and undoubtedly remain in the area. We hope to find them soon. Perhaps they are well armed enough to impress you, Sheriff, should you have the bad luck to encounter them."

"No bows or arrows on these two, though," Saint said. "No lances or war clubs?"

"No, just as you see. Shall we take the bodies away now, Sheriff? The flies are already descending upon them."

"We'll wait just a bit," Saint said. "I'd like Doc Chau to look them over first."

Misterio grimaced. "These *indios* are dead. Why is further examination necessary?"

"Since Apaches are the enemy, we need to know everything about them that we can. If you would, Señor Misterio, please pull the canvas back over the bodies. That'll discourage the flies until Doc gets here. Could somebody go and get her?"

McLendon volunteered. He went to the laundry, but Sydney wasn't there. Her mother still held a grudge from the dance. She glowered at McLendon as he kept repeating, "Sydney—where's Sydney?" Finally the old woman heaved an extravagant sigh and gestured in the direction of the river camp. McLendon set out, passing the wagon with the bodies of the Apaches. A few prospectors, having heard the news, were attempting to pull off the tarpaulin to gawk at the corpses. Saint was trying to keep them away. Misterio and his vaqueros stood nearby, smoking hand-rolled cigarettes.

McLendon found Sydney weeding a vegetable patch. When he told her why she was needed in town, she asked him to wait while she washed dirt off her hands. Then they hurried back to Glorious.

"Doc, can you look these bodies over?" Saint asked. "Maybe we can take them into the saloon so you can do it in some privacy."

"Keep those goddamn things out of my place," Crazy George snapped. "You think people will want to drink where dead Apaches were?"

Mulkins volunteered a room at his hotel: "I've got no guests right now, and Mrs. Mendoza can clean up afterwards."

Misterio grudgingly ordered the vaqueros to take the bodies out of the wagon and carry them into the hotel. The vaqueros weren't big men, but they hefted the canvas-wrapped Apaches over their shoulders without much effort. They carried them through the lobby and dumped them on the floor of the room that Mulkins indicated. Sydney and the sheriff went in and closed the door. Everyone else waited in the lobby. Mulkins brought them coffee. In a while Sydney and Saint emerged. The sheriff asked the vaqueros to bring the bodies outside. By then about a dozen prospectors were gathered there. They yelled for the dead Apaches to be displayed.

"Most of these boys are scared of Apaches but probably never seen a wild one," Mulkins whispered to McLendon. "You got your tame 'Paches lingering around the Army camps, offering to sell their squaws for a drink, but it's not the same thing."

The prospectors kept demanding to see the bodies. Saint consulted with Mayor Rogers, then said, "Okay, boys, you can have a look, but make it quick." He and Bob Pugh pulled off the canvas cover and the prospectors pushed forward. McLendon heard remarks about how scrawny the corpses were. Then a prospector tried to yank down one of the Apaches' breechclouts.

Saint grabbed the man's arm. "What are you doing?"

The prospector grinned. "I'm gonna cut me off an Apache whanger and keep it for a souvenir."

"No you're not," Saint said. "Respect the dead."

"Fuck that—the Indians don't respect who they kill. You recall Tommy Gaumer, how they carved him up so terrible?"

"Step away," the sheriff said, and once again McLendon noticed that his voice trembled a bit. "We're better than that."

The prospector stepped toward Saint. He dwarfed the skinny sheriff. Pugh and Mulkins moved to Saint's side, and McLendon was surprised to find himself doing the same. The prospector looked at them, paused, and spit on the ground near the Apache bodies.

"Goddamn Apaches," he snarled, and walked away.

"All right," Saint said, his voice still shaking. "Señor Misterio, will you please have your men take these bodies away and bury them?"

"We don't bury Apaches, Sheriff," Misterio said. "We leave their bodies out for the buzzards."

"As you please, but at least take them well out of sight before you do."

Misterio barked out orders in Spanish, and the vaqueros went over to the bodies. One, just as eager as the tall prospector for a grisly momento, took a knife and severed one of the corpse's ears. Misterio looked at the vaquero, glanced back at an obviously disgusted Sheriff Saint, then moved forward so fast that his body seemed to blur. In what appeared to be a single motion he snatched the ear from the vaquero's hand, pulled his pistol from its holster, and smashed the gun into the side of the man's head. The vaquero groaned and crumpled. Then Misterio delicately tucked the ear inside the dead Apache's calico shirt and muttered orders in Spanish to the other vaqueros. They picked up the Indian bodies and tossed them back into the bed of the wagon. The dazed vaquero was dragged off to his horse and helped into the saddle.

"Profound apologies, Sheriff," Misterio said. "My *muchachos* sometimes lack manners. We will now dispose of these bodies."

"Well, Bob, I hope you feel satisfied that there is, indeed, increased Apache threat," Mayor Rogers said to Pugh. "Your bellyaching was misguided. Now, how about making up for it by buying me a drink?"

"It's possible that I was mistaken," Pugh admitted. "Everybody over to the saloon for a round on me."

"I'll pass on this one, Bob," Saint said. He looked and sounded troubled. "I'm heading back to the jail. Doc, could you come with me? I need to think through things some more."

"What's the sheriff's problem?" McLendon asked Sydney.

"Come along with us," she said. "Your opinion might be helpful." Saint was so preoccupied that he didn't seem to notice McLendon walking along with them.

Though McLendon had seen the adobe jail before, he had never been inside. Much like Bob Pugh's livery office, it had a desk, three chairs, a woodstove, and a chest to hold Saint's personal items. Two cells took up the back of the room. Their barred doors looked rusty but stout. Each had a bed. The blankets on one were rumpled; the sheriff apparently slept there.

Saint dropped into one chair and gestured for Sydney and McLendon to take the others. "Doc, are you sure about what you told me?"

Sydney nodded. "That one Apache was shot in the chest, from the front. The other was shot from the front and the right. There's no doubt."

"Misterio said they were shot while trying to run," Saint mused. "So it seems like they should have been hit from the back."

"Maybe they were twisting around to return fire," McLendon suggested.

Saint glanced over, apparently surprised to see him there. "Well, that's possible," he said. "But there are other things. No war paint, for one. When Apaches are out on a raid, they generally paint up their faces. It's a ritual, and important to them. But I looked closely at those bodies, and there wasn't a trace of paint on either. If they were part of a war party, they surely would have been painted up."

"You seem to know a lot about Apaches," McLendon observed.

"When I first was out here in the territory, I spent time at Camp

Grant," Saint said. "They had a considerable number of Apaches there who'd turned themselves in. So I talked to some of the ones who spoke English, and also a few of the Army vets. That's how I learned some things about Apache traditions and culture."

"Maybe you could ask some of those Camp Grant Apaches about the war paint thing," McLendon suggested. "There might be a reason that these two were in a war party but weren't wearing any."

"I can't do that. About a year ago, some hotheads in Tucson got the notion that the Camp Grant Apaches were raiding, then running back to the Army post and pretending to be tame. They got up a bunch of vigilantes, rode up to Camp Grant, and wiped the Apaches there out. Not many escaped. Those calico shirts our two dead ones were wearing, they might have come from the Camp Grant sutler. They might have been two massacre survivors. The ones that got away, some of them are still out in the Pinals. They try to avoid whites as much as they can."

McLendon was intrigued. "If they wanted to avoid us, what were they doing so close to town?"

"That's another thing," Saint said. "Misterio claimed that they took them in the mountains just north of the creek. Saw 'em, chased 'em, shot 'em. You remember how loud your shotgun sounded when you blasted away at that jackrabbit?"

"Jackrabbit?" Sydney asked.

"I thought it was an Apache," McLendon said. "Go on, Sheriff."

"Did you notice that when the prospectors came back in and looked at the bodies, none of them said they'd heard shots? Sound carries out there. That close to town, somebody should have heard the shooting. And then there's the weapons, or the lack of them. Apaches setting out to fight carry lances and quivers. They may have guns, too, but they can't use them much because they have trouble getting ammunition. Misterio said these two each had a knife and one had a shotgun. They weren't going to attack this town by running up at us waving knives. Even if they were just out hunting, they'd have had bows and arrows. So where are those?"

"They might have dropped them as they ran from the vaqueros," Sydney said.

"Maybe so," Saint mused. "Maybe it all happened the way Misterio says. Say, McLendon, don't I recall Bob Pugh telling me he got drunk the other night and might have wondered out loud in the Owaysis whether there really were Apache war parties about? And that Misterio swore to him that there were?"

"That's what happened."

Saint shook his head and tilted back in his chair. "There's no way to be sure, but here's what I think. Misterio and his bunch went out Apache hunting. They didn't scare up any near here, so they rode way out until they found a couple of Indians hunting game, not people. They ambushed them and brought the bodies all the way back to town to shut up doubters like Bob."

"Even if that's true, it still doesn't mean there aren't Apaches lurking nearby, waiting for a chance to attack," McLendon said.

Saint nodded. "But the deception bothers me. That's a lot of trouble to go to, if the story's made up. And where are the bows and arrows?"

No other townspeople seemed to share Saint's doubts. The consensus was that Glorious had been saved from an Apache raid by the Culloden Ranch vaqueros. Mayor Rogers had made a visit to thank the reclusive Collin MacPherson on behalf of the town, and reported back that the rancher had been gracious though abrupt.

"He said that he's doing whatever he must to ensure that everyone here is safe," Rogers said. "He was too busy to talk longer, having letters to write to the legislature in Tucson. It's Mr. MacPherson's expectation that we'll be granted official town status very soon."

For a few days everyone was especially wary when venturing outside of town. Though no other Apaches were sighted, the memory of the two killed by the vaqueros was enough to keep prospectors working closer in than usual. They gradually began to range farther into the mountains again, but by the end of June there were still no silver strikes beyond occasional discoveries of promising float. One or two prospectors began drifting away with each successive week until fewer than twenty remained. Archie and Old Ben left, following a rumor of silver strikes in southwest New Mexico. Bossman Wright said that he and Oafie would stay only a week or two longer "if we don't find any color," and even Preacher Sheridan talked about going somewhere else.

"I can't sow seeds for God on barren ground," he told McLendon. "It seems increasingly likely that silver and souls to save are both too scarce here in Glorious. I'm praying on whether to stay or leave, just waiting for the good Lord to send me a sign."

Though his friends among the town founders continued expressing optimism that someone would find silver any day, McLendon now knew them well enough to realize that they, too, were quickly losing faith. At the current rate of prospector attrition, the population of Glorious would be reduced to its founders, Sheriff Saint, and the Chinese by the end of the summer.

The decreasing numbers were most obvious at night in the Owaysis. Now there were always tables available. Ella was particularly disheartened. She redoubled her efforts to coax McLendon into taking a paid turn with her.

"Most days now I earn no more than a dollar or two," she complained to him. "Fare back to Britain is very dear, several hundred dollars alone for stage and rail to New York City, and of course the cost of ocean passage from there. If you're willing, I'll express my gratitude in a very energetic and pleasing manner. In fact, if no one else is waiting, as is most often the current case, we can ignore the fifteen-minute limit and be together longer. With business so depleted, Miss Mary won't be watching the clock."

McLendon said that he sympathized but couldn't comply. "I've told you that I can't. It's no reflection on you, Ella. You're charming. In another place or under other circumstances, I'd be a regular customer."

"Pining for your fine lady is futile," Ella said, toying with her hair and leaning close. McLendon caught the sweet scent of rosewater. The girl had been using the fancy soaps peddled by William Clark LeMond, the traveling salesman he'd met on the stage from Florence to Glorious. "Come to bed with me and you'll forget all about her."

"But I don't want to forget," McLendon said, and was surprised by his honesty.

"Well, then," Ella said, "if you won't lay with me, perhaps you could loan me some money? I so desperately want to go home, and I promise to pay you back someday."

"I'm sorry, but no. I may be leaving myself soon, and I need what I have to make my own fresh start."

Ella nodded. "If you won't pay for pleasure with me and you won't loan me money, will you at least buy me a beer? It's fearfully hot, and a girl does get thirsty amid all the dust."

After she drank her beer, Ella left McLendon and circulated

among the half-dozen prospectors scattered around the saloon. McLendon watched as she perched on laps and cooed in ears, trying to attract business. She had no luck. Most of the remaining prospectors were down to their last few dollars. After a while she gave up and sat sullenly beside Girl, who as usual was smiling but silent in a corner of the room.

In a bit Bob Pugh came in with Major Mulkins, and later Mayor Rogers arrived. They joined McLendon at his table and talked about the heat, the purple tie Mulkins was wearing, the mule that kicked Pugh in the dangles that afternoon as he tried to pull burrs out of its tail—anything but the looming demise of Glorious. Later Joe Saint arrived. McLendon guessed that he had just finished eating supper with the Tirritos. Since listening to the sheriff express his doubts about the dead Apaches, McLendon found himself grudgingly liking the man. He was with Gabrielle, which was hard to forgive, but he was also smart and honest. Gabrielle may have even been right when she claimed that Saint was brave. Maybe his voice sometimes shook, but he stood up for what he believed.

"You're lately having a quiet time of it, Sheriff," Pugh said joshingly. "I don't recall that there's been a drunken fight in town for weeks."

"People are being quiet," Saint agreed. "You may soon decide that you don't need a sheriff at all."

"Don't talk that way," Mayor Rogers said. "Before you know it, we'll be a boomtown with lots of fights, and Joe here will have to hire deputies to help him subdue the combatants. Let's drink to that happy day."

"To more brawls than a sober man can count," Pugh said, and raised his beer mug.

After they drank, Mulkins said, "Bob, I believe that's the most foolish toast ever."

Pugh smiled ruefully. "Well, we needed to drink to something. C.M., what say we get back to the livery and take some rest? For all we know, we might be knee-deep tomorrow in prospectors wanting to rent mules, and need all our strength."

ONLY THREE PROSPECTORS rented mules in the morning, but that evening Angel Misterio came by. Pugh was already at the Owaysis. McLendon was slouched behind the desk in the livery office, writing up an order for oats to be sent into Florence on the next stage. He was startled when Misterio came in—whenever the head Culloden vaquero came to town, he invariably visited Saint in the sheriff's office or Mayor Rogers in his farrier's shop or the saloon.

McLendon asked, "Señor Misterio, how can I help you? Are you here to rent one of Mr. Pugh's fine mules?"

"Thank you, but at the Culloden we already have sufficient mules," Misterio said. "I come to extend an invitation. My employer wonders if you might be free to come to his home for a conversation."

"Now?" McLendon asked, surprised by the request.

"I have another horse with mine in front of this building. We could ride back to the ranch at once, if you find it convenient."

"How does Mr. MacPherson even know my name?"

"Señor MacPherson is always well informed. Will you ride with me to see him now?"

McLendon was too curious about what MacPherson might want to refuse. "I'll just change my clothes."

The Mexican waved his hand. "There is no need. Mr. MacPherson understands the wardrobe of a workingman. He also looks forward to your arrival. Shall we be on our way?"

"I suppose," McLendon said. He went outside, washed his hands in the trough, and then walked with Misterio to where the horses were tethered in front of the livery.

THIRTEEN

McLendon had always assumed that riding horses was easy, but it wasn't, starting with the unexpected complications of getting onto the saddle. Back in St. Louis he'd ridden in horse-drawn carriages but never on a horse's back. The mount Misterio brought for him was one of the small, agile Mexican breeds, and it wouldn't stand still while McLendon tried to get his foot into the stirrup and hoist himself up. He kept missing the stirrup, kicking it away in the process, and then he had to wait until it swung back from under the horse's midriff to try again. Misterio, who seemed to vault onto his horse, watched impatiently as McLendon failed several times to get seated.

"Grasp the pommel and step into the stirrup, *señor*," he said. "It should be one smooth movement."

When McLendon was finally in the saddle, Misterio wheeled his own mount around the back of the corral, away from the few main buildings in Glorious. He apparently wanted them to make their way to the ranch unobserved. In the purple glow of the high desert twilight, they trotted behind the farrier's shop, the mayor's small house, and the Tirritos' dry goods store. No vaqueros were posted at the guard hut because it was getting dark. They were almost to Turner's small, isolated shack when Misterio made a sharp turn south. McLendon almost didn't follow, because his horse seemed determined to keep going west. He yanked on the reins and finally the horse turned and started trotting faster, which made McLendon bounce uncomfortably on the hard saddle. Night was falling fast and he could barely discern Misterio only a few yards ahead.

"How far?" McLendon called.

"Another mile and a little more after we ford the creek," Misterio said, and then they were briefly in the water. McLendon's legs were splashed. The ground leveled out and he did a better job keeping his seat. That allowed him to wonder again what Mr. MacPherson wanted to see him about.

With only the light of a quarter moon in otherwise pitch-blackness, McLendon had no sense of direction. Peering ahead, he thought after a while that he saw pinpoints of light. These gradually grew larger, and he realized that they were torches flickering behind a high stone wall. There was a wooden gate built into the wall, and Misterio rode up to it. He called out something in Spanish; there was the sound of metal bolts being pulled, and the gate swung open.

"Come along, *señor*," said Misterio, and he and McLendon rode into the compound. There was sufficient light from the torches for McLendon to see that the nearly head-high wall surrounded several adobe buildings and a large, sprawling main house also made of stone. A woman carrying a basket piled with laundry crossed from one of the adobe structures to another. Guards with rifles lined the interior wall.

"Señor MacPherson awaits you in here," Misterio said, pointing at the stone house. He dismounted and gestured for McLendon to do the same. It wasn't easy. When he tried to swing his leg over the horse, he discovered that his crotch and thighs were cramped and aching. As McLendon awkwardly clambered down, he almost fell. He took a few moments to stretch; he didn't want to limp when he met Mr. MacPherson. When he was finally able to stand up straight, Misterio ushered him inside.

The interior of the house was brightly lit. The lamps and the kerosene burning in them were of better quality than in Glorious: there was no smoke coming from the flaming wicks. The furniture caught McLendon's eye. This was the first time he'd seen upholstered chairs and elegantly crafted tables since he'd fled from Rupert Douglass's mansion in St. Louis. Standing in the center of the room was a smiling man in a well-tailored suit.

"Come in, Mr. McLendon," he said in a deep voice tinged with a faint New England accent. "I'm Collin MacPherson. Thank you for this visit; please sit down."

Still feeling achy, McLendon made his slow way to a chair and dropped into it, luxuriating in the nearly forgotten pleasure of thick cushions. MacPherson sat in another and crossed one leg over the other. McLendon saw that he was wearing laced shoes buffed to a high shine.

"I've asked the housekeeper to prepare coffee and light refreshments," MacPherson continued. "I hope they're to your liking." He reached for a small bell on the table next to his chair and shook it. Before the sound of the chimes faded, a stately-looking Mexican woman in a black dress and white apron appeared with a tray. She served McLendon and her employer coffee in delicate china cups, offering milk from a silver pitcher and lumps of sugar. McLendon took plenty of both. MacPherson pressed him to sample the cookies on the tray. "Carmen's gingersnaps are delectable." McLendon had one, though MacPherson did not. The crisp gingersnap tasted fine, and he couldn't resist helping himself to another. While he chewed, he studied his host. Collin MacPherson was not a large man, but even sitting he maintained ramrod-straight posture. His smile was unnerving because the warmth of the grin did not extend to his eyes. These remained cold and calculating; McLendon had the sense that MacPherson was trying to stare into his soul.

"Your invitation was unexpected," McLendon said. "I know from conversations with Mayor Rogers how little time you have to socialize."

MacPherson drank some coffee. As he raised the cup to his lips, McLendon saw that the back of his hand was thick with coarse dark hair. "I always enjoy making the right new acquaintances. You come to us from somewhere back east, I understand. And now you've decided to stay?"

"You're well informed, sir. I can't say that I'm permanently in Glorious. All I know is that I'm staying on longer than I originally anticipated."

"It's an interesting little town with great possibilities," MacPherson said. "Its founders are good people. Major Mulkins, the mayor and Mrs. Rogers, the people running the saloon, and the Italians with the dry goods store."

"Don't forget Bob Pugh, who operates the livery."

MacPherson set his cup on the table. "Yes, him too. He wondered whether there were really Apaches near town."

McLendon put down his cup as well. "After the two bodies that your vaqueros brought in, I believe that he's convinced."

"He'd better be," MacPherson said. "And now you work for Mr. Pugh."

"He was kind enough to offer me a job when I needed one."

MacPherson stopped smiling. He fixed McLendon with a particularly penetrating gaze. "I prefer that our conversation this evening remain private. Would you oblige me in this?" It was a command rather than a request.

"Certainly," McLendon said. "I admit I'm curious as to this meeting's purpose."

"We'll come to that in a moment. I'll begin by telling you something of myself. I'm descended from an ancient Scottish clan. In 1746 my forebears aligned with Bonnie Prince Charlie against King George II, a German claiming the throne of England. They believed the prince when he promised them great wealth and power in return for their support. But instead the scoundrel abandoned them, fleeing Britain after losing a disastrous battle to the Royalists. He left his loyal followers to suffer at the vengeful hands of the English bastards. Do you know where that battle took place?"

"I'm sorry, I don't."

"It was on the plains of Culloden. I've named my ranch for it, as a reminder never to place faith in any authority other than myself. After Culloden, the MacPhersons were brought low as England made Scotland part of its empire. We were hunted like animals. Those who survived eventually escaped to the New World, many settling around Boston. It takes generations to recover from such defeat. My father, a good man, was a cabinetmaker. Cabinets! I swore I'd regain our previous good fortune. I made my way west, and three years ago I came to Arizona Territory and found this place and bespoke the 160 acres allowed me by the American government. That's the way their so-called Homestead Act is written. Everyone receives the same piddling amount. But now I have over a thousand acres, and there will be much, much more."

McLendon knew what he was expected to ask. "How did you increase your holdings?"

MacPherson rose and paced as he continued telling his story. There were already four other ranchers in the valley, he said, each with his allotted 160 acres, and also a few Mexican homesteaders claiming bits of land as their own. Everyone was under constant attack by the Indians. The Army was no help. The other white land-owners soon gave up, and when they did, MacPherson bought their ranches "at a fair price, considering that they were so eager to be gone. And so the best grazing land in the valley became mine."

"What about the Mexican homesteaders?"

"Oh, I soon convinced them that they should leave too. I have considerable respect for Mexicans if they keep their proper place. They make good servants, but most are intellectually suited to take orders rather than give them. And their superstitions—well, my vaqueros are all veteran Indian fighters, and they'll charge any number of Apaches without the slightest hesitation. But almost to a man they also believe that the Devil walks the earth after dark, and they tremble at the thought of encountering him. Sometimes I need them working at night. That's why it was necessary for me to hire the one Mexican who's oblivious to that nonsense. I found Angel Misterio in Sonora. I think that the men have come to fear him more than Satan."

Once he had his Indian fighters and Misterio to lead them, MacPherson said, he began raising a great herd of cattle: the beef shortage in Arizona Territory was acute. It was at this time that a small group of settlers hoping to found a town on the north side of the valley came to ask his blessing. He gave it gladly, and more, hiring additional vaqueros to sweep the nearby mountains for hostiles: "From the start, I wanted to make that town succeed. There's silver in the mountains, and someone's going to find it soon."

"I've heard that since I arrived in Glorious," McLendon said. "But in recent days I sense optimism is fading."

MacPherson returned to his chair. "Is there talk of giving up among the businesspeople? What have you heard?"

"It's obvious that the prospectors have begun to drift away," McLendon said. "No new ones are arriving. If there's no silver strike soon, the town will die. No one wants to give up. They just fear they may soon have no choice."

MacPherson nodded. "A valid concern, of course. Let's have more coffee, or would you prefer something stronger? I can offer an excellent brandy."

"Coffee is fine." MacPherson rang for the housekeeper, who replenished their cups. Then McLendon broached the subject of their meeting: "Mr. MacPherson, I continue to wonder why you invited me here tonight."

MacPherson's mouth stretched into its widest smile yet, though his eyes still lacked a corresponding glow. "Why, I wish to employ you, of course."

McLendon couldn't help laughing. "Honesty compels me to admit that I'd be of no use on your ranch. I had great difficulty even mounting the horse you sent, which suggests that I'd not be adept at herding cattle."

"Oh, I've no need for you here on Culloden," MacPherson said. "But you might prove of value to me in town."

"In what manner?"

"You're a man of cool calculation. I was impressed to hear how you stepped into that foolish squabble between my vaquero and a prospector. You didn't panic, you didn't bluster. You made a quick, accurate assessment of the men involved and you acted accordingly. I've invested considerable effort into building a good relationship between myself and the town founders. Had that prospector been done in by my Mexican, as surely would have happened, that relationship would have been jeopardized. So you earned my gratitude that night."

"If you seek someone to periodically intervene in brawls, I recommend you look elsewhere. I was astonished by my own actions that night, and doubt that they'll ever be repeated."

MacPherson shook his head. "You misunderstand me. I value your ability to accurately discern intentions, motivations, what to say to bring others around to your way of thinking. Your powers of persuasion, in sum. People naturally confide in you. You're even making inroads with the sheriff, and he fears your intentions regarding that Italian girl."

"And you know this because . . . ?"

"Oh, I have people who go into town and *see*. What I want is someone there who *listens*."

There was a sudden sinking feeling in the pit of McLendon's stomach. "Would you elaborate?"

MacPherson leaned forward. Now there was a gleam in his eyes. "This is a critical time in little Glorious. Something must happen soon. Either silver will be discovered or the town is done for. One or the other, or so the people there think. I guarantee that Glorious is going to survive and, more than that, grow to impressive proportions. Its leaders hope for a silver strike. I promise you that there will be one. And when there is, I intend to benefit. Why should I not? Without me, the Apaches would have wiped the place out long ago. Even the most ambitious prospector could never have safely set foot in the Pinals. So when the grand moment comes, as the man most responsible, I should prosper from it. Don't you agree?"

"It's only right," McLendon said, sick with memory. Rich, unscrupulous men in Arizona Territory were the same as in St. Louis, offering similar justification for insatiable greed. "You'll have made their prosperity possible, so you deserve to share in it."

"You understand!" MacPherson said exultantly. "When the discovery is made, mobs will flood into this valley—*mobs*. They'll want shelter and food and entertainment. Money flows in mining boomtowns. Everyone will spend and spend. And I intend for them to spend it in *my* shops, *my* saloon, *my* hotel."

"Which means the founders must sell their businesses to you."

MacPherson pounded his fist on the table where the housekeeper had set the coffee tray. One of the china cups fell to the floor and broke. The ranch owner ignored it.

"Exactly! And they'll benefit too. I'll pay fair prices, enough so they can go somewhere else and start fresh."

"Just not in your town."

"Mr. McLendon, it's a pleasure to talk to a man like you. I'm sure you see your role in all this. Go back into Glorious, be my ears, get a sense of who's discouraged and wants to sell now, who's decided to hold on and see what happens, who may prove too stubborn to be reasonable and so requires additional persuasion. Then, as the town grows, you'll be my inside man on the scene, passing along helpful information. Of course, you'll be handsomely compensated. If it's your wish, I might even see my way clear to let you operate a business of your own, with a proper percentage accruing to me, of course."

"Of course," McLendon said. "All this depending on whether they discover silver."

"And you've heard me guarantee it. They will. I won't allow the town to die. I've invested too much in it."

McLendon sighed. "I'm sure."

"Have we an agreement, then? Shall we discuss immediate wages, something for your pocket tonight?" MacPherson stood over McLendon's chair, ready to close the deal.

"That won't be necessary," McLendon said. Both his head and heart were aching.

"You prefer remuneration at a later date? Of course—for the moment there's little worth buying in Glorious."

"I decline your offer, Mr. MacPherson."

"Do you doubt the generosity of my terms? The amount I had in mind—"

McLendon stood. "The amount doesn't matter. I can't do it. These people are my friends."

"Ah, you're a canny negotiator, playing the friendship angle. So let's say two hundred in gold now where I might have intended to offer a hundred. Then, each time I acquire a business or key property with your assistance, two hundred more. That, plus a guarantee of well-compensated, permanent employment when the whole town is under my control. Are we agreed?"

"You're mistaken, Mr. MacPherson," McLendon said wearily. "I wasn't trying to negotiate. The founders of Glorious really are my friends. I can't act against them."

MacPherson hunched his shoulders forward like a man ready to throw a punch. "If they're really your friends, then on their behalf you ought to accept the inevitability of this. Whether you're with me or not, I'll have what I want."

"I'm sure that you will, but I won't be part of it."

"Well," MacPherson said, shaking his head. "You're decided?" McLendon nodded. "Then let me remind you that you gave your

word to keep this conversation confidential. If I find that you've
slinked back to town and informed your precious friends of my intentions, I'll be so displeased that no one could guarantee your personal
safety. Am I clear?"

"You are."

"I hope that your friends in Glorious are more reasonable than
you've proven to be, Mr. McLendon, for those who will not reason
with me are fools." MacPherson rang the bell again, and when the
housekeeper came he whispered in her ear. She left, and MacPherson
sat down in his chair. He picked up some papers and began reading
them. McLendon still stood a few feet away, but MacPherson made
no further acknowledgment of him. It was as though he'd ceased to
exist.

Moments later Angel Misterio came in. He took McLendon's arm,
not gently, and said, "Come." He led McLendon outside and motioned
for the guards to open the gate in the stone wall. *"Vamos,"* Misterio said.

"Are you coming? Where are the horses?" McLendon asked.

Misterio laughed disdainfully. "There is no guide or horse for you.
Make your way back to town if you can." The head vaquero shoved
McLendon forward; as soon as he was beyond the wall, the gate shut
behind him and he heard bolts being slammed home.

The inky night enveloped McLendon. He knew that Glorious was
somewhere in front of him, but he couldn't see anything. He shuffled
ahead, trying to stay positive. Two miles or so wasn't that far. There
weren't any mountains between him and town, just the creek, which
wasn't deep. If he kept walking he'd be in Glorious soon enough.

He'd thought the valley was quiet at night, but he quickly became
aware of noise all around him. McLendon recognized the low moan of
the wind, but the other rustlings and creakings dismayed him. He
remembered someone telling him that Apaches didn't attack at night.

He hoped that was right. He hadn't thought to bring his gun when Angel Misterio summoned him to Culloden. McLendon knew that there were mountain lions and bears in the Pinals. Did any ever venture down this far? The threat of Indians and wild animals aside, it was difficult just to keep walking. He kept stumbling on soft spots in the ground, and several times he walked right into clumps of cactus. The spines dug into his shins. When he tried to blindly pick them out of his lower legs, they tore open his fingers. He'd never felt so miserable.

After a while McLendon felt certain that he must be nearing Queen Creek. Glorious wasn't that far beyond it. He kept hoping to see the lights of the town, then remembered that there weren't that many lights. It was possible, even probable, that if he didn't walk in exactly the right direction he'd miss Glorious entirely. How could he know? All he could see for certain were the stars overhead, and while there were those who could tell directions from the stars, McLendon wasn't one of them. He wondered how long he'd been walking. It seemed like an hour, but surely it wasn't. Where was goddamn Queen Creek?

McLendon sensed movement to his left and panicked. Even though he couldn't see anything, he knew it was human—Apache, or maybe Angel Misterio following along to kill him. He tried to shout, "Get away!" but he was so terrified that his voice squeaked rather than roared.

"No, no, it's me," a voice called softly, and then someone was right beside him. It was so dark that even then McLendon had trouble making out the newcomer's features.

"It's me," the man said again. "Juan Luis. You know me from town, the night that I almost killed that man."

"Yes," McLendon said, sagging with relief. Then he reconsidered. This vaquero worked for Collin MacPherson. "What do you want?"

"Keep your voice down. Noise carries out here at night."

"What do you want?" McLendon asked again, quietly this time.

"Careful, you're going right into a cactus," Juan Luis said. He gently guided McLendon to the right. "You're walking the wrong direction if you're going back to town. Here, this way."

"I've been thinking I'm about to cross the creek," McLendon said. "It's got to be nearby."

"No, it's farther. You aren't that distant yet from the *rancho*."

McLendon peered back over his shoulder and saw the flickering torches. They seemed disgustingly close. "Can you help me get back to Glorious?"

Juan Luis tugged on McLendon's sleeve. "Let's go, it's this way. But try to be quiet. I don't want Angel Misterio to know I'm helping you. It would make him angry. After they closed the gate behind you, he told everyone that you were now an enemy of the *jefe* and no one was to have any more to do with you."

"Then why risk this?"

"If, in my rage, I'd killed that drunken *gringo* prospector, Misterio would have killed me. So I'm in your debt. *¡Vámonos!* Come on!"

They made steady progress, though McLendon still occasionally stumbled over plants and outcrops of rock. To his great relief, the water didn't lap over the tops of his boots when they stepped into the shallow cut of Queen Creek. Then McLendon saw a few dots of light ahead, kerosene lamps or candles flickering behind oilcloth curtains. For once, he felt that Glorious lived up to its name.

"Can you go on your own from here?" Juan Luis asked. "If someone in town sees me and tells Misterio, it would be bad for me. He punishes anyone who disobeys."

"I'll be all right. Juan, thanks. I don't think I would have made it back without you."

"No, you would have been food for coyotes," the vaquero said matter-of-factly. Then, in a more urgent tone, he added, "*Amigo*, you've got to get out of here. Go away, leave tomorrow. Bad things are going to happen."

"What do you mean?"

"I don't know for sure, but real bad. All those people in town are scared of the *indios*, but there are worse things than Apaches."

"What things?" McLendon asked, but he was talking to the night. Juan Luis had disappeared into the darkness.

MCLENDON WALKED into town and headed for the saloon. Just outside the door he checked his pocket watch: it was only a little after nine. He could have sworn that he'd been gone all night. He went into the Owaysis and saw Pugh, Mulkins, and Mayor Rogers at a table. His immediate instinct was to tell them about Collin MacPherson's plans, but then he thought better of it. What good would telling them do? MacPherson would have his way anyway, and he'd order McLendon killed with no more hesitation than swatting a pesky fly.

"C.M., come join us," Pugh called. "We've missed your company this fine evening. Where have you been hiding yourself?"

"I took a little walk around the valley," McLendon said. "Here, let me get the next round." He'd always had a gift for feigning good humor when he felt the opposite.

THE STAGE FROM Florence wasn't due again for another four days. McLendon's experiences going to and from Culloden Ranch had convinced him that he couldn't ride or walk out of Glorious on his own. The morning after McLendon's meeting with MacPherson,

Angel Misterio rode into town. When he saw McLendon in front of the livery, one of his eyebrows cocked in fleeting amazement. Then he passed by without a further glance.

THE MORE MCLENDON thought about it, the more certain he felt that, despite Juan Luis's warning, he didn't have to go right away. Prospectors were still leaving and Glorious was dying by the day. MacPherson's plans might be thwarted after all. It made McLendon feel that he wasn't betraying his friends with his silence. Probably in a matter of weeks, not months, they would have to give up anyway, whether or not they sold out to MacPherson. Maybe that would be the end of Gabrielle and Joe Saint. He thought that it was worth waiting to find out.

EVERYONE IN TOWN knew the end was looming. Their sense of it was reinforced when they noticed that sour-spirited Turner was gone.

"If he's left, that's it," Mulkins proclaimed gloomily. "No one believed in the silver possibilities more than him. But the only prospector to buy breakfast at the hotel this morning said Turner ain't been seen since two nights ago. It's got the rest of them spooked. I don't doubt there'll be a procession of 'em heading out of town by tomorrow."

Mayor Rogers agreed. He brought out some crates and began packing his farrier's tools. In the Owaysis, Ella sobbed.

"I haven't nearly the necessary money saved," she mourned to McLendon. "What's to become of me?"

Mary Somebody overheard and patted Ella's shoulder. "You're still young and pretty. Somewhere, men will pay for you a good while longer."

"But I don't *want* to be a whore anymore," Ella wailed. "I just want to go *home*." McLendon, still uncertain of his own destination after Glorious, reflected that Ella at least knew where home was.

That night in the Owaysis, the mood was glum. Toasts were drunk to good times that no one any longer believed were really coming.

"Cheer up, boys, maybe things'll look different in the morning," Bob Pugh suggested.

They did.

FOURTEEN

The dwindling population of Glorious was up before sunrise. The prospectors emerged from their tents, many stumbling down to the creek for morning ablutions. There were only a dozen still in town, but the Tirritos opened the dry goods store for those who wanted canned fruit or buttons or hard candy. Major Mulkins set up for breakfast in the dining room but had no takers. Mayor Rogers waited hopefully in his farrier's shop, but none of the prospectors brought tools for him to mend. At the livery, Bob Pugh and McLendon rented out one mule; the prospector paying two dollars for use of the animal told them that he'd either bring it back that evening loaded with promising ore samples, or else he'd be leaving town for good the next day.

Not much after six, the first early rays of daylight edged over the lower mountain peaks to the east. McLendon, Pugh, Mayor Rogers, and Mulkins stood outside the livery and watched the prospectors disappear into the Pinals and the canyon.

"This is the last day," the mayor predicted. "It's over. Goddamn it, we tried so hard."

"God knows we did," Mulkins agreed. "What the hell. I've got fresh biscuits and coffee going to waste back in my dining room. There's plenty of bacon, too, and a batch of hen eggs I bought from the Chinese. Let's at least go have ourselves a mighty breakfast."

They had just turned to walk to the hotel when Bob Pugh, the sharpest-eyed among them, pointed west down the valley. "What's that coming?"

They squinted, trying to see past the guardhouse patrolled by the MacPherson vaqueros. The light was still dim, but it seemed to McLendon that several tiny dots were moving toward town. "Apaches?" he asked nervously.

"No, 'Paches wouldn't approach out in the open," Pugh said. "It's white men for sure. Six, maybe seven, all on foot. I wonder what's their purpose."

Thirty minutes later the first walked past the guard post, looking curiously at the two armed vaqueros. He carried a huge pack on his back. A pick and a shovel were lashed to the sides of the bulky bundle.

"How do," called Mayor Rogers. "Welcome to our town. My name is—"

"No time for introductions," the newcomer barked. "Which way is the strike?"

"What strike?" the mayor asked.

"Shit, you're trying to keep the information to yourselves," the man said. "I'll find it in spite of you. Where can I rent a mule?"

"Why, right this way," Pugh said. "Let me escort you to my livery and supply you with the finest mule in Arizona Territory."

"I want that mule pronto."

"Pronto it shall be, all yours all day for the meager fee of three dollars."

"It was two dollars just a few minutes ago," McLendon whispered to Mulkins.

"Hush," Mulkins hissed. "A man should always charge what the market allows."

Pugh hustled his customer to the livery. While he was gone, three more men walked into town from the west, all of them prospectors, two carrying their blankets and tools and the third pushing his possessions along in a wheelbarrow.

"We've been walking two days and nights from Florence," the wheelbarrow man announced. "Point us to the silver."

"I'd very much like to, but I don't know what silver it is to which you refer," Mayor Rogers said politely. "It would be a kindness for you to inform us."

"Jesus! Look!" One of the miners pointed to the first prospector who'd arrived, who now was leaving the livery in the direction of the Pinals, leading the mule he'd rented from Pugh. "That bastard's ahead of us. Hurry!" All three dashed to the livery, the man with the wheelbarrow trailing.

"Ol' Bob's gonna make him a fortune today," Mulkins predicted. "I better get back to the hotel. Some of those boys may desire a room with a view tonight."

When two more prospectors walked into town and made their way straight to the livery, McLendon thought he ought to assist Pugh. Leaving Mayor Rogers as a one-man welcoming committee, he walked behind the livery to the corral, where Pugh was frantically currying his seven remaining mules.

"Let's get these critters all presentable as quick as we can," he told

McLendon. "What with the sudden demand, I believe I can ask three fifty apiece."

"What's all this about a silver strike?" McLendon asked.

"Damned if I know, and also, at this particular moment, damned if I care. We got customers is all that matters. Get your curry comb flying."

Within half an hour, all the mules were rented. Pugh smiled contentedly, gloating over the small pile of coins and bills on his desk.

"This calls for a serious celebration tonight," he told McLendon. "For now, we'll limit ourselves to a beer at the Owaysis. Maybe George or Mary's picked up some information."

They had. Eager as they were to hurry out into the Pinals, a few of the newly arrived prospectors stopped in at the saloon for a quick, refreshing drink first, and they'd talked about how, two days earlier, word spread in Florence about somebody in Glorious bringing in ore samples the assayer claimed were among the richest he'd ever seen. Almost immediately, the men loitering around the assay office grabbed their tools and started northeast, having to come on foot because the stage wasn't scheduled for another five days. There was no time to waste.

"According to these first boys to get here, we'll have a hundred more in town before we know it," Mary Somebody exulted. "We're still vague on the details, but who cares? It's happening, and just in time."

Prospectors continued to arrive throughout the day, all of them eager to go out in search of ore. The Tirritos sold most of their supply of canned fruit. Mayor Rogers wore himself out mending tools at his forge, and Pugh could have rented fifty more mules if he had them.

"This keeps up, we'll have to go to Florence and buy us up a whole passel more," he said to McLendon. "But being as the current supply is so limited, four dollars a day—that's what we'll be charging tomorrow. Might think about five. I do love being prosperous."

"You sound like Major Mulkins."

"Well, a man should benefit from the good example of his friends."

Mulkins was a happy man that night. Most of the newly arrived prospectors pitched tents, but five rented rooms at the Elite, the first paying guests Mulkins had since McLendon had checked out.

"I went with three seventy-five for an upstairs room, four and a half for downstairs with windows," he reported that evening when he, Mayor Rogers, Pugh, and McLendon met at the Owaysis. "Three of them rented upstairs and two downstairs. Next round's on me, but I can't stay late because I need to prepare for the big breakfast crowd tomorrow."

"So all the dreams are coming true," McLendon said, wanting to be happy for his friends but distracted by thoughts of Collin MacPherson. How would the day's events affect his plans?

"Oh, we never doubted it," said Mayor Rogers.

"Didn't I hear you say just this morning that it was over?" McLendon asked.

Mayor Rogers grinned. "Do you know, I just can't recall."

THAT NIGHT the Owaysis was jammed. Girl was pressed into helping Mary serve drinks. Ella couldn't because she was too busy out back. One of the arrivals from Florence told the story as everyone else gathered around. Bossman Wright and Oafie were right in front. McLendon was surprised to see Preacher Sheridan hanging back on the periphery. To his knowledge, except for the Sunday dance, this was the first time Preacher had been in the saloon.

"I was in the assay office, passing the time of day with ol' Held, the assayer, and in comes this raggedy-ass looking back over his shoulder like the Devil's chasing him," the prospector recounted. "He says to Held, 'Clear the room and see what I got here,' which, if he don't want to attract attention, is about the worst way to go about it. Ever'body heard him and all ears pricked right up. Held says to hold his water, let's see what you got, and the raggedy-ass, a man with a sniffer the size of Texas, spills out this sample and it ain't even dark-lined float, it's fucking horn silver!"

His listeners gasped.

"Pure horn," another of the recent arrivals called out. "Held said afterward that it was so soft, he pushed a silver dollar into it and it left the imprint of the eagle."

"It wasn't a silver dollar, it was his thumb," the storyteller grumbled. "Who's relating this tale, anyway? So Held tells the raggedy-ass the obvious, that it's pure and rich, and he better get himself over to the courthouse and officially file his claim. So he cuts out and everybody follows to watch him fill out the documents, trying to read over his shoulder to get the location. And somebody sees him write about the Pinals outside of Glorious, and Old Man Billings at the stage depot tells where this town is and we all light out, and here we are. Horn silver's the surest sign of a massive lode. Soon the news will spread all over the territory and beyond. You folks here is about to become a boomtown. Now I want one more whiskey, then it's off to sleep. Got to get out into the mountains early tomorrow. There's more silver to be found, and I intend to be the next lucky one."

Mayor Rogers stood up and waved for attention.

"As mayor of Glorious, I feel responsible to inform you that we are presently under particular Apache threat. It need not be of overriding concern if you all go out in groups."

"No groups!" shouted a grizzled prospector. "I ain't sharing a rich find."

"It is, of course, a matter of individual decision," the mayor said, and sat down. "I was obligated to make the announcement and suggestion," he said to his three companions. "The silver frenzy is so upon them that I felt the Apache information wouldn't drive them away."

"Nothing will drive away a prospector with the scent of a strike in his nostrils," Pugh agreed. "Say," he called out to the man who'd told about the scene at the assay office, "did you happen to catch the name of the fellow who made the horn silver discovery?"

"I believe that he was named Turner."

"Turner," Mulkins said. "Well, it's only right. He got here first and stayed the longest. Good for Turner."

"The surly bastard'll have to be back here soon so he can sell off the claim," Pugh said. "I hope at the least he'll buy a round of drinks for the house."

"Why would he want to sell his claim?" McLendon asked. "Wouldn't he just dig all the silver out of it himself?"

"It don't work that way," Mulkins explained. "You get horn silver when pressure in the rock squeezes a few bits out, but mostly the silver's going to be part of mineral deposits way down deep. So you need miners to dig underground shafts, and then machines to crush all the rock into sand and washes to extract the ore and finally it gets processed into what you'd recognize as silver. The whole setup costs considerable, half a million or more, and no prospector's got that kind of scratch. So Turner's got to sell his claim to some outside company that'll come in and build and run the working mine. They'll make the profit off the finished silver."

"That hardly seems fair."

"Oh, Turner'll come out of it just fine. With horn silver, he'll get a considerable number of bids, and he'll walk away a rich man. Don't you be fretting for Turner."

The new prospectors in the Owaysis quizzed everyone about where Turner might have found his horn silver. Did the man usually work high up in the mountains, or maybe along the top of Apache Leap? The locals couldn't help them. Turner always went out alone and never talked about anything, let alone the locations where he went prospecting.

"We'll keep an eye out for his markers," one prospector said. Pugh and Mulkins explained to McLendon that prospectors staking out a claim marked the 1,500-by-600-foot area allowed by territorial law with piles of stones set up on each corner.

"What's to keep someone from moving someone else's markers?" McLendon asked.

"With no silver finds up to the present, that hasn't been a problem," Pugh said. "But in light of today's news, I predict that it soon will be."

McLendon sidled over to where Martin Sheridan stood near the bar. Preacher was drinking coffee, not beer or whiskey, but his eyes were shiny all the same.

"It's odd to see you in the Owaysis," McLendon said.

"This is it," Preacher said.

"The change in fortune for the town?"

"The sign from God that I'm meant to stay."

McLendon looked around the room; everyone in it seemed to radiate near-hysterical energy. "I doubt that for a while there will be too many people willing to sit and discuss their salvation. They'll all be out in the mountains, frantically looking for silver."

"And I'll be there with them," Preacher said. "Horn silver! The ways of the Lord are mysterious and full of wonder."

McLendon looked at Preacher and then at the prospectors clustered in excited, babbling groups all around the saloon. The avaricious glow radiating from Sheridan was identical to theirs. "Well, good luck to you," he said, and went back to the table where Mulkins, Pugh, and Rogers sat.

"Preacher's got silver fever same as the rest of them," McLendon said.

"Don't sound so disapproving," Pugh said. "Ol' Sheridan was a hardscrabble prospector long before he got to preaching. Godliness may come and go, but once you catch it, the silver itch never does get cured."

THE NEXT MORNING Mayor Rogers estimated that at least fifty prospectors had arrived in Glorious over the last twenty-four hours. Many wanted to buy supplies and rent mules. The dry goods store and livery did brisk business. They all sallied out into the Pinals and, during the day, more kept coming into town, a few now arriving from the south because word of Turner's strike had reached Tucson. Then, around three in the afternoon, Turner himself reappeared, seated on the bench of a fine buckboard and holding the reins to a team of two mules. The taciturn prospector who never smiled or spoke was grinning so widely that the corners of his mouth seemed to extend all the way to his ears.

"Hello, my good friends," he said to Mulkins, Pugh, Mayor Rogers, and McLendon, who were too stunned by the warm greeting to respond beyond wide-eyed nods. "I'm glad to be back in your company."

"Sir, you closely resemble a man that I know as Turner, but you can't possibly be him," Pugh said. "Turner's a foul-spirited sort who'd sooner spit in your eye than wish you good day. Do you know what might have become of him?"

Turner cackled. McLendon noticed that he was wearing a fine new shirt and pants of gabardine rather than his usual denim.

"Oh, Bob, all that's behind me now," Turner said. "Let me get this rig put up in your livery, and then I'd admire to join you fine folks over at the Owaysis. I wonder if Ella's going to be free."

"If you have fucking in mind, you best get to it," Pugh said. "Come evening, Ella's likely to be kept busy with some of those that your news has attracted to town. Your time might be better spent going out to guard your claim. They're all on the hunt for it, and someone unscrupulous might mess with your markers."

Turner didn't seem fazed by the suggestion. "Let 'em try. A Culloden vaquero is there standing lookout for me."

"That's curious," McLendon said. "Why would he be doing that?"

"Let me get my buckboard and team put up, then we'll all sashay to the Owaysis and I'll tell you. Of course, the drinks will be on me."

"Well," Pugh said, "I would think so."

After Turner stabled his mules, there was further delay at the Owaysis while he went off with Ella. He told Crazy George to serve his friends beer while they waited. Ella's customary fifteen minutes stretched into twenty, then twenty-five. When she and Turner finally returned, he was red-faced and gasping.

"That young lady gives your money's worth," Turner said. "About the best five dollars I ever spent."

"I thought it was three," McLendon said. "But I suppose like every other price in town it was bound to increase."

"What the market will bear," Mulkins reminded him. "That's the choicest of philosophies. Now tell us your story, Turner. We all want to hear it."

Turner drank some beer and launched into the tale. Four days earlier he had set out from Glorious in the early morning to prospect along the east canyon bisected by Queen Creek.

"Just where we went on your prospecting excursion, C.M.," Pugh pointed out to McLendon.

For most of the morning Turner searched in vain for promising float. Then, just about the time he was thinking about breaking for lunch—leftover biscuits from breakfast and a cucumber purchased the evening before at the Chinese camp—Lemmy Duke came riding up to him. Turner knew Lemmy from some years back. Though it was well known in and around Glorious that Turner didn't indulge in social conversation, Lemmy hopped down off his horse and started chatting anyway, going on about how there had to be silver somewhere close, just had to be. Turner grunted inhospitably, wishing the man would go away and let him eat his lunch in peace, but Lemmy kept yammering, and what a good thing that turned out to be. He insisted that Turner take a look about a half mile farther east: there was this outcrop just around the bend in the creek, and if Lemmy wasn't so occupied patrolling for Apaches, he'd go there and take a gander himself.

Turner thought Lemmy was full of shit. He knew that outcrop, most of the prospectors did. There wasn't anything there. Lemmy came back at him, saying that was how the prospecting game went. You looked at a place over and over and then one day you saw something that was probably there all the time. Turner figured that if he wanted Lemmy to shut up and ride away, he'd have to go inspect the goddamn outcrop, which he said he'd do if Lemmy would just leave him alone. So Lemmy rode off and Turner walked to the bend in the creek and poked around the outcrop. And all of a sudden he saw it.

He paused and took a long drink of beer.

"Well, goddamn, Turner, get on with it," Pugh urged. They were all leaning forward, wanting to hear.

All right, Turner said. At a slightly sharp angle on the upper portion of the outcrop, there was some shine. Maybe the angle was what kept anyone from noticing before. Turner clambered up and twisted around to look and his heart nearly stopped, because it was horn silver, a dozen bits of it spread over the rock like they'd been fired out of a shotgun. He'd heard of horn silver but like most people had never seen any before. He pushed at the bits with his thumb and damned if they didn't squish at his touch just like the stories claimed. Turner let out a whoop—he couldn't help it—and worried right away that he'd called the Apaches down on himself, but instead Lemmy Duke came riding up, asking what had happened to make Turner holler so.

"Lemmy must have been close by," Pugh said. "That canyon just swallows sound and spits it out in odd directions."

"Probably so," Turner said. "Anyway, Lemmy helped me hack out the horn silver and mark my claim. Then he told me to head out for Florence right then. I said I wanted to look around some more—there might be more silver nearby. But Lemmy reminded me there were other prospectors at work in the area, and I'd better get my samples assayed and my claim legally filed before they saw what I'd seen and beat me to it. He said he'd put a guard on the spot quiet-like while I was gone, so nobody could jump my claim, and off to Florence I went."

"Your actions there precipitated a frenzy," Mayor Rogers said. "As a result, our town is going to flourish. What's next for you, Turner?"

"Mr. Held in the assay office telegraphed some mining concerns in California," Turner said. "They're sending representatives out here immediately. Major, I expect they'll want lodging at the Elite. They'll have their own assayers inspect my samples, and then they'll bid on my claim. I'll sell to the highest. Held predicts rich offers. I'll be set for life."

"We're grateful to you," the mayor said. "You've saved Glorious."

"Hellfire, I only made my discovery because Lemmy Duke wouldn't leave me alone. Should I see Lemmy, I'm going to stand him to drinks and a turn or two with young Ella. As you might imagine, I now hold him in considerable high regard."

When the Florence stage arrived on Tuesday, it was so crammed with passengers that two had to ride on the roof. All eight arriving men represented mining companies. They booked rooms at the Elite through the entire week, and didn't blanch when Major Mulkins charged six dollars a night for upstairs and nine for downstairs with windows. They ate dinner in the hotel dining room and asked Mulkins to send to the saloon for postprandial whiskey. Mayor Rogers and his wife, Rose, greeted them in the dining room, and the mayor reported afterward at the Owaysis that these were exactly the kind of businessmen Glorious wanted to attract.

"When they buy up claims and their companies build mines, then we'll have engineers and the like moving to town," he said. "They'll bring their families, and before you know it, we'll have to be opening a school. Joe Saint will be teacher, of course. That's always been his hope, an eventual return to the classroom."

"I remember that was his calling back east," McLendon said. "I still don't know how he ended up in Glorious."

"That's Joe's story to tell you, if he ever so chooses," Mulkins cautioned. "Out here a man's past is his own business."

"Even so," McLendon grumbled. He was in a terrible mood. So many customers flocked to the Tirritos' dry goods store that they were sometimes packed two or three rows deep in front of the counter. When McLendon came in and tried to catch her eye, Gabrielle said that she was too busy to visit. But to his dismay, she still managed to make time for daytime chats and evening meals with Joe

Saint. McLendon glumly reflected that he should go ahead and leave town. Because so many people wanted passage to Glorious, a daily route to and from Florence had been established; he could go anytime. With no town collapse imminent, and daily reminders that Gabrielle had chosen the sheriff, there was nothing to keep him. With Killer Boots still undoubtedly trying to track him down, McLendon knew that it would be smartest to keep moving until he reached the relative anonymity of some major California city. But he surprised himself by choosing to stay awhile longer. For better or worse, McLendon wanted to see what happened next in Glorious.

TURNER MET INDIVIDUALLY with mining company representatives in their rooms at the Elite. After a final early morning meeting with representatives of Sears and Sons, a renowned mining concern headquartered in San Francisco, he emerged, beaming, and marched to the Owaysis. He asked Mary Somebody to bring him a full bottle of whiskey. Turner sat alone at a table and drank it all, continuing to smile and ignoring everyone else in the saloon. When the last drops in the bottle were gone, Turner stood and walked unsteadily to the livery, where the stage was about to depart on the return trip to Florence. Still grinning, and without carrying any luggage, Turner climbed into the carriage and the stage clattered off. No one in Glorious ever saw him again. Rumor had it that he'd sold his claim to Sears and Sons for $80,000, maybe more. Bob Pugh stabled the carriage and mule team that Turner had brought back to town. After a week went by, he announced that they were now his property, and he began renting them out.

The men from that company and the other mining concerns kept their rooms at the Elite. They had their own assayers with them, and they made it known that they were ready to examine samples and, if warranted, make purchase offers for claims on the spot.

That drove all the prospectors into heightened frenzy. There were almost two hundred of them now. Everyone wanted the next $80,000 deal. At daylight they swarmed into the Pinals, ignoring the threat of Apaches. Where earlier it was possible to hunt ore in relative isolation, now men jammed promising locations within a few feet of each other and bickered about who was in which spot first. Fights broke out in town at night between prospectors accusing each other of moving claim markers. Joe Saint couldn't get the fighting under control. Pugh, Mulkins, Mayor Rogers, McLendon, and even Crazy George with his lead pipe had to assist him. They'd drag the combatants off to the adobe jail; with only two cells, most nights it couldn't hold all the brawlers. Angel Misterio brought a welcome offer from Mr. MacPherson: the overflow could be held overnight in the guard posts on either end of town. MacPherson also said he'd supply vaqueros to serve as deputies should the sheriff need them.

The fights weren't the only problem. Prior to Turner's strike, Glorious had been a relatively clean place. There weren't enough people living there to create much trash. But now there were, and the town was littered with empty cans, discarded boxes, and drained bottles. The refuse attracted great waves of rats. Major Mulkins's feral cats were filched by prospectors who tethered the felines in their tents. Glorious began to smell bad too. Previously, two outhouses—one behind the saloon, the other behind the dry goods store—had been sufficient. But now they overflowed, and it became a common sight to see prospectors relieving themselves out in the open. No one had time to construct additional facilities.

The most constant concern was shortages of everything. Every room at the Elite was taken, and Major Mulkins got three dollars apiece each night from a dozen more men who rolled up in their blankets and slept on the lobby floor. The tent camp on the west side of town now extended all the way down to the creek and a quarter mile beyond the guard post. Sydney Chau and her mother couldn't keep up with the mounds of dirty clothes accumulating daily at the laundry, and couldn't recruit other Chinese to help because they were all needed growing, harvesting, and selling vegetables from their camp gardens. Fresh-picked onions became especially prized treats, bringing a dollar apiece. The prospectors peeled the onions, then gnawed them like apples.

Feeding the town was a constant struggle. Every day, supply wagons arrived alongside the stage from Florence, their beds packed with boxes of comestibles. But never enough. Major Mulkins regularly ran out of flour and coffee. The Tirritos could never stock sufficient canned goods. Fresh meat was also scarce. Before, it was usually possible for hungry prospectors to pot deer or jackrabbits. Now the waves of men spreading out into the Pinals scared off much of the game.

At the Owaysis, beer and red-eye ran out at some point every night. Crazy George increased his liquor orders, but no matter how many barrels he ordered daily from Florence, thirsty prospectors drained them all and clamored for more. There wasn't enough of Ella to go around, either. The English girl could have worked twenty-four-hour shifts of fifteen-minute sessions and still not satisfied demand. Mary Somebody announced that Ella would only be "on the job" from seven p.m. to midnight daily, at ten dollars a turn. Anyone wishing a special appointment during the day would pay twenty dollars for the privilege, and then only if Ella felt up to it.

"She's terrible worn-out at the end of every night," Mary told McLendon. "She fears that if the pace continues, she'll walk crooked for the rest of her life. I tell her that she ought to be pleased. Every one of 'em she takes on brings her that much closer to steamship passage home. Of course, I've upped her share of the proceeds. Now she gets two dollars per."

With Ella constantly occupied, Girl was also in demand. Before sending them back to one of the whores' cribs with her, Mary spoke to each of her customers, stressing that only the most basic sex act was allowed. The charge for Girl remained one dollar. As soon as the initial rush of arriving miners was over and there was time to get a breath, Mary said, she'd take trips to Florence and Tucson and recruit more whores. It wouldn't be easy; she wanted them to be young and fresh, and Mary believed that there were few such in the entire territory. She wanted her saloon to build a reputation for having the finest pleasure girls around. Until she recruited additions, the two current Owaysis whores had to work nonstop. Even so, some nights men had to leave the Owaysis unsatisfied, since Ella and Girl were so booked up.

Bob Pugh predicted that the first additional business to open in Glorious would be a full-scale whorehouse, and briefly he was right. A hustler from Phoenix arrived with five tired-looking Mexican whores in tow. He set up shop in a patched tent next to the prospectors' camp and charged two dollars a turn. The new enterprise did booming business for a few days; then a customer complained to Joe Saint that someone had stolen the wallet out of his pants while he was with his whore. The wallet was found in the proprietor's possession. The sheriff returned the wallet to its owner and told the whoremonger to leave town. Afterward several of the men who'd dallied with his whores found themselves afflicted with groin itch. They went out prospecting every day anyway, frantically scratching all the while.

TEN DAYS AFTER the Turner news broke, there was the first murder in town history. Prospectors Kid Barson and Willie Ward argued over a claim site. Each swore he'd put down markers first. They first quarreled in the Owaysis, screaming and shoving until Crazy George pulled the lead pipe from his boot and chased them outside. The next day they harangued each other outside the dry goods store. Joe Saint separated them. Ward went to the dry goods store to buy some canned goods, and when he came out Barson stabbed him to death. He pulled his dripping knife from the body of his victim and told the stunned onlookers, "I'm justified because the sumbitch provoked me." Barson offered no resistance when Joe Saint arrested him. The sheriff took Barson to the town jail and locked him in a cell.

"Now what?" McLendon asked Pugh. "Does the man get a trial? There's no court here."

"Joe will send word with the Florence stage driver for the sheriff there to telegraph Tucson," Pugh said. "There's a court there, Judge Palmquist's, and the deputy U.S. marshal will be dispatched here to collect the killer. Then Barson'll be tried in Tucson, all good and legal. It's a speedy process. Hunky-Dory will no doubt be here within a few days."

"'Hunky-Dory'?"

"Hunky-Dory Holmes is the deputy marshal, and a fine, cheerful fellow he is. He gets his name from the song he sings when he arrives anywhere. He composed it his ownself, and changes the words around to suit the location. Hunky-Dory's famous for it. When he arrives we'll make a point of being on the spot—it's something not to be missed."

Four days later, Hunky-Dory Holmes arrived, driving a buckboard behind the Florence stage. Holmes was a thin-faced fellow with dark, scraggly eyebrows. He hitched his mules near the livery and walked across to the jail. Pugh and McLendon tagged along.

"Have you had a spot of bloodletting, Joe?" Holmes asked Saint. "The miscreant in the cell there, is he the perpetrator?"

"He is," Saint said. "I suppose a murder was inevitable, given the town's new crowded circumstances."

"I've heard your happy good news," Holmes said, and broke into song:

"Oh, when a town is poor,
All the people stay away.
They head for dear ole Tucson,
If they're of a mind to play.
But Turner made his strike,
Now it's quite a different story.
And in the town of Glorious
All things are hunky-dory."

"Told you he'd sing," Pugh said to McLendon. "Ain't he a wonder?" McLendon agreed that he was. The next day, Hunky-Dory Holmes followed the stage back to Florence. Barson, in shackles, rode up on the buckboard bench with the deputy marshal, who was singing as he left town.

McLENDON FELL into a funk. It had a combination of causes. Gabrielle was apparently lost to Joe Saint. Collin MacPherson had designs on McLendon's friends in Glorious. McLendon was also tormented by thoughts of Ellen Douglass. The more he tried not to think about her, the more the memory of her pale, dead face haunted him. Collin MacPherson and Rupert Douglass seemed so much alike—was it McLendon's fate to always attract the wrath of such powerful, ruthless men? How much of his trouble was his own fault? What things should he have done differently?

One afternoon when his mood was especially dark, he told Bob Pugh that he had a headache and needed to sit down for a while. Instead of closing himself in the livery office, he went over to the Owaysis, thinking that if he couldn't force troubling thoughts from his mind, then he'd flush them out with alcohol.

Except for Crazy George behind the bar and Girl and Ella sweeping around tables, the saloon was empty. Mary Somebody was in Tucson scouting whores, and all the prospectors were off in the mountains. McLendon had a few drinks, feeling simultaneously guiltier and sorrier for himself with each swallow of red-eye. He brooded about MacPherson, about Ellen, about Gabrielle and the sheriff. He was so lost in miserable contemplation that he was startled when Ella touched his arm and asked if he was all right.

"You generally don't drink so hard, especially in the afternoon," she said. "It's causing me concern."

McLendon was moved by her words. Somebody cared about him. Her hand on his arm stirred him too. It had been so long since he'd been with a woman. That was with Ellen. He suddenly remembered with particular clarity how Ellen would reach for him, eager and desperate at the same time.

"I know that you require an appointment in the afternoon," McLendon said. "Is there any possibility that you might make time for me now?"

"I thought you felt obligated to abstain," Ella said. "Aren't you worried that your fine lady in town might hear of it and be offended?"

"She's not my lady, as you and everyone else well know. And I don't care what she thinks."

"In that case, let me put up my broom," Ella said. "I'll just inform George that I'll be otherwise occupied for a bit."

The whore's crib where she led him made McLendon feel even worse.

It was cramped and dreary, with just enough room for a bed and wash-basin. But Ella was adept at her craft. Correctly assessing McLendon's mood, she took the initiative and skillfully proceeded until physical plea-sure temporarily overwhelmed him. Afterward they lay twined together.

"Don't worry about the time," Ella murmured. "Miss Mary is away, and George can't make out the face of the clock. We're all right for a while. Relax and tell me why you're so troubled."

McLendon didn't mean to say too much. But to his own amaze-ment he began talking about St. Louis, his early life there, how he came to work for Rupert Douglass and then met Gabrielle and loved her, and then Douglass's offer of his daughter. Ella was a good lis-tener, drawing him out with requests to tell her more. He did, describing his brief, troubled marriage and the circumstances of Ellen's death, how he'd had to run because he knew for certain Dou-glass would send Killer Boots after him. Ella was fascinated. She murmured comforting things while McLendon described his flight from New Orleans when Killer Boots showed up there.

"No wonder you seem so bothered," she said. "Just the thought of this Boots person makes me tremble. But at least you can feel confi-dent that he'll never find you here. Perhaps your father-in-law will have called off pursuit by now?"

"He never will. I'm certain of that. Rupert Douglass has all the money in the world, and he'll be prepared to spend it. Men like him never give up until they get what they want."

Ella nodded. Then she said that as much as she was enjoying her time with McLendon, she had to get back to the saloon. Soon it would be evening and the prospectors would rush in, eager for whis-key and fifteen-minute turns with her.

"Are you close to saving the amount needed for passage back to England?" McLendon asked. "I know how eager you are to go home."

"I'm still short of funds, but due to recent circumstances I feel confident that I'll soon be sufficiently solvent," she said. "The good Lord willing, I'm not long for Glorious."

McLendon suddenly thought about Gabrielle. He didn't want her to know that he'd had sex with the town whore.

"Here's your twenty dollars," he told Ella as she dropped her dress down over her head. "Promise me you won't tell anyone about this."

She took the folded bills and winked. "I won't tell a soul. It shall be our secret. Do you feel better now?"

McLendon did, a little.

THE TOWN FOUNDERS bubbled over with renewed optimism. Mayor Rogers predicted full town status would be granted at the next session of the territorial legislature in Tucson. Territorial governor A. P. K. Safford himself was rumored to be coming out for a look at Glorious. With all his rooms consistently spoken for, Mulkins anticipated bringing in a work crew soon to finish the second floor of his hotel. He briefly promoted himself to colonel, but the new rank didn't take. Everyone continued calling him Major. And Bob Pugh informed McLendon that the two of them would go to Florence to buy mules.

"What with our recent run of customers, I've got enough to purchase six or seven," Pugh said. "There's a fellow in Florence who charges ninety dollars for a broke-in, healthy mule, but I think I can get him down to eighty or even seventy-five. With the new ones we'll be bringing back, that gives us eighteen or nineteen mules to rent by the day—handsome profits. I might find myself feeling obligated to pay you a salary besides room and board."

"Would it be just the two of us going to Florence?" McLendon asked. "What about Apaches along the way?"

"Not to worry. We'll take the buckboard and trail along with the Florence stage. That should be sufficient to discourage the Indians."

They set out the next morning, staying close enough to the stage to maintain contact and far enough behind to avoid choking on the dust kicked up by its mule team and wheels. Pugh was in a merry mood. He regaled McLendon with stories about his colorful life roaming the frontier. Pugh claimed he'd been in California for the big Sutter's Creek gold rush, and in Virginia City, Nevada, during the lush era of the Comstock Lode. What happened in those places was happening now in Glorious, he said. The first big strike, the rush of prospectors, then more strikes and more people flooding in.

"We'll soon be a destination for traveling actor troupes and circuses," he predicted. "There'll be shops selling the latest fashions and treats like iced cream. Maybe even a racetrack, a baseball nine, and a bowling alley. Anything's possible now."

The trip to Florence took most of the day. They rolled in just before dusk.

"There's the big city!" Pugh whooped.

Florence would not have comprised a good-size neighborhood back in St. Louis, but after his time stuck in Glorious, it still looked impressive to McLendon. Even the stage depot seemed sizable and sophisticated with its posters and ticket counter. Pugh steered the buckboard past the depot and down a real street with buildings lining each side.

"We'll stable the team and then get ourselves a hotel room," Pugh said. "After that, it's time for fun. We'll purchase our mules in the morning, follow the stage out, and be home in Glorious in time for supper."

They had a fine evening, dining on chili and enchiladas in a real restaurant. Then they enjoyed fancy mixed drinks in a Florence saloon that sold liquor other than the generic red-eye served at the Owaysis. The next morning they met with a livery owner. He and Pugh haggled in a chummy way, and Pugh purchased six mules for eighty-two dollars apiece. Each man loudly claimed that the other had robbed him blind. McLendon helped Pugh tether the mules to the back of the buckboard, and then they hurried to the depot just in time to connect with the stage departing for Florence.

"Mission accomplished, C.M.," Pugh said. "Now let's get the hell home and start making money off these damnably expensive beasts."

They rode for a while, never in silence, Bob Pugh being addicted to making nonstop conversation. He nattered on about the rising price of curry combs, wondered at length how Mary Somebody was faring in her search among territory whores for some worthy ones (Bob personally favored blue-eyed blondes), and predicted that soon Crazy George would have to start serving a finer brand of liquor in the Owaysis because a better class of customers would demand it. McLendon listened for a while, then became distracted by his own thoughts. Pugh eventually noticed his lack of a polite response and demanded, "C.M., what exactly ails you? Why ain't you enjoying my stimulating conversation?"

"I'm disturbed by the Turner strike," McLendon said. "You surely must have noticed that there's something bothersome about it."

"What the hell do you mean? What could be bothersome about a hardworking man experiencing great good fortune?"

McLendon shifted on the buckboard bench so he could face Pugh directly. "It's possible, isn't it, to fake the presence of valuable ore and minerals?"

"You mean salt a fake claim?"

"Yes, that."

Pugh spit over the side of the buckboard. "Now, you really believe Turner did that? He'd been bustin' ass prospecting for years. If he meant to do some salting, he surely would have done it sooner."

"I don't suspect Turner." McLendon wiped sweat from his forehead with his shirtsleeve. The sun was straight overhead in the cloudless sky. "If you think about the story he told us, he could have been set up himself. Lemmy Duke told Turner exactly where to look. He nagged at him until he did. Was that a coincidence?"

"It very well might have been. Besides, silver ain't like gold. You can salt a gold claim by tossing a few nuggets in a stream or inside a cave. The silver's underneath rock. You got to look for discoloration. How the fuck do you salt that? You can't."

"But Turner found shiny horn silver, not discolored rock or float. Couldn't somebody have planted that horn silver there, forced it on the rock some way, maybe pounded it there with a hammer? Turner said the pattern of it looked like a shotgun blast. Maybe they loaded some bits of silver in a shotgun and fired it into the rock. Could they do that?"

Pugh snapped, "C.M., why the hell would they? The cost of salting horn silver—who could afford it?"

"Collin MacPherson. Glorious was about to die, and he didn't want it to. Isn't it obvious? I've suspected it since I heard Turner's story. MacPherson has his men salt a spot, then somebody has to be lured there. Turner was perfect; he was the only prospector who went out alone. It's easier to persuade one man than several. Lemmy Duke gets him there, knowing Turner will find the silver. Then he urges him to rush to Florence to file right away—a Culloden vaquero will guard his claim so nobody jumps it. This, when the vaqueros were on alert for increased Indian threat."

"We've known all along there's silver in the Pinals," Pugh said. "Somebody finally found some. That's all there is to it."

"Consider the timing and the circumstances. Remember when you doubted there were Apaches lurking? There's been something off about this all along. Think, Bob, please."

The livery owner fell silent. For a mile or more, the only sound was the hooves of the mule team clopping on the ground. Finally Pugh said, "I'm not saying that you're right, but why would Mr. MacPherson do such a thing?"

McLendon pondered how much to tell. "He owns his big ranch. Maybe he wants to own a town too."

Pugh sighed, and suddenly he wasn't perpetually jolly Bob Pugh anymore. He seemed to McLendon to turn into a bent, worn-out man whose exhaustion was evident in his voice as well as his posture.

"It don't matter," Pugh mumbled.

"What?"

"I said it don't matter. It don't matter if Turner made an honest strike or if him or Collin MacPherson or Satan hisself faked it. A few of us put all we had left into starting a town, and we did and it was dying. Now it's becoming ever'thing we hoped for, and as far as I'm concerned, it don't matter how or why. I'm fifty-one years old and I been scraping along on the frontier since I was fifteen. I can't count the places where I tried to set up and it didn't take. Now I got a chance to make my pile and I'm done scrambling. I'm gonna stay in Glorious and run my livery and ain't anybody gonna discourage me or run me off. All of us feel the same—Mulkins, the mayor, Crazy George and Mary. Life's pushed us all this far and we ain't gonna be pushed farther. So shut up about salting. Nobody wants to hear it."

"Bob, there's more that I can tell you. Things that will help you understand what's happening."

"I said shut up."

AFTER A WHILE, when they'd passed Picket Post Mountain and Glorious was just a few miles ahead, Pugh started talking again: about the good time they'd just had in Florence, and how over the next week or so they'd have to enlarge the corral and build stalls for the new mules. He sounded just as cheerful as always.

FIFTEEN

By early July, Turner's was still the only significant strike near Glorious. There were three much smaller finds, where prospectors offering marginal samples were each paid $2,500 for their claims by mining companies willing to invest small sums—there was always the possibility that limited traces of ore in surface rock signified larger underground deposits. Some of the prospectors who'd rushed to town immediately following the Turner news decided that the Glorious pickings weren't promising after all. They packed up and left. But for each one departing, two or three more arrived. Word of Turner's horn silver discovery was still spreading, and some of the newcomers came from Nevada or California or even as far away as the Dakota Territory.

The Californians included Newman Clanton, his wife, and two grown sons, Phin and Ike. There were also some younger offspring, the first children to live in Glorious. The Clantons arrived late one morning in a wagon overflowing with household goods and prospecting tools. For their first few nights in town they stayed in tents. Then they moved to Turner's old wooden shack on the hill beyond where the other prospectors camped. It had stood empty since Turner left, and no one complained when the Clantons took possession. Mrs. Clanton bought a broom and bucket from the Tirritos and spent several days cleaning the place. Gabrielle and Rose Rogers, making a joint social call a week later, reported that the shack was now spick-and-span. The Clanton children, they said, were well mannered and quiet, particularly the little boy named Billy. Mrs. Clanton, who never told them her first name, gave her guests coffee but, much to Rose's dismay, failed to offer snacks. After that first encounter, Mrs. Clanton never socialized with the other two women again, except for innocuous chat with Gabrielle while she made purchases at the dry goods store.

Newman, Phin, and Ike Clanton went out prospecting by day and drank in the Owaysis at night. The Clanton patriarch was a heavyset man who never drank to excess and gave the impression of knowing a great deal that he had no intention of revealing. Mayor Rogers and Bob Pugh found him intriguing. They did their best to draw Newman out, but failed.

"He makes occasional reference to land investments," Rogers told McLendon and Mulkins over breakfast biscuits at the Elite. "I suspect he and his grown sons are prospecting just on the off chance that they might find something. But in the long run they must have some sort of entrepreneurial plans."

Dark, shaggy-haired Phin Clanton was secretive like his father. But Ike, about twenty-five, was Newman Clanton's polar opposite. Ike wore an elegant Vandyke beard and mustache and, in Bob Pugh's words, was "overfond of his own voice." He spouted opinions about politics, bragged about his prowess as a lover, bare-knuckle brawler, and gunfighter, and laughed uproariously at his own mostly humorless jokes. When he drank too much, which was almost every night,

Ike got into arguments that invariably ended with him challenging someone to fight. But before verbal insults escalated into physical violence, Newman and Phin Clanton would grab Ike and drag him back to the family cabin. The next night Ike would be back in the saloon, acting for all the world like no previous unpleasantness had occurred.

"We were bound to get a jackass in town sometime," Pugh said to McLendon. "And the real problem with Ike is that he don't know he's a jackass. He truly believes that he's a fine fellow and everybody admires him. He's like trying to scrape off stubborn cow flop that's stuck on your boots—you just can't rid yourself of someone like Ike."

McLendon was preoccupied sketching the proposed corral expansion. Pugh was going to buy cottonwood logs from the Chinese camp and they had to determine how many were needed. "Oh, Ike just enjoys the sound of his own voice too much, that's all," McLendon said. "The same could be said of others around here."

"Don't be comparing me to Ike Clanton. At least my talk entertains rather than annoys."

THE BIG NEWS in Glorious that week concerned whores rather than silver. Mary Somebody returned from Tucson with two new girls in tow. Sally was skinny, but with a pleasantly sassy way about her. Abigail's stupendous bosom more than compensated for a missing front tooth. Both were new enough to the game to seem fresh rather than shopworn, and most of the men in town were eager to try them out. That led Ella to announce that, despite her eagerness to earn passage home to England, she would treat herself to a short vacation. According to Mary Somebody, she wanted relief of discomfort "from overuse," and Mary agreed to Ella's break. The English girl took the stage to Florence and was gone for several days. When Ella returned, she seemed happy to let Sally and Abigail take most of the evening turns with prospectors. McLendon thought that was odd: If Ella wanted to get home so badly, why wasn't she taking advantage of the constant demand to earn the necessary money as quickly as possible? But after all, it was her business and not his.

WILLIAM CLARK LeMOND returned to Glorious on the same Tuesday stage as Ella. The soap salesman, dressed in another loud checked suit, was surprised to see McLendon when he dropped his bags off at the livery.

"You stayed after all! Does that mean you won the heart of Miss Gabrielle?"

"Hardly," McLendon admitted. "But it turns out that you were right about the potential of this town."

Around sundown, LeMond had a beer in the Owaysis and passed along territorial news. President Grant's peace commission had signed treaties with some minor Apache chiefs, but warriors led by Cochise continued to terrorize towns and ranches southeast of Tucson.

"We continue to be told of substantial Apache presence in this area, but there have been no incidents lately," Mayor Rogers said.

"That's surprising, given the number of prospectors who must be out daily in the Pinals," LeMond said. "Perhaps the Indians from this area have moved down to join Cochise."

Lemmy Duke, drinking at the next table, overheard. "Wish it was true, but it ain't. Our Culloden vaqueros keep finding sign. Apaches are all around here."

"Then they must be more cautious than the rest of their quarrelsome tribe," LeMond said. "That, or else you're running in incredible luck.

I'd best be on my way. I've an errand tonight, a sales call in the morning, and then I'm off on the stage back to Florence." He gathered up a small, square package wrapped in brown paper and nodded to everyone.

"I think I'll have an early night too," McLendon said. "I'll walk out with you, LeMond."

When they were outside, McLendon asked, "What's your errand?"

"I have to drop something off to Miss Gabrielle. I'm sorry to hear that things with her didn't work out to your satisfaction. She's a fine young woman."

"She is. Are you going to the dry goods store? I'll come with you."

Gabrielle was still behind the counter, selling sundries to some prospectors. "Mr. LeMond!" she said cheerfully. "Just in time! Were you able to find it?"

LeMond handed her the package. "I was. They had a few in one of the Tucson general stores."

"How much do I owe you?" she asked.

"We can settle up in the morning, when I'll show you some samples of a fine new lemon-scented soap. You'll want a dozen, at least."

Gabrielle looked over LeMond's shoulder and said to McLendon, "I'm going to close up now. Was there something you needed before I do?" Her tone was friendly, but no more than that.

McLendon shook his head. "I was just keeping LeMond, here, company. We'll be on our way."

When they were outside, McLendon said, "If you don't mind me asking, what did you bring Gabrielle?"

"Just a book that she wanted, *Roughing It*, by some journalist calling himself Mark Twain. It's about his adventures here in the territories. I've read some of it—very funny stuff."

"Well, that's Gabrielle for you," McLendon said. "She always did love to read."

LeMond yawned. "I'm tuckered from the stage ride. I don't think Miss Gabrielle wanted the book for herself. She wants to use it for the other thing—the class."

"What class?"

"The one she has for the prospectors who want to learn to read. I understand that she hosts it a couple of nights each week."

"Tuesdays and Thursdays," McLendon mumbled.

"You know, I think that's right."

Back at the livery, McLendon tried to concentrate on mending a bridle, but he couldn't. After an hour he tossed the bridle on a table and walked back to the dry goods store. A half-dozen prospectors, including Bossman Wright and Oafie, were sitting cross-legged on the floor. Gabrielle stood in front of the counter with Joe Saint at her side. A small chalkboard McLendon remembered from St. Louis was propped on the counter. Gabrielle was reading to her scruffy pupils from *Roughing It.*

"'I had already learned how hard and long and dismal a task it is to burrow down into the bowels of the earth and get out the coveted ore,'" she read, "'and now I learned that the burrowing was only half the work; and that to get the silver out of the ore was the dreary and laborious other half of it.'"

"That's the truth," one of the prospectors called out, and everyone laughed.

"Let's consider the letters in 'dreary'—how the *e* sounds out, but the *a* is silent," Gabrielle said. "Sheriff Saint is going to write the word out on the chalkboard so that we can study it. Sheriff, would you take over for a moment? I need to talk to Mr. McLendon." She took McLendon's arm and guided him outside.

"What do you want?" Gabrielle asked. "I need to return to the class."

McLendon thought he'd experienced every possible terrible feeling since Ellen died and he fled St. Louis, but now he hurt in a new way. "So the sheriff is your helper," he said.

"Yes. He was once a teacher himself, and he's still a good one. These men, and of course Oafie, too, have their pride. They want to learn to read but couldn't abide feeling demeaned in the process. Joe treats them with respect and courtesy. I think we make an effective team."

That was exactly what McLendon didn't want to hear. "Why the Twain book?" he asked, trying not to show how devastated he felt. "It's thick with pages and, from what I heard you read, has long, difficult words. It may be too advanced for these pupils."

"Possibly, but the tales Mr. Twain relates about prospecting and mining and towns in the territories are all familiar to them," Gabrielle said. "They relax when they hear the stories, and when they're relaxed, they're better able to learn."

"And now the sheriff helps you," McLendon said again. "Back in St. Louis, weren't we an effective team?"

"Yes. For a while we truly were. Despite all that happened later, I treasure the memory. And now I really must get back inside."

THERE WAS new construction in Glorious. The stage line built a formal depot, and Sears and Sons, the San Francisco mining company that bought Turner's claim, put up an office. Both structures were wood rather than adobe. The companies had the planks freighted in from Tucson and hired builders from Florence. Sears and Sons had a plate-glass window in front that was big enough to make Major Mulkins jealous. Walking past, the prospectors could see assayers sitting at desks, waiting to evaluate rock samples. Mayor

Rogers met with Don Jesse, the Sears and Sons manager, and Jesse said the company intended to start blasting tunnels at the Turner site soon, possibly in another month. This was exciting news, Rogers reported at the Owaysis that night.

"They've got to bring in experienced dynamiters to set the charges, and then specialists to dig the tunnels," Rogers said, his face flushed with excitement as well as red-eye. "Then they need carpenters to build wood supports, and engineers to place the supports properly in the tunnels, and others to build a waterworks down by the creek for a smelter and a stamp mill. A couple of months after that, they'll bring in miners. Come late fall, this town will really be a-bustle."

McLendon had no idea what a stamp mill was, and wasn't interested enough to ask. But the news excited Major Mulkins enough to call in another work crew from Florence to finish off the second floor of the hotel.

"I'm going to start leasing rooms by the month," Mulkins said. "Eighty dollars with a window, seventy without. With all that's required to get a mine up and running, those engineers are going to have to stay awhile."

THE NEWS THAT miners would soon be arriving in Glorious encouraged a builder named Merrill to come from Florence with a dozen workers in tow. Merrill announced in the Owaysis that he was building homes to rent to the miners. He and his men began constructing small adobe huts on the low hill just west of town, across from the prospectors' tents and between the Tirritos' store and the shack now occupied by the Clantons. Two were in place and a third was almost completed when Lemmy Duke rode up and talked with the builder. Then Duke rode off and Merrill hurriedly called together his crew. They loaded their tools in wagons and left town immediately without speaking to anyone. After a day or two, Bossman Wright and Oafie moved into one of the huts. With so much else going on, no one paid much attention except McLendon. A prominent company like Sears and Sons of San Francisco was one thing, McLendon knew, because they were bringing money into Glorious. But Collin MacPherson wouldn't tolerate an interloper like Merrill taking money out of *his* town.

MAJOR MULKINS continued to lend his dining room to Preacher Sheridan for Sunday worship. With the influx of new citizens, Mulkins was concerned that now there wouldn't be enough room, but it wasn't a problem. Many of the Sears and Sons employees came to the service, but there was plenty of space to accommodate them because, with the exception of Preacher himself, no prospectors came anymore. Being far more concerned with finding silver than God, even on Sunday mornings they were out in the mountains. As soon as each service was concluded, Preacher rushed to join them.

IKE CLANTON drank so much one night in the Owaysis that he was still staggering the next morning. His father and Phin went prospecting without him. Ike made a nuisance of himself at the livery, wandering in and babbling to Pugh and McLendon as they worked on the corral expansion and sweated in the brutal summer heat. He jabbered suggestions about which logs to place where until Pugh lost patience and told him to get his sorry drunk ass lost. That infuriated Ike, who challenged Pugh to fight. The livery owner was much older and smaller than Ike, but he was still ready to fight. McLendon pushed Pugh back and walked toward Ike himself, swinging a heavy mallet. Ike backed away, muttering threats about taking the mallet and bashing McLendon's head in. Then he stumbled off.

"A goddamn yellabelly is all he is," Pugh grumbled. "I'da taken him easy."

"Sure you would," McLendon soothed. "I intervened to keep you from hurting him. Now let's get back to work."

It was a difficult day for Ike. Soon after leaving the livery he was chased from the Owaysis by Crazy George in full blind, lead-pipe-waving fury after Ike tried to pull Abigail's top down. Ike's excuse was that he wanted to "inspect the goods before paying for them." Abigail screamed and Crazy George charged. Then Joe Saint escorted Ike from the Tirritos' store after Gabrielle complained that he was harassing her. The sheriff walked Ike to the jail and told him to go sleep awhile in one of the cells.

"He's snoring there now," Saint told Pugh and McLendon as the three men ate lunch at the Owaysis. Mary Somebody served them tomatoes and beef jerky. The jerky was too stringy, but the tomatoes were perfectly ripe.

"We ought to run Ike Clanton out of town," Pugh suggested. "He's a boil on our backsides."

"Oh, men like Ike are mostly all talk and no action," Saint said. "I'll let him sleep it off and see where we are after that."

Pugh and McLendon worked on the corral until late afternoon, at which point Pugh announced he was going to treat himself to a bath at the Elite. McLendon said he'd take their sweaty work clothes to the Chinese laundry. They changed in Pugh's office, and McLendon scooped up the dirty garments. As he stepped in front of the livery, he heard Joe Saint speaking to Ike Clanton outside the jail.

"I won't allow any more rude, drunken behavior, Ike," Saint said.

"One more incident and I'll lock you up, then send for Hunky-Dory Holmes to take you off to trial in Tucson."

Even after his long nap, Clanton still looked the worse for wear. He propped himself up against the adobe wall and nodded feebly.

"My word as a gentleman, Sheriff. I just got on the outside of too much whiskey."

"Then on your way," Saint said, and went inside. Ike shook his head as though to clear it and began walking slowly west, past the livery and saloon and farrier's shop. McLendon followed with his arms full of smelly, wet clothes. He thought Ike must be going back to the Clanton shack, but instead he looped behind the Elite Hotel and walked into the laundry. McLendon, fearing trouble, hurried after him, and saw that Ike had Sydney Chau pinned to a wall while her horrified mother cowered in a corner.

"Gimme a kiss," Ike snorted, pushing his face toward Sydney's. McLendon dropped the clothes and leaped at Ike. He grabbed his shoulder and yanked him away from the young Chinese woman.

"What the hell?" Ike screeched. "Lemme alone, she's just a Chink." He cocked a fist and McLendon crouched, ready to defend himself. From the corner of his eye, he saw Sydney adjusting her dress and comforting her mother. Then she straightened and turned around.

"You can stand down, Mr. McLendon," Sydney said. "I'm capable of dealing with this myself. Mr. Clanton, leave this place immediately and never come back."

"I respect no commands from Chinks," Ike said. He snatched at Sydney again. Small but quick, Sydney ducked under his arm, kicked the back of his knee to knock him off balance, then pulled a thin-bladed knife from her belt and held it to Ike's throat.

"I'm sure you don't want to die, Mr. Clanton. Now, be on your way."

Ike's eyes widened. He clearly was trying to decide what to do next. Fully sober, he could easily have broken free of Sydney before she could use the knife, but in his present muddled condition it was doubtful.

"Best be going, Ike," McLendon suggested. "Doc Chau will slit your gullet like a chicken's, and since you've so offended her, she won't sew it up afterwards."

Ike glowered at him. "I'll take her down, and then you." Sydney pressed the knife into his neck and he flinched. "Ah, fuck you both." He stepped away from Sydney and picked up his hat, which had been knocked to the floor. He said to McLendon, "You better not spread lies about some Chink woman getting the best of me."

"Wouldn't think of it," McLendon promised, but that night at the Owaysis he told everyone, and acted it out besides. Bob Pugh proposed a toast to Doc Chau. Ike was nowhere to be seen.

But the next day he went out prospecting with his father and brother, and that night he was back in the Owaysis, swilling beer and telling stories about facing down three men at the same time in a San Bernardino saloon. A few prospectors jeered at Ike and asked him to tell about how Doc Chau whipped him at the laundry. Ike shot a quick glance at McLendon, then laughed and said that Chink women just had a stealthy way with a blade. That got the prospectors laughing, and they bought Ike his next mug of beer.

"Old Ike's a choice one," Mulkins observed.

Mayor Rogers, seated at the table with the hotel owner, Pugh, and McLendon, agreed. "That's the one unfortunate thing about town growth. You're bound to get some Ike Clantons."

"Joe Saint had dinner at the hotel," Mulkins said. "He told me that a bit earlier today, Newman Clanton dropped by the jail. Said he'd heard his son had raised some hell and although Ike was mostly all right he sometimes acted up. Anyway, the old man promised that Ike would behave from now on. Told Joe that if he didn't, let him know and, full-grown though Ike might be, Newman'd beat the tar out of him."

"You should have let me take Ike on, C.M.," Pugh complained. "But you backed me off and let Doc Chau have all the fun."

"I'm a spoilsport of the worst kind," McLendon agreed, and excused himself to visit the outhouse. When he emerged, buttoning his pants, Ike Clanton was waiting. McLendon balled his fists, but Ike extended his hand.

"I apologize for my earlier shitheadedness," he said. "I sometimes get foolish from drink. No hard feelings, then?"

"I suppose." McLendon didn't want to shake Ike's hand, but the man was apologizing and he felt obligated. As they shook, Ike squeezed hard.

"I'll be seeing you around, McLendon. Indeed I will." He winked. "For now, I wish you the pleasantest of good evenings."

THE NEXT MORNING, McLendon went to the laundry to see if Sydney was all right. She wasn't there. Her mother indicated that she was down in the creek camp. McLendon walked there and found Sydney helping several Chinese who had just come to town unload a wagon.

"We're growing just like the town is," she told him. "There's more demand for our vegetables, and Mother and I need help at the laundry. So we've been in touch with relatives and friends, saying they should join us, that there are opportunities."

"I'm sorry about Ike the other day," McLendon said. "Your response was impressive."

"I was able to take him by surprise, that's all. He thought a Chinese woman would be defenseless. And unnecessary as it was, thank you for preparing to defend me. It was chivalrous. Now, if you'll excuse me, I need to finish here and go help Mother. Starting tomorrow, we'll have three more of our people working with us in the laundry. By the way, there'll be no charge for the clothes you dropped off."

"There's no need for that. I'm glad to pay."

"And every other time, you will. It's a onetime courtesy. Take advantage, because starting tomorrow we're raising our prices."

On his walk back to town, McLendon found himself admiring the jagged-edged Pinals and towering Apache Leap. They still were predominantly blood red, but now he noticed subtle shadings of other colors—tan and gold and even purple where certain vegetation flourished in crevices and cracks in the rock. The various species of cactus on the slopes added a full palette of green, from pale olive to almost iridescent emerald. Above him, the sky was vivid blue, streaked with cotton-white threads of clouds. This far from the smells of town, the scent of sage perfumed the air. Though the morning was hot, the wind was brisk and refreshing. *I'm getting used to this place,* he thought. *I like it.*

IN ALL THE EXCITEMENT about silver, the Apache threat had been mostly ignored in Glorious, though never entirely forgotten. One night in mid-July, Lemmy Duke called for everyone's attention in the Owaysis.

"While there's no cause for immediate alarm, our Culloden vaqueros are again finding Indian sign," he announced. "Increased vigilance is necessary. Remember there are always likely to be Apache about. Few are prospecting in groups just now, I know, but you might at least try to work in sight of some others. And should you happen upon any Apache sign, notify me or anyone else from Culloden or the sheriff."

"Nice of him to include you," Pugh said to Saint.

"Well, it never hurts to remind people about the Apaches," Saint said. "We don't want to lose anyone else to them."

The sheriff sat and drank a beer with Pugh and McLendon. They watched as Duke circulated, chatting briefly with various prospectors before settling at a back table with Newman, Phin, and Ike Clanton. Duke signaled to Mary Somebody, who brought them a full bottle of red-eye. Duke poured generous drinks for himself and the other three. Then they settled into intense conversation.

"I wonder what Lemmy has to say to that crew," Pugh said. "Perhaps he thinks they've been extra careless in regard to Apaches and is pointing out the error of their ways."

Saint finished his beer and excused himself to return to the jail, where he'd left two prospectors locked in separate cells. They'd gotten into a fistfight earlier in the evening, and the sheriff hoped that they'd calmed down enough to be released. He usually slept on a cot in one of the cells and would have to settle for the floor that night if his prisoners weren't sufficiently calmed down. Pugh and McLendon stayed and drank beer awhile longer. When they finally left, Lemmy Duke and the Clantons were still talking.

TWO DAYS LATER, McLendon and Pugh sweated in the mid-afternoon sun as they nailed up trimmed cottonwood logs to expand the livery's corral. Their heads snapped up at the sound of shots echoing out of the Queen Creek canyon into the valley.

"Running gunfight," Pugh said. "Apaches attacking some of the prospectors, sure as hell. Get your pistol; I'll fetch my shotgun."

Sheriff Saint hurried out of the jail, buckling on his gun belt as he came. Crazy George emerged from the saloon with a shotgun. Major

Mulkins bolted from the hotel lobby; he carried a rifle. The gunfire continued, and the echoes of wild screams and shouts reached the town too.

"Let's get out that way—we've got to provide cover fire for anyone on
the run here," Mulkins said, and for the first time McLendon thought
that "Major" might be a real military rank rather than an affectation.
"All men with guns, follow me. Everyone else, take cover inside."

The four vaqueros stationed at the two guardhouses leaped on
their horses and galloped toward the canyon. Mulkins led everyone
else with guns in the same direction on foot. Before they'd gone a
hundred yards they saw three prospectors—Bossman Wright, Oafie,
and Preacher Sheridan—running hard out of the canyon toward
town. The quartet of mounted vaqueros raced past them, forming a
protective line. The gunfire back in the canyon slowed to occasional,
sporadic shots.

The prospectors, short of breath from physical exertion and fear,
reached the armed townsmen. "What happened back there?" Mulkins
demanded.

"We were all working on a ledge maybe a mile back in there and
all of a sudden there was whooping and some gunshots," Wright
gasped. "One nearly hit Oafie, and Preacher got cut with some rock
splinters from the ricochet. We ducked down but couldn't see any
Indians, couldn't tell for sure where the shots were coming from.
Then Lemmy and a half-dozen vaqueros ride up, just hauling ass to
reach us. Lemmy says, 'Sounds like too many to take on, but we'll
hold 'em off as long as we can. Run!' And we did."

"We better go on and reinforce Lemmy," Pugh said, but Mulkins
disagreed.

"Shooting's done back there. I think the fight's over," he said.
Moments later Lemmy Duke and the Culloden vaqueros came trotting out of the canyon.

"They're gone," Duke reported. "I guess there were enough of 'em to take on three prospectors, but not for a full fight after all."

"How many, Lemmy?" Sheriff Saint asked.

Duke leaned back in the saddle and wiped his forehead with his hat brim. "Shit, I don't know. Five, six, something like that. Apaches, of course, with war paint on. Surprised they had guns. Maybe they took them off other white men they ambushed."

"Kill any?" Bob Pugh asked.

"No, but they got one of ours, damn it." Duke gestured toward a vaquero leading a horse with a body strapped across its saddle. McLendon recognized the bullet-riddled corpse of Juan Luis.

Duke saw McLendon staring at the body and said, "He went out where he shouldn't have been."

AFTER THAT, everyone was on constant guard during daylight for another Apache attack. The prospectors once again went out into the mountains in groups. McLendon and Pugh continued work on the corral but kept their guns handy. They were in a hurry to finish. Every mule they had was rented daily, and Pugh talked of returning to Florence to buy some more.

"Anytime now, somebody will come to town and set up another livery," he said. "I need to be prepared for the competition."

"Would having a competitor rile you, Bob?" McLendon asked. "After all, you've been here from the beginning. You nearly lost everything. Now you're finally making money and someone might waltz in and take your play away."

"All I ever asked for was a fair chance," Pugh said. "If somebody else offers better mules at better prices, more power to him. Of course, I don't mean to make it easy for the bastard. Whoever comes and attempts it had better be ready to dig in and scrap. We got the corral all bigged up, we'll get some more mules, we're gonna be ready. Which reminds me: You've worked hard here, and I'm of a mind to invite you to be my partner in the business. You wouldn't need to buy in right up front. We'd figure a way for you to pay me back out of your part of the profits."

"Why, hell, Bob." McLendon was genuinely moved. "That's a generous offer."

"It's not generous at all. I'd expect a partner to do all the hard work while I take my ease in the saloon. So, what do you say?"

"It's tempting. In some ways I've very much enjoyed my time here in Glorious. But soon I'll be leaving. I've said as much all along."

"Because of the girl? People are moving in. There'll be other girls."

McLendon shrugged. "Partly that. And there's the other thing. I've tried to tell you about Collin MacPherson, and you don't want to listen."

"No, I don't. And I'll say this much: There's damn-all he can really do. I'm not selling my business. If he wants, he can start up his own livery here, but he ain't getting what's mine. Though he's got you spooked, he has no such effect on me."

"You don't understand men like him."

"I understand all that I need to. At least I don't waver. You're always saying you're about to be leaving and you never do. Make up your damn mind. If you're staying, be my partner. If you're going, get the hell gone. Now, let's have some beer."

GABRIELLE WANTED to know McLendon's plans too. She confronted him one afternoon when he dropped into the dry goods store to buy work gloves.

"You arrived in May, made it clear you were only staying for a week until the next Florence stage, now it's more than two months later and you're still here. Why?"

"I don't know. But it won't be too much longer."

Gabrielle chewed on her lower lip, a signal McLendon recognized. She was furious. "It's inconvenient having you around."

"That's not entirely true," McLendon said. "I've done such a fine job at the livery that Bob Pugh offered me a partnership."

"What? Don't tell me you accepted." She seemed horrified at the prospect.

"No, I told him I'd be leaving. I meant it. You've made it clear that you're with the sheriff, so I have no reason to stay. Does Joe Saint still find my presence so bothersome? He hasn't indicated such to me, but of course you know him better."

Gabrielle began sorting combs in a box, putting the smallest ones on top. "Joe is a gentleman as always. It's just that when you arrived you said you'd changed, and now you do things like assist Bob Pugh at the livery, and you helped Joe break up that fight, and you attempted to rescue Sydney Chau from that brute Ike Clanton."

"She told you about that?"

"Of course she did. We talk. But the idea of you doing things for the benefit of others and not just yourself—it's troubling."

"I don't see why. I've admitted past mistakes and am attempting to improve myself."

She pushed the box of combs to the side of the counter and began folding a stack of bandannas. "I really think you're trying to change, and respect you for it. But you need to continue doing your improving elsewhere. That remains my wish, if it matters to you. Now, if you're in need of no other purchases, you might leave. Joe will be dropping in soon. I'd rather that he not see us talking."

"It hasn't been much of a conversation."

"Well, you'll have to settle for it, because it's all you're getting."

McLendon was irked. He couldn't blame Gabrielle for not loving him anymore, but she didn't have to be so prickly.

WHEN MCLENDON brought more dirty clothes to the Chau laundry, he was surprised to see Ike Clanton there. Ike handed some clothes to Sydney's mother and walked out, nodding to McLendon as he passed.

"I thought you barred Ike from this property for life," McLendon said to Sydney.

"I did, but then a few days ago he came to see me at the camp and handed me a note. He said he'd leave and let me read it. There were only a few lines, about how much he regretted his act. He can't spell at all—he wrote 'akt,' with a *k*. But the letter seemed sincere. So I said that we would do his laundry again. Grudges are impractical when running a business. I'd like us to make enough money so that Mother can eventually live in San Francisco in some comfort. She has sisters there, but it's an expensive city."

IKE SEEMED DETERMINED to be on good terms with everyone. At night in the Owaysis he made a point of calling all the whores "ma'am" and politely asking if they had time for a turn with him. When the saloon was especially busy, he helped Mary Somebody serve beer and whiskey to the impatient customers. Where he once tried to entertain everyone with tall tales told in a loud voice, he now sought one-on-one conversations, often with town founders. Bob Pugh pronounced himself astonished by Ike's curiosity regarding the ins and outs of the livery business. Mayor Rogers enjoyed an eve-

ning's chat with Ike so much that he invited him to share coffee and
sweets with him and Rose in their home the next morning.

"There are good qualities in Ike that I hadn't previously recognized," Rogers said. "He had some insightful thoughts on the future
of the farrier trade. Thinks there's about to be a pressing need for it
down in the southeast territory, where the population will explode
once the president's peace emissaries get things squared with old
Cochise. I told him that I had a cousin who wanted to try his hand in
the profession, and I'd pass the suggestion along."

"That's odd," said Major Mulkins. "I passed an hour yesterday with
Ike, just the two of us sitting in my hotel lobby, sipping lemonade. Ike
predicted that once Cochise was pacified, there'd be sizable new com-
munities sure to spring up in the San Pedro Valley down past the
mountains, since the rumors of silver and copper lodes are so prevalent
there. He was saying how a man who had the first fine hotel down
there could make a fortune, even more than here in Glorious. Not that
I'd be looking to move, of course, and I told Ike so."

"Why do you suppose Ike's suddenly so boosterish on other parts
of the territory?" McLendon asked.

"As I have it from Ike, he and the other Clantons are looking to
found a town of their own," Mulkins said. "That's the big plan his
daddy Newman's keeping secret. My opinion is that Ike and his kin
want to use Glorious as a jumping-off point, learn what they can
about how we succeeded here and then apply the knowledge on their
own behalf elsewhere. It's a sensible approach."

"And Ike Clanton's nothing but sensible," McLendon said sarcas-
tically. "Beware his ulterior motives."

"Be a cold day in hell when Ike Clanton outfoxes me," Pugh said,
but McLendon was puzzled. That night he left the Owaysis early and
waited out of sight around the side of the hotel. By eleven p.m. most

of the saloon's other customers were gone. Ike was the last to come out. McLendon watched as he walked north toward the shack where the Clantons lived, then abruptly toward the west guard post where MacPherson vaqueros were stationed during the day. McLendon followed at a discreet distance. The town was still. Ike didn't look back. There was movement by the guardhouse and McLendon flattened himself on the ground. Angel Misterio appeared, leading two horses. He mounted one and Ike took the other. They rode off quietly in the direction of Culloden Ranch.

Now McLendon understood. Collin MacPherson had his spy, and was ready to make his next move.

SIXTEEN

I t took Ike Clanton less than two weeks to completely overcome his previous bad reputation with everyone in Glorious but McLendon. Whereas his friends were charmed by Ike's fascination with and responses to whatever they had to say, McLendon recognized it as a gifted conniver's art; he'd used the same technique himself back in St. Louis to gain the trust of people he would later betray.

"Don't try your tricks on me, Ike," McLendon told him when Clanton approached him in the Owaysis and said that they ought to chat. "I'm familiar with the game, and I know your intent."

"I only intend enjoying your company," Ike said, sounding hurt. "Let me buy you a drink and discuss any differences that remain between us."

"Shall we discuss your recent alliance with Collin MacPherson?"

Just for a moment Ike's eyes narrowed. "You wouldn't want to be spreading that rumor about. I'd take it hard if you did."

"What's your gain from it, Ike? What's the plan?"

Ike took a breath, and then the smile was back on his face. "Why, my only plan is to enjoy my stay in this fine town and to hopefully share in its good fortune. I regret that your hard feelings toward me prevent us from being friends. And since there's no satisfaction to be gained from further talk with you, I'll bid you good evening and hob-nob instead with my dear pal Bob Pugh, who I see has entered the saloon. He, at least, is always agreeable."

Ike waved at Pugh, gesturing him over to a table. Then he yelled for Mary Somebody to bring him and thirsty old Bob "a pitcher of your finest lager, or at least the warm horse piss Crazy George always serves." But he winked broadly to indicate that he meant to be enter-taining rather than insulting, and when Mary brought the beer he gave her a dollar tip. He whispered something to her and she laughed. Then Ike turned his full attention to Pugh, who was soon yammering away while Ike listened, leaning forward and apparently hanging on every word.

McLendon sat at a nearby table with Mulkins and Mayor Rogers. He did his best to participate in their conversation about the latest wave of newcomers and how the Major no longer had even a few feet of lobby floor left to spare. Mulkins started telling about the crew from Florence that would be coming in mid-August to finish off the Elite's second floor. He was thinking of having them go ahead and add a third.

"Don't you think that'd be wise, C.M.?" he asked. "Say, C.M., did you hear me? Are you listening?"

"Sorry, Major," McLendon said. "I heard you. A third floor. Why not?" He was preoccupied watching Ike and Bob Pugh. Among all of McLendon's Glorious friends, the livery owner was proving most sus-ceptible to Ike. There was something in Pugh's makeup, McLendon realized, that craved admiration or at least respect. Ike had recognized this and now expertly played on it. He and Pugh sat together at the table in the Owaysis for hours, and later when Pugh and McLendon were bedding down in the livery office—McLendon was wrapped up in blankets on the floor, since it was Pugh's night for the bed—instead of falling right to sleep, Pugh talked about Ike's latest comments.

"He thinks I ought to damn well dominate the livery business in the territory," Pugh said. "The idea would be get out ahead of the next strike, set up in the southeast maybe well past Tucson, and have plenty of mules ready when all the prospectors arrive in the San Pedro Valley. Not, you see, get caught unprepared and have to catch up like I'm doing here. It makes sense."

McLendon sat up. "Bob, what exactly did Ike say? Did he suggest how you should go about it?"

"Oh, he said something about how I should divest myself of my operation here so I could give full attention to the new venture. How a man can't be in two places at once. Then he got to describing the new setup, how much I could charge for each mule and so forth, so I never did mention to him how you and me are going to be partners. I thought you could stay on here and run this place while I went off to establish a new branch of the business. Don't worry, C.M., I ain't about to cut you out of anything. Now we better get some sleep."

"That's not what I was worried about," McLendon said. After a moment he continued, "You need to think about this carefully—"

But Pugh was already snoring.

EARLY THE NEXT AFTERNOON Lemmy Duke came to the livery office. He greeted Pugh warmly and made a perfunctory nod in McLendon's direction.

"Bob," he said, "Mr. MacPherson wonders if you might pay him a call. He'd admire the opportunity for conversation. I could escort you to the ranch right now if it's your pleasure."

"Well, now," Pugh said. "Mr. Collin MacPherson wants to see me?" He sounded very proud. "Lemmy, I've got some important paperwork to finish up. Maybe you could drink a beer over to the Owaysis, and in an hour or so I'll be right along."

"Sounds just right," Duke replied. "See you there, Bob."

As soon as Duke was gone, McLendon said, "What was that malarkey about paperwork? All you're doing right now is rolling smokes and bullshitting."

"Never let on that you're at anyone's beck and call," Pugh said, a self-satisfied smirk on his face. "It won't hurt Mr. MacPherson none to wait awhile. Don't you wonder what he wants with me?"

"I know exactly what he wants. He wants this livery. He's going to offer to buy it and tell you all about the great opportunities elsewhere, just like Ike Clanton did in the saloon last night."

"Is he, now? Well, won't that be interesting."

"Bob, I wish you wouldn't go."

"Why is that?"

McLendon knew he was risking his life by telling Pugh about his own meeting with MacPherson, but he told about it anyway—the preliminary coffee and compliments, the discussion of Glorious's glowing prospects, the offer of brandy and a paid position as MacPherson's town spy.

"He means to own all the businesses here, Bob. He was open about it. He figures on buying everyone out and running off anybody who doesn't do what he wants. He's picked you out to start on because you've been playing so chummy with Ike Clanton. Ike took the offer that I turned down. He's working for MacPherson now. They figure he's softened you up and you're ripe for cooperating. And after they get your livery, they'll go after the Major and his hotel, and George and Mary with the Owaysis, Charlie Rogers's farrier shop, even the

Tirritos' dry goods store. Once a man like MacPherson starts, he never stops. Don't go, Bob. I fear for what might happen to you."

Pugh looked thoughtful. "You say you got offered brandy?"

"Christ, Bob, I'm talking about a bad man with sinister intentions, and all you care about is brandy?"

"Well, I've never had any. I've heard brandy spoken of, even seen others drink it, but it was always too dear for my pocketbook. Look, C.M., I know your concern's well intended. But it strikes me that you're one of those who always thinks the worst of rich men. You think I don't know why Collin MacPherson's so wealthy? It ain't because he happened to be standing outside with plenty of empty buckets on the day it started raining gold. No, he's a man who sees opportunities and takes them. Sure, he wants my livery and the other businesses here, but he ain't gonna get 'em. None of us will sell out to him. We'll never be fuck-you rich like MacPherson, but we're finally in place to get some of our own. He can offer me all the money he wants and I'll turn him down. He don't like it, well, it won't cost me any sleep."

"If you're not going to sell, why even go out there? It can't be just for brandy."

"Shit, no, it's not brandy, though I hope I get some. It's that a rich man's asking to see me, ordinary ol' Bob Pugh. All my life, rich men stepped on me or ignored me altogether. Now I got something one of them wants. I'm going to enjoy the moment."

"Don't go, Bob," McLendon pleaded. "I've known other men like MacPherson. No good will come of it."

"Well, I guess we'll see. Now I'm gonna cut a mule out of the corral and go meet Lemmy Duke. I expect I'll develop a thirst on the ride out to the ranch."

"Be on your guard."

"Oh, I won't tarry that long. By dark at the latest I'll be back here buying you a beer and telling you all about it. If I'm somewhat delayed, commence to drinking without me."

BOB PUGH didn't return to the livery that afternoon, or show up in the Owaysis that night. McLendon considered saddling a mule and riding out to Culloden Ranch; then he imagined the less-than-warm welcome he was likely to receive there. So instead, when it was past ten and Pugh still wasn't back, McLendon walked over to the town jail. For a change, the two cells were empty of drunks and brawlers. Joe Saint, his eyeglasses pushed up on his forehead, was nodding off at his desk.

"I need a word, Sheriff," McLendon said.

Saint blinked a few times and lowered his glasses in place. "Is there trouble?"

"I think so. This afternoon Bob Pugh went out to see Collin MacPherson at Culloden Ranch and he never came back."

The sheriff had trouble waking up. He yawned and said, "Maybe Bob stayed there for dinner and they're still talking. Bob can converse for a long time without pause."

"No, I don't think it can be that. He said he was coming right back to town, by dark at the latest."

Saint rubbed his face. "The Culloden hands have been saying again that they've seen fresh Apache sign."

McLendon didn't think Pugh had come to harm at the hands of Indians, but thought better of saying so. "Hadn't we better go look for Bob?" he suggested.

"I suppose that we should. You're right, this is worrisome." Saint buckled on his gun belt. "If we ride out to Culloden, we'll need mules from the livery. Can you saddle a pair?"

They rode slowly out to the ranch, because of both darkness and frequent stops to call out Pugh's name. McLendon lost any sense of direction shortly after they splashed across Queen Creek, but Saint knew the way. When they approached the gates, the sheriff called out, "It's Joe Saint and McLendon. Let us in."

After a few moments the gates swung open. Angel Misterio waited for the riders just inside the compound.

"You come calling late, Sheriff," he said. "You, too, Señor McLendon. What is the cause of this visit?"

"Bob Pugh is missing," Saint said. "I understand he came here earlier in the day."

"Indeed, he did. But he left long since, riding his mule back in the direction of town. I cannot recall the exact hour, but it was well before dark."

"He never got there," Saint said. "I wonder if we might speak for a moment to Mr. MacPherson?"

Misterio frowned. "The *jefe* has retired. I prefer not to wake him. There's nothing to be done in the darkness anyway. As soon as the sun rises, if your friend is still missing I will send out some of our vaqueros as search parties to assist you. But in the meantime it would be best for you to return to town. Perhaps Señor Pugh has arrived there in your absence."

"We want to talk to your boss," McLendon said.

"It is not possible at this time," Misterio said. "You would be wise to leave now."

McLendon started to argue, but Saint said, "He's right, McLendon. At night we might ride within a few feet of Bob and never see him. Señor Misterio, we'll gladly accept any help you can give us in the morning. Let's go."

As the gate shut behind them and they rode back toward town, McLendon said, "There's something wrong, Joe. You know there is."

"I do, but we've got to stay sensible. Maybe Bob will turn up yet."

McLendon sat up all night in the livery office. Mayor Rogers and Major Mulkins learned that Pugh was missing, and they joined in the vigil. Just before dawn there came the clopping sound of hooves on hard ground and the three men rushed outside. Bob Pugh's riderless mule was drinking from the corral trough, its reins dangling in the dirt.

"Shit," Mulkins muttered. "This is bad."

As soon as it was daylight, McLendon and Saint rode out again. They were joined by Sydney Chau, who told them that she needed to come along.

"It's possible Mr. Pugh may be hurt, and I could be of some assistance," she said. "He's always been kind to me. I can handle a mule if you'll saddle one for me."

Saint said they should begin by riding back toward Culloden Ranch. "We know Bob was there yesterday."

McLendon was so concerned for Pugh that he didn't notice any discomfort during the ride. He and the sheriff and Sydney continually twisted in the saddle as they rode, scanning for Pugh in all directions. About halfway to Culloden they met a party of vaqueros led by Lemmy Duke.

"I'm heartsick about old Bob," Duke said. "Let's hope his mule pitched him or some such thing and he's laying somewhere with maybe a broke leg, just waiting to be found."

They looked most of the morning. When the sun was almost directly overhead, Duke sent out his vaqueros separately to widen the search area. McLendon, Saint, and Sydney stayed together.

"This is going to end badly," McLendon said. "I tried to talk him out of it, but he wouldn't listen."

"Talk him out of what?" Saint asked, but before McLendon could reply, one of the vaqueros galloped up.

"Señor Duke says to come at once," he said. "They have found Señor Pugh."

BOB PUGH lay behind a rock in a deep wash perhaps three quarters of a mile north of Culloden and a few hundred yards from Queen Creek. Three arrows protruded from his body, two in his back and one in the center of his chest. His throat had been cut.

"Fuckin' Apaches," Lemmy Duke growled. "Slaughter a man like he's an animal. Damn it, Bob should have known better than to be out alone."

McLendon felt overwhelmed by grief and guilt. He stood beside his mule while the sheriff and Sydney examined the corpse. A vaquero tried to pull out one of the arrows and Sydney stopped him. She whispered to Saint and he looked up at Duke.

"Could you have someone from the ranch send over a wagon?" Saint asked. "We'd like to transport our friend back to town." When the wagon arrived, the vaqueros lifted Pugh into it and covered his body with a blanket. They had to lay him on his side because of the arrows in front and back. The ends of the shafts poked out from under the cover.

"We'll escort you back to town," Duke said. "Can't take the chance that the Apaches are still nearby."

They made a solemn procession. No one spoke. A few tears trickled down McLendon's face. Even in his sorrow, he was struck by Sydney's expression. She seemed puzzled. He noticed that Joe Saint did too.

When they arrived back in town, Saint told the vaqueros to bring Pugh's blanket-covered body into the jail and lay it on the floor. Word had reached town and there was a crowd of people waiting. Saint asked them to disperse: "There's nothing good to see here."

Mulkins, Rogers, and Mary Somebody lingered, and Saint told them that if they'd wait back at the hotel or the saloon, he'd come talk to them as soon as he could.

"Bob will need a proper funeral service," Rogers said. "Find Preacher Sheridan and ask if he'll hold off prospecting to handle it."

Saint and McLendon joined Sydney inside the jail. She had pulled the blanket off the corpse and was bent over it, using the embedded arrows to tug the body this way and that. Saint squatted beside her. McLendon couldn't bring himself to look at his dead friend. The sheriff noticed his reticence and suggested, "Why don't you join the Major and the mayor while Doc Chau and I study on this?"

"No, I'll stay." McLendon swallowed hard. "What are you looking at?"

"These wounds make no sense," Sydney said. "The arrows, and the slashed throat."

"I don't understand."

"Two of these arrows—the one to the chest and one of them in the back—would have killed Bob," Sydney explained. "So if the Apaches surprised him and shot him with their bows, he would drop dead on the ground."

"I'm sick at the thought of it, but still fail to grasp your meaning."

"Then why cut his throat if he was dead already?" Sydney asked. "Or, if his throat was cut first, why shoot him afterward with arrows?"

"Whoever slit Bob's throat did a masterful job of it," Saint added. "It's a long, clean cut accomplished with a strong arm and razor-sharp blade. Apaches frequently mutilate the bodies of their victims, but why would they shoot their arrows into a dead man? They'd cut him up instead, like they did that prospector Tom Gaumer. They weren't chased away from Bob's body. It was all night and some daylight hours before we found it. Why waste the arrows, if that's what they did?"

"It's the mule that bothers me," McLendon said. "The way it showed up at the corral without Bob."

"Mules have a good sense of direction," Saint said. "Sometimes when they lose their riders they have the sense to return to where they're stabled."

"Well, a while ago when I tried to rent a mule from Bob and ride it back to Florence—this was before the daily stage, of course—Bob said that he wouldn't do it because the Apaches would not only get me, they'd eat the mule too. He said they loved mule meat."

"I believe that's correct."

"So, if Apaches killed Bob, why would they let his mule run off?" McLendon asked. "That and the arrows—*Jesus. I see it.*"

He told the sheriff and Sydney about his visit to MacPherson and the offer he turned down, MacPherson's threats of what would happen if he didn't keep quiet, Ike Clanton's recruitment by MacPherson to serve as a spy in town, and Bob Pugh's subsequent invitation to Culloden Ranch.

"Bob wouldn't sell, so MacPherson had him killed," McLendon said. "The way you say his throat was cut—Angel Misterio did it. He carries that long knife, and we've all seen how quick he can move. Bob didn't stand a chance. Then they shot some arrows in Bob and tossed him someplace where he'd eventually be found."

"That can't be right," Saint said. "The arrows are Apache for sure, with turkey-feather fletching like they use. You're thinking someone at Culloden made Apache arrows?"

McLendon thought for a moment. "Didn't you wonder where the bows and arrows were when they brought in those two dead Apaches?

MacPherson was planning something like this, and he had his people keep them to use later."

"But why pretend it was Apaches?" the sheriff persisted. "If they killed Bob, they could have buried him somewhere out there and no one ever would have found him."

"Keeping the rest of us scared of Apaches is the way MacPherson's been taking control of the town," McLendon said. "That prospector who got killed, well, the vaqueros could have done it and made it out to look like Apaches, just like they did with Bob. All this Apache sign we've been hearing about—only MacPherson's men ever saw any of it. But as a result, we've got guard posts on either end of town with armed Culloden hands in them. When Bossman and Oafie and Preacher came running into town thinking Indians were after them, only Lemmy Duke claimed to have actually seen Apaches. Long as people here believe MacPherson's all we've got between us and an Apache massacre, that makes us beholden to him, more likely to do whatever he wants. And that horn silver Turner found that started all the current commotion, MacPherson had it planted. It's been his plan all along, from the time the town founders first came here and met him. He's let them establish the town, and when he had to, he stepped in to bring attention to it with the salted claim. Because he believes that real silver strikes will happen anytime, he means to have Glorious all to himself."

"That's too much," Sydney protested. "No one could be that terrible."

"Some are," McLendon said. "They take what they want by whatever means necessary. Sheriff, you know it makes sense, don't you?"

"This is all just guesswork," Saint said. "There's not a lick of proof. We can't go accusing someone of murder without any."

"So you're going to let this go?" McLendon demanded. "You're going to allow Bob Pugh to be murdered and not lift a finger?"

Saint didn't immediately react. He sat at his desk and stared out a window cut into the adobe wall. Finally he said, "I'm going to ride back out to Culloden and ask Mr. MacPherson some questions. Doc, while I'm gone, will you and Mr. McLendon assist Mayor Rogers with burial arrangements for Bob? We haven't a cemetery here in town, so something will have to be figured out."

McLendon said, "I'll go back to the ranch with you."

"No, your presence wouldn't be helpful."

"MacPherson may refuse to see you. Misterio wouldn't let us talk to him last night."

"I'm an officer of the law investigating a death. He'll see me."

"Don't pussyfoot. Put him on the spot."

Saint looked at McLendon, not glaring, but regarding him carefully. "Just as you did, agreeing not to inform us of his plans out of concern for your own safety?"

McLendon looked away. "I'll help with Bob's burial."

JOE SAINT rode out toward Culloden on the same livery mule he'd used on the initial search for Bob Pugh. Sydney Chau removed the arrows from Pugh's corpse and washed the body while McLendon sat with Rogers and Mulkins in the Owaysis and discussed where Pugh might be buried.

"One of the prospectors found some wood and is making a casket," the mayor said. "Many of those boys were fond of Bob. He drank with them here in the evenings, and sometimes if they didn't have the coin to spare he let them use a pack mule for free. Just a fine, generous man."

"We can't lay him to rest outside of town," Mulkins said. "If coyotes get a scent of him they'll dig right down. But if we locate him in too close, then we have to worry about all the new construction. We wouldn't want some shop built right over Bob."

They were drinking coffee, not beer or whiskey, and Mary Somebody brought over a pot to replenish their cups. "Put him in the ground right behind here," she suggested. "Between the hotel and the whores' cribs. We won't expand much in that direction because of the creek."

"Bob would like lying near whores and a saloon," Mulkins said, and in spite of their grief everyone smiled, because it was true. McLendon and Rogers dug the grave. Mulkins went back to the hotel to fetch one of his suits so Pugh could be buried in appropriate finery as soon as his coffin was ready.

Around mid-afternoon, the prospector lugged the coffin over to the jail, and Mulkins and Rogers lifted Pugh's blanket-covered body in.

"Last look," the mayor said, and many of Pugh's friends leaned over to peer at his face. Sydney had thoughtfully secured the blanket above the gaping throat wound. McLendon couldn't bring himself to look. The mayor nailed the coffin lid down and suggested that they proceed with the funeral.

"We should wait for the sheriff, who has gone to Culloden Ranch," Preacher Sheridan said. "He would want to be here."

"We can't wait too long," Rogers cautioned. "The heat's effect on the body won't allow it."

Everyone milled in front of the hotel. McLendon was surprised to see that a number of prospectors had broken off their day's explorations to attend. The Owaysis whores were careful to keep a respectful distance between themselves and Gabrielle and Rose Rogers, who stood together in the Elite doorway. Salvatore Tirrito looked uncomfortable in a shirt with a high collar. It was a gloomy gathering. Everyone talked about Bob Pugh and the Apache threat and why it was always the best people who had to die.

In about an hour, just after the mayor suggested for the second time that they had to be getting on with it, Joe Saint rode in. He took in the situation with a glance, tethered his mule in front of the livery, and walked over to join the group.

"What did MacPherson say?" McLendon whispered.

"Later," Saint said. McLendon thought that the sheriff seemed frustrated.

McLendon, Mulkins, Bossman Wright, and Crazy George Mitchell served as pallbearers, lifting the coffin up on their shoulders and following Mayor Rogers to the grave. They rested the casket on the ground while Sheridan officiated in a short ceremony. As Preacher described Bob Pugh's warm heart and sense of humor, a carriage rattled up. Collin MacPherson, dressed in a black mourning coat, jumped down and walked to the graveside. He was escorted by Angel Misterio and Lemmy Duke. There was some muttering among the crowd; no one had ever seen MacPherson in town before. McLendon couldn't help glowering at him. MacPherson stood silently, holding his hat respectfully over his heart.

"We must keep in mind that each day is a gift," Preacher said. "As we commit our friend Bob Pugh to the Almighty, we also commit to honoring his memory by building this town to the heights it deserves." He nodded at the pallbearers, who lowered the casket into the grave.

"And now let's sing," Preacher instructed. Dinges, the prospector who'd led the band at the Owaysis dance, said, "'Rock of Ages.'" He lifted his fiddle and began to play while Sheridan called out the words. They sang "Nearer My God to Thee" next. When the song was over, Crazy George shouted, "In honor and memory of Bob

Pugh, one free beer for all," and the crowd trooped into the Owaysis. MacPherson shook hands with the mayor, climbed back into the carriage, and rattled off back to Culloden. Joe Saint walked back to the jail. McLendon and Mulkins stayed behind to shovel dirt over Pugh's coffin, and after that they piled small rocks high atop the grave.

"I'll fashion a cross tomorrow and commission a proper headstone in Florence," Mulkins said. "Now let's show proper respect to Bob in the way he'd most prefer: by drinking beer."

"I'll be along in a bit," McLendon said, and went to the jail. Saint was sitting there behind his desk, polishing his glasses on his shirtsleeve.

"I expected you'd be coming," he said.

"Did you see MacPherson? What did he say?"

Saint gestured at a chair. "Sit down. Yes, we talked. In terms of any confession, it was less than satisfactory."

"How do you mean?"

"It went like this. I got there and asked to see him. Somebody called over Angel Misterio and he told me to wait, he'd check with the *jefe*. I stood out in the courtyard for a while and then Misterio said to come in. It's an impressive house."

"I know," McLendon said impatiently. "I've seen the inside myself. What did MacPherson do when you asked about Bob?"

Saint's lips compressed in a grimace. "He told me that he'd heard Bob might be interested in selling the livery, so he asked him to the ranch to learn what price Bob might be asking. He said they had a good long talk, 'satisfactory' is how he termed it, and then Bob said he had to be getting back. Mr. MacPherson offered to have a vaquero or two escort him on account of Apaches, but Bob was real insistent on returning by himself. He said he felt bad when he heard what happened—that he wished he'd insisted Bob let a couple of his men take him back to town. He says that, in a way, he feels responsible."

"He ought to, because he is. Tell me that you didn't let him off that easy."

"No, I didn't. I repeated the story that you told me, about Mr. MacPherson planning to take over the town and asking your help— then, when you said no, threatening your life if you told anyone."

"And he denied it?"

The sheriff picked up a canteen by the side of his desk. He pulled two pewter cups out of a drawer, filled them with water, and pushed one across to McLendon. "He said that you were twisting his words, trying to make him look bad. You seemed like someone with some smarts, so he offered you a job and you turned it down. He said that he didn't think offering a man employment was against the law."

"What about him wanting to take over all the businesses in town, driving the founders out?"

"I asked, and he didn't exactly deny it. He said that was the way successful men did business, trying to acquire companies and property with potential. He made his fortune through such deals. Sure, he wanted you to provide him with inside information, and when you wouldn't, he turned to Ike Clanton. Mr. MacPherson said that's the way business works. He claims he told you that he would offer fair prices to everyone. True?"

"It is, but did he neglect telling you what he said he'd do if his offers weren't accepted?"

Saint sighed. "That part he denies. He says he doesn't know why you hold a grudge against him, but you clearly do. According to him, all he's ever tried to do was be a good neighbor to everyone in Glorious, spending a good deal of his own money on the town's protection.

He suggested that I should investigate your background. He feels that a deliberately deceptive man like you must have dark secrets in his past that are likely of a criminal nature."

McLendon tried not to flinch. He sipped some water to conceal his discomfort. "So you're leaving it at that?"

"What else can I do? All I've got is some suspicions and his word against yours."

McLendon set down his cup. "But what do you *think*?"

"I think that Collin MacPherson is an evil man, and people have died by his order. But he's been too clever and we'll never prove it. Now it's necessary to protect those who are left."

McLendon said skeptically, "And how do you propose to do that? You against MacPherson and Misterio and the rest? You're a school-teacher, not a gunman, and you recoil from violence besides."

"I'm the sheriff, and so I accept the responsibility. You, on the other hand, have none. You've shared with me what you know, so you should feel free to board the stage tomorrow and save yourself from whatever MacPherson intends next. This is our trouble and none of yours."

McLendon thought of Gabrielle and his Glorious friends and, most of all, Bob Pugh. "It's my trouble too. No, don't shake your head. Just tell me what you intend to do."

Saint drank some water and set his cup on the desk. "The others—George and Mary, Major Mulkins, Mayor Rogers and Rose, the Tirritos—deserve to know the situation as we see it. I'll summon them to a meeting tonight."

"MacPherson has eyes everywhere, Ike Clanton chief among them," McLendon said. "Word of any such meeting would surely reach MacPherson and might incite him to immediate action."

"You're correct. I'll be discreet. I'll set the meeting time late, and in a place that should escape notice. Not the saloon or the hotel. I think the living quarters in the dry goods shop. There's sufficient room for us there."

As you well know, McLendon thought bitterly. He reminded himself that any jealousy he felt toward Saint was insignificant compared to the current threat posed by Collin MacPherson.

"I'll attend to chores at the livery, then," he said. "The mules should be fed and stabled, and there are Bob's things to get together. I don't know if he has any family to send them to. I'll look through what there is and see what I can find. What time will we meet at the Tirritos' store?"

"Eleven should suffice. That's late enough that most of the prospectors will be in their tents." Saint paused, then said grudgingly, "It's good of you to stay."

McLendon shrugged and left for the livery.

AFTER THE MULES were fed and in their stalls, McLendon went into the livery office that doubled as living quarters. When he had shared the place with Bob Pugh he always felt cramped. Now the room seemed too large.

Though he wasn't hungry, McLendon thought he ought to have supper. With the late meeting in the dry goods store, it would be a long night, and he hadn't slept at all during the previous one. There was kindling for the woodstove if he wanted a hot meal, but lighting a fire and cooking seemed like too much trouble. He had peaches instead, stuffing the fruit in his mouth with his fingers and drinking the juice from the can. That took only a few minutes. Then McLendon opened Pugh's trunk and began looking through his personal effects. There wasn't much, just some clothes and two belts, one of them fancy, and a battered book about sailboats. McLendon wondered why Bob had it—he'd never mentioned living near a lake or the ocean, let alone an interest in sailing. Then, near the bottom of the chest, tucked underneath a flannel shirt, McLendon found a photograph of a young woman. It was a formal studio portrait; she posed sitting on a chair, resting a parasol on her shoulder. She was very pretty. Written on the back of the photograph in a flowing, feminine hand, was "All of my love forever, Sophie." McLendon tried to imagine Sophie with a younger Bob Pugh and couldn't because it made his heart hurt too much. What had happened to keep them apart?

Nowhere in the chest or the office was a letter or anything else from Pugh's family that included an address. McLendon felt at a loss about what to do with his friend's things. Perhaps the clothes could be given to prospectors clearly down on their luck. But what about the photograph of the girl named Sophie? She'd clearly meant a great deal to Bob, because he'd kept the picture. McLendon didn't want to keep it himself; that felt somehow like an invasion of Bob's privacy. But he didn't want to throw it away, either. He put it in his pocket, then sat on the bed and thought about what he should do.

McLendon's reverie was interrupted by someone pulling open the door. Ike Clanton barged in, lugging blankets and some pans.

"What do you want, Ike?" McLendon asked sharply. "What have you got there?"

Ike dropped his armload on the floor. The pans clanged together. "It's my gear. I'm moving in here."

"Why would you be doing that?"

"Just prior to his unfortunate demise, Bob Pugh sold this livery to Mr. MacPherson, who's been kind enough to ask me to take over and run it. So I'm living here now and you need to leave. I want to arrange my new quarters and then get some sleep. The prospectors will be wanting to rent mules early tomorrow morning."

McLendon shook his head. "That can't be true. Bob told me before he left to meet with Mr. MacPherson that he had no intention of selling."

"I guess he changed his mind. Get up off the bed. I want to see if the blanket on it's thicker than mine. If it is, that's the one I'll use."

"Leave the blanket alone and get out. Bob never sold this place and we both know it."

Ike reached in his pocket and pulled out a folded paper. "Not according to this."

McLendon snatched the paper from Ike's hand and read it. Written at the top in dark ink was BILL OF SALE and then came a short description of transactional details. For the sum of $7,500, in the form of a draft to be drawn from a company in Tucson, Bob Pugh sold Pugh Livery and all its property and contents to Collin MacPherson, possession by new owner to take place immediately. The document was signed by Pugh and MacPherson and witnessed by Lemmy Duke and Ike Clanton.

McLendon was stunned. "There's something wrong with this. Bob would never sell. He said so."

"Ain't that his signature there?"

"I'm sure it's not. It's a forgery."

Ike looked stern. "That's a harsh accusation, and might bring down trouble upon the one making it. Mr. MacPherson, Lemmy Duke, and myself, all good men and true, were present when ol' Bob signed the paper. It'll hold up in any court. Your friend being dead at the hands of the Apaches and all, Mr. MacPherson stands ready to send the money to Bob's relations if someone knows how to contact them. It's a very fair price. Bob did right by himself when he made the deal."

"When MacPherson talked to the sheriff today, he never mentioned this."

"Did he not? It must have slipped his mind on account of his grief concerning Bob's passing. That's understandable. But now you've seen the bill of sale, and it's time you were on your way. Pack up all of your things, but be careful not to include any of Bob's. As I read that agreement, Mr. MacPherson now owns everything of Bob's on this property, up to and including the bed, the cookstove, and that chest I see there, including all of its contents. You won't object if I watch you closely while you pack, I hope. There are so many who would take advantage of this unfortunate situation."

McLendon felt as though a tight band were constricting around his skull. "You won't get away with this, Ike."

"Get away with what? I'm merely taking possession of my employer's property. Now get to packing up."

McLendon began jamming clothes in his valise. As he did, there was the sound of hammering outside.

Ike grinned. "That'll be some of the ranch hands at work. Got your bag packed? Then I'll just escort you from the premises."

They went outside and McLendon saw two Culloden hands working by torchlight. One held a large sign in place while the other attached it with nails to the top of the building's wooden doorframe: MACPHERSON LIVERY. "The boss had that one prepared in advance of his negotiation with Bob," Ike said, chuckling. "Mr. MacPherson likes to think ahead. As I understand it, he's got some more signs already made up for other places here in town."

"God-d-d-damn you, Ike," McLendon snarled, so agitated that he stammered. "You're taking pleasure in this, you sick bastard."

"Just doing my job," Ike said pleasantly. "Nothing personal in it. Say, I hope you don't have to sleep in the street tonight. I hear the hotel's absolutely full up. And Mr. MacPherson asked me to pass along a message to you. He says he knows that you've told all you have to tell, and you see it makes no difference. Out of generosity, he's willing to pay your stage fare out of town anywhere you want to go, so long as you leave right away. The offer's withdrawn if you stick around. So, simply put, if you go, Mr. MacPherson pays. Stay, and you'll pay. You'll certainly pay."

"Fuck you, Ike."

Ike dropped his genial pose. "I'm not the one who's fucked, McLendon. I personally hope you're foolish enough to stay. I'll enjoy seeing what happens to you then, maybe even be part of it. Now, get away from Mr. MacPherson's livery."

SEVENTEEN

Fuming and more than a little shaken, McLendon trudged away from the livery, carrying his valise. His immediate concern was where he would sleep that night. He walked toward the hotel. As he passed the Owaysis, he saw that most of the customers were leaving. There was enough light from the kerosene lamps inside for him to check his pocket watch: the time was just after ten. Then, looking through Major Mulkins's prized glass window into the lobby of the Elite, he saw that the place was jammed with men curled up on the floor. Sleeping space was at a premium in Glorious. Maybe he would have to spend the night on the ground. There were still some campfires flickering among the prospectors' tents. Perhaps he could sleep there. Preacher Sheridan would probably be willing to share his tent. For the time being, he leaned against the wall of the Chinese laundry and thought about the ways Collin MacPherson might find to kill him if he remained in Glorious.

When he felt enough time had passed, McLendon walked to the dry goods store. The town was dark. A coyote howled somewhere out in the valley. McLendon stumbled over a rock and nearly dropped his valise. He regained his balance and tapped on the shop door.

Gabrielle opened the door and whispered, "Come in." It was dark in the store and he bumped into the counter. "We've got candles in the back room," Gabrielle said, and held aside a blanket in the doorway separating the shop from the living quarters. There was enough light there to see Mulkins, Crazy George, Mayor Rogers, and Salvatore Tirrito sitting in chairs by a table. Mary Somebody sat on the edge of a bed. Gabrielle pulled out another chair and gestured for McLendon to sit down. Then she joined Mary on the bed.

"Joe should be here any moment," Gabrielle said.

McLendon blinked as his eyes adjusted to the dim light. "All right," he said. "Something's just happened."

"Let's wait for Joe," Gabrielle said. "We don't want you having to say everything twice." Everyone sat silently until there was soft knocking on the front door and Gabrielle let in the sheriff.

Saint stood by the table rather than sitting down. "We needed everyone together because Cash McLendon and I need to tell you what we believe is happening. I realize that they're only suspicions, but they're well grounded in fact. When you hear what we have to say, I think you'll agree."

"Can you get on with it, Sheriff?" Rogers asked. "What with Bob Pugh's death and burial, we've all had a terrible day, and I dislike leaving Rosie alone. She's prone to bad imagining and nightmares."

"I believe that we've got our own real-life nightmare, Charlie," Saint said. "As McLendon and I see things, here's the way of it. I'm going to let him speak first."

McLendon told about his belief that Turner had discovered a salted claim, his meeting with Collin MacPherson and MacPherson's frank description of his intentions, and how, when Bob Pugh left for his own visit to Culloden, he swore that he had no intention of selling his livery. Saint explained how he and Doc Chau were puzzled by Pugh's wounds, and that the two dead Apaches brought into town earlier by Culloden vaqueros were missing the bows and arrows that they should have had.

"As McLendon pointed out to me, it's certainly possible that MacPherson's men tried to make it appear that not only was Bob killed by Apaches, but Tommy Gaumer also," Saint said. "There's a pattern to it."

McLendon recounted Ike Clanton's appearance at the livery and the bill of sale that Ike claimed proved Pugh had sold the livery to MacPherson prior to his death. When he described the new sign nailed up over the livery door by Culloden ranch hands, Mulkins cursed under his breath.

"Taken together, all this indicates that Collin MacPherson intends to take your businesses whether you wish to sell to him or not," Saint said. "He's killed to get to this point and will kill again if anyone doesn't let him have his way. By my count, because of his greed, at least four people are dead, maybe five."

Mayor Rogers cleared his throat. "Come now, four? Who are they?"

"Tommy Gaumer, Bob Pugh, and the two Apaches. Possibly a fifth—that vaquero killed in what Lemmy Duke claimed was an Apache attack."

"Then really only two. Apaches don't count, nor a Mexican. And besides, Joe, you admit that this is just something you think and not anything that you can prove. Up to now we've all had ample cause to feel grateful to Mr. MacPherson. He's protected our town—you can't deny that."

"We don't know that he actually protected us. He wanted us to believe that he did."

"Everyone knows that there are Apaches all through this region. Are you telling me that there aren't?"

"Yes, there are Apaches," Saint said. "No one knows how many. But MacPherson has used that fact as the basis for his plan to trick us."

"That's your opinion, Sheriff."

"Yes."

McLendon said, "It's my opinion too. I've worked for a rich man like Collin MacPherson. They think that because they have wealth and power, whatever they do is all right, no matter who else suffers in the process."

"It's true," said Gabrielle. "I can personally attest Mr. McLendon knows all about that."

"He wants the hotel, and the Owaysis, and the dry goods store and the farrier shop," McLendon said. "He'll do whatever he must to get them."

"Come now, it may not be as dramatic as that," Rogers said. "You make it sound as if we don't sell, then he'll murder us."

"He murdered Bob Pugh," Mulkins said. "The son of a bitch killed our friend. I believe the sheriff and C.M."

"Same here," Crazy George said, and Salvatore Tirrito grunted in what seemed to be agreement, although McLendon guessed that, because of his very limited English, Gabrielle's father hadn't been able to completely follow the conversation.

Mary Somebody waved her hand for attention. "All right, let's get down to it: What do we do now? I'll tell you this, George and me ain't selling the saloon. We've worked too long and hard. We dreamed of a successful place of our own and no rich man's scaring us into giving it up. If he wants to try to kill us, let him come on. We've been in fights before."

"Same goes for me, Mary," Mulkins said. "I've got the hotel I always wanted, and it's going to have glass windows in every room."

"Let's not forget the Chinese," Gabrielle cautioned. "Are Sydney and her people also in danger from Mr. MacPherson?"

"Sydney is aware of the threat," McLendon said. "Though I doubt MacPherson is concerned with the river camp and laundry now, eventually they'll come to his attention. For now they should be safe."

"What about you and Salvatore, Gabrielle?" Saint asked. "Would you consider selling out to Mr. MacPherson?"

Gabrielle spoke to her father in Italian. He replied vigorously and at length, shaking his finger for emphasis.

"Papa says that we're here, this is our home now, and no rich bastard is going to take it away from us," Gabrielle said. "He made some references to past incidents in St. Louis that I won't repeat. But the gist is that, no, we're not selling."

"But what do *you* think?" Saint asked.

Gabrielle smiled at him. "This is where my heart is now."

"Well," Saint said, smiling back, "I'm gratified to hear it."

"I feel obligated to mention something," McLendon said. "Odd as it seems, men like Collin MacPherson believe themselves to be observing a code of honor. Prior to engaging in dubious acts to gain what they want, they make arguably fair financial offers—even, sometimes, generous ones. This allows them to feel that they've been reasonable and, if the offers are refused, then it is the other parties who are being unreasonable. Your lives are in jeopardy here. Each of you still has the option of calling on MacPherson and asking his terms for your business. There's no doubt he'll offer substantial sums, enough for any of you to leave Glorious and set up nicely somewhere else."

Gabrielle said, "And that's your recommendation? What a surprise."

"I'm not recommending it. But it's an option to be considered."

"You might consider it," Gabrielle said. "We won't." She turned to Joe Saint. "What's to be done next?"

Saint lifted his glasses off the bridge of his nose and rubbed his eyes. "The immediate thing, I think, is to stay together or in sight of each other as much as we can. Bob Pugh went out to Culloden alone. Here in town, at least, there are always some prospectors about, the people from the mining company—enough potential witnesses to prevent MacPherson from arranging Indian attacks or accidents involving us. Perhaps that will be enough to discourage him."

McLendon felt certain that MacPherson couldn't be discouraged, but he knew there was nothing further to be accomplished that night. At least everyone had been warned.

"It's very late," he said. "Let's all sleep on this."

"Speaking of sleep, now that Ike's evicted you from the livery, where will you bed down?" Mary Somebody asked. "We've got the floor of the saloon if you don't mind some spit and spilled beer. We mop up in the mornings, not after we close for the night."

"I could try to find someplace in the hotel, C.M.," Mulkins offered. "Problem is, every inch is spoken for and everyone's asleep by now."

"Maybe I can find a place out among the prospectors in their tents," McLendon said. "Or I might sneak back into the livery stalls with the mules. Ike's not likely to be standing watch."

Gabrielle whispered something to her father, who snarled an angry reply. She whispered again. Salvatore Tirrito, clearly unhappy, shrugged and glowered at McLendon.

"You can stay in the store for a few nights," Gabrielle said. "Not back here with Papa and me, of course, but I'll get you some blankets and you can sleep under the counter. It won't be perfect, but at least it will be clean and dry."

"I couldn't," McLendon said, thinking that of course he could. By far, it was preferable to sleeping on the slimy floor of the saloon or sharing a prospector's tent. "Well, if you really don't mind . . ."

"No," Joe Saint said. "That won't do."

McLendon said, "I promise that nothing—" He was interrupted by Gabrielle, who said sharply to Saint, "It's not your decision."

Saint said, "But I have a better idea. McLendon can stay with me at the jail. If the cells are occupied, we'll sleep on the floor. But tonight, at least, there are no prisoners, so there's a bed available. All right?"

"I suppose," McLendon said. "Thank you, Joe."

Everyone stood up and pushed past the blanket into the dark outer room of the store.

"You go on ahead," Saint said to McLendon. "There's a basin by my desk if you want to wash up. I'm just going to take a moment with Gabrielle."

McLendon, valise in hand, trudged away. As he did, he heard Gabrielle ask Saint incredulously, "Are you his *friend* now?" and the beginning of what seemed to be a protracted denial by the sheriff. Saint didn't return to the jail for almost an hour, and when he did, McLendon pretended to be asleep on the bed in one of the cells.

EIGHTEEN

Except for running the livery, Ike Clanton acted as though nothing had changed. If anything, he was friendlier than ever. At the Owaysis, Ike made an evening habit of buying a round of drinks for the house, which he could afford, since he'd raised the price of daily mule rentals from four to six dollars. Ike was respectful to the whores, and he paid particular attention to Girl, chatting with her pleasantly and frequently causing her to dissolve into fits of giggles with his silly jokes.

"I keep expecting Ike'll attempt some unpaid indecency with her, but as yet he's done nothing untoward," Mary Somebody confided to McLendon as they watched Ike and Girl huddled in a corner of the saloon. "She's such a shy thing, and he brings her out of herself. If I didn't know he was a scoundrel, I'd consider his attention to her a blessing."

"The ones like Ike never act without purpose," McLendon cautioned. "I doubt it's sex, since if that was the basis of his interest in

JEFF GUINN

her he could pay and have it. But he has something in mind. Don't allow Girl to become too attached."

"I'll do my best, but it will be hard. Sense is generally beyond her. Me and George found her living in a Tucson alley, just a young slip of a thing foraging in garbage and mostly starving for want of it because the dogs beat her to the edibles. How she came there, who her people were, we never have found out. Once we fed her, she followed us like a stray kitten. So we cleaned her up and took her with us. There are those who'd say we're taking advantage of the simpleminded in turning her out, but at least she's clean and cared for. If we'd left her in that alley, she'd have starved or been raped and left for dead. George and me have been good to her."

"No need to defend yourself," McLendon said. "Just keep her away from Ike as best you can. Meanwhile, it's getting late. If you announce last call, I'll help you distribute the drinks."

With nothing else to do after being evicted from the livery, McLendon filled the time by assisting his friends. In the morning he had breakfast at the Elite with Major Mulkins, then helped him and Mrs. Mendoza, the maid, clean the hotel. Charlie Rogers had more blacksmith's work than he could handle, and although McLendon had no skills in that regard, he could still write up job orders and help the mayor collect payment for completed work. In the evenings he pitched in at the Owaysis, serving drinks and washing glasses and reminding patrons to patiently wait for their turns with the whores. When Joe Saint had prisoners in the jail, McLendon watched them while the sheriff made his rounds. The only place where he didn't lend a hand was at the dry goods store. It was obvious to him that Saint wouldn't approve, and McLendon couldn't risk alienating his host. Sleeping in the jail was the best alternative he had, though it was seldom restful: most nights both cells were occupied by noisy drunks. Then Saint and McLendon had to roll up in their blankets on the floor and hope that the prisoners would eventually quiet down.

Despite the tension between them, the two men found themselves getting along reasonably well. One night when things had been relatively quiet and the sheriff was able to enjoy several beers at the Owaysis before they retired to the jail, Saint even talked a little about his life before Glorious. Lying on the cot in one cell and talking across to McLendon lying down in the other, Saint said that he'd grown up in Pennsylvania. From childhood he'd loved books and arithmetic. It was natural to become a schoolteacher: "I loved helping children, seeing their faces light up when they learned something new. There's just nothing else like it in the world."

McLendon had consumed enough beer himself to disregard frontier custom regarding questions about someone's past. "If you were so happy, how did you end up here?"

Saint didn't answer right away. Just when McLendon thought the sheriff might have fallen asleep, he said, "I married a girl. We had a daughter and lived just outside Philadelphia. She and the baby caught the bloody flux and died. I couldn't stay there after that."

"Oh," was all McLendon could say.

He drifted to Ohio first, Saint said, and then to Indiana and down to Tennessee and Georgia. Whenever he'd stop somewhere and try to settle in, the memory of his family overwhelmed him and he had to move on. He had heard a lot of talk about the western frontier and how you could lose yourself in it, and he wanted that to happen. He asked around, wanting to know where it was still wildest, and Arizona Territory sounded just right. He came there with no expectations,

no hopes beyond a bone-deep longing to get so far away from anything familiar that the pain of losing his family would be forced from
his soul.

"I was in Maricopa Wells, thinking of taking the stage to Arizona
City. My money was about to run out. I figured I'd find some temporary job. Charlie Rogers was in Maricopa Wells buying some tools.
We crossed paths and he told me about this town he and a few others
were founding out in the middle of nowhere. He asked: Did I want to
come take a look? Maybe I'd want to stay. So we came out here,
though I never thought I'd remain more than a week or two. And
then there she was."

"Gabrielle," McLendon prompted, not wanting to say the name
but unable to resist.

"Gabrielle. When I was with her, my heart started aching in a different way. She'd been hurting too. And we helped each other heal.
They wanted a sheriff here and I agreed to serve. Everything was
fine—"

"Until I came."

"—until you came." Saint was silent for a moment. "You're such a
selfish bastard, McLendon. You spurned her in the worst way possible. Why couldn't you have the decency to leave her alone afterward?"

It was dark in the jail, but McLendon could see the cracked,
cobwebby ceiling of the cell by the moonlight shining through the
barred window. He'd have to find a broom and brush off the cobwebs in the morning. "I don't know. I suppose I didn't think, or at
least think of others. I'm trying to do better now."

"You still have intentions toward Gabrielle." It was a statement,
not a question.

"I don't. I mean, I don't know that, either. Right now I'm mostly thinking about MacPherson. That takes precedence. You're the sheriff. We've got to work together on this. You could make me your deputy."

"There's only the one badge."

McLendon lay pondering the ways that his life had changed. A wife had died, he was on the run, he was in a tiny primitive frontier town instead of a modern city. He'd probably lost Gabrielle to a scrawny, bespectacled schoolteacher turned sheriff. Then he realized that he hadn't thought about his life in St. Louis for days. Those regrets and fears had been superseded by the current crisis, which, except for the setting and the death of Ellen, was virtually identical to the previous one. A rich man was using any means necessary to impose his unwelcome will on decent, hardworking people. Collin MacPherson was Rupert Douglass. Angel Misterio was Killer Boots. It made McLendon sick to realize that, in St. Louis, he had in many ways been the equivalent of Ike Clanton in Glorious.

After a while McLendon slept. When he woke in the morning, Saint was already up and gone. Later he told McLendon that he'd enjoyed an early breakfast with the Tirritos.

LESS THAN A WEEK after Bob Pugh's death, there was a second significant silver strike outside of town. Boze Bell and Johnny Boggs, two veteran prospecting partners, staked a claim about three miles northeast of town near a curve in Queen Creek. Unlike Turner, who'd been eager to sell out to mining company interests right away, Bell and Boggs took their time. They distributed samples to the assayers of Sears and Sons and the other three mining companies that had set up offices in the Elite Hotel. The samples were black-lined float rather than soft horn silver, but they indicated a rich deposit just the same. All four companies made immediate offers—rumor pegged them in the range of $50,000. Bell and Boggs coolly said they'd think about it and perhaps take additional samples all the way to San Francisco or Philadelphia to see if other mining concerns might care to bid higher.

"They're wise ones," Mulkins said to McLendon over morning coffee in the hotel dining room. It wasn't yet eight, but everyone else had already breakfasted and headed out into the mountains. The latest strike had left the rest of the prospectors more frantic to find a fortune in silver for themselves. Even Ike Clanton had brought in two Culloden vaqueros to run the livery while he joined his father and brother Phin out in the Pinals, searching for signs of ore. "Boze and Johnny'll goose up their offers considerably. I predict they'll top Turner's eighty thousand before all's said and done."

"At least this one seems legitimate," McLendon said. "There were no Culloden hands anywhere around—nothing suspicious at all."

Mulkins drained his coffee cup and poured himself more. "Sad thing is, this find came right where the Apaches caught and butchered poor Tom Gaumer. I know, you think it wasn't Indians. But whoever it was, they prevented Tommy from making the fortune he wanted so bad. All that's sure to be forgotten. I wish to hell I had a third story on my hotel, maybe even a fourth. This town's in for another rush of newcomers. It'll take a few weeks for word of this latest strike to spread, maybe another month, since the samples have been evaluated here but not in Florence or Tucson. But the next rush is coming."

McLendon stared gloomily out of the window. "What's coming is more from MacPherson. He knows what this latest news means. More than ever, he'll want to own this town."

"I suppose, and there seems to be little we can do about it. Say,

here are Charlie and Mr. Jesse from Sears and Sons. Gentlemen—
will you join us for coffee?"

"No time for coffee," the mayor said. "Mr. Jesse has exciting news."

"Has your company purchased the claim from Boze Bell and
Johnny Boggs?" Mulkins asked.

"No, though I predict we eventually will," Jesse said. He was a
small, wide-shouldered man with a craggy face. "Any sensible prospectors would do business with us. We pay fair prices, which is more
than can be said for those of some competitors. In any event, the
bosses back in San Francisco have decided we're to begin excavat-
ing the Turner claim next Tuesday. Just blasting to get under the surface rock, of course, but that will soon be followed by tunneling.
We're bringing in a contingent of expert Cornish miners, perhaps
fifty in all."

"Pay them each four dollars a day is what they do," Rogers said.
"All fifty of 'em will spend a good deal of that on housing and meals
and entertainment right here in Glorious. And after the miners will
come engineers to build wood supports in the tunnels, and all manner of other workers to extract the silver from the rock and so forth.
Call in that building crew, Major, and get the second floor of this
hotel finished pronto. You're going to need every room."

"With pleasure, Charlie," Mulkins said. "I'll do that and send in
an order for glass windows on the Florence stage today. I'll have that
second floor available in two weeks, and maybe a third floor besides."

Jesse cleared his throat. "Perhaps I'll have some of that coffee
after all, Major Mulkins. And now we come to the news that immediately concerns you. It seems you'll need to have your finest current
room clean and ready on Tuesday for a very distinguished guest."

"One of the big bosses from your San Francisco headquarters?"
Mulkins asked.

"An even bigger boss than that." Jesse took a slow, theatrical sip of coffee. "Major, in four days' time you'll host the territorial governor. The Honorable A. P. K. Safford has consented to come to Glorious and see this exciting new town and Sears and Sons excavation site for himself."

"It's such a blessing," Mayor Rogers enthused. "The governor is a considerable force in the business world, and should he feel impressed by our community, he's certain to recommend it to all the right people. Major, C.M., we must go all out for his visit. It's a tremendous opportunity. Every effort should be made to ensure that Governor Safford sees us at our best."

"Well, I'll leave you gentlemen to it," Jesse said genially. "I believe I'll hunt those rascals Bell and Boggs, see if they might not want to come to an agreement we can announce during the governor's visit."

When the mining company manager was gone, McLendon said, "You're right, Charlie. This is the opportunity we've needed."

"To impress the governor with our town?"

"No, to tell him about MacPherson, what he's trying to do. As mayor, you can take Safford aside and share our concerns, ask him to send in some lawmen to discourage Misterio and the vaqueros."

Rogers made a fluttering motion with his hand. "Don't you see, C.M., that there's no longer anything to worry about regarding MacPherson? The governor's coming and he'll see how we're all established here. MacPherson may think himself a mighty man, but if we make the governor our friend, well, what can MacPherson do to us then? Governor Safford's said to be a canny investor himself. Why, hell, maybe we can interest him in partnering up in one or more of our businesses, like the Elite or the Owaysis or even my farrier shop. He may well see the advantage of getting in on the ground floor, so to speak, before the next wave of people arrives and the next strike hits."

"Instead of warning the governor about MacPherson, you want to ask him to go shares in your business?"

"Don't sound so disgusted, C.M. I'm just trying to take advantage of a rare opportunity."

McLendon reminded himself to set, rather than slam, his coffee cup down on the table. "It's up to you, Charlie, but I'm going to talk to the governor about MacPherson."

The mayor fixed McLendon with a hard stare. "C.M., be careful about bothering the governor with such notions when we're trying to give him a good impression of our town and its prospects. Bob Pugh's death was unfortunate, but as you and the sheriff have both admitted, we've no proof it was MacPherson's men and not the Apaches. The more I think about it, the more unlikely your suspicions seem. Don't you agree, Major?"

Mulkins looked uncomfortable. "There's merit in what both of you say. Why don't we just set up as best we can for the governor's visit and see what transpires? Four days isn't long to prepare. We'll need bunting to drape over the doors and on the fences. I'll want some new pillows and sheets—best take myself to Florence on today's stage to select the finest. C.M., will you take care of the hotel in my absence? Mr. Jesse has my best room—will you ask him if he'll double up with one of his employees so we can have it for the governor? The floors will need to be thoroughly scrubbed. Mr. Jesse does dribble more than his share of tobacco juice. There's just so much to do. . . ."

McLendon, disgusted, stalked back to the jail and told Saint about the governor's pending visit and the unexpected reactions of the mayor and Mulkins to the news. "I guess I can understand Mayor Rogers going all goggle-eyed—at heart he's mostly an opportunist. But the Major? I thought he had more sense."

"Try to understand," Saint said. "Mulkins and the mayor want so badly to make successes of themselves. For them, the chance to cozy up to the governor might well be their equivalent of a big silver strike. He's about as likely to go partners with them as he is to believe what we have to say about MacPherson. What will we tell him? That Culloden vaqueros are pretending to be Apaches, and slaughter people so their boss can take over all the businesses in town? Do you really think Governor Safford is going to believe that?"

"I have some ability in the way of persuasion."

"Yes, so I understand. I agree that we should try. At some point you can share our suspicions with the governor. As for me, Hunky-Dory Holmes is likely to be in the governor's traveling party, and I'll bring up MacPherson to him. They'll likely laugh us off, but the attempt must be made. For now, go see the Major off on the stage to Florence. Wish him a successful journey. It doesn't hurt you any to let him feel hopeful."

THE NEXT MORNING, when McLendon walked Mulkins to the Florence stage in front of the renamed MacPherson Livery, they saw another passenger. Ella, a cloth carryall in hand, stood by the carriage.

"Treating yourself to a day or two of recreation in Florence, Miss Ella?" Mulkins asked. "You're a young lady who's certainly earned herself some time off, no disrespect intended."

"I'm leaving for good," Ella said. "As it happens, I've secured my passage home to England." Though she was answering the hotel owner, Ella looked past him at McLendon, who thought she seemed distressed for someone who had achieved a long-sought goal.

Mulkins didn't notice. "George and Mary never mentioned this."

Still looking at McLendon, Ella said, "I only informed them this morning. I have no liking for extended farewells."

McLendon said, "I wish you well, Ella. It was a pleasure to know you, and I hope that you have a happy life."

She seemed suddenly on the verge of tears. "Thank you. I wish you the same."

Mulkins gallantly helped Ella up into the stage carriage. McLendon swung the door shut behind them. The driver cracked his whip over the heads of the mule team and the stage lurched forward. Mulkins leaned out the window to wave; McLendon saw that Ella, sitting opposite him, had her face buried in her hands. *She's sorry to leave,* he thought. *Maybe she cared about me more than I knew.*

Later, in the Owaysis, McLendon asked Mary Somebody why Girl was acting so mopey.

"She's distraught over Ella's departure," Mary said. "I myself find it inconvenient. A little notice so that we could have brought in a replacement would have been appreciated."

McLendon swallowed some beer. Over the months in Glorious, he'd come to savor the warm, bitter brew. "Weren't you aware that she would leave just as soon as she had enough money saved for passage back to England?"

"That's the thing of it—she hadn't. I held the money for her, and the total was just under three hundred dollars, which would get her to New York but not across the Atlantic, unless she's a prodigious swimmer."

"Wait," McLendon said. "I met her as she was about to board the stage, and she said that she had the money she needed to get home."

Mary shook her head. "She's got her pride, don't she?"

"So why did she leave before she had enough money? Wasn't her purpose in whoring to secure the necessary finances for returning home?"

"Oh, it's something I doubt a man can understand," Mary said.

"For whores with any spark of spirit remaining, there arrives a time when you just can't keep on spreading your legs on demand. It comes sooner to some than to others. I expect that as much as she longed for England, Ella couldn't make herself do it anymore. God bless and good luck to her, wherever she may go."

"Amen to that," McLendon said, and raised his glass in a toast.

WHEN MAJOR MULKINS returned Monday on the Florence stage, he brought an update on the governor's visit. Safford would arrive in Glorious the next day by buckboard, accompanied by an honor guard led by Deputy U.S. Marshal Hunky-Dory Holmes. The party would come in tandem with the daily stage, which would leave for Glorious several hours earlier than usual. Upon arrival, the governor hoped to meet leading town citizens and also visit the Sears and Sons excavation site. He would stay overnight and return to Tucson the next day.

"It's the talk of Florence," Mulkins reported. "I believe a good many residents there are considering a move out here to Glorious. There's no limit to what we may achieve. Given a few years, we might very well replace Tucson as the territorial capital."

Much of Monday was spent preparing the town for the governor's arrival. Mulkins brought back several bolts of red, white, and blue bunting. Gabrielle and Rose Rogers took charge of draping the decorations over doorways and windowsills and even hitching posts. The usual strong winds cooperated by dwindling to gentle though still dusty zephyrs. All feral cats were gathered and set loose in the Elite, lest a stray rat remain to spoil the governor's sleep in Mulkins's best room, which was amiably vacated by Mr. Jesse. Mulkins remade the

bed with smooth new sheets; he claimed that they cost him three dollars in a Florence general store. After the governor left town, Mulkins
mused, he might cut the sheets into small squares and sell the squares
for two bits apiece to those desiring souvenirs of the historic visit.

At the Owaysis, Mary Somebody counseled Sally and Abigail, the
remaining whores, on proper conduct in the governor's presence.
They were to wear high-necked dresses, fetch promptly any drinks
that he and his entourage required, neither swear nor spit, and, above
all, not mention available sexual services unless the governor asked
first.

"It's unlikely that he will, but you never know," Mary said. "Despite the title and all, he's still a man. And should he request a tumble,
inform him promptly that there'll be no charge, as he's a guest of the
saloon."

MAYOR ROGERS called a town meeting in the Owaysis on Monday night. Most of the prospectors were more interested in drinking
than in talking about how to impress the governor. Rogers had
trouble quieting them down. Then Gabrielle, who was attending
along with her father, requested silence and the men immediately
complied.

"Now, folks, tomorrow is the most important day in the history of
Glorious," Rogers said. "We want Governor Safford to leave here
eager to tell all his businessman friends that this is the place to come
to and invest. He must feel welcome. To that end, let's have everyone
in a big cheering crowd when he and his party arrive tomorrow afternoon, which I expect will be around two o'clock, since they're departing Florence before dawn."

"At two tomorrow afternoon, most of us will be busting rock," Bossman Wright interrupted. "Damned if I'm going to be standing around waiting on a governor while everybody else is out finding silver."

"That's a valid point, Bossman, and so no one gains unfair advantage, I'm asking everyone to refrain from prospecting tomorrow," the mayor announced. There was a chorus of groans and boos. "It's a sacrifice, sure, but it's for the good of the community as a whole. We need to convince the governor that we're just the dandiest, most promising town in the entire territory."

"And while you wait, I'm going to dish out complimentary biscuit-and-bacon sandwiches for all, and George and Mary will serve free beer," Major Mulkins added. "Just one beer apiece, of course. We don't want the governor's first impression to be that we're a passel of drunks."

The promise of free food and drink seemed to please everyone. Mayor Rogers took advantage. "Let me announce the schedule of tomorrow's festivities. Everyone will gather outside Bob Pugh's livery—"

"The MacPherson livery," Ike Clanton corrected. He was sitting with his father and brother at a table near the back of the saloon. "You need to identify it right. But don't worry, Your Honor. No offense taken."

"Well, I'm glad of that, Ike," Rogers said. "No offense was intended. All right. We'll gather outside the *MacPherson* livery just before two. When the governor's party comes into sight, we'll raise the first cheer, which ought to be audible at considerable distance if the wind stays down. I think Major Mulkins brought back some small American flags from his Florence trip, correct, Major?" Mulkins nodded. "Well, we'll distribute these flags beforehand, so when the mayor's buckboard enters town, we'll cheer again and all the flags will be waved."

"The hell you say," another prospector interjected. "I fought proudly for General Lee in the past war, and I will not flourish Yankee colors."

"Those who don't wish to be flag-wavers can confine themselves to cheering," Rogers amended. "So, after the governor alights, I'll greet him in my capacity as town mayor. I understand Mr. Jesse of Sears and Sons is having some of his men erect a temporary platform outside the livery?"

"We are," Jesse confirmed.

"The governor and I will mount the platform. I'll offer words of welcome that emphasize the business potential of this town. Please, everyone, cheer loudly when I do. Then I'll invite the governor to make some remarks. Again, receive them with loud enthusiasm. Mr. Jesse will then lead the governor's party and the rest of us off to the site of the excavation. Ike Clanton has donated a carriage for the ladies. Most everyone else will have to walk, but it will be an easy pace. After the governor inspects the excavation site, we'll return to town. Major Mulkins will serve a private dinner for Governor Safford and certain dignitaries—myself, Mr. Jesse, the other town founders—in the Elite Hotel, and then the governor will have the choice of retiring to his room or perhaps enjoying some of our soon-to-be-legendary hospitality here in the Owaysis. Should the latter be his preference, I beg everyone to be on their best behavior. And then in the morning Governor Safford will return to the territorial capital, where we all pray that he will sing our town's praises and bring upon us the prosperity we have worked so hard to gain. Well, I believe that's all. Does anyone have anything to add?"

"Over here," Ike Clanton called out.

"You've got the floor, Ike," Rogers said.

Ike stood up and walked out into the middle of the room. He pushed his hat back on his head, hitched his thumbs in his belt, and said, "Even with the commotion about the governor and all, everybody needs to remember the Apaches out there. Me and my father and brother went out today toward the north, looking for float along the far base of the Pinals. I guess we got maybe four miles out of town, the three of us with a pack mule, and off another mile or so in the distance we spied what looked to be a war party, two dozen of the devils at least. Biggest damn bunch of Apaches I ever saw. I doubt they glimpsed us, or we wouldn't be here to tell the tale. Thing is, if they're bunching up like that, then trouble is brewing. This town needs to be on its guard. That's all."

Sheriff Saint was seated at a table with Gabrielle and her father. "Wait a minute, Ike," he said. "You saw a war party this afternoon and you're only getting around to reporting it now?"

"I figured the mayor would call a meeting tonight about the governor and all. It just seemed best to hold off until everyone was gathered to hear me."

"But two dozen Apaches, Ike? Walking along right out in the open? You saw them, but they didn't see you?"

Ike frowned. "That was the way of it. My daddy and brother saw them also."

Saint asked, "Mr. Clanton? Phin? Will you swear to the same thing?"

Phin Clanton shrugged. His stocky father, Newman, rose from his chair and said, "Maybe more like fifteen than two dozen. But they were Apaches. Must have thought their medicine was so strong that they could sashay out as they pleased. My boy Ike's right. Renewed caution is required."

Before Saint could respond, Mayor Rogers said, "Well, then, thanks for the warning, Ike and Mr. Clanton. We'll all be on our guard. Now, everybody get some sleep. Big day tomorrow."

"Drinks all around on me!" Ike hollered, and there was a surge toward the bar. Saint walked out with the Tirritos, and McLendon and Mulkins followed them out the door.

"I wonder what Ike's up to, Major," McLendon mused. "Another warning about Apaches—MacPherson's planning something."

"After tomorrow, he can plan all he wants," Mulkins said. "Once the governor's our friend, he won't allow MacPherson to trifle with us."

"Men have already died, Major. That's considerably more than trifling."

"I realize that," Mulkins said, sounding hurt. "I just want tomorrow to go perfect, and then we'll be all right."

THERE WERE FOUR DRUNKS crammed in the Glorious jail that night, two in each cell. One repeatedly howled like a wolf and another vomited copiously into a bucket the sheriff gave him. Saint and McLendon tried to sleep on the floor and couldn't. They went outside and sat with their backs against the adobe wall.

"Something feels wrong, Joe," McLendon said. "The new strike, the governor coming to town—MacPherson's not the kind to wait and see what happens. Did you notice that Lemmy Duke and Angel Misterio weren't at the meeting? MacPherson usually sends them in to keep watch on such things. Why not tonight?"

Saint took off his glasses and rubbed his eyes, his typical gesture when tired or exasperated. "Maybe MacPherson figured Ike could be his eyes and ears."

"So what about that Indian business? Once again, it's only MacPherson men who see Apaches."

"Ike works for MacPherson, but I don't think his father and brother do. And Newman corrected Ike on the number of Apaches they saw."

"That was a clever touch." The drunk in the cell howled again and they flinched. "MacPherson's about to act, Joe. I wish I could predict how."

The sheriff yawned. "Well, they can't shoot us down in front of Safford and claim it was Apaches. All we can do is follow our own plan. Major Mulkins has invited you to the private dinner for the governor, right? You can get him aside and speak about MacPherson then. While you're in there, I expect that Hunky-Dory will be nearby, maybe in the kitchen, standing watch. I'll seek him out wherever he is and share our concerns. Perhaps one or both of them will be moved to help. Perhaps we'll be sent a contingent of lawmen to stand between us and MacPherson, or else the governor might request that the Army set up a temporary post nearby. At the very least, MacPherson will be warned to leave us alone."

"I hope so," McLendon said. "But men like Collin MacPherson seldom acknowledge any authority higher than their own."

"Well, as the Bible says, 'Sufficient unto the day is the evil thereof.' Let's go back inside and try again for some shut-eye."

They still weren't able to sleep, at least soundly or long. The one drunk kept howling and the nauseated prisoner repeatedly woke them with demands to come empty the vomit bucket because it was near to overflowing again.

TUESDAY DAWNED bright and beautiful. The wind was soft, and white, fluffy clouds blocked the harshest rays of the late-summer sun. McLendon and Saint were awakened from fitful dozes by the sound of pounding hammers. The Sears and Sons crew was erecting a low platform in front of the livery. Ike Clanton watched them, offering suggestions as though he were their foreman.

Saint stretched, then took a set of keys from his desk and unlocked the cells. "You're free to go, boys," he told the prisoners. "Behave while the governor's here."

McLendon spent some of the morning helping Mulkins and Mrs. Mendoza prepare biscuits and fry bacon for sandwiches. Mulkins estimated that they needed two hundred: "We don't need somebody bitching instead of cheering because he wasn't fed as promised." When they were finally done, they loaded the sandwiches on trays and took them over to the Owaysis, where Crazy George was washing every glass in the saloon.

"You don't need to fill them to the brim when you're passing out the free libations," Mary Somebody reminded him. "You might consider making them mostly foam."

"I pride myself in pouring honest glasses of beer with minimal foam," George protested.

"That's in the case of paid-for beer. Our free beer comes with generous foam portions."

McLendon spied Charlie Rogers at a table in a far corner of the saloon. The mayor of Glorious was bent over several sheets of paper, jotting notes and then scratching some of them out.

"I usually extemporize, but on this occasion I feel obliged to prepare my remarks in advance," he explained. "Have a listen, C.M. How does this sound?" Rogers donned reading glasses and consulted what he'd written. "'Governor Safford, honored guests, beloved citizens: As mayor of aptly named Glorious, I welcome you to the Eden of Arizona Territory, a veritable garden of neighborly regard and investment potential.'"

"You've got a subtle touch there, Charlie," McLendon said. He meant to be sarcastic, but the mayor took him seriously.

"Damn it, you're right," Rogers said. "As an inexperienced public speaker, eloquence apparently eludes me. Perhaps 'neighborly regard' isn't strong enough? I want to emphasize that good people live here."

"And some not so good. Sheriff Saint and I were kept up most of the night by boisterous drunks in the cells."

Rogers glowered. "Well, we don't need to be distracting the governor with any of that." He crumpled the pages that he held and held his pen over a clean page. "I must compose remarks that are grander, a full half hour's worth at least."

"I believe President Lincoln spoke for only a few minutes at Gettysburg."

"Lincoln was a common Kentucky-born cracker, and Gettysburg was just another battle. Today's visit by the governor is a far more critical event."

THOUGH SAFFORD wasn't expected to arrive until at least two that afternoon, people began gathering in the Owaysis by eleven. They demanded their free beer and sandwiches. Mulkins and Mary Somebody consulted with Saint, who announced that lunch would be served at one. Some of the prospectors passed the time drinking. Mr. Jesse of Sears and Sons and the mayor worried about drunks.

"Can't you order them not to imbibe, Sheriff?" Jesse asked.

Saint shook his head. "If I try to prevent these men from drinking, sir, they're likely to tell me to go to hell. They may get a bit tipsy, but at least they'll be in pleasant moods when the governor finally arrives."

McLendon suggested that Jesse and Mayor Rogers inspect the stage that had been built in front of the livery. He and Saint accompanied the two men, who stepped up onto the wooden platform and peered in all directions.

"I believe this will do," Jesse said. "The height is such that everyone gathered around can get a good look at the governor."

"How loudly should I speak, to be certain that all in the throng can hear me clearly?" Rogers inquired. "Should I perhaps rehearse?" He withdrew his speech from a suit pocket, put on his glasses, cleared his throat, and read, "'Most honorable Governor Safford, it is with the greatest gratitude and deeply profound hospitality that I, on behalf of the most promising town in all of the West and perhaps the nation, welcome you—'"

"Pardon me, Mayor Rogers." Sydney Chau was at the side of the stage. A small group of Chinese stood behind her. "My people were wondering: Will we, too, be allowed to greet the governor when he arrives?"

Mayor Rogers was not pleased by the question. He removed his reading glasses and exchanged glances with Mr. Jesse, who violently shook his head. The mayor said, "As much as I wish it were possible—"

"Of course you can, Doc," Joe Saint said. "I believe Gabrielle will have some small flags available if you folks feel like waving them. Why don't you go see her about that?"

"But when the time comes, be certain not to have your people standing out in front," Jesse said. "We don't want you to be the first thing that the governor sees."

"Thank you, Sheriff," Sydney said. She pointedly ignored Jesse and Mayor Rogers as the Chinese walked off to the dry goods store.

AT ONE O'CLOCK Mary Somebody announced that lunch was being served in the Owaysis. There was some arguing over the sandwiches.

Several prospectors were accused of taking two. Mary stood behind Crazy George, making certain that the free beer was half foam. When anyone protested, she snapped, "Do you also want to complain about the price?" Sally and Abigail, the whores, appeared in modest dresses, and Girl was proud of several brightly colored ribbons in her hair.

A half-dozen prospectors with their own mules volunteered to ride west out of town and stand lookout for the governor and his party. When they spied them, they would ride back in and alert everyone to get ready. Mayor Rogers said that it was a fine idea and sent them off.

"This is it," he predicted, nervously hugging his wife, Rose, whose voluminous dress featured lots of ruffles that made her look even wider than usual. "We're going to do it, boys. We're going to have it happen, just as we hoped."

At two the crowd drifted out in front of the livery. McLendon thought they might number more than two hundred—there were more prospectors than he'd realized. By two-thirty everyone was restless, but a few minutes later the lookouts came trotting in on their mules to report they'd observed a wide cloud of dust about two miles out of town: "It's the governor for sure."

Mayor Rogers shouted for everyone to take their places. The town founders had places of honor directly in front of the stage. Major Mulkins insisted that McLendon stand beside him: "You're one of us now, C.M." Everyone stared west. Soon they saw the dust cloud for themselves, and then tiny specks grew into the distinguishable shapes of riders, the Florence stage, and a long buckboard.

"Let's go, friends, and raise the first cheer," Rogers cried, and they did, a loud whooping chorus that seemed to echo off nearby

Apache Leap and rebound down the valley in the direction of the approaching procession. The rider leading the way waved his hat in response.

"I believe that's Hunky-Dory in front," Saint whispered to McLendon.

As the newcomers drew closer, Mayor Rogers called for a second cheer, and the crowd, caught up in the excitement, roared happily. A man on the bench of the approaching buckboard stood and waved.

"Governor Safford himself!" Mayor Rogers cried. "Welcome him, everyone, welcome him!"

Then, perhaps a hundred yards before the governor's party would have passed the cluster of prospectors' tents and entered town, riders appeared from the south. They splashed across Queen Creek and intercepted the procession.

"Those are Culloden vaqueros," Saint said. "Look, Lemmy Duke's yammering with Hunky-Dory." The U.S. marshal seemed confused. Duke turned his horse and trotted to the buckboard. He leaned over in the saddle and spoke to the governor. The governor called out something to Deputy Marshal Holmes, and then the buckboard swung south, following Duke and the vaqueros across the creek in the direction of Culloden Ranch, with Hunky-Dory Holmes and several other riders trailing behind. The Florence stage continued into town. The crowd moved aside as the stage driver pulled up his team beside the stage.

"What's going on?" the mayor demanded. "Where did the governor go?"

The driver spit tobacco juice and replied, "From what little I overheard, the man with the Mexicans told the governor that the party to welcome him was to be at this ranch nearby, and when the governor

said, 'Really,' the man said, 'Your friend's waiting there for you,' and
the governor told his driver to follow the man along."

"This can't be," Rogers blustered. "We're the official hosts. Governor Safford's come to see Glorious, not Culloden Ranch. I won't
tolerate it!"

"I believe that you will." Ike Clanton appeared at the mayor's side.
He was smiling. "As it happens, Governor Safford and Mr. MacPherson
are great friends of long standing, and so of course Mr. MacPherson
has laid on a considerable greeting for his chum. But don't despair, Mayor,
you or anyone else. The boss invites the whole town to join them at the
ranch for barbecue and entertainment. I've got a buckboard for the
ladies, so they don't have to walk and dirty up their nice dresses. Step
to—this will be a most festive occasion." Ike jumped up on the stage
next to Rogers and bellowed, "A fancy free feed, and entertainment
besides! Everyone over to the Culloden!" A few in the crowd looked
uncertain, but most took the change of plans in stride and set out for
the ranch.

"We've been outsmarted," Mulkins said to McLendon and Saint.
"Collin MacPherson's just plain took the play away from us. Might as
well go over there and see what's doing."

"I can still try to talk to the governor, and you can get with Hunky-
Dory," McLendon told Saint. "MacPherson can't stop us from talking to them."

Ike brought the buckboard over and extended his hand to help
Gabrielle and Rose Rogers climb up. He had to tug hard with Rose,
but Gabrielle got up by herself without Ike's help. Mary Somebody
asked Ike, "Can they come too?" gesturing at Sally, Abigail, and Girl.

"The more, the merrier," Ike crowed, "but this pretty one's got to
sit up on the bench by me." He took Girl by the waist and tossed her
up. She squealed with laughter. Mary, Sally, and Abigail joined Gabri-

elle and Rose in the bed of the buckboard. Ike took up the reins, but Gabrielle called for him to hold up.

"You and your mother should ride with us too," she said to Sydney. Ike didn't object, and Gabrielle helped Sydney get her mother in. Then Ike clucked at the mule team and the buckboard lurched toward the ranch, with everyone else from town following.

NINETEEN

Decorations at Culloden Ranch put the bunting and small flags of Glorious to shame. Great hand-painted banners proclaiming WELCOME, GOVERNOR hung from the compound walls, and huge bouquets of colorful wildflowers festooned windows and doorways. A Mexican band played welcoming fanfares; McLendon thought that MacPherson must have brought the musicians in from Tucson. The air inside the compound was redolent with the smell of cooking beef. A deep pit had been dug in one corner, and in it two whole beeves roasted on spits over glowing coals. Young Mexican women wearing long, formal dresses welcomed each arrival with a drink—tequila shots for the men and lemonade for the ladies. They also offered treats—sections of orange and quince, and wedges of several types of cheese. Under a canopy in front of the main house, Collin MacPherson and Arizona Territory governor A. P. K. Safford sat comfortably in cushioned chairs, sipping their own drinks and surrounded by a phalanx of Culloden vaqueros. Angel Misterio stood behind their chairs, eyeing the newcomers as they entered the compound through the front gate. His fingers brushed the hilt of the knife in his belt.

"So much for speaking privately to the governor," McLendon said to Saint. "MacPherson and Misterio clearly don't intend to let us near him."

"I should be sitting with them," Charlie Rogers complained. "I'm the mayor. Say, there," he said to Lemmy Duke, who was standing nearby. "Take me over to the governor and Mr. MacPherson."

Duke smiled and shook his head. "Can't do it, sir. The two gentlemen have emphasized that they desire some private conversation. Perhaps later."

"But I'm the mayor of Glorious!"

"So you are. But you're on MacPherson land now."

Mayor Rogers fumed and everyone else milled about until Angel Misterio signaled for quiet by firing a pistol in the air. All eyes turned to the shady spot where Collin MacPherson rose from his chair.

"Governor Safford, visitors, and neighbors, welcome to Culloden Ranch. We've got a splendid time planned, with food and entertainment, but first, if you'll allow, I'll make some brief remarks."

"I have remarks prepared too," Mayor Rogers grumbled, but no one paid attention to him.

"We who have come to this wild, wonderful region have poured our money, sweat, and on occasion blood into the land, always with the goal of building a thriving community," MacPherson said. Standing erect, resplendent in a well-cut suit, he was an imposing figure. "We're now close to achieving that goal. The good things happening now are only the beginning. In partnership with the territorial government, we will move on and up, always grateful to God and government for our blessings. Today's visit by the governor marks the conclusion of one era and the bright beginning of the next."

"It'd seem a damn sight brighter with some more tequila!" a prospector shouted, and everyone laughed, including MacPherson.

"Someone refill that fellow's glass, and everyone else's besides," MacPherson commanded. "A little patience, my thirsty friends. There's just to be a bit more talk, then food, then some fun. I've always tried to be the best of neighbors, today is no different. And now let's hear from our distinguished guest, the governor of Arizona Territory, the Honorable Anson Pacely Killen Safford."

Everyone clapped, and then gasped as the governor stood beside MacPherson.

"The man's a *midget*," someone near McLendon hissed. It didn't seem far from the truth. Though he, too, was dressed in a splendid suit and sported a magnificent low-hanging beard, the top of Governor Safford's head barely reached Collin MacPherson's shoulder. Some in the throng couldn't help laughing, and Safford smiled and nodded as though to acknowledge the mirth.

"It's a *tall* order, following a speech by Collin MacPherson," he said, and everyone felt free to guffaw. "It's obvious I'm a small man in stature, but I have big plans for this territory." McLendon, himself skilled in the use of self-deprecation to engage others, admired the governor's approach. And though Safford was diminutive, he had a deep, booming voice. He was in control of his audience. Everyone listened raptly.

"Arizona Territory is God's gift to America," Safford continued. "We're growing to where statehood is inevitable, and in the process we're extending civilization in the best of ways. There'll be good roads into every town, and telegraph lines, enough prisons to hold all the bad men and enough high-paid jobs for all the good ones. You're all for that, am I right?" There were cheers. "Of course you are. None but fine people here today. There's been silver found and the first local mine is about to begin excavation and it's an exciting time. The legislature in Tucson is well aware. For those of you living across the creek in Glorious, official certification as a town will soon be forthcoming. Good times, golden times."

The governor paused, then raised his right forefinger in warning.

"Remember, though, that while success is looming, it is never guaranteed. There remain impediments. I note specifically the ongoing presence of Apaches. We're working hard to root them out, I'm cooperating all I can with President Grant's peace commission to them, but at present they're still dangerous and they're all around you. My good friend Collin MacPherson has informed me that at least one war party has been recently spotted in the vicinity. I urge you to observe great caution as you venture out in search of ore. God willing, the day shall come soon when the Apache threat is no more. But for now, remain alert, and in particular cooperate with Mr. MacPherson's fine men as they endeavor to keep you safe from the savages."

McLendon and Saint looked at each other and shook their heads. "MacPherson's foxed us," the sheriff said. "He got to the governor first."

"We can't give up. Let's see how it plays out."

The governor spoke a little longer. He reminded everyone to support local businesses, be mindful of obeying territorial laws, and, above all, "always vote Republican." Then he waved and sat down. Collin MacPherson announced that dinner was served. Everyone lined up for plates of thick, juicy steak along with fresh-baked tortillas and frijoles. The musicians played and some of the women who lived on the ranch danced.

Afterward, MacPherson instructed everyone to walk through the gate to an area just west of the compound, where they found targets attached to hay bales and several dummies made of white sheets and stuffed with straw that were suspended from T-shaped supports.

"My vaqueros are now going to demonstrate their skills in the warlike arts," he said. "Benches are provided for our much-respected town founders." Ike Clanton and Lemmy Duke escorted Charlie and Rose Rogers, Crazy George and Mary Somebody, Major Mulkins, Salvatore and Gabrielle Tirrito, and Joe Saint to seats in front. Sally and Abigail, the Owaysis whores, weren't included, but Girl clung to Mary and sat next to her.

"You, too, McLendon," Ike snickered, grabbing his arm.

McLendon jerked free. "I'm not a founder."

"Tough shit. Boss says you sit up there with them. He wants you and your friends to get real good looks." There seemed little use in arguing. Most of the crowd stood behind the benches. The Chinese were herded off to one side, where the late-afternoon sun shone directly in their eyes.

The demonstrations were impressive. MacPherson and Governor Safford sat on a bench apart from everyone else. Before each event, MacPherson explained what everyone was about to see. First came basic pistol marksmanship. A half-dozen vaqueros blasted away at hay bale targets, and afterward the targets were passed around so all could see the holes blown squarely in the center of the bull's-eyes. Then Angel Misterio threw knives with such incredible speed and precision that the blur of his arm seemed simultaneous with the *thunk* of the blades burying themselves in hay.

Cattle were driven in front of the crowd, and the vaqueros demon-

strated their roping skills. Then MacPherson announced the grand
finale.

"Please observe this closely, friends, especially the ordnance
involved. I have a business acquaintance back east named Oliver
Winchester. His company manufactures the repeating rifles with
which I believe you're all familiar. Within a year Ollie hopes to market his latest model. Not to bore the women, but these will be center
rather than rim fire, in regards to where the firing pin strikes the
cartridge. That means the Winchester '73s will fire more powerfully
and accurately than any previous rifle. Ollie had some sample weapons he wanted tested, and so he sent them to me at Culloden Ranch.
My men now have superior firepower to anyone, anywhere. As a
fighting force, they are virtually invincible. See for yourselves." He
barked an order and ten vaqueros led by Lemmy Duke raced from
the compound past the crowd. They were all mounted on wiry Mexican horses and had Winchesters in one hand. Duke signaled and the
riders dropped their reins, aimed their rifles, and from their galloping horses opened fire at the dummies hanging from the supports.
The dummies seemed to almost instantly disintegrate. One moment
they dangled, and the next they were reduced to scraps of material
and wisps of straw floating down into the dirt. Even after the shooting was over, McLendon's ears rang uncomfortably.

"That concludes our program—almost," MacPherson said. "Governor Safford has one more announcement."

The governor rose and smiled. "First, let's all express appreciation
to our most gracious host, Collin MacPherson." He clapped his
hands and the crowd dutifully joined in the applause. "Well, now. I
believe we are next scheduled to depart this fine ranch and journey
to the site of the Sears and Sons mine excavation. But before we do, I

have exciting news. Promising as it may be, one mine alone won't be the making of the town of Glorious. More are needed."

Ike Clanton led two men through the crowd. One was tall and grizzled. The other sported a brushy mustache and wore a particularly wide-brimmed hat.

"Why, it's Boze Bell and Johnny Boggs," Mulkins said. "Why are they being brought up to the governor?"

Safford dramatically shook hands with the two prospectors, then gestured for Collin MacPherson to join them.

"Isolated as you've been, no one could blame you good people for wondering if your governor was even aware of you and whether he and the territorial legislature have your best interests at heart," Safford said. "Well, here's confirmation in its finest form. Mr. Bell and Mr. Boggs have made a significant strike, and I hereby announce that they have sold their claim—to myself and Collin MacPherson. The Safford-MacPherson Mining Group will begin excavation within weeks. So never doubt that I hold Glorious in the highest esteem, for, from this moment and by way of investment, I am one of you. Now, if you will, form a line, for before we set off to the Sears and Sons site, I want to personally greet each of you and shake your hands."

"Son of a bitch," Major Mulkins mumbled. "MacPherson's got the governor in his pocket too."

"We might as well get back to town," Saint said. "There's nothing we can do here." But the Culloden vaqueros, some of them carrying Winchesters still warm from firing, herded everyone into a single-file line to greet the governor. The Glorious founders were among the first. Crazy George nodded to Safford, and Mary Somebody said, "Pleased, Your Honor," and made a sort of clumsy curtsy. Salvatore

Tirrito shook hands firmly, and McLendon thought Safford smiled a bit too intimately at Gabrielle. Major Mulkins, too furious to pretend, briefly touched the governor's hand with his and walked away as quickly as he could. Safford greeted Saint with "It's the local lawman," and Joe managed a weak smile. The governor kissed Rose Rogers on the cheek. Her husband said mournfully, "I had some remarks to deliver," and Safford said smoothly, "I'm sure there'll be another opportunity."

Then it was McLendon's turn. The governor held out his hand. McLendon took it and pulled himself in close. "We have concerns, sir," he whispered.

Safford pulled away. His eyes widened for a moment. Then he said, "Good to see you."

"Governor, it's about Collin MacPherson."

"Good to see you," Safford repeated.

Angel Misterio appeared beside the governor. His dark eyes burned into McLendon's as he softly murmured, "Please move along, *señor*. The governor has many more people to greet."

McLendon saw Collin MacPherson standing a few yards away, smoking a cigar. He walked over to him, with Misterio just a step behind.

"Oh, McLendon," MacPherson said. "You should have left as I suggested. Perhaps you still could. No promises, of course."

"Why do this, MacPherson? You don't have to."

"What do you mean?"

"It's not necessary to destroy these decent people. No one has to be hurt. Instead of taking their businesses, you could just start your own in town, build a bigger and better saloon and hotel and dry goods shop and farrier's. Undercut their prices, take all their customers, and they'll give up and go. You proved your point today with the guns and the governor. If you'll just wait, it wouldn't take long."

MacPherson regarded McLendon like a scientist contemplating where to drive the pin through a bug. "No," he said presently. "I want it now. Waiting any longer would be inconvenient. Good-bye, Mr. McLendon."

TWENTY

That night, Ike Clanton visited the founders: Crazy George and Mary Somebody at the Owaysis, Charlie and Rose Rogers in their cabin behind the farrier's shop, Major Mulkins in the office of the Elite Hotel, and Salvatore and Gabrielle Tirrito in their dry goods store. McLendon and Saint, leaning on the outer adobe wall of the jail, watched as he went to each in turn.

"It's an ultimatum from MacPherson, wait and see," McLendon predicted. "Say, I was so unnerved by MacPherson and the governor that I never thought to ask: Did you get your moment with Deputy Marshal Holmes and share our suspicions with him?"

"I tried, but he didn't let me tell much. Hunky-Dory just said that Safford considers MacPherson to be not only a business partner but a close friend, and the governor doesn't like to hear words spoken against his friends."

"Then we can't hope for any assistance from Hunky-Dory?"

"He's going to do what he can, which is to try and come through here every ten days or so to make sure we're all right."

Ike went to the Tirritos' last, and when he was done there he strolled back to the livery, nodding pleasantly as he passed McLendon and the sheriff.

"Good evening, both," Ike said. Saint nodded back. McLendon didn't.

"Come on," he said to the sheriff. "Let's collect everyone and see what Ike's been up to."

When everyone was gathered in the family area of the dry goods store, they had the same tale to tell. Ike had made to them what he emphasized was a onetime offer from Collin MacPherson to buy their businesses. The proposed purchase prices were adequate though not overwhelming: $8,000 for the Owaysis, $7,500 for the farrier's, $12,000 for the Elite Hotel, and $5,000 for the dry goods store. In each instance there were the same conditions: all tools, goods, furniture, and other items directly connected to the businesses must be left intact for the new proprietor, and the old owners would leave Glorious immediately after receiving the agreed-upon bank drafts.

"'Out with the old' was the way Ike termed it," Mulkins said. "He said Mr. MacPherson expected we'd want to make our fresh starts somewhere else as promptly as possible."

"He also stressed that our answers were expected quite soon," Gabrielle said. She sat on a corner of one bed. Saint sat beside her and openly held her hand. "He said that Mr. MacPherson was not a man of infinite patience."

"Fuck if I'll do it," Crazy George spluttered. "Goddamn rich man saying, 'Take some money and haul ass.' Let the sumbitch and his Mexicans try to take my saloon away from me. I'll cave in all their heads. I'll die before I roll over like they want."

"Don't rule out that possibility," McLendon cautioned. "We've seen what happens to those who don't agree to MacPherson's demands.

Your lives hang in the balance, make no mistake. The money on offer is reasonable. You're surrounded by armed men and clearly cut off from assistance by the territorial government. Weigh your responses carefully."

"Mary and me ain't selling out," George declared. "I'll die before I give in."

"Same for me," Mulkins said. "Let MacPherson do his worst and be damned."

"Papa and I won't sell out, either," Gabrielle said. Salvatore Tirrito, seated at the table, set his mouth in a grim line and nodded.

Everyone turned to Mayor Rogers, who swallowed hard and looked regretful.

"I'm choosing to accept Mr. MacPherson's offer," he said. "Tomorrow I'll go to Culloden and tell him so. Me and Rosie will depart on Thursday's stage to Florence."

"You can't do that, Charlie," Mulkins protested. "You're the mayor, you're the leader of this town. If you knuckle under, that will encourage MacPherson all the more to stampede the rest of us."

"I know, Major, and I regret it with all my heart. But, you see, it's Rosie. She's of a tremulous disposition in the best of times. If I turn down MacPherson and events grow ugly, why, I know she'd react poorly. And if violence ensued—well, I just can't risk losing my jelly bunny. I hope you understand."

Mulkins and Crazy George began to protest, but Gabrielle interrupted. "Of course you must do as you think best, Mayor Rogers," she said. "Rose is your primary consideration and you place her welfare above that of all others. That's how it should be." She looked meaningfully at the others in the room. "Let no one attempt to persuade you otherwise."

"Thank you, Miss Gabrielle," Rogers said. "Well, I suppose I should go home to Rosie now. While Mr. MacPherson's offer encompasses the tools and such in my shop, I don't believe he wants our personal possessions in the cabin. So there's packing to do. I'll say my final farewells to you all on Thursday, before we depart."

"But what will we do for a mayor?" Mulkins asked.

"You be mayor, Major," Rogers said, and left the shop.

After Rogers was gone, Mulkins said, "I don't want to be mayor. All I want to do is run my hotel. One of you others be mayor. Mary, how about you?"

"God, no," Mary replied. "I've got enough trying to keep the saloon in order."

"Nobody needs to be mayor right now," McLendon said. "It's the least of concerns. MacPherson's made his offers and he's not going to be pleased by refusals. As soon as you turn him down, you can count on him to act. Maybe the Apaches will strike right here in town. He's surely got something in mind."

Joe Saint had been silent, but now he leaned forward. "Apaches. Wait a minute. Let's think about the Apaches."

"But there aren't any, Joe, at least not war bands poised to attack us," McLendon said. "MacPherson and his men have set it up to appear that way. We've already agreed on that."

"I know, but there may be a way we can turn it to our advantage. MacPherson's vaqueros supposedly guard us, but, by definition, who ideally protects civilians from the Indians? It's the Army. And the Army is separate from any territorial control."

"But there's no specific Indian threat," McLendon protested. "MacPherson made it all up. That's what we wanted to tell the governor."

"Yes, I know. But what if we took the opposite tack with the Army?

What if we told them that MacPherson was right, that we were in grave danger of immediate attack and resulting slaughter?"

McLendon considered that for a moment, then understood the point the sheriff wanted to make. "You're right, Joe. If the Army sent a cavalry contingent to provide additional security, it would be impossible for MacPherson to fake Apache deprivations here, at least while the soldiers were in place."

Gabrielle said, "That would gain us some time, even if Mr. MacPherson was furious at us for spurning his offers."

"Yes," McLendon said, his mind racing now. "And there's been the second silver strike. Word's spreading about it—has to be. Remember after the first one how prospectors flocked here, and that fellow set up the whorehouse in a tent?"

"A tent full of poxy Mexican girls," Mary Somebody said.

"Yes. And we said it was only a matter of time before more businesses got started, competition for you founders. All right, then. So we get the Army here, and that stalls MacPherson, and if we can keep the soldiers here long enough, just a month or even a few weeks might be enough, then more people will come flooding in and additional businesses might be established—another saloon or two, stores selling dry goods stock, even a hotel. Under tents to begin with, maybe, but businesses just the same. MacPherson couldn't buy out or murder them all. And that would mean there would be no advantage to him of killing any of you. It could work, Joe, it could work."

"Another hotel," Mulkins mused. "Well, let it come. I'll match my service and fine windows against any competitor, and may the best man win."

"Damned if I'll serve gaudy mixed drinks," Crazy George huffed. "The other fellows can serve ladylike concoctions."

"Let's not look that far ahead," Saint said. "We've got a plan with potential, but we need to move fast. It all begins with alerting the Army. I know the area commander is at Camp McDowell, north of Florence, near Maricopa Wells. He needs to be alerted to the masses of Apaches gathered just outside town. I'll get a mule and start for the camp tomorrow."

"Hold a minute," McLendon said. "We can't forget MacPherson's watching our every move. I suppose you'd rent the mule from Ike Clanton? Well, once you do, what's to stop him from scurrying to Culloden and informing MacPherson that the sheriff's bound out of town, probably trying to get help? A squad of vaqueros would set out on your trail. They'd find you and cut you down. You're not a fighter, Joe. You'd not stand a chance."

Saint's brow furrowed. "Don't waste time with petty insults."

McLendon noticed that Gabrielle was glaring at him too. "I intended no insult, only honest appraisal. I'm not a fighter, either. None of us are."

"All right, then, I'll borrow a mule from a prospector. Ike Clanton need not know."

"Don't forget the guards at either end of town," McLendon said. "They'd still see you ride off. We can be certain that they've all been instructed to immediately report any of our comings and goings. The sheriff setting out alone? MacPherson would know it in minutes."

"Doesn't have to be the sheriff," Mulkins said. "I could go. If anyone asked, I could say I'd been stricken with silver fever and couldn't resist doing some prospecting."

Crazy George said, "I'll go, and take the pipe in my boot to the skull of the first fool who disputes me."

Mary touched his arm and said gently, "Darlin', with your poor vision there's simply no way. You'd set out for the Army camp and end up in Canada or Mexico City."

"No," McLendon said. "It can't be any of you. It can't look like anything out of the ordinary. The right person to go is me."

"Why is that?" Gabrielle asked. "Must you always consider yourself superior to us ordinary folk?"

"It's not that. It's logical. You know MacPherson's been warning me to get out while I can. This afternoon at the barbecue he said it again. When the mayor and Rose take out on the Florence stage tomorrow, MacPherson will see two people he frightened enough to quit and run. If I get on the same stage with my valise in my hand, he'll just assume I'm a third."

"Self-preservation would be an obvious motive with you," Gabrielle said. "Of course, I intend no insult, only honest appraisal."

"The vaqueros won't track the stage. It will be obvious where I'm bound—to Florence—and if you all come out to bid me and the Rogerses farewell, I'll loudly declare that I'm heading on to California after that. Then, when I get to Florence, I'll find my way north to, what, Maricopa Wells?"

"It's some forty miles to the north, and there's a daily stage there from Florence," Mulkins said. "Then from Maricopa Wells it's another thirty miles, maybe thirty-five, to the Salt River, then fifteen more to Camp McDowell. You can rent a mule in Maricopa Wells and make the ride, or perhaps join an Army group going from town to the camp. It would be a day on the stage to Florence, a half day's stage travel from Florence to Maricopa Wells because the way is easier, and whatever time it took you to get from there to McDowell. In all I'd estimate three days at least."

"And then time to meet with the camp commander; I'd hope to persuade him quickly. How long will it take for me to bring the soldiers here to Glorious from McDowell?"

Mulkins mused, then said, "I estimate it's near seventy miles as the crow flies, but you aren't crows. There's rugged country along the way. If the Army'd ride all night, you might arrive late the following day, but I doubt they'll go on in the dark. Too many holes to fall in."

"All right," McLendon said. "Thursday, Friday, and Saturday to get to the Army camp. Sunday to persuade the commander to send us troops. A late Monday return here at the earliest, more likely Tuesday. Wednesday on the outside. So you might have to hold out against MacPherson for a week."

"We can say we need more time to consider his offers," Gabrielle said.

Mary said, "That might gain a day or two, but never a week."

"We'll stay grouped up when we can, and where witnesses abound," the sheriff said. "That will help."

"The important thing is to try and not arouse suspicion," McLendon cautioned. "Ike and the rest of MacPherson's spies will be watching for anything out of the ordinary."

"As you would know," Gabrielle said.

"As I would know. Do your best to appear resigned rather than rebellious. The better that you give this impression, the better the chances that MacPherson will believe he's about to get what he wants, and so delay any violence. Though he'll do whatever he thinks he must, he'll prefer as little fuss as possible. You must keep your wits about you, and your nerve."

"We'll do it," Mulkins said. "Count on us. Just use your way with words and convince the McDowell commander to send soldiers."

"If we're agreed, let's all get some sleep," McLendon suggested. "Ike's sure to come around tomorrow asking what you've decided. The mayor will say he's ready to sell, and the rest of you must stall. I'll talk up my own departure on Thursday's Florence stage. And I'll be back as soon as I can."

"You know, that may not be necessary," Saint said. "You're under no obligation to return. If you can get the Army sent our way, you've fulfilled any moral obligation that you might feel. There's nothing to keep you from getting on a stage and continuing on to California. As I understand it, that was your original destination before you made this lengthy sojourn in Glorious."

"I'll return here from the camp, with the soldiers or, if I fail in the effort, without them. I think I'm a better man than I was when I left St. Louis, and I'm going to prove it. I'm in this to the end."

Saint removed his glasses, rubbed his eyes, and put the spectacles back on again. "It's not really your fight, is it? No one will blame you."

McLendon looked at Saint, then Gabrielle. He said, "You'll see. I'm coming back."

TWENTY-ONE

On Thursday morning, McLendon put on his good suit and packed his other belongings in his valise. He thought about wearing his Navy Colt in its holster, but decided against it because going out openly armed might arouse suspicion among MacPherson's men. But he put the weapon on top of everything else in the valise.

Just before ten o'clock, he left the jail and walked across to where the Florence stage waited in front of the livery. Charlie and Rose Rogers were already there. They had a heavy trunk that the driver and shotgun guard were struggling to lift into the baggage bin at the back of the stage. Two Sears and Sons officials were traveling to Florence too. Like McLendon, they had valises that they handed to the driver to stow after the Rogerses' trunk was finally heaved up into the bin. McLendon shook his head when the driver asked if he wanted his valise stowed away as well. Even though he was certain he'd never hit anything he aimed at, there was still some comfort in knowing his gun was handy.

Ike Clanton lounged in front of the livery office, taking in the scene. Across the way, Lemmy Duke perched on the front steps of the hotel. MacPherson's lookouts were in place. Crazy George, Mary Somebody, Girl, Major Mulkins, Salvatore and Gabrielle Tirrito, and Joe Saint were all outside the livery, there to say good-bye to the Rogerses and, McLendon knew, to carry out the charade that he was also leaving. Mulkins in particular proved to have skills as a thespian. He dramatically hugged Rose Rogers, pumped her husband's hand, and said, "Now, Charlie, you linger in Florence for a while. I suspect the rest of us might be joining you there soon, and then we can go out and found ourselves another town."

"I suppose we could, for we're in no hurry," Rogers replied. He seemed relieved that his friends weren't resentful of his selling out to MacPherson. "Rosie wants a few days of leisure before we contemplate our future."

"You rest yourself well, Rose," Gabrielle said. "I know you've been under considerable strain." She handed the other woman a paper parcel. "Papa and I thought you might want these for the ride today."

Rose twisted open the package and peered inside. "Hard candies! Bless you both!"

The stage driver called, "All on, time to depart," and the mining company men climbed into the carriage. Everyone lined up to hug the Rogerses before they climbed aboard—Rose needed considerable help managing the high step up into the stage—and then it was McLendon's turn for farewells. Mary Somebody and Girl hugged him, and after she did, Girl began to sob. Mary patted her arm, and then Ike Clanton came over and led Girl away.

"Don't be mournful, lovey, because you've still got Ikey," he said. Then, glancing back, he added, "Best board that stage, McLendon."

"Well, C.M., it's been a pleasure," Mulkins said. "I hope our paths cross again down the road."

"I feel the same, Major," McLendon said. "I hope everyone considers making those fresh starts out in San Francisco. Look me up when you get there."

He shook hands with Crazy George and Joe Saint. Salvatore Tirrito hesitated, then held out a gnarled hand. McLendon briefly touched it, knowing the elderly Italian wouldn't want any extended contact. Then Gabrielle stood before him. One of the things McLendon had always loved about her was her complete openness of expression. It was always easy to tell what she was thinking. Now she was obviously torn. She limited herself to a handshake rather than a hug; he thought it was because Saint was there. But then she stepped close and whispered in his ear, "Once you alert the Army, don't come back. Go to California. Be safe."

He held her hand a beat longer than strict propriety allowed. Looking over her shoulder, he saw Saint stiffen. Then he gently pushed her away and said, "You'll see." He thought that he saw in her eyes faint glimmers of tears that she would never allow herself to shed, and then, in the next instant, her eyes were dry again. How did women do that?

"Everyone on," the driver said again. Knowing Ike and Lemmy Duke were watching, McLendon took a long look around—at the tiny town and the cluster of prospectors' tents, the jagged Pinals and the intimidating sweep of Apache Leap.

"Tell Sydney that I sent my regards," he said to Gabrielle, and then he jumped up into the carriage and pulled the door shut behind him. The driver cracked his whip over the heads of the mule team and the stage lurched forward. Even though he fully expected to return, McLendon still felt sad. He kept the window curtain open so he could see Queen Creek, and then Picket Post Mountain looming ahead.

BECAUSE OF THE increased passenger traffic between the towns, the stage was a nine-seater rather than the smaller six-seat model that initially brought McLendon from Florence to Glorious. The two mining company executives took one bench. They spread papers between themselves and pored over them, ignoring their fellow passengers. Rose and Charlie Rogers occupied the middle bench, with McLendon facing them on the third. Because of his wife's bulk, the former Glorious mayor was squashed against the side of the carriage. McLendon almost suggested that he join him on the third bench, but realized just before he did that Rogers would never want to separate himself from his beloved jelly bunny. So he and Rogers talked, mostly about Florence and the various amenities there. Rose Rogers said very little, contenting herself with eating the candy that Gabrielle had given her. Rose consumed the candy one piece at a time, crunching it between her teeth, swallowing, and immediately inserting another piece in her mouth. There was a certain rhythm to it.

As he and Rogers chatted, McLendon maintained the fiction that he was on his way to California. Rogers probably wouldn't have any means of informing MacPherson otherwise, but there was no sense taking chances.

"California's the place to be," McLendon said. "Unlimited opportunity. Lots of room to grow. No Apaches to speak of."

"You're a man who'll be happier in the city, C.M.," Rogers said. "I never thought you well suited for the high desert and Glorious."

They discussed McLendon's route to the West Coast. Rogers helpfully noted that he'd have to take the stage from Florence to Maricopa

Wells, because all Florence stages went north and south. Longer east–west lines were routed through Maricopa Wells, which had a larger depot than Florence.

"But the road between Florence and the Wells is a good one, so that trip will only take you four hours, at most five," Rogers said. "So after you spend tonight in Florence, you can depart for the Wells in the morning, and if your timing's right, you might be on a California stage by mid-afternoon."

"That's a pleasant thought," McLendon said, but his mind was on something much different. He spent much of the long day remembering that Gabrielle had almost cried when he left that morning. Maybe Joe Saint hadn't won yet.

McLendon spent the night in a small, smelly Florence hotel. He still had almost seven hundred dollars, but he didn't want to spend any more of it than necessary. When he was done in Glorious, stage fare on to California would be almost a hundred dollars, and maybe, just maybe, there'd be Gabrielle's fare too. They'd need money to live on in California while they got settled, and what if she insisted that her father come with them? The addition of the old man's stage fare and other travel expenses would just about deplete McLendon's money. But the Tirritos would undoubtedly have some money of their own. Salvatore could pay his own way.

The Maricopa Wells stage was scheduled to depart at eight a.m., so McLendon turned in early. He'd declined Charlie Rogers's invitation to dine with him and Rose, choosing instead to eat a bowl of greasy chili at a café near the stage depot. During the unsatisfactory meal, he was overcome by a sensation he recognized from the early weeks after he'd fled St. Louis, the feeling of being stalked. Surely MacPherson wouldn't have sent anyone to Florence after him with orders to kill. Yet on the short walk to the café from his hotel, and again on the way back, McLendon sensed someone lurking. There was an unwelcome but familiar prickling on the back of his neck. But when he stopped and nervously peered into the shadows, no one was there. He shook his head and reminded himself to keep his imagination under control.

By the time McLendon crawled into the lumpy hotel bed, the chili was rolling uncomfortably in his stomach. He spent too much of the night squatting over a chamber pot. It was, he thought, an inelegant posture for a man engaged on a heroic mission. Then the rest of the night he lay awake wondering what was happening back in Glorious. How long could the founders put off MacPherson? What if he returned with the Army, only to find they'd given up and sold out, or something worse? MacPherson was capable of anything.

IN THE MORNING McLendon walked to the Florence stage depot and purchased a ticket to Maricopa Wells. He bought the ticket, which cost five dollars, from Mr. Billings, the depot manager who'd tried to discourage him from going to Glorious three months earlier. Mr. Billings apparently didn't recognize him. He took McLendon's money, handed him a paper ticket, and said, "Maricopa Wells stage is boarding outside to the left. Step lively."

There wasn't time for McLendon to get breakfast at the depot, but he really didn't want any. The thick taste of the previous night's chili was still in his mouth. The stage to Maricopa Wells was another nine-seater. He was one of five passengers, all men. Three of the other four appeared to be business travelers. The other was a soldier. There were two stripes on his uniform sleeves and McLendon thought that meant he was a corporal, probably stationed at Camp McDowell and returning after being away on leave. Nobody felt like talking. The carriage was quiet during the five-hour trip. The ride was smooth. Charlie Rogers had been right about the good road.

MARICOPA WELLS surprised McLendon. He'd expected a town like Florence, maybe a little bigger, with hotels and cafés and adobe houses. But Maricopa Wells was the equivalent of a civilian fort, one massive building spread over two acres, with individual businesses and residences built in. There was a stable with horses and mules for rent, a blacksmith, and several cafés and shops, all under the same roof and separated by wooden walls. Smells of manure, burning coals, and cooking food mingled, not unpleasantly. The stage pulled up outside the building and the occupants climbed down.

Now that he'd arrived in Maricopa Wells, McLendon faced the dilemma of how to go on to Camp McDowell. Mulkins had said it was about fifty miles northeast. McLendon looked and there were mountains in that direction. It was hard to tell how far away they were, but it seemed a considerable distance. There was no stage service. Probably he'd have to rent and ride a mule. The thought made him wince. He remembered how much it had hurt to ride a horse the two miles from Glorious to the Culloden Ranch. It was already almost three in the afternoon. He didn't want to wait to set out until morning. With MacPherson poised to strike back in Glorious, every hour counted. But McLendon couldn't see himself riding through the night. Even if he didn't collapse from pain, he was certain to get turned around in the dark. And how long would it take to ride fifty miles on a mule? He had no idea.

"You aiming for McDowell?"

McLendon, who'd been lost in his thought, was startled to find the Army corporal standing beside him. "That's correct. I was wondering the best way to get there."

The corporal was chewing tobacco. He spit a great blob of brown juice at the base of a cactus and held out his hand. "Name's Stowers. I'm stationed there. A rough go to McDowell is what it is, particularly if you ain't used to saddle travel."

"I'm Cash McLendon. What little experience I've had riding has proven painful. Is there any other way?"

Stowers squinted at the mountains to the northeast, apparently lost in thought. McLendon noticed that the corporal had a great deal of gray in his beard. He seemed old to hold such a low rank.

"Thing is," Stowers finally said, "there's a sutler here hauling some beer out to the camp, leaving this afternoon and going all night. We're friends. He knew I was to arrive today and could accompany him. Another gun in case the Apaches get feisty. Every one helps. Would you have a weapon in that bag of yours?"

"A Navy Colt," McLendon said, feeling hopeful.

Stowers spit more tobacco juice. "I expect I could ask him if you could join us. He's got a wagon. The beer barrels'd take up much of the space, but there might be room for you to sit, even stretch out and sleep a bit during the night if you wished. We leave in another hour or so, and if we make steady progress all night, we'll fetch up at McDowell by mid-morning. What business have you there?"

"A message for the camp commander from the people of Glorious."

"I've not heard of anyplace named Glorious, but then, I ain't heard of lots of places."

"Will you ask your friend on my behalf?"

Stowers grinned. "You know, a man out here often runs short of tobacco. I'm down to my last chew. Now, if someone was to buy me a few twists so I'd be well supplied for a while back out at my post, I'd feel kindly toward him."

"Help me ride in a wagon rather than on a mule, and you can have all the tobacco that you want."

"There ain't enough money in the world for that, but you can buy tobacco inside. Feel free to purchase with a lavish hand. I'll go talk to my friend."

Ninety minutes later McLendon sat wedged against several heavy beer barrels in the bed of a wagon pulled northeast by a two-mule team. Corporal Stowers rode another mule alongside the wagon, which was driven by a sutler named Blackman.

"Just push those barrels off a little if they're squeezing you," Blackman, a hefty, jolly man, advised McLendon. "You don't need your balls mashed."

"My balls are better here than they would be riding a mule," McLendon said. "Are we really to travel all night?"

"It's the best way," Blackman said. "The Apache tend toward quiet at night. It's an easy trail. We ought to make good time, get to McDowell in the morning."

"But how will you find your way in the dark?"

"Easy. You just sight on the North Star. Don't you worry, I'll get you to McDowell."

McLendon felt certain that he could never sleep in the cramped wagon bed, but after a brief rest stop where they relieved themselves and then Blackman cooked biscuits in a Dutch oven, he felt himself nodding off. The next thing he knew, the first thin pink rays of daylight peeped above the horizon to the east.

"Two hours more and we're at McDowell," Corporal Stowers told him.

"Have you been riding that mule all night?" McLendon asked. "Didn't you want some sleep?"

"Oh, I can sleep comfortably as I ride," Stowers said. "All that matters is, the mule needs to stay awake."

They stopped one more time to water the animals—Blackman had brought a cask of water for the mule team and the corporal's mount—and once Stowers thought he'd detected suspicious movement ahead. He drew his Army handgun and clucked to his mule to advance, while Blackman pulled up his team and rummaged in the wagon bed for a shotgun. McLendon took the Navy Colt out of his valise and nervously scanned the land in every direction until Stowers returned.

"Just some ground birds, maybe turkey," he reported. "But it's always better to be careful. Apaches will sound turkey calls to fool you, but I found claw scratchings and some droppings, so we're all right."

McLENDON'S FIRST IMPRESSION of Camp McDowell was disappointing.

The camp consisted of some dozen buildings surrounded by a fence so low that any able-bodied man, let alone an Apache warrior, could easily clamber over it. The buildings themselves seemed well constructed of chinked wood and stone, but several lacked roofs. Soldiers lounged about the grounds, many of them only in partial uniform or completely in civilian clothes. Clumsy-looking Morgan horses cropped yellow grass inside a rickety corral.

Corporal Stowers noticed McLendon's expression of dismay. "Yessir, we're the nation's finest," he said. "This is the army that stands between you and the Apaches. Which, I suppose, is a matter of considerable merriment to the Indians. You say you want to see the commander?"

"I do."

"Headquarters is that building there to the left, the one with the flagpole in front. Captain Smyth is the man you're seeking."

"A captain is the camp commander?"

"At least he's usually sober. You should have seen some of the daisies that came before him. Thanks for the tobacco, and best of luck."

McLendon walked over to the headquarters building. His legs and back were stiff from riding in the sutler's wagon for so long. The door to the building was ajar, but he wasn't certain that he could simply walk in. He stood on the porch and rapped his knuckles against the doorjamb. There was no response. He poked his head inside and saw a small man in uniform slumped over a desk, his head resting on his arms. "Hello?" McLendon called tentatively. "May I come in?"

The soldier raised his head wearily and said, "You woke me up, so you might as well. Who the hell are you, and what do you want?"

McLendon went inside. There was sufficient light from several window openings—no glass—for him to see that the man was sweating profusely, with a gray pallor to his skin. "I'm looking for Captain Smyth," McLendon said.

"You're looking at him. I repeat, what the hell do you want? If you're another liquor salesman, I'll inform you that it's my intention to ban bottled spirits among the enlisted men, and the officers have suppliers of their own. Does that conclude our business? If so, remove your sorry ass from this camp."

"You mistake me. My name is Cash McLendon, and I've come from Glorious on urgent business."

Smyth dragged a stained handkerchief from his pants pocket and mopped his dripping face. "Where the fuck is Glorious? Never heard of it."

"Glorious is a small town east of Florence, right at the base of the Pinal Mountains."

"Oh, near old Camp Picket Post. Never should have closed down that camp. Some civilian convinced the brass that his ranch hands could fight the Apache in that region better than the Army. Hell, he might be right. But it was a good camp, well situated. Made no sense to close it, not that the Army ever makes much sense."

McLendon sensed that Smyth was prepared to rail indefinitely about the Army's incompetence. "I'm sure you're correct, but I have information to report. It can't wait. Lives are in the balance."

"They often are." Smyth gestured at a chair on the other side of his desk. "Take a pew and tell me about the problem in Glorious."

McLendon sat down. "For several weeks—actually, for several months—signs have indicated that substantial numbers of Apache are gathering to attack. Two of our people have been slaughtered in an appalling manner just outside town. A few days ago, prospectors saw a full-blown war party. We're still a small town and would be unable to defend against any substantial onslaught."

Smyth sighed and leaned back in his chair. "And why, exactly, have you come to tell me this?"

"I would think it's obvious. We need the Army to come out to protect us, to drive off or at least discourage the Indians."

"I see." Smyth mopped his sweaty face again. "You'd like me to dispatch a significant number of soldiers to keep your people safe. Open-ended as to time, of course. They'd stay as long as you felt they were needed."

"That sums up my request."

"And do you suppose that yours is the only such request I've received in recent days? That Glorious is the only town in Arizona Territory that feels threatened by the Apaches?"

McLendon didn't like the turn that the conversation had taken. "Perhaps not, but I'm certain the urgency of our plight trumps any other pleas you've heard. The Indians are poised to swarm down upon us. You can't let helpless people die. You're the Army—it's what you're here in Arizona Territory to prevent."

Smyth sighed again. "Let me ask you: How many troops do you suppose I have here at my disposal?"

"I have no idea."

"Currently, Camp McDowell serves as the headquarters of the Fifth Cavalry. I'm sure that sounds impressive. But if I include cooks and other support staff as well as full-fledged soldiers, my garrison numbers just under one hundered seventy men. We're called cavalry, but we have fewer than seventy-five horses fit to ride. Another fifty or more are too broken-down to be saddled, let alone ridden off after Indians."

"That's appalling," McLendon said, and meant it.

"There are, Lord, a dozen or more other Army camps in the territory, but McDowell is the one the brass dips into for foolish fucking assignments and wild-goose chases. The president has a peace commissioner visiting such Apache chiefs as can be found. Twenty McDowell cavalrymen ride with him. Some legislator down in Tucson has his ranch raided and some of his cattle run off by Indians. Nothing will do but thirty McDowell cavalry must ride down in an attempt to recover beeves that were butchered and eaten by the Apaches long before the first word even reached me. And not three days ago, an Apache war party was sighted less than four miles from here. They may be plotting to attack this camp. And if they do, they'll likely find much of the garrison drunk on their asses, too boozed up to fight back. I've got a camp full of fucking alcoholics is what I've got. I'm trying to tamp down the drinking. One of the more recent commanders before me got falling-down drunk every single day. The men took it as encouragement to do the same. So I'm probably down to a few dozen effectives, and here you are asking me to send troops to some goddamned place in the middle of nowhere. What troops, mounted on what horses? I can't conjure help for you out of fucking thin air. This civilian with all his men, the one that got Camp Picket Post shut down last year by promising to defend the area himself. Turn to him. He'd seem your best hope." Smyth's diatribe was cut off as he began coughing. They were deep, wet coughs. Coupled with the man's ghastly pallor, McLendon thought that the captain must be very sick.

"Are you all right?" he asked. "Can I get you some water?"

"No, just give me a moment," Smyth choked. "The desert doesn't agree with me."

They sat silently for a few moments. McLendon racked his brain. What could he say to persuade Smyth to send troops when he apparently had none to spare? He remembered from former negotiations that when facts couldn't prevail, empathy sometimes did.

"It must be hard being stationed here, even for someone in the best of health," McLendon said. "All the dust, and the tedium. The mess left behind by former commanders. The brass and its outrageous demands."

Smyth coughed again, but the spasms were milder. "That's the truth of it. I hate this place."

"You seem an accomplished man. Why not resign and find a more tolerable situation?"

"It's not that easy. I've a wife and baby. They're here in camp with me, God help them. It's my heart that's giving out on me. If I stay in the military, when I'm gone, at least my widow gets a pension. But that's nothing to you."

"It is. You're bearing up under a terrible burden. You have my compliments for that."

Smyth studied McLendon, who tried to adopt a concerned expression. "What's the name of the civilian with the gunmen?" the captain asked.

"Collin MacPherson. But his men are otherwise occupied and currently not in a position to offer any protection," McLendon said.

"Can't this MacPherson be persuaded?"

McLendon reminded himself to stick to the truth as much as possible. "He's a hard man to talk to—just sees things his own way."

Smyth nodded. "Yes, the big shots are like that. There's no making them see what's really what."

"He's been even worse since a recent visit by the governor. They've gone into business together, buying a local silver claim and planning to build a mine."

"The governor? Fucking Safford himself?" Smyth said, eyes widening. "He's got business interests in your town?"

McLendon thought, *An opening!* "That's a fact."

"Shit, the governor," Smyth said. He'd begun sweating heavily again, but was too preoccupied now to use his handkerchief. Perspiration dripped down from his chin onto the desk. "The Apaches overrun the town, the governor's business is wiped out, he's the kind of powerful bastard who holds a grudge."

"This is certainly so."

"He'd blame the Army, of course, and the Army would blame me. I could be cashiered."

"Your wife's pension gone, just like that. Hard times for her and your child."

"Shit." Smyth frowned. McLendon sat quietly, waiting. "All right," Smyth finally said. "Here's what I can do. Though I've precious few men to share, I'll send down six, and there's a corporal just back from leave who's less of a drunkard than most of the rest. I'll place him in charge."

"Just six? Against war parties of Apaches?"

"Seven, counting the corporal. Don't dispute me on this, for I could change my mind. I'll call Stowers in, explain what he's to do, which is go to this Glorious, have a scout around, ascertain the situation. If the Apaches are in truth skulking about, he can send word back and I'll dispatch more men as soon as I get the troops back from that waste of time down Tucson way. It'll take an hour or so to get the expedition together. You might visit the stores here, get yourself some food. You've a long journey ahead. And if ever you're asked, testify that I looked out for the governor's interests as best I could." Smyth stood and shouted for an orderly. He shook hands with McLendon. The captain's palm was slimy with sweat.

McLENDON BOUGHT bread and bacon from the camp sutler. He fashioned a rudimentary sandwich and washed it down with brackish well water. Standing on the porch in front of the store, he watched as Smyth's orderly fetched Corporal Stowers. The corporal was inside with his commander for about ten minutes. When he emerged, he saw McLendon looking in his direction and shook his fist at him. Clearly, Stowers wasn't pleased to have to lead troops against the Apaches so soon after returning from leave.

Blackman, the Maricopa Wells sutler who'd brought McLendon to the camp on his beer wagon, came into the store. "Have you finished your business here?" he asked. "If you have, I mean to depart in short order. You're welcome to ride back to the Wells with me. You can pretty much catch a stage to anywhere from there."

For a long moment McLendon was tempted. He'd done his duty by Glorious. Seven soldiers weren't much, but at least he'd tried. Gabrielle was probably going to marry Joe Saint anyway. McLendon could ride back to Maricopa Wells and, with a clear conscience, climb on a stage for California. Returning to Glorious with a handful of drunken soldiers was probably the equivalent of signing his own death warrant.

"Well?" Blackman asked.

"No," McLendon said. "I'm needed elsewhere, damn it."

THE SMALL EXPEDITION left Camp McDowell for Glorious just after four o'clock. Stowers said they had three or four hours of daylight remaining. He and five of the soldiers rode Morgan horses. The sixth soldier drove a small wagon pulled by a two-mule team. There were supplies in the bed of the wagon, and room for McLendon.

"I figure you're not up to seventy miles in the saddle," Stowers said, and McLendon gratefully agreed.

"We don't exactly know the way from here to your town," Stowers added. "None of us have been to or even heard of Glorious. But Captain Smyth says it's near Picket Post Mountain, and I guess we can find that big old pile of rock."

Shortly before eight, Stowers called a halt. McLendon argued that they shouldn't stop for the night—the Apaches might descend on Glorious at any moment. But Stowers said that the horses needed to be fed, watered, and rested. "We've still got more than fifty miles ahead of us, some of it hard going. If we keep a steady pace tomorrow, then we should reach Glorious by the following afternoon."

McLendon had trouble sleeping that night and the next. He kept imagining MacPherson's men sneaking into town and murdering the remaining founders in their beds. He had particularly unsettling visions of Ike Clanton manhandling Gabrielle while Joe Saint looked on, too panicked to intervene.

Both mornings they set out while stars still were visible. The Morgans were unsuited for speed in the desert sand, but they could hold an even, if plodding, pace. Stowers let another trooper take the lead while he dropped back beside the wagon and pointed out to McLendon some of the sights they were passing. The most impressive was a high, thin mountain spire Stowers said was known as Weaver's Needle. "You can just see the tip of it from Picket Post Mountain," he said. "So remain patient, for we're making progress."

They skirted through part of the Pinto Mountains. Stowers sent two men ahead to look for Apache sign. When they returned they reported that they hadn't found any. McLendon fumed through what he considered an unnecessary stop for lunch; Stowers pointed out that his men would be of no help to the citizens of Glorious if they arrived exhausted and starving. McLendon suspected that the half-dozen troopers quietly passed around a flask during their meal break. How could this unimpressive bunch intimidate Collin MacPherson?

Then they rode on again, and finally they entered the long valley. McLendon could see the specks that made up Glorious at the base of Apache Leap.

"Let's hurry," he said to Stowers. "My friend Crazy George will gladly stand you and your men to drinks in his saloon, and a slap-up dinner at the town hotel will be on me."

Stowers shook his head. "No time for that. I've got my orders. Now that we're in sight of town, I'm going to send you and the wagon on ahead. You can make sure that your people are still safe. The rest of us have a different responsibility."

"You're going to scout around for Apaches?"

"Perhaps we will, but our immediate task is to meet with this civilian named MacPherson. Captain Smyth was real specific about it—that I should inquire of him about the situation and assure him that his and Governor Safford's interests are being protected."

McLendon was stunned. "What about the interests of the people in Glorious?" he demanded. "What about their safety?"

"We're here to do our best about that. But the captain don't want the governor mad and climbing up his ass. Let me hear what MacPherson has to say, and then I'm sure we'll go looking for your Apaches."

"Don't do this. Come with me into town. Let everyone there see you so the word of your presence spreads."

"Mr. MacPherson's to see us first. I've got my orders. You go on and tell them in town that we'll arrive presently. Is that MacPherson's place across the creek?"

McLendon watched Stowers and the five soldiers splash across. "We going on into town?" the private driving the wagon asked.

"We are," McLendon said. "Try to look impressive."

The Culloden vaqueros at the town's west guard post stared as the wagon with McLendon aboard rolled past. One of them jumped on his horse and rode off in the direction of the ranch; McLendon knew the Mexican was reporting his return to town. As the wagon came to a stop in front of the Owaysis, Crazy George and Mary Somebody, the Tirritos, Major Mulkins, and Joe Saint all came hurrying outside.

"Where's the Army?" Mulkins asked.

"They did send some soldiers," McLendon said. "Not as many as we hoped, but some. Seven, counting the private here." He was still so shaken by Stowers's orders to report first to MacPherson that he failed to notice whether or not Gabrielle seemed surprised that he'd returned.

"Where are the others?" Saint inquired.

"At Culloden, checking in with MacPherson."

"Christ Jesus, no," Mary said. "The Army works for MacPherson too?"

"It's more like they work for the governor," McLendon said. "I'll explain. Private, I guess you want to stable your mules at the livery. You can see a man named Ike Clanton right over there, staring at us from the doorway. Everybody else, let's have a moment inside the saloon."

McLendon told about his meeting with Captain Smyth and how the camp commander was only convinced to send any troops at all when McLendon told him about MacPherson's business partnership with the governor.

"I think we can still work this to our advantage," he said. "How do all of you stand with MacPherson just now?"

"He sent Ike around again this morning to tell us he'd waited long enough," Gabrielle said. "We have the rest of the day to agree to sell. After that, Ike says, Mr. MacPherson won't ask again."

"But he can't act while the soldiers are around," McLendon said. "The longer they can be persuaded to stay, the better. While I was gone, were there many newcomers?"

"A few," Saint said. "Just prospectors, though—no one out to open new businesses."

"But they're coming," McLendon said. "They have to be. It's inevitable. So what we have to do is keep the soldiers here."

"What do you think MacPherson is telling them?" Gabrielle asked.

"What can he tell them? It's his men who've reported seeing all the Apaches. If he claims they're miraculously gone now, the soldiers will still have to look for themselves. Their commander at McDowell can't risk the governor losing his precious investment. A Corporal Stowers is in charge of the men sent here. When he comes back to town, all of you talk to him. Lie to him. Tell him you've seen Apaches too. Anything to convince him that we're in imminent danger."

But when Stowers rode into town soon afterward, he needed no convincing.

"Mr. MacPherson confirms that the Apaches are all around," he told McLendon. "He's got his men on alert. Have you seen their weapons? All of them have double-action pistols, and they also have these Winchesters—"

"Yes, we know about the Winchesters," McLendon said impatiently. "But what about the Apaches? What's your plan in this?"

Stowers set his lips in a thin, grim line. "As I said, Mr. MacPherson's bunch are alert, but he admits that, well armed as they are, they still may not be able to hold off the number of savages about to descend. The best they can do is protect his ranch, which as I'm sure you understand has to be Mr. MacPherson's primary concern. Which leaves you folks open and vulnerable to the Indians."

"But you're here. Hell, send back to McDowell for more help. Captain Smyth said he'd be prepared to supply it."

"There's no time for that. Two days for the messenger to make the ride, a day to gather and prepare the men, another two days to make the march here—the way it seems based on Mr. MacPherson's information, you people would be buzzard food by then."

"What are you saying? That you're going to ride off and leave us?"

"Christ, no. There's a plan, a sensible one. Mr. MacPherson suggested it."

Heart sinking, McLendon asked, "And what's that?"

"Since you can't be protected here, you'll be loaded up in wagons and transported under our guard to Florence, where you'll be safe until this Apache threat subsides. Mr. MacPherson has kindly offered to write a letter to the governor telling him the Army acted with great foresight and dispatch. Captain Smyth will be pleased. Tonight my men and I will stand watch along with some of the Culloden hands. Meanwhile, everyone living in town is to pack a few necessities and prepare to leave first thing in the morning. Glorious is being evacuated."

TWENTY-TWO

Word of the evacuation spread quickly. All afternoon and evening, the founders were kept busy. The Sears and Sons employees and the prospectors staying at the Elite Hotel demanded dinner, then lined up to pay their room bills. The Tirritos' dry goods store was crowded with jostling men anxious to purchase candy, beef jerky, and canned fruit to eat on the way to Florence. The shop's small supply of pistols and ammunition was completely depleted; as one customer told Gabrielle, "If the Apaches attack as we're traveling, I mean to return fire." The Owaysis was busiest of all. Everyone in town, it seemed, intended to be hungover when they departed.

It was very late, almost midnight, before the saloon crowd thinned and McLendon, Saint, Mulkins, Crazy George, Mary Somebody, and Gabrielle had the opportunity to sit down together in the Owaysis and talk. A few prospectors, including Bossman Wright and Oafie, were still huddled around tables, but they were so deeply into drink that they seemed unlikely to eavesdrop or interrupt.

"So we'll have to be away for a while," Mary said. "I've got the girls packing up. It can't be longer than a few days, can it?"

"What's MacPherson's intent?" Mulkins asked. "How does he benefit from everyone leaving?"

"I expect that you have some idea," Gabrielle said to McLendon. "You understand how people like him think."

"Sadly, I do," he said. "MacPherson's outmaneuvered us again. It's terrible and brilliant, what I believe he plans to do next. In the morning everyone leaves for Florence. The town stands deserted. As soon as it is, MacPherson sends in his men to take over the hotel and this saloon and your shop, Gabrielle. They nail up signs announcing new ownership, MacPherson Hotel and MacPherson Saloon and MacPherson Dry Goods. I see they put up 'MacPherson Farriers' the minute Charlie and Rose left town."

"They started hammering as your stage departed," Mulkins said. "But how can he have his men come in and claim businesses that are legally ours? We're going to come back. Unless we agree to sell, they're our businesses, not his. It's the law."

"Not entirely," McLendon said. "Remember the bill of sale for the livery that Ike Clanton showed me after Bob Pugh's death? When you return, MacPherson can produce more forged sales documents that he'll claim you signed. You can call him a liar all that you want, but he'll be in possession of the property while you're taking him to court. He can afford as many lawyers as he likes to draw out the process, while you struggle to pay off your own lawyers and still have something left over to live on. Even if you can hang on, you'll have to hope that the judge rules in your favor. Given MacPherson's money and political connections, I don't think that's likely."

"Judge Palmquist in Tucson is supposed to be honest," Saint suggested. "We could take the matter before his court."

Mary Somebody snorted in disgust. "Joe, you know there ain't an honest judge in the territory. All of them have been bought and paid for by somebody. Mr. MacPherson's got us, don't he? I can't see any way past this."

"Me, either," Mulkins admitted. "He's too rich and too smart. We're done. What pains me most is feeling so helpless. We work hard and we're honest and still whatever we have can be taken away on a rich man's whim. I know it happens all the time back east, but it wasn't supposed to be that way out here. The West was going to be a place where anything was possible, where there were better lives for ordinary people."

"Agreed," said Crazy George. "Hell. Wait a minute." He rummaged behind the bar and produced a bottle. "Fine blended whiskey. Let's all have some."

"Why, George," Mulkins gasped. "I thought you only served red-eye."

The saloon owner grinned. "Just because I sell that piss don't mean I have to drink it myself. I always have a little of the finer stuff on hand for personal consumption." He poured generous measures for them all.

Even Gabrielle sipped the whiskey. After they sat for a few moments, drinking silently, she said, "Well, I'd best get back to the shop. Papa is trying to pack, and he's terrible at it. The one travel bag that the Army allows us will be overflowing with things we won't need in Florence. Joe, will you come and distract him while I set the packing straight?"

"Of course," Saint said. "I guess there's nothing more to be done here." He and Gabrielle stood up, and as they did, Bossman Wright jerked to his feet at the prospectors' table.

"Sheriff, wait a goddamn minute," he demanded.

"Bossman, it's very late," Saint replied. "All of us have to prepare for morning departure. I suggest you get to it."

Wright exhaled boozy breath and shook his head. "I ain't departing. Today I caught sight of promising silver sign and I'm not walking away from it, Apaches or no."

"You must leave. All of us must. The Army's ordered it."

"The Army, you say." Wright regarded Saint curiously. "Is the Army the law in town, or are you? Ain't you the one wearing the badge?"

"I am," Saint said. "But I believe a military edict supersedes civilian law."

"Say what?"

"I mean the Army has authority over a sheriff."

"That's not always so," McLendon said. "Joe, Bossman's making a valid point. When martial law is proclaimed, the military runs everything, but even Collin MacPherson doesn't have the authority to declare martial law in conjunction with an Army corporal. Glorious no longer has a mayor, but it still has a sheriff. Legally, I think you're unquestionably in charge."

Wright unleashed a mighty belch. "Like I said."

Saint looked thoughtful. He said to Wright, "Well, Bossman, in any event I'd advise you to at least go off and get some sleep. Tomorrow promises to be challenging." Wright, Oafie, and the other prospectors left the saloon. When they were gone, Saint said to the founders and McLendon, "All right. Tomorrow when everyone else evacuates, I'm staying."

Gabrielle snapped, "You can't. Don't be foolish. What can you do against MacPherson?"

Saint shrugged. "I'm the sheriff. When I took the job, I promised to uphold the law. It would be a crime for MacPherson to take advantage of your absence and claim he bought your businesses when he didn't. If he tries and I'm still here, I can prevent it."

"How?" Gabrielle asked. "Will you stand in my shop doorway

and forbid his men to enter? They'll shoot you down and claim it was the Indians."

"I'm the sheriff. It's my responsibility to try."

"You alone against MacPherson's men," Gabrielle said, attempting sarcasm but sounding horrified instead. "You're not a fool. Don't act like one. Self-sacrifice accomplishes nothing."

"Well, fuck it," Crazy George said. "Joe, I mean, *Sheriff*, you say you're not leaving?"

"That's correct, George."

"And that corporal can't make us go?"

"Not as far as I'm concerned."

"Goddamn, then I'm staying too. Let them try to take over my place. They'll pay for it with blood."

"Think about it," McLendon cautioned. "Aren't your lives worth more than your businesses? MacPherson's in earnest. He won't be dissuaded by anyone standing up to him."

"Probably not," Mary said. "But me and George have had some hard times, and this place is what we've ended up with. We'll send Girl and the two whores away with the soldiers in the morning, but we've been pushed out enough in our lives, and we ain't going to be pushed no more."

"Amen," Mulkins said. "Not long ago I fought for this country, all the way down to Cold Harbor and Richmond and Appomattox. I'm staying, and I'll fight if I must."

"You really *are* a major?" McLendon asked.

"Union Army. George, pour us another shot of that fine liquor. Let's toast spitting in Collin MacPherson's eye."

Everyone but Gabrielle raised a glass. She said to Saint, "Are you determined to do this? You can't be talked out of it?" The sheriff shook his head. "All right, then. I'll go help Papa pack, and in the morning I'll send him on to Florence while I stay behind with you."

"What? You can't," Saint spluttered.

"Why not? Don't I have the same right as you to be stupidly noble?"

The sheriff took her hand and said, "Gabrielle, be sensible. This is going to be no place for a woman."

She yanked her hand away. "Mary's staying with George. Isn't she a woman?" Gabrielle looked at Mary as though seeking support.

"It's different," Mary said. "I'm old. Glorious has always been the end of the line for me. You've got a fine life ahead. Don't throw it away."

"Mary's right," Saint said. "Gabrielle, I forbid you to stay. You'll leave tomorrow. And that's the end of it."

A dark expression swept across Gabrielle's face. McLendon recognized it from their time together in St. Louis. Saint's attempt at male mastery was the worst possible response. *I still understand her better than he does,* he thought, and it made him proud. He, too, was determined that Gabrielle shouldn't stay, but, unlike Saint, he knew how to persuade her.

"Gabrielle," he said. She and Saint were glaring at each other. "Gabrielle. Think about your father."

"What about him? He'll go with the Army to Florence."

"No, he won't—not without you," McLendon said gently. He knew he had to avoid any hint of confrontation. "I know this—that your father loves you more than anything else in the world. If you stay, he will too."

"I'll tell him that he has to go."

"You know better. Think about it. He won't leave you, any more than you'd let him stay while you were evacuated. It's going to get bad here after everyone else is gone. There's going to be fighting, shooting. People are going to die. Your father is brave, but he's old. If he stays, he won't survive. He'd probably be the first one down. And if you do stay and send him away, what will become of him if you're killed? You know that, for all his pride, he's not able to take care of himself. He's loved you and done his best to protect you. Now it's your turn to protect him. You have to go to Florence with Salvatore. You know that."

Saint, recognizing a compelling argument, chimed in. "Your father's your responsibility. Save him."

Gabrielle chewed on her lower lip, then addressed McLendon and Saint collectively. "You bastards." She whirled and ran out of the saloon.

"She'll go with her father in the morning," McLendon told Saint. "No need for further concern in that regard."

"And when word reaches Gabrielle in Florence of what's going to happen here, you'll be there to comfort her," the sheriff said bitterly. "At least this turns out well for you."

"I don't see how. I've had enough of bending to the will of rich men. I'm not going to Florence, either."

CORPORAL STOWERS took it hard the next morning when Saint told him that he and some others weren't leaving.

"You have to," the bearded enlisted man insisted. "I represent the Army, and I'm telling you what's so."

"Unless martial law has been formally declared, as sheriff of this town I'm not under your command." Saint and Stowers stood outside the livery, where several buckboards and wagons, all on loan from the Culloden Ranch, were ready to transport evacuees to Florence. The daily Florence stage was waiting too. "If Apaches are about to attack, then you'll not want to risk them descending while you waste time in fruitless argument." He gestured at everyone milling around. "Get these people on the wagons and be on your way."

"Mr. MacPherson may be unhappy with this when he learns of it,"

Stowers protested. "He'll likely protest to the governor, who in turn will take action against Captain Smyth. The captain's a good commander. Have you any idea of some of the incompetents who've commanded my camp?"

"First of all, Mr. MacPherson is undoubtedly about to be informed," Saint said. "I just saw his man Lemmy Duke observing us, then riding out to Culloden. Whatever form Mr. MacPherson's wrath may take is already beyond your control. Second, I sympathize with your commander, but I have more pressing concerns. The morning is passing— organize the evacuation."

Stowers called for quiet. Those holding tickets on the stage to Florence should get on board, the corporal instructed. It would be part of the evacuation procession. Mr. Jesse of Sears and Sons and the representatives of several other mining concerns climbed aboard. Then the corporal explained to the crowd that women and children had first claim on space in the wagons. Mrs. Clanton came forward with her brood and they were helped up. Bossman Wright took Oafie firmly by the arm and dragged her to the next wagon.

"I won't go, I won't," she wailed.

Wright said, "Keep me in your heart, darlin'," and kissed her. Then, embarrassed at displaying tenderness in public, he grunted, "Git up there, woman," and literally tossed Oafie into the wagon bed. She covered her face with her hands and sobbed.

Sally and Abigail, the Owaysis whores, followed Oafie into the wagon. They called down to Mary Somebody that they'd wait to hear from her in Florence. She had given them money for food and a few nights' lodging in an inexpensive hotel. Girl was supposed to go with them, but she screamed and refused to get up in the wagon, even when Mary and Crazy George tried to push her into it. Finally Mary sighed and said that she could stay.

"Older men next in the wagons," Stowers ordered, and some gray-haired prospectors and all of the mining company clerks clambered on. Most of them weren't even middle-aged, but as professional men they felt that they had the right to pride of place. Salvatore and Gabrielle Tirrito stood by a wagon but still didn't get in. Gabrielle might be leaving, but she would wait until the last minute to give Saint and McLendon the satisfaction of knowing for certain that they'd prevailed.

"Thanks to the generosity of MacPherson Livery, we also have some riding mules available," Stowers said. "There's not enough room for all on the wagons and there aren't enough mules for everyone else, but able-bodied men can take turns riding and going on foot. We'll keep a steady pace, but slow enough for brisk walking. I know many of you walked here from far-off places, anyway." The men who wanted to ride first rather than walk hurried to the mules. McLendon noticed that Newman and Phin Clanton claimed the best ones. He saw Ike standing nearby and called, "Aren't you going with the rest of your family?"

Ike tried to smile, but it seemed to McLendon that the resulting expression was a nervous grimace. "If others are staying, I will too."

Besides Saint, McLendon, Mulkins, Crazy George, Mary Somebody, and now Girl, not many others besides Ike chose to remain. About ten prospectors besides Bossman refused to go, and many others left their tents intact as a sign that they planned to return soon. Preacher Sheridan was leaving. Just before he mounted a mule, he called to McLendon, "I've said a prayer for all of you who decided to stay. Place your trust in the Lord, and He may protect you in unexpected ways."

"Thanks for the thought," McLendon replied. "I'm surprised to see you evacuating. Is it God's will that you do?"

Preacher said solemnly, "Martyrdom is for worthier prophets than me. Given my poor record at soul saving, at present I'd be ashamed to stand before my maker. And I can't spread the Good Word if I'm dead."

Just as everyone was ready to depart, Sydney Chau and the rest of the Chinese arrived from their river camp.

Sydney walked directly to Stowers and asked, "Are we to be evacuated under Army protection as well? We just learned of it. Why did no one inform us earlier?"

Before the corporal could respond, Saint said apologetically, "I'm sorry, Doc. I truly meant to. I guess there was so much going on that I forgot."

"Chinese are used to being forgotten," Sydney said. "Yet here we are. Are we allowed to join you?"

"I don't know," Stowers said. "Nobody mentioned Chinks to me. There's no more room in the wagons or available mules. I've only made arrangements for white people."

"Most of us can walk," Sydney said. "A few of our older people, though, will need to ride."

"I don't think I can do it," Stowers said. "Space is too limited." Then Gabrielle approached, and the corporal tipped his hat. "Good morning, ma'am. I see you're with an elderly man, perhaps your father? You two should get in that last wagon. One of my men will assist you if required. We need to be going."

"I agree that we do, and my father could, in fact, use some assistance getting up in the wagon. I myself will walk alongside with my friend Sydney Chau. After the soldier helps my father, please ask him to aid Sydney's mother, who must ride in the wagon as well."

Stowers looked uncomfortable and said, "The wagons are for whites only."

"Is this a military regulation?" Gabrielle asked. McLendon, listening, couldn't help but grin. Corporal Stowers was about to be stampeded.

"No, ma'am, I guess not officially," Stowers said. "But it's understood."

"Understood by whom?"

"Well, by everyone."

"Not by me. If Mrs. Chau, who is elderly and in delicate health, is forced to walk the whole way to Florence, then I'll ask my father to walk, and everyone else of good character and conscience in the evacuation party. Some won't make it all the way to Florence. They'll collapse. Won't the territorial legislature and the newspapers be interested to learn the details of how—excuse me, are you a corporal? All right—of how a corporal was responsible for this tragedy? Your superiors will be called upon to act. Not being in the military, I have no specific knowledge of the process of a court-martial. I'm sure it's unpleasant in the extreme for the accused. But no one wants that. Allow Mrs. Chau and whatever other older Chinese require it to ride in the wagons."

Stowers, thoroughly flummoxed, said shakily, "Yes, ma'am. Fine. Get them up there."

Sydney embraced Gabrielle and led her mother and a few other Chinese to the wagons. Gabrielle watched as her father, Salvatore, was helped in by a soldier. Mr. Tirrito waved at his daughter, gesturing for her to join him, but she didn't.

"Well," said Gabrielle. She turned to McLendon and Saint. "You're both fools." She hugged Saint. "Don't die," she told him. She looked at McLendon for a moment, walked toward the wagon, then abruptly turned, walked back, and hugged him, too, though she didn't tell him not to die. It was a hard rather than a tender embrace.

His ribs hurt a little from the force of it. Still, he wanted badly to extend the contact, the feeling of Gabrielle's body pressed against his, but as soon as his arms tightened around her in response, she pulled away.

Stowers called for everyone to mount up. The motley procession moved west out of town, passing the guard post. The last McLendon saw of Gabrielle, she was walking beside Sydney Chau and not looking back.

Ike Clanton rode past on a mule. For a moment McLendon thought he was trying to catch up to the wagons, but he turned left across Queen Creek, heading for Culloden. Led by Bossman, the remaining prospectors drifted back to their tents. Major Mulkins, Crazy George, Mary Somebody, and Girl stood watching McLendon and Saint, waiting to be told what to do. McLendon didn't say anything. It was Saint's place to take charge.

For another long moment, the sheriff watched the evacuees recede farther in the distance. Then he said, "Well, I guess we better get ready for whatever's coming."

Twenty-three

McLendon took the Navy Colt and its holster from his valise. He'd spent the night at the jail and had left his belongings there. He attached the holster to his belt; the weight of the gun was comforting. He took the box of cartridges from the valise and tried to wedge the box into his pants pocket, but it wouldn't fit.

"Take the shells out of the box and put them in your pockets," Joe Saint advised. He was checking his handgun too.

McLendon jammed a handful of cartridges into his pocket. There were still some left in the box. "Would you like these?" he asked Saint.

"No, you've got that Colt, and I have a Smith & Wesson. The ammunition isn't compatible."

"I suppose I'll leave the rest of my things here," McLendon said. But he pulled a roll of bills from the bottom of the bag. His stay in Glorious hadn't been expensive. Almost seven hundred dollars was still left from the original two thousand he'd had when he left St.

Louis. McLendon tucked the money into his pants pocket with the cartridges. He wondered if he would ever have the opportunity to spend it.

Major Mulkins came into the jail carrying his rifle. "Forty-four Henry repeater," he said. "Might be handy if we have to do any distance shooting, though I'm the farthest thing from a marksman. Have you a rifle, Joe?"

Saint shook his head. "Never had any need for one before now. I guess I'll have to make do with a handgun."

The three men walked from the jail to the Owaysis. Some prospectors who'd stayed, including Bossman Wright, were out in the mountains, defiantly looking for silver sign despite the supposed Apache threat. The others lingered around their tents. They had guns, too—Henrys like Mulkins's, and shotguns. McLendon didn't see any pistols. No vaqueros were manning the guard posts on either end of town. MacPherson had apparently withdrawn them.

The office door to the livery swung open in the wind. "Ike Clanton seems conspicuous by his absence," Saint observed.

"He's probably still at the Culloden, plotting with MacPherson," McLendon said. "They're deciding what they're going to do, how they're going to do it."

Inside the Owaysis, Crazy George was washing plates and beer mugs. Mary Somebody tried to soothe Girl, who was clinging to her and softly whimpering.

"She senses our discomfort," Mary said. "Let loose, child. I've things to do." But Girl wouldn't let Mary go, and finally the older woman sat down with her at one of the tables, holding her hand and talking to her quietly.

"You got those items good and clean, George?" Mulkins asked. "It hadn't occurred to me that crockery was of such paramount importance in time of trouble."

The saloon owner peered nearsightedly in Mulkins's direction. "Well, Major, on the off chance we get past this, there might be some who want a drink or food afterward. What time is it, anyway?"

McLendon checked his pocket watch. "Nearly noon. MacPherson's had time to think. We need to work out our own plan."

"I thought we'd each set up in our proper places," Mulkins said. "Me at the hotel, George and Mary here, maybe you at the dry goods store, since the Tirritos aren't present. The sheriff to work in wherever he thinks best."

"What I think is, we'd be wise to stay together," Saint said. "If we separate, that makes it easier to pick us off one or two at a time. Let's choose a place and make our stand there."

"Can it be my hotel?" Mulkins asked. "I'd like to protect my windows, try to keep them intact."

"The hotel's too big, Major," Saint said. "We'd have to spread out inside too much defending it. MacPherson's men could shoot right through those windows. The dry goods store won't work, either. There's just the one door and one window opening out in the shop area. They could charge us from the other directions and we'd never see them coming. But there's the jail, maybe. Windows cut in all the walls, good vantage points."

McLendon walked around the saloon, looking through window openings, and then peered into the back corner where Crazy George stored his casks and barrels. He asked, "George, you got any water in those?"

"One keg, for those who prefer water or coffee to beer and whiskey. It's fairly fresh water, drawn yesterday from a town well."

"Good. Mary, what food is on hand?"

Mary extricated herself from Girl's grasp, thought a moment, and said, "Not much. Some jerky and a jar of pickles."

"All right, that's better than nothing," McLendon said. "I propose that we hole up right here. It's just one big room, really, but there are windows and the front entrance and the back door. There are just enough of us to keep those covered. And if there's a siege, we've got water and food to hold out for a while. Corporal Stowers planned to take everyone to Florence, then ride on to Camp McDowell to get help sent here. Maybe we could hold out until the Army comes to relieve us."

"In terms of a siege, remember the Alamo," Saint said. "As I recall, all those defenders died waiting for relief. We're on our own." The tremor in the sheriff's voice that emerged in moments of stress was back. McLendon was first annoyed, then sympathetic. Saint was afraid, but he had good reason to be.

"Well, Joe, we've still got to try," McLendon said. "I think our best option is staying here. George, have you a weapon? The Major's got his rifle, and the sheriff and I have pistols."

Crazy George reached under the makeshift bar and pulled out a shotgun. "I've got this, and a box of shells."

"I'm heeled too," Mary Somebody said. She reached into the bodice of her dress and extracted a derringer. "Over-and-under, two shots. It's not good at any distance, but effective at close range, should it come to that."

"All right, then," Saint said. His voice still quavered, but McLendon could see that the sheriff was attempting to reexert his authority. "We've got arms, we've got supplies. Let's station ourselves appropriately and be prepared. The attack can come anytime."

"Now that we know what we're doing, Joe, don't you think we might as well drink a little water and take a bite or two?" McLendon said, making a point of asking permission rather than correcting. "Whatever

MacPherson's going to do, he's likely to wait until dark. Besides us, there's the prospectors, some of them outside of town. That's too many potential witnesses in daylight. He could try to kill everyone, but all it would take is one man getting away. Don't you think he'll wait 'til nighttime?"

"That's true," Saint said. "All right, I guess we should eat."

Nobody felt hungry, but to keep their strength up they all nibbled jerky and sipped water, not taking too much of either in case they needed their limited supplies to last for several days. Crazy George offered beer or whiskey instead of water, but Saint said sharply that everyone needed to keep their wits fully about them. McLendon was pleased that the sheriff's voice sounded steadier.

After the meal they took up defensive positions: the sheriff at the front door, Mulkins at the back entrance, McLendon at one side window, and Crazy George at the other.

"I can't see anything clear even in daylight, but I believe I'll detect movement," the saloon owner said.

"Just hold your place for a few minutes, George," Mary Somebody said. "I'll get Girl settled and then I'll add my eyes to yours." Mary sat Girl at a table and placed a deck of playing cards in front of her. "Lookie here, darlin'. The cards with the pictures. You study them real careful. I'll be right over here." Girl began shuffling the cards, her hands in quick, precise motion. Then she began placing the cards faceup on the table, stopping each time she set out a face card, bending over to study the visage of the jack, queen, or king.

"She can occupy herself that way for the longest time," Mary said. "Make room for me, George. I'll look out that window for you."

FOR SEVERAL HOURS there was no movement outside the saloon and little inside it except for Girl shuffling her cards and placing them down on the table in front of her. The snapping sounds of the shuffling and the slaps of the cards on the table were distracting, but not as much as Girl's nervous whimpering would have been without her attention otherwise occupied. The others spoke very little; each was wrapped up in personal thoughts. McLendon found himself trying to remember St. Louis, the Douglass mansion that he'd lived in, the details of Ellen's face. He found that he couldn't. Everything that had happened since took precedence. He pictured Gabrielle earlier that day, facing down Corporal Stowers so that Sydney Chau's mother could ride to Florence instead of walk. Gabrielle. What might have been—what would have been—if Cash McLendon had been a better man? He glanced over at Joe Saint. The sheriff had pulled a chair up to the front door of the saloon. He had the door cracked open and seemed to be intently keeping watch. McLendon felt certain that Saint, too, was thinking about Gabrielle.

In late afternoon Crazy George declared, "I need a piss break." He walked toward the back of the saloon and Mulkins asked, "George, where you going?"

"To the outhouse, of course."

Mulkins looked at Saint and McLendon, who shook their heads.

"You can't risk it, George," the sheriff said. "MacPherson might have men with rifles waiting to pick us off if we go outside."

"Damn it, I got to piss," George growled. "I can't hold it and I don't mean to soak my pants."

"Go in the corner and use a glass or one of the serving bowls," Mary told him. "Nobody'll look. When you're done, I need to go. If any of the gentlemen are squeamish, they can avert their eyes."

"It'll smell," George said. "I can't abide piss smell."

"Then we'll pour it out one of the windows. Is that all right, Sheriff?" Mary asked. When Saint nodded, Crazy George took a wide bowl and retreated to a far wall. "He's modest," Mary whispered to the others. "It's so sweet."

When Crazy George was done, everyone else took turns and felt better for it. Afterward they had small sips of water. Girl went back to her cards, content to play with them for as long as Mary allowed. Mulkins mused about how much it would cost to complete the second story of his hotel, adding that he'd wait awhile longer before adding a third. Then he said, "Well, if I even have a hotel after today." They were quiet again after that.

MCLENDON HAD just checked his watch and seen that it was half past six when someone in front of the saloon began shouting, "Hello, the town! Hello, the town!" It was Ike Clanton.

"Come out with me, McLendon," Saint said. "Everyone else, keep watching. This may be to distract us so they can storm in from the other sides." The sheriff and McLendon went slowly out the door, looking carefully around them as they did. They didn't see anyone except Ike, who stood in front of the farrier's shop. He was holding the reins to his mule.

"All of you shut up in the Owaysis?" Ike asked. "Going to fight off the Apaches from there?"

"We're ready for anything, Ike," Saint said. McLendon was annoyed because the sheriff's voice was shaky again. He knew that Ike noticed it too.

"Apparently so," Ike said. "Let me put up my mule and I'll join you."

McLendon hissed to Saint, "Don't let him. He means to survey our defenses and count our guns."

"What's that, McLendon?" Ike inquired. "Don't whisper. There need be no secrets among pals."

"Where've you been, Ike?" McLendon asked. "Run out of things to tell MacPherson at the Culloden?"

"Now, that accusation hurts. Since there's no stock at the livery to guard—as a good citizen, I lent all but this one mule to the evacuation—I've been out scouting around, on the lookout for the Indians. I'm sorry to say there's sign, considerable sign—more footprints and so forth than I could count. Let me inside the saloon with you. I'll reinforce you with another gun."

"A new Winchester, just like the rest of the Culloden mob," McLendon observed. "We know whose side you're on, Ike. Stop pretending."

Ike shook his head. "Sheriff, I appeal to you," he said. "Let me inside. McLendon has always opposed me. I don't know why. But I've friends in there. Don't I observe my slow-witted sweetheart at the door, just delighted to see me?"

The sheriff and McLendon turned to look. It was true. Girl was trying to wedge past Mary Somebody, who stood in the saloon door, blocking her way.

"Ike," Girl shrilled.

"Right here, lovey," Ike called back. "Give me leave to join you, Sheriff."

"Get away, Ike," Saint said. "Go back to your boss and tell him to leave us alone. We'll fight if we're forced to."

McLendon sensed movement to the right, past the jail in the direction of Queen Creek and the Chinese camp. He saw Angel Misterio, mounted on one of the nimble Culloden ponies, ride briskly past the jail and around the livery corral before he disappeared behind the farrier's.

"Misterio watching out for Apaches too?" McLendon asked. "Just do your dirty work and be damned, Ike."

Ike smiled unpleasantly. "I'm not the one who's about to be damned, McLendon. Well, Sheriff, if you won't have me, I'll resume my scouting." He got back on his mule and rode west out of town.

"We'd better get back inside," Saint said to McLendon. "You were right to predict they'd wait until tonight, but it's getting on to dusk now."

THEY WATCHED through the saloon's front door and side windows as the prospectors who'd gone out for the day returned to their tents. McLendon cautiously went over and invited all of them to join the group in the saloon, but they refused.

"If I got to fight, I want to do it out of doors," Bossman said. "It makes running easier."

"While you were out today, did you see anything suggesting Apaches?" McLendon asked him.

"Not a sign. Couldn't have been quieter."

WHEN IT WAS fully dark outside, Mary Somebody began lighting kerosene lanterns inside the Owaysis. Saint cautioned her not to light more than one.

"Too much illumination will make us better targets," he said.

Mulkins leaned against the saloon's back door and rested his rifle stock on the floor. "My arm aches from holding this weapon all day," he said. "But the hardest thing is the waiting. I don't want to die, but I wish to hell that if they're going to attack, they'd do it and get it over with."

"What do you think, McLendon?" the sheriff asked. "Are they going to get on with it?"

"Probably soon," McLendon said. "We have to remain alert."

But hours passed and nothing happened. Girl, wrapped in blankets, slept on the saloon floor. Everyone else sat in chairs by the windows and doors. In spite of themselves, they fell into fitful dozes. McLendon snapped awake and held his pocket watch up to the single lighted lantern: two o'clock. He looked out the side window and couldn't detect any movement around the prospectors' tents. They, too, must have fallen asleep.

"Are you awake, Joe?" McLendon asked.

"Just barely. There's nothing going on at all. I wonder if MacPherson is going to allow the night to pass."

Then there came the sound of gunfire to the west, and bloodcurdling screams. The others in the saloon came quickly awake.

"Where is it?" Mulkins asked.

There were many more shots and howls. "Outside of town, I think," McLendon said. He looked out the window and saw the prospectors tumbling out of their tents, rifles in hand.

Girl began shrieking, a high-pitched counterpoint to the screaming outside. Mary Somebody rushed to comfort her.

Saint, crouched by the front door, said, "Someone's coming—I think it's Ike." He raised his pistol and called, "Stand to, Clanton! I'll shoot if you don't." McLendon, peering over Saint's shoulder, saw Ike stop just a few feet away. It was too dark to tell if anyone was behind him.

"It's the Apaches," Ike cried. He moved forward again, pushing right up to where Saint guarded the door. "They're coming fast—you got to get out of there. Girl, honey, can you hear me? Come out to Ike."

"Move along, Ike," Saint said. He tried to push Ike away. Girl stopped screeching and rushed toward the door, moving too fast for

Mary Somebody to intercept her. She squeezed between Saint and McLendon and ran outside to Ike. He grabbed her hand and shouted back to the others in the saloon, "Follow me! You'll be safer!"

"It's a trick—don't do it," McLendon warned, but Mary Somebody was already past him, too, calling for Girl to come back inside. Ike spun and ran, yanking Girl behind him. He pulled her past the dry goods store and up the hill.

"We got to get her," Mary shouted, and set off in galloping, clumsy pursuit. McLendon and Saint ran behind her. So did Mulkins and Crazy George, who kept bellowing that he couldn't see and would someone tell him what was going on. The gunfire just outside town seemed to spread to all sides, but whoever was shooting was too far away to be seen, only heard as they fired and shouted.

"It's Apaches! Keep running!" Ike called back. There were lights ahead, and McLendon saw that he was running for the old wooden shack where the Clantons lived after Turner left town.

"We can't follow Ike, he's up to something," McLendon called to the others, but Mary, breathing hard, gasped, "I got to keep Girl safe." She clearly wasn't going to stop, and so the others didn't, either. There was gunfire all around them now, and still they couldn't see who was shooting. Whether it was the Culloden vaqueros or even the Apaches, McLendon wondered, why weren't they closing in?

Ike flung open the door of the cabin and shoved Girl inside. Then he stood in the doorway, gesturing for the others to come in as well.

"It's safer here, away from the main part of town!" he yelled, and McLendon, Saint, Mulkins, Crazy George, and Mary all hustled inside. A half-dozen kerosene lamps lit the interior. A table and some chairs stood in the center of the one-room dwelling, and several straw-stuffed tick mattresses were stacked in a corner. McLendon had an immediate sense of claustrophobia. It was a very small cabin.

"Everybody stay down," Ike commanded. "I'm going out for a look."

"You're what?" Saint exclaimed, and grabbed Ike's sleeve, but Clanton yanked away and ran back down the hill.

"What the hell?" Mulkins exclaimed, and McLendon went outside to chase after Ike, but as he did several shots rang out from very nearby, and he heard the whiz of the bullets and the smack of them hitting the wood beside him. McLendon dove back inside, colliding with Mulkins. They went down in a heap as Saint slammed the door.

"Douse those lamps!" Saint yelled. "Then everybody with a gun to a window." His voice shook terribly, and he swallowed hard, trying to control his panic. "We're surrounded. They're shooting at us from all sides." Everyone scrambled to blow out the lamps, and then the cabin was as pitch-black as the night outside. The sheriff pulled the door open an inch. McLendon and Mulkins rushed to the windows. There were only two, one in the front of the shack and the other in the back. Crazy George joined Mulkins at the back window. Mary Somebody pulled Girl to the floor and held her there. Girl was still shrieking, and her howling added to the confusion.

"It's too dark to see," Mulkins complained. "What's going on out there? Why did Ike lead us here?"

"Who knows?" Saint said. "Everyone do your best. If you think there's something out there moving toward us, don't hesitate. Shoot at it."

"I feel like George, because I can't see what to shoot," Mulkins said.

"Blast away at the muzzle flashes," the sheriff snapped. He fired his pistol, and the room was filled with the acrid scent of gunpowder. Then there was a near-deafening boom to McLendon's right: Crazy George had fired the shotgun. Mulkins chimed in with two shots from his Henry, and even though McLendon couldn't see much as he craned his neck to peek out the window, he cocked his Navy Colt and prepared to fire too. There was a muzzle flash from a few dozen yards down the hill, so McLendon pointed the Colt in that direction and pulled the trigger. The gun bucked in his hand as he fired, hurting the base of his thumb. When he tried to fire again, he found that his hand was trembling, so much so that it was difficult to get his thumb on the hammer to draw it back.

The assailants' shots didn't completely subside, but they decreased in frequency. There were occasional thuds as bullets hit the wooden walls, and a few times they whizzed through the two window openings and struck interior walls, spraying splinters everywhere.

"Why have they slackened the shooting?" Mulkins asked. "Do you think we hit some of them?"

"It's unlikely," McLendon said. "I think that for the moment they just want us pinned down here. Be ready—they may be preparing an all-out assault." Behind him, he heard Girl sobbing, and Mary Somebody attempting to comfort her.

"Is it the Cullodens for sure?" Crazy George asked Saint.

"I'm certain of it," the sheriff said. "Ike's the one who sprung the trap."

"Fuckin' Ike," the saloon owner growled. "I'd like one last chance to take my pipe to his skull. I'd mash that bastard—"

A new fusillade erupted at the bottom of the hill, and then there were flames.

"They're burning the prospectors' tents," Mulkins said. "My God, they're shooting them as they run from the fire!"

The conflagration lit the night. Those in the cabin peered out the door and windows and watched with horror as Culloden horsemen, visible now in front of the flames, rode down and shot fleeing prospectors.

"Maybe they won't get them all," Mulkins said hopefully. "A few could escape in the confusion."

"MacPherson's murderers are efficient," McLendon replied, and thought but didn't say out loud, *It will be our turn next*. He was right: as the last prospector fell—it looked like Bossman Wright—the riders turned their horses about and dismounted. With the burning tents at their backs, more than a dozen began walking up the hill, moving slowly but purposefully.

"They're out of pistol and shotgun range," Saint said. "Major, can you reach them with your Henry?"

Mulkins moved from the back window to the front door. "Reach them, yes, but hitting them is another matter." He aimed and fired. The men on the hill paused, but no one fell or gave any other sign of being wounded. Mulkins fired a second time, with no better result.

The flames from the burning tents were high in the air, and by their light McLendon recognized some of those below. "There's Misterio and Lemmy Duke, and Ike Clanton's off to the side. What have two of those vaqueros with them got? Bows and quivers?"

"They took them off those dead Apaches they brought in a while back," Saint said. "Are they setting up to charge us, do you think?"

"No, they seem to be waiting for something. There are a couple of vaqueros coming up behind them. They've got buckets. What the hell?" McLendon pulled the door wider to get a better look, and instantly bullets smacked into walls again. The new Winchesters used by the Culloden hands fired more accurately than Mulkins's vintage Henry.

"Yes, they mean to pen us up here," Saint said. "Why this cabin?"

McLendon, squinting hard, saw another vaquero coming up the hill. He carried a torch. "Damn it. They got us here because the cabin's made of wood. They mean to burn it down—and us with it."

"Can't be!" Mulkins protested. "My hotel's wood too. If that's what they intended, why not trap us in there?"

"MacPherson wants your hotel, Major," McLendon said. "He has no further designs on this cabin. We've got to shoot, got to keep them back. They've got kerosene and a torch. We can't let them get near."

Mulkins fired the Henry again, and McLendon and Saint used their pistols. Crazy George cut loose with his shotgun. But it had no real effect. Most of the Culloden men stayed where they were on the hill, returning fire with their longer-range Winchesters until the defenders in the cabin had no choice but to stop shooting and duck. As soon as they did, the vaqueros toting buckets of kerosene ran up the hill. Saint and McLendon snapped off shots, but the vaqueros dodged to the sides of the cabin where there were no windows and then there were sloshing sounds as the kerosene splashed against the wood. Then the men on the hill threw down heavy covering fire as the vaquero with the torch sprinted toward the cabin. Those inside had no chance to prevent him as he pitched the torch against the outer wall. The kerosene ignited and flames instantly crackled. Girl began shrieking again, and Mulkins moaned, "We got to get out of here before we fry."

"Back window," Saint suggested. "Maybe we can climb out there, keep the cabin between us and them," but when Mulkins tried to squeeze through the window there were shots from behind the cabins. MacPherson's men had anticipated that escape route and had riflemen placed to block it.

They huddled together in the middle of the cabin, cringing away from the heat of the flames that were already eating through one wall and part of the roof.

"Out the front door, then," Mulkins said. "We don't want the agony of burning."

"We do that, and they'll shoot us down right there," Saint said. "Either way, when it's over they'll stick some of those arrows in us and claim it was Apaches."

Mary Somebody let go of Girl and grabbed McLendon's arm. "Soames," she shouted.

McLendon, distracted by the fire, said, "What?"

"Soames. My real name is Mary Soames and I hail from Burkburnett, Texas. If I'm going to die, I want someone to know who I really am."

Then Ike Clanton, standing down the hill, called for Girl. As she had earlier at the Owaysis, she shook free of Mary and ran toward the door. As soon as she stepped outside there was a series of shots, and Girl's body came flopping back inside, entirely limp as though she had no bones. In the light from the flames on the wall and roof, they could see a round hole in the middle of her forehead. Mary Soames began to sob. Crazy George dropped his shotgun and wrapped his arms around Mary. "She's safe now," he said. "She's with Jesus and we'll join her directly."

The flames had spread enough so that part of the roof began crumbling. McLendon looked at Saint. "All right," the sheriff said, and McLendon was surprised that there was no longer a quaver in his voice. "Time's come. The Major's right, it's an easier death from bullets than flames." Crazy George tried to pick up Girl's body, but the rest of the roof came tumbling down in blazing chunks and he had to jump back. They all went through the front door, moving quickly, ready to get it over with. When they were outside, they drew themselves up to die with dignity. Crazy George and Mary Soames held hands.

Twenty yards down the hill, Angel Misterio barked an order, and Lemmy Duke and the Culloden vaqueros snapped their Winchesters up to their shoulders and aimed. McLendon thought, *Firing squad*. He took a deep last breath and then it happened. Lemmy Duke, standing immediately to Misterio's left, levitated. His feet came off of the ground and his Winchester dropped to the ground. McLendon wondered how a man could fly and then he realized Duke had been lifted off the ground because there was a burly shape behind him. Duke dropped his rifle, his body shook violently, and McLendon thought that a grizzly bear must have wandered down from the mountains and attacked. Then Duke was flung aside and there stood Patrick Brautigan—Killer Boots—who immediately turned his attention to Angel Misterio. The Culloden vaqueros gawked at the burly giant, frozen in place by his unexpected appearance, but Misterio was tougher-minded. He reached for the throwing knife in his belt, his hand moving as always at amazing speed. Brautigan didn't seem to move quickly at all in contrast to Misterio's blurriness, but somehow before Misterio could pull and throw his lethal blade the hulking Brautigan made a graceful pirouette. His right leg rose up and the steel toe of his massive boot caught Misterio under the chin. Misterio's head snapped back and even twenty yards away McLendon could hear the *crack!* as his neck broke. Brautigan whirled, picked up the Winchester dropped by Lemmy Duke, and began firing at Ike and the remaining Culloden vaqueros. Terrified by the death of their leader, the Mexicans shrieked, *"¡El Diablo, El Diablo!"* and fled. Ike Clanton vaulted onto his mule and galloped away.

Brautigan walked up the hill. McLendon, Saint, Mulkins, Crazy George, and Mary stood and watched him come, all of them working through what they'd just seen, stunned to the point of immobility by the unexpected sensation of still being alive. Before McLendon could even think of fleeing, Brautigan clamped a meaty hand on his shoulder, his thick fingers crushing McLendon's collarbone. With his other hand, he yanked the Navy Colt from McLendon's grasp and tossed the gun aside.

"Got you," Brautigan said in the flat, emotionless tone McLendon remembered too well.

Joe Saint, struggling to regain control of himself, wheezed, "Who are you?"

Without relinquishing his tight grip on McLendon, Brautigan said, "This man's wanted for murdering his wife in St. Louis."

Saint, Mulkins, Crazy George, and Mary all looked startled. Saint said, "McLendon? What's this?"

"Not true," McLendon gasped, and grunted in agony as Brautigan tightened his grip. "I didn't kill anyone. I was never accused of murder."

"It's no concern of yours," Brautigan said to Saint. "I've got horses ground-hitched just down the way, and I'm taking him now."

"Don't let him take me, Joe," McLendon pleaded. "He'll kill me."

"I'm the sheriff here," Saint said to Brautigan. His quaver was back, and McLendon couldn't blame him. Saint had just narrowly escaped certain death, and now he was face-to-face with Killer Boots. "What's your name, and under what authority do you make this arrest? Can you show me a warrant?"

Brautigan peered down at Saint. "I'm Patrick Brautigan, representing the St. Louis law, and I have no truck with paperwork." With his free hand he gestured at the bent, broken star pinned to Saint's shirt. "I wear no fine badge such as your own. But this man McLendon has crimes to answer for in St. Louis, and I'm going to take him there."

"Don't listen, Joe. He's going to kill me as soon as we're out of sight."

"He'll make it back to St. Louis alive, Sheriff," Brautigan said, then bent and whispered in McLendon's ear, "And you will, because Mr. Douglass wants to watch you die." McLendon panicked and tried to twist out of Brautigan's grip. The giant swatted his open hand against his captive's head, and McLendon, stunned, dropped to the ground. Brautigan reached down, grasped McLendon's shoulder again, and hauled him back to his feet. McLendon swayed on unsteady legs.

"I've got to think about this, Mr. Brautigan," Saint said. "Are you telling me that you're an officer of the law?"

"He isn't a lawman," McLendon mumbled, trying to focus his eyes and concentrate. "He's a goon working for a man who was my father-in-law." Brautigan raised his hand to strike McLendon again, but Saint reached up to stop him. The sheriff's fingers weren't long enough to wrap around the giant's massive wrist, but the contact was enough. Brautigan put down his hand and looked at Saint curiously.

"What do you require of me?" he asked. "Is it a matter of money?"

"Show me a badge or some other proof of your official capacity."

"I've been deputized by St. Louis chief of police Kelly Welsh. If you wire him, he'll confirm this."

McLendon said desperately, "Welsh has been bought off. You heard how Brautigan just offered you a bribe." Brautigan shook him and McLendon's teeth rattled.

"Wire Chief Welsh," Brautigan repeated. "Let his word settle it."

Saint said, "The problem is, the nearest telegraph service is down in Tucson. So that's not an option. Meanwhile, I have a strong suspicion that you're impersonating a lawman, and that's a crime. Release that man. Until I get proof otherwise, I'm placing you under arrest."

"You're going to try to arrest me? That would be a mistake."

McLendon said quickly, "Careful, Brautigan. Remember your boss's rule? Never openly break the law. What are you going to do, kill us all? All those vaqueros saw you before they ran away. Murder a sheriff and there'll be a manhunt, and they'll have those vaqueros to identify you. Does Rupert Douglass want that kind of notice?"

"Let loose of McLendon," Saint ordered. Behind the sheriff, Major Mulkins stepped up with his Henry. Crazy George raised his shotgun, and even Mary Soames had her derringer. Brautigan released McLendon, who dropped to his knees and kneaded his throbbing shoulder. "Now take a step back," Saint told the giant. "I'm going to hold you in the town jail. Deputy U.S. Marshal Hunky-Dory Holmes is due here soon. When he arrives I'm going to place you in his custody. He'll take you back to Tucson and you can wire your St. Louis police chief from there. If he vouches for you, you'll be released at once. I expect that in all it will be a matter of four or five days."

Brautigan said, "This is a mistake, Sheriff, one you'll regret."

"That may be, sir. Please stand where you are." Brautigan folded his arms and waited.

Saint said to McLendon, who was being helped to his feet by Mulkins and Crazy George, "Did you hear what I told him? You've got four or five days, and that's probably all. Get as far away as you can."

"Wait," McLendon said. He asked Brautigan, "How did you find me?"

"It was the English girl. She wrote to Mr. Douglass in St. Louis, offering your whereabouts in exchange for first-class passage back to Britain. You always talked too much, McLendon. I thought I saw you the other night in Florence, but I couldn't be sure. Go on, run. I'll find you again, and next time no one will save you from me."

"Major, would you bring up one of those Culloden mounts?" Saint asked. Mulkins hurried down the hill to where some of the lithe Mexican ponies were tied. "Mary, can you find McLendon's gun? It got thrown somewhere over there." Mary retrieved the Navy Colt and handed it to McLendon, who slipped it into his holster.

"I don't know that it's right to leave you," he said to Saint. "MacPherson won't take what's happened well. He'll lie his way out of tonight somehow and then he'll try again."

Saint said, "It's no longer your problem. Whatever he does, we'll deal with it. You've got your own life to save."

"I can't just set off in the dark. I have no idea which way to go."

"For now, any direction will do, but you can't delay. This man Brautigan clearly means business, and you need all the head start on him that you can get."

Mulkins led over the Culloden horse. McLendon said, "You know that I have no talent for riding."

"Acquire it," Mulkins said, smiling. "It's mostly a matter of keeping your feet in the stirrups and your ass in the saddle."

Mary Soames asked for a hug, and she and McLendon embraced. Crazy George and Mulkins shook his hand. After Mulkins helped him climb up into the saddle, McLendon hesitated.

"Joe," he said. "Sheriff Saint. Thank you."

Saint looked hard at him, the flames from the cabin reflecting on the lenses of his glasses. "I'll tell Gabrielle that you said good-bye."

"All right, then," McLendon said. He tugged on the reins and, already jouncing painfully, rode down the hill, past the burning tents and into the night.

Acknowledgments

————•+•————

Thanks above all to Ivan Held, who called to ask if I might be interested in writing some western fiction. (I was.) Jim Donovan, as usual, was a great literary agent and friend. This was my first chance to work with editor Christine Pepe at Putnam, and she's every bit as good as Robert B. Parker once told me.

I'm grateful for all of my friends at Putnam, past and present.

Jim Turner and Sara Tirrito provided solid research, and I received plenty of moral support from Major Kevin "Cap" Mulkins, Bob Pugh, Bob Palmquist, Bruce Dinges, Tom Gaumer, and Anne Collier. Mike Blackman, James Ward Lee, and Carlton Stowers read the chapters as I wrote them, and offered constructive criticism as needed.

Settings in real life are identical to those described in this story. Fictional Glorious is in about the same spot as the actual town of Superior, just a little distance west down the road from Globe. If you take Highway 60, you'll see Queen Creek, Apache Leap, and Picket Post Mountain. The scenery is gorgeous and well worth even a long drive.

Cash McLendon will be back soon.

Everything I write is always for Nora, Adam, and Grant.